WORDS OF LOVE

"Hasn't anyone ever told you you're absolutely beautiful?"

Delilah shook her head. "Pretty, but not absolutely beautiful."

"That he lies awake at night thinking about you?"

She shook her head again.

"Then I'm certain no one ever told you what wonderfully expressive eyes you have."

"No."

Nathan moved closer. "Or that to have you within reach and not be able to caress your skin is a temptation almost greater than a mortal man can endure."

"No."

He moved closer still. "That your lips are an irresistible invitation to kiss you."

"No." Her response was a little breathless.

"I've spent days thinking of ways to get you out of the kitchen so I can see you as much as possible. Every beautiful woman should know she's appreciated." He reached out and touched her cheek.

"How would you do that?"

"It's very simple." He drew so close she could almost feel the heat of his body. "You let her know what you like about her."

Delilah felt paralyzed. She had never had a man court her this way.

"I particularly like your lips," Nathan murmured. Their lips were now so close they almost touched. "They are so full and red and wanting to be kissed." His fingertip traced the outline of her mouth. Then he leaned closer and

Rebel Enchantress

Leigh Greenwood

LOVE SPELL NEW YORK CITY

LOVE SPELL®

February 2006

Published by

Dorchester Publishing Co., Inc.
200 Madison Avenue
New York, NY 10016

ISBN 0-505-52656-5

The name "Love Spell" and its logo are trademarks of Dorchester
Publishing Co., Inc.

Printed in the United States of America.

Visit us on the web at www.dorchesterpub.com.

Rebel Enchantress

Chapter One

The closer Delilah came to Maple Hill, the more nervous she became. Public opinion labeled Ezra Buel a mean, sour-tempered, stingy old man, a River God, one of the rich men who'd built their mansions along the banks of the Connecticut River, but his reputation had never mattered to her before. Nothing he did had touched her directly. But that would no longer be so.

Gossip had it Ezra built the mansion from profits made during the War of Independence, but it was the sheer size of the white clapboard structure that overwhelmed Delilah. It sat atop a hill overlooking the river, dominating the country-side like a sleeping giant.

Odd that a house could be so intimidating. Even more unusual that it should give the people inside an importance they wouldn't have had by themselves. She might tell herself Serena Noyes and her daughter were ordinary people like herself, but as she stood gazing at the house, an outsider about to ask for something they could give or withhold, they didn't seem like ordinary people.

Still, she couldn't afford to give in to her fears now. Only Reuben's oxen stood between them and hunger.

She stopped at the bottom of the shallow steps. Who would answer her knock? Did rich people open their own doors, or did they get somebody else to do it for them? It seemed a waste of time to set anybody such a simple task,

5

but then, rich people were different. They couldn't live in a house like that and not be changed.

She would be if she lived in such a house. She'd stay in bed until noon. That pleasant thought soothed her nerves until she found herself on the porch. Then she started to tremble. Hundreds of reasons why she should go back home flashed through her mind. She didn't want to be here, she had fought against it most of the spring and summer, but the thought of her two little nephews wondering why they should have to leave the table hungry, the fear on their faces at the tense silences between their parents, stiffened her resolve. She might be afraid—well, she was afraid—but she wasn't a coward.

Her first, tentative knock made almost no sound. The massive door appeared to have been sculpted from a single piece of wood, though Delilah knew it had been pieced and carved by skillful hands. Taking hold of her courage, she grasped the brass knocker and gave it a strong whack. The report of metal against metal sounded so loudly she involuntarily jumped back. But after several moments passed and still no one came, Delilah began to wonder if anyone was home.

Was she supposed to go to the back door? If a farmhouse had a second door, it led to the barn or the cow pen, and no one expected a guest to use it. But these people were different. Maybe their front door was just for other rich people.

Well, she might be poor and she might be offering herself to do a servant's work, but until they offered her a job and she accepted it, she would enter by the front door or no door at all. Pride bolstering her courage, she reached for the knocker once more. The door opened without warning.

"Can I help you?"

Delilah felt as if she'd been turned to stone. The most attractive man she had ever seen stood before her. For the moment not even his heavy British accent registered. She frantically searched her mind for who he might be. She had prepared herself only for Ezra Buel, his sister, or his niece. She didn't know what to say to this man.

He had beautiful eyes. Light blue and clear as a summer

6

sky. His gorgeous mouth, full lips smiling now, parted to show strong white teeth. He had a splendid face—clean-shaven, clear-skinned, handsome.

He was tall, with broad shoulders, slim hips, and was dressed in a style unlike anything Delilah had ever seen. Rather than the usual brown waistcoat and plain coat, he wore a white embroidered waistcoat with a blue broadcloth coat. Instead of a carelessly knotted cloth at his throat, his silk neckcloth was tied into a small, neat bow. His blond-brown hair was not long and gathered at the back of the neck by a ribbon, but was cut short in a style she found new and most attractive.

Whereas the men Delilah knew wore rough boots and loose or ill-fitting breeches, he wore low-cut leather shoes decorated with silver buckles, stockings which clung to his muscled calves, and tight-fitting fawn-colored breeches which emphasized his muscular thighs.

And everything else!

Delilah felt a rush of heat surge through her. Good God, his breeches were indecent. The English must be depraved to go about dressed like that.

He looked her over with a critical eye, his expression becoming less welcoming as his gaze took in the quality and cut of her dress, the dusty condition of her shoes, the absence of any means of transportation or an accompanying servant. He scrutinized her exactly as Ezra Buel would have done.

"Are you certain you have the correct house?" he asked.

Delilah bridled instantly. The implication was unmistakable: No one at Maple Hill could possibly have anything to do with the likes of her.

"I'm certain," she said with a confidence she didn't feel. "I wish to come in."

For a moment she thought he was going to close the door in her face. But after a slight pause, during which Delilah was sure he wondered if she had come to steal the silverware, he stepped aside to allow her to enter.

As his gaze wandered over her person—Delilah had undergone this kind of scrutiny too many times before to mis-

7

understand—his expression began to indicate curiosity, even speculation. Delilah refused to let herself think about what must be going through his mind. She could deal with that later.

Her step was firm and confident, even though her mind still grappled with the unexpected meeting. A slight feeling of uneasiness settled about her when he closed the door and plunged them both into near darkness. A moment later he opened the door to a sunlit drawing room.

Delilah had never even imagined such a room. An Aubusson rug echoed the delicate pink of the tinted walls. Three circular inlaid mahogany card tables, separated by mahogany side chairs upholstered in pink damask, stood against the wall. The windows were adorned with mull curtains crowned with pink, blue, and gold brocade swags. A massive rolltop desk stood between the far windows. A table bearing a Sèvres tea set stood in the center of the room, surrounded by four brocade-covered chairs. An enormous gilt mirror over a pink marble fireplace magnified the splendor of the room. The heavy fragrance of tuberoses, underlaid by a hint of lemon-oil beeswax, filled her nostrils.

"My aunt and cousin are away from home at the moment," the young man said as he helped her to a seat.

Staggered by the double shock, Delilah had to fight to regain her wits. The young man didn't help. His gaze never left her. Having finished his study of her body, he focused on her face as though by sheer force of will he could unlock the secrets of her mind. She felt breathless, distracted.

"I came to see Mr. Buel," she managed to say.

"My uncle is quite ill," the young man said. "The doctor won't allow anyone to see him at present."

"But I must see him," Delilah replied, reeling from still another shock. "It'll only take a moment." She was so nervous she felt nauseated.

"You could come back in a few weeks."

"That'll be too late. I've got to see him now."

His gaze was unrelenting. How was she supposed to concentrate when she felt the barriers to her mind were being burned away by the heat of it?

8

"I'm afraid that's impossible."

"Ask him."

"No."

The word was short and sharp, uncompromising, his expression only slightly altered. Delilah decided he looked vaguely apologetic, interested, less censorious.

"I'm sure if you tell him Delilah Stowbridge is here to see him on a matter of utmost importance he'll see me."

"He won't."

The change in the man's voice and expression shocked Delilah. No longer did a physical heat, maybe even a sensual interest, live in his gaze. The coldness in his eyes would have daunted a much more intrepid heart than hers.

A desperate fear of failure made Delilah's temper flare. "How do you know? Where is he? I'll ask him myself."

"He's upstairs in the front bedroom on the left, but he won't answer you." The man stood when Delilah started to rise. "My uncle fell from his horse three weeks ago. He's been in a coma ever since."

Delilah sank back into her chair. "Will he recover?"

"There's no way to tell. The doctor says he looks sound of body, but his mind is gone. He could be like this for months."

"That'll be too late," Delilah groaned. "I've got to talk to him now."

"Maybe I could help."

Delilah looked at him, and her mind faltered. Why had she never before noticed the way a man's breeches clung to his body? She averted her eyes. If she kept looking at him, she'd never be able to think.

"How?"

"I'm Nathan Trent."

"So what does that make you?" Delilah asked before she realized what a rude question it was. She expected him to be angry, but she saw a look of melancholy briefly cloud his eyes.

"Nothing much, I'm afraid. It's not much of a name."

"I'm sorry," Delilah said, a blush turning her cheeks quite hot. "I didn't mean to say that, but Mr. Buel's illness has up-

9

set all my plans. I can't think what I'm about." Not as long as she looked at him, she couldn't. "How can you help me?"

"I can't possibly know until you tell me why you've come."

"I didn't mean that," Delilah said, a trifle more impatiently than she wished. "I mean what can you do about his affairs?"

"Quite a lot as it happens. I'm my uncle's heir."

Delilah didn't know how many more shocks she could endure in one day. Everyone had assumed Ezra Buel's estate would go to Serena Noyes and her daughter.

Nathan seemed to be cynically amused by her discomfiture. "I'm his nephew," he explained. "I was about to have tea. While you compose yourself, I'll have Lester bring in the tray." He walked over to the bell pull but turned as his hand reached out to grasp the long silken rope. "You colonists do drink tea, don't you?"

Between the effect of his smile — so condescending, so intolerable — and the sight of his handsome face and taut body, Delilah quite forgot her good sense.

"Every day." She meant it to be sarcastic. She'd never had tea. She and Jane drank coffee. Reuben drank ale or cider. But apparently her companion took the remark for irritation.

"What kind would you prefer?"

Good God, were there different kinds? "Whatever you prefer," she replied. And sit down, she pleaded silently. Seeing the lower half of his body, encased in those skin-tight breeches, was making her utterly distracted.

In the uncomfortable silence that followed, Nathan did take a seat, but Delilah continued to feel the need of a fan. She suspected a telltale blush might have stained her cheeks. Nathan cast her a look which showed he was puzzled, and her tension increased when a black man entered the room and placed a Sèvres teapot before her.

Delilah would have kicked herself if she could. She should have asked for coffee, but no, she had had to be sarcastic. Now they were both staring at her, waiting for her to do something. Did he expect her to make the tea? She didn't know how, and she wasn't about to make a fool of herself by proving it.

Fight fire with fire. She folded her hands in her lap, settled back on the chair, and brazenly stared back at Nathan. When it became clear that she didn't intend to make the tea, Lester made it for them.

"Sugar and cream?" he asked.

Delilah nodded her head. She had no idea what one was supposed to put in tea, but she wasn't about to let them know that either. She noticed Lester eyeing her askance. *He knows I've got no business drinking tea with the likes of Nathan Trent, but he has to treat me as if I belong here.* She took courage from that.

"Not too much cream," she said. Lester had already put two large lumps of sugar in the cup. Delilah hoped it wouldn't taste like syrup. She waited until Nathan had been served, then took a sip. The tea was hot and strong. The bitter taste made her wish she had asked for more sugar. She would have much preferred coffee.

"Now tell me why you need to see my uncle," Nathan said.

Delilah was distracted again, this time by his hands. They were so slim, his fingers so long and elegant. So different from Reuben's massive paws with their thick, hairy fingers. *Suitable for a thin-blooded English aristocrat but terribly attractive.*

Speculation was back in his eyes, and Delilah knew it had nothing to do with Reuben's oxen.

"It's about my brother's debt."

"Forty shillings, isn't it?"

Delilah's expression showed her surprise.

"I have become acquainted with my uncle's affairs," Nathan explained.

"Reuben can't pay it."

His expression turned wintery, and the speculative glint disappeared. "Then I shall have to ask the sheriff to fetch his oxen." His words were like pinpricks in her skin.

"You can't do that," Delilah exclaimed. She started up from her seat, spilling tea on her dress. Nathan rose from his seat as well, but Delilah didn't pause. "He won't be able to put in the crops or anything," she told him as she dabbed

11

at her skirt with unconscious skill. "He'll lose the farm."

"I can't do him any more favors. My uncle has already extended the debt twice."

Delilah's pride turned to anger as she watched him settle back in his chair, the expression on his face even more cold than before.

"I'm not here to beg for special favors. I mean to work for Reuben's debt."

Nathan was in the midst of a swallow. Delilah saw that the hot liquid caught in his throat before it went on down.

"How?" he asked when he could talk.

"Here, in your house."

"Doing what?"

She didn't know whether he was stalling or he really wanted her to tell him what work she could do. His expression was beyond interpretation.

"I can cook, iron, sew, clean. I could even help take care of your uncle." Odd. What could she have said to cause him to look relieved? "I'm really quite good with sick people." The speculative look reappeared. She had hit a soft spot there.

"We are rather shorthanded as it turns out, but I'm not sure you are the right person."

The word "please" almost escaped Delilah's lips, but she held it back. "Reuben's got two little boys with Jane swelling up for another come spring. If he loses those oxen, he'll lose the farm."

She could tell he was undecided now. The expression on his face was set, like a mask kept firmly in place, but his eyes gave him away. He couldn't keep the interest out of his gaze.

"Reuben's a good farmer, and Jane's very frugal, but it's the taxes. They've gotten worse every year since the war. Last year Reuben had to borrow money. He was sure he could pay it back this spring, but farm prices are too low."

"I can't speak for my uncle. . . ."

He was softening. She couldn't let up.

"Do you know what it's like to look into the eyes of hungry children and know you have nothing else to give them? Of course you don't, not living as you do in this great big

12

house, but I do. They don't ask questions. At least not with words. Only their eyes ask. Their eyes tear me apart. I can't go back there knowing I failed."

She was aware that he didn't know how to refuse her. She had him cornered. Just a little bit more.

"I couldn't face Reuben either. He took me in after Mother died and our farm went for debt. He's never begrudged me a mouthful, even when he sees his own children hungry. Neither does Jane. Could you watch your children go wanting while someone ate their fill?"

"No, but then I don't imagine you would eat at all unless they made you."

Delilah blushed furiously. The only time she had fought with Reuben was the time he had found her trying to give her food to the children.

"What makes you say that?"

"You are the kind of young woman who would deny herself to help others."

"I am not." From anybody else, that would have been a compliment. Why didn't it seem so from him?

"Then why are you here? Did Reuben send you? Does Jane know you hold back food for your nephews? Anyone can tell you haven't been eating enough."

"What you imagine is quite beside the point — and impertinent."

He accepted her censure with a nod.

"Are you certain your brother can't repay the loan?"

"The tax collector demands coin, but we haven't seen any gold or silver in years. The merchants give only credit. That's why Reuben had to borrow from your uncle."

"But if I let you work off your debt, what will the other people say?"

"Do many people owe you money?" She didn't mean to sound impertinent, just curious.

"They owe my uncle. No one owes me anything, but that's not the issue. I can't allow debtors to work off their debts. I couldn't possibly find jobs for hundreds of people."

"Good God! Do that many people owe your uncle money?"

13

Nathan looked as if he wanted to say something rude and final, but he must have changed his mind. "We need coin, too. The government doesn't want goods or services from my uncle either."

"Then it's good business to give me the position," Delilah said, trying to bring him back to the purpose of her visit. "Anyone else would want to be paid in coin. I only want Reuben to have his oxen."

"Have you thought of how long it would take you to work off forty shillings?"

Delilah swallowed. "Would it be very long?"

"About four months."

Four months! She had thought in terms of weeks, not months. She tried not to think of being in the same house with Nathan for such a long time, but she was unsuccessful. She might be able to pretend his presence had no affect on her for an hour, but how could she stand to look at him in those breeches for four months! The shocking thoughts popping into her head made her breathless.

Still she didn't have any choice. Regardless of how witless he made her feel, she couldn't turn her back on Reuben.

"That's only about two shillings a week. I'm worth more than that."

"Not when I can get a grown woman for two and a half."

"I'm a grown woman."

"You're no more than a young woman at best, and I doubt your brother knows you're here. Furthermore, I don't know if my aunt will take you on."

"If you're the heir, you ought to be making the decisions."

"That's an opinion not shared by anyone else in this household."

He looked angry with himself. Delilah could tell he hadn't meant to say anything that personal.

"I'm newly arrived, and my aunt has been running my uncle's house for years."

Delilah could see her advantage melting away. His sympathy for her plight seemed to be fading.

"You may not find anybody else who wants the job," Delilah said, thinking quickly. "People around here don't like

14

your uncle. They won't work for him, not if they can do anything else. Considering all the men the Redcoats killed in the war, and you being fresh from London, people are more likely to spit on you than work for you."

Nathan flushed.

She hadn't said that to hurt his feelings, but she had to have the job.

"If that's so, why would you work for me?"

She might as well be honest. "Because I have no choice."

"Have your brother and sister-in-law given their permission?"

"There was no point in asking before I had the position."

"I couldn't take you without it."

"Then you will take me on?"

When he didn't answer right away, she thought he was trying to decide whether she was suitable. But the look in his eyes told her he was thinking of something else.

"I think we ought to have a trial period, and you must have your brother's permission."

"I meant to tell him as soon as I got home," she said. "It only made sense to talk to Mr. Buel first."

"And you found me instead."

Relief made her careless of her words. "I near'bout swallowed my tongue."

"Was I that much of a surprise?"

"What do you think, with me expecting your uncle or your aunt to come to the door? Instead you showed up looking like I don't know what."

"I take it I was a disappointment."

"Oh, no." She corrected herself. "I mean, yes. I thought at first they'd hired you to help out and wouldn't have a place for me."

"There's not much difference," Nathan muttered.

Again he looked irritated with himself. He might be as much of a stranger in this house as she was. That made her feel a little less nervous. And a little curious.

Nathan stood up. "I'll have someone take you back. Sorry, I forgot. My aunt and cousin have the buggy. It will have to be the cart."

"I can walk," Delilah said, rising to her feet. "It's not much more than five miles."

"I may be a Redcoat," he said, anger momentarily flashing in his eyes, "but I don't force females to walk home. Finish your tea."

He disappeared, leaving Delilah alone to assimilate the shock of finding that rather than working for a grasping, cruel, ugly old man, she was going to be in daily contact with the best-looking man she had ever seen.

But she was a levelheaded girl. Nothing ever fazed her for long, and she didn't doubt she would have herself completely under control soon. Working for Nathan Trent, or living in the same house with him, wasn't going to upset her.

And he seemed to be interested in her. The speculative look never left his eyes for long. He had been swayed by her story, and everybody knew sympathy often preceded a warmer feeling.

Stop this! What honorable interest can a man of his station have in the likes of you, a yeoman farmer's daughter? If he was interested, it had to be only physically, without regard for her as a person.

And he was an Englishman. That alone ought to make her dislike him, make her hate being his servant. She had been only eight when that famous declaration was written in Philadelphia, but she remembered the fighting, the men who never came home; she remembered her father dying of his wounds. She couldn't forget. She wouldn't forgive.

Chapter Two

With a muttered oath, Nathan pushed away the papers he had been studying. He rested his elbows on the desk, head in his hands, his slim fingers digging into thick, blond-brown hair. With a second muttered oath, he lurched up from the high-backed armchair and walked over to the window, his lower lip wedged between his teeth.

He barely noticed the beauty of the manicured lawn as it fell away to the water's edge or the luxuriant foliage of maples, elms, and willows that shaded the grass or leaned out over the slow-moving waters of the Connecticut River. He was only vaguely aware of the lavish display of color in the formal rose garden, the carefully tended beds of dahlias, canna, and tuberoses, or the less controlled growth of morning glory and trumpet vines. Even though the open window let in the soft, late summer breeze, on it the fragrance of freshly scythed grass, he was aware primarily of the unfolding disaster on his uncle's desk.

The door behind him opened. He turned. Serena Noyes, a tall, thin, faded woman with bad skin and a penchant for choosing colors accentuating her pallor, stood squarely in the doorway. Her long, bony fingers clutched the handkerchief with which she habitually dabbed at angry eyes, eyes Nathan had never seen produce a single tear. Skin cobwebbed with fine wrinkles, wisps of escaping dull-brown hair streaked with gray, and a surfeit of lace in her cap, around her bosom, and at her cuffs made her ap-

17

pear fragile. Her sharp, penetrating voice gave a different impression.

"Have you finished going over the accounts?" Not even her tone could hide her fear.

Nathan nodded.

"Well, are we ruined?"

"We have very little cash," Nathan replied with a weary sigh, "but Uncle Ezra is wealthy enough to support a dozen people."

"God be praised," Serena cried and collapsed onto a high-backed settle liberally furnished with gold brocade cushions. "Ever since I found the cash box empty, I've suffered the most awful nightmares. Ezra never tells me anything."

"You can relax now."

"Relax?" Serena responded, the anxiety in her voice replaced by bitterness. "You're the one who's rich."

"You'll always have a home here."

Serena sat forward and glared at him without any trace of family affection or liking. "But I don't want to live here."

"I'm sure if you spoke to Uncle Ezra, he would provide you with a sufficient allowance to—"

"How? Him lying like the dead!"

"The doctor says he could recover his wits any day."

"That doctor wouldn't know weak lungs from loose bowels," Serena snapped angrily. "I think Ezra's brains are addled. If he ever does wake up, he'll be a complete idiot. We'll be ruined.

"*You* don't know anything about making money. He should have left Maple Hill to me," she continued when Nathan remained silent. "I'm his sister. I'm the one who's lived with him, taken care of him. What are you but a Redcoat? It's a shame you never joined the army. Someone might have shot you."

A hot flood of anger jolted Nathan. "Why don't you shoot me, Aunt Serena? You could tell the sheriff I was a burglar come all the way from London to steal the cash

18

box. I'm sure these patriotic, *law-abiding* colonials wouldn't disbelieve you."

"Don't mock me, Nathan Trent," she hissed angrily. "There're times when I'm angry enough to shoot you both. I could run this place better than either of you."

"I can learn."

"What's there to learn? Those people owe us thousands of pounds. Make them pay or take everything you can."

Nathan started to tell his aunt about Delilah, about how there might be another way, but changed his mind. He didn't want to share Delilah with her. Up until now his only identity in Springfield was as an extension of Ezra and Serena. But with Delilah, Serena and Ezra were *his* aunt and uncle.

He was surprised to find he didn't want to share anything else about Delilah either. He pointed to the papers scattered on his uncle's desk. "Uncle Ezra's done that rather often already. It can't make him very well liked around here."

"Liked?" Serena repeated, incredulous. "Ezra never cared whether anybody liked him or not. Why should he? People only came around when they needed money."

"But what's the point of taking more cows and wagons and bedsteads? Do you know we have a dozen butter churns?"

"If they can't pay, Ezra takes what they have. If they don't have anything, he puts them in jail."

"They'd come closer to settling up if they could earn a living. We have no use for those churns. I can't even sell what we have without a court order."

"I suppose you'd let those shiftless farmers keep owing money?"

"No," Nathan said, thinking of what had happened to his family, "but they need their livestock and farm equipment. We need cash. As things stand, nobody is getting what he wants."

"You sound like Sam Adams," Serena said with a deri-

19

sive laugh. "That kind of talk was all right before the war, but it won't do now."

Nathan bit his tongue. There was no point in trying to explain anything to his aunt. She wouldn't understand because she didn't want to. He walked over to the window.

"I'm going to fight you for Maple Hill," Serena said after a slight hesitation, "Ezra couldn't have been in his right mind when he made that will. I'm sure I'll win if I take it to the General Session. They'd never decide in favor of a Tory."

Nathan's anger boiled over. He was tired of being treated as an outcast. He swept his fingers through his hair before turning on his heel to face his aunt. "If you so much as speak to a living soul about challenging the will, you'll leave the house with no more than the clothes on your back."

Serena blanched. "You wouldn't dare. I have my rights . . . You can't threaten me. This isn't England where you precious lords can do anything you please."

"I'm not a lord, and I have no more freedom than you, but I will not be robbed."

"This should be mine," Serena said, flinging out her arm. Her gesture took in the whole library, its oak-paneled walls, its shelves filled with leather-covered books, its furniture crafted with skill and tended with care. "You have no right to it."

"As long as Uncle Ezra is alive, it's neither mine nor yours," Nathan said. "We would make better use of our time if we turned our minds to solving this tangle."

"There's nothing to solve. They borrowed money from your uncle. When the time is up, they pay it back or we take something of theirs in exchange. Can you do that?"

Nathan thought of the hundreds of colonists whose unpaid debts had ruined his father and caused him to commit suicide. He also thought of his mother, broken in spirit and frail of mind, living out her last years with a hired companion. He tried to stamp down his thirst for revenge; he attempted to choke down the feeling of satisfaction at knowing these people now suffered as he had suffered; he endeavored to remember he didn't want to be like Uncle Ezra or Aunt Serena.

He tried, but he failed.

"Yes," he said, feeling ashamed of the tremor of satisfaction that skittered along his spine.

"Good. Still, it's a good idea to send the sheriff. They'll try to talk you out of it. That awful bully Reuben Stowbridge might even threaten you."

Nathan remembered the shame of hearing his own father beg the sheriff to spare their home, to leave his wife a few of her favorite possessions. He remembered even more clearly the cold refusal, the methodical carting away of everything that could be moved, dismantled, or ripped up.

"I'll go," Nathan said, his eyes as cold as his aunt's.

"Don't be so thick headed," Delilah snapped. "Do you think I want to work for Nathan Trent?"

Ezra Buel had died three days after she'd visited Maple Hill. Reuben was furious that she would even have considered working for the old man, but he was adamantly opposed to her working for Nathan Trent.

Delilah faced her brother and sister-in-law across the table, her hands on her hips, an expression of fierce determination molding her features into the look of a woman much older than her nineteen years—she hoped.

"I won't let you be a servant to anybody, especially not to a damned Englishman," Reuben shouted.

"There's no use kicking against what can't be helped," Jane told her husband philosophically. "The young man can't be worse than his uncle."

"I won't have it," Reuben repeated mulishly.

"You didn't object when I helped Mary Nunn," Delilah interjected.

"Mary is a God-fearing woman, even if I can't say as much for Bradley Nunn," Reuben said. "But I wouldn't

21

trust any female in the same house as a damned Redcoat."

"Serena Noyes and her daughter live with him," Delilah pointed out. "That should be sufficient protection."

"No!" Reuben shouted.

"Then tell me how you plan to run this farm without a yoke of oxen?" Delilah demanded, her patience growing thin. Didn't Reuben see she couldn't stand around and watch him lose everything he had because of his stubborn pride?

"The sheriff is going to be here first thing in the morning. What are you going to do when it comes time for spring planting—put Jane in harness?"

Reuben tried to protest, but Delilah swept on.

"And what are you going to do when you lose everything you've got? Tell me that, Reuben Stowbridge, because you will lose it if you can't carry flax to market or haul lumber or plant spring crops. It won't do your boys a particle of good to starve just so I can avoid the shame of working as a servant. And what about the baby?"

Backed into a corner, Reuben reacted as he often did. "Tom Nutting won't take my oxen," he shouted. "I'll break his head first. Maybe I'll shoot him. I should have shot Ezra Buel."

Delilah wanted to scream with frustration. Would Reuben ever forget he had been a war hero? Once he had charged a redoubt of British soldiers and single-handedly killed every one of them. Now he thought shooting somebody was the answer to everything.

"What good will that do?" Delilah demanded. "They'll only send more men the next day."

"Dammit, Delilah, I can't let my sister pay my debts. I couldn't hold up my head if I did."

"I don't mind."

"Well, I do!" he thundered. His shouts woke the boys and they started to whimper.

"You go to them, Reuben," Jane said.

Reuben disappeared up the ladder to the small loft where the two lads slept.

22

"It's unaccountable," Jane shook her head. "He's ready to break the sheriff's head and shoot Nathan Trent, but he's as gentle as a woman with those boys."

She paused and looked away. "Reuben isn't the only one who feels shamed that you should have to do for us what we can't do ourselves." She turned her gaze back to Delilah. "But I'll not tell you to go or stay. You must decide for yourself."

Delilah knew what she had to do, and she knew Jane would somehow bring Reuben to accept it. She slipped outside.

The sky was unusually bright for this late in the evening. A bank of low-lying clouds deflected the last rays of the sun to the earth, immersing everything in a rosy glow. She loved being outside at dusk. She enjoyed feeling the bite of the cool, invigorating air after a hot day, the spring of the earth beneath her feet; and she liked hearing the birds in the treetops squabble over roosting places.

The evening air was heavy with the musty odor of ripe grapes fallen to the ground under the arbor next to the house. Even the rank odor of the animal yards was not wholly unpleasant. There was a comfort in familiar sounds and smells.

It really wasn't much of a farm—at less than fifty acres it was too small to support a family of five-about-to-become-six—but Delilah only had to think of the hours of solitary backbreaking labor Reuben had put in to know how much he loved it. Except for a cow lot and pig pen at the edge of the woods, a vegetable garden behind the arbor, and a barnyard and chicken coop beyond that, nearly every foot of cleared land was under cultivation.

Unlike most of the yeomen, who farmed only enough land for their own needs, Reuben had cleared extra land to grow crops to sell. But prices had fallen so low it was all he could do to buy a few necessities for his family. She *had* to work for Nathan Trent.

What was wrong with her? Why couldn't she say his name without feeling a twinge of excitement. He had probably taken her into that fancy drawing room just to show her how far below him she was. Okay, so she didn't hobnob with members of London society and she didn't drink tea every afternoon from bone china, but that didn't make her a social outcast. She was just as good as he was. A war had been fought to prove it.

It galled her to have to reenter his house as a servant. She had made the choice to sacrifice her pride, not her family, but she didn't have to like it.

Anyway, it was a waste of time thinking about Nathan Trent. She'd probably never see him again once Reuben's debt was paid. Still, even if she did not, she wouldn't forget him. No woman could forget a man like Trent.

Daniel Shays, captain of the local militia, stopped by later that afternoon. Shays was one of the most famous people in Massachusetts. He had fought at Lexington, Concord, Bunker Hill, and Stony Point. Because of his bravery, General Lafayette had given him a fancy sword. But brave as he was, Daniel Shays was just a poor farmer, and he'd had to sell the Lafayette sword to pay his taxes.

Reuben told him what Delilah wanted to do.

"Ought to have it paid up before Christmas," Shays said.

"I won't let her put one foot inside that house," Reuben exploded. "I'll find some other way to pay."

"I wasn't thinking of your debt," Shays replied. "I was thinking how useful it would be to have somebody at Maple Hill on our side." They all looked at Shays in surprise. "Something has to be done soon," he explained, "or the courts are going to take all our property. Abel Tucker's place was sold up last month. It only brought thirty cents on the dollar, not enough to cover Abel's debts, so they threw him in jail. Before that they sold a farm out from under a sick widow. Even sold the bed she was lying on."

Reuben made a furious, strangled noise.

"People won't stand for it much longer, and Nathan

Trent and his like know it. They'll be planning something in return. A smart young woman like Delilah might over-hear some plans or get a glimpse of important papers."

"Do you mean spy on him?" Delilah asked. She couldn't believe he was asking her to do it. Women were never al-lowed to do anything dangerous.

"They can confiscate our property, but they can't sell it without a court order," Captain Shays explained. "I have a plan to stop them from holding court, but they're bound to try to stop us. If we know what they mean to do, we might be able to stay ahead of them until elections next spring. We intend to put someone up against every one of them. Then the General Court will change the laws that let merchants get rich while the farmers, who fought for everybody's freedom, starve."

So it was decided Delilah would go to Maple Hill.

But now that she was to become a spy, she didn't want to go.

Nathan cracked the whip above the horse's head. The quicker he got out of Springfield, the better. After his uncle's funeral, he had deposited Serena with her friends and had headed straight for his buggy. Much as he wasn't looking forward to picking up Delilah, it had to be better than standing about waiting for condolences from people who clearly had no desire to speak to him. Nathan saw hate in the eyes of the people who lined the path outside the church.

Now that Ezra was dead, it was directed toward him.

He wondered if Delilah felt the same way. It had been a week since he had seen her, but not a single detail of the visit had escaped his memory.

He could still see her face, rounded with the freshness of youth, her deep, blue eyes open and curious. Except for her generous lips, her features were finely drawn, her lashes long, her eyebrows narrow and thinly sketched. Her skin was unfashionably tanned, and she parted her thick, dark brown hair in the middle, allowing it to fall unrestrained over her shoulders. The coarse material of Delilah's loose-fitting dress had neither revealed the rounded contours of her figure nor concealed the fact that her body had outgrown the shapelessness of youth. Nathan's imagination had had no trouble filling in the details.

It had been doing so over and over for the last three nights.

He didn't understand what it was about this country maiden that aroused his senses when more sophisticated women had failed to do so. Brazenly forcing her way into his home and using every means at her disposal to coerce him into letting her work for him, she had irritated him. Yet she attracted him so strongly he had given her the job without asking for a character reference.

He knew it wasn't a good idea to take a stranger into his household, but he'd been unprepared for Delilah's effect on him. Having a lovely woman in his parlor begging him to give her a job put everything in an entirely different perspective.

Besides, he lusted after her.

Lusted, for God's sake! Not simply liked her or sympathized with her or thought she was beautiful or admired her courage. The thought of her in his bed, naked in his arms, kept him tossing, half-awake, half-tormented, even in sleep. She had seldom been out of his mind for as much as five minutes in the last seven days.

He did understand this attraction. It was a common, primitive desire for a woman unlike any he had known. A challenge of a sort. A woman of the land, of the earth, whose hips swayed like a wind in the treetops, whose eyes danced like a brook across rocks, whose lips moved like the ocean against the shore, whose mere existence mesmerized him.

But seeing Delilah in much the same situation he had been in a few years earlier aroused his sympathy as well as his admiration. Most women would have looked for a husband, a way out. Not Delilah. Having found a solution,

26

she was determined to shoulder the burden despite her family's objections.

He was glad he could help her and himself at the same time. Indeed, he was so attracted to her that at times he had been tempted to forgive the obligation altogether, but he didn't dare. That would invite everybody who owed him money to come hammering at his door, demanding the same thing, and he'd end up as poor as he'd been before he left London.

But Nathan hadn't always been poor. In fact, until five years ago, he'd been the pampered only son of a rich father. Then, without warning, he had been thrown into a desperate struggle to keep his father from going bankrupt.

Yet similar as his and Delilah's situations were, he was as far removed from her as from an enemy in war. Her brother and hundreds of colonials just like him owed Nathan thousands of pounds they didn't want to pay back. These same people, or people like them only four years earlier had destroyed his father's business by refusing to pay their English debts. Well, he wasn't going to let them deprive him of a second fortune. If anybody was going to be ruined, it would be these bloodthirsty colonists.

Still, when he remembered the way the people had looked at him outside the church, he felt less sure. His uncle might not have minded being a social leper, but Nathan did.

One look at the Stowbridge farmhouse made Nathan feel like a villain. How could his uncle mean to foreclose on such a pitiful holding? And Ezra Buel had certainly meant to do that. Nathan had found explicit directions to the sheriff in his uncle's desk.

The family he saw standing in front of the mean dwelling aroused his sympathy even more. A powerfully built young man, his pregnant wife, and his two small sons stood facing Nathan, who despite all his vows to the contrary, knew he could never dispossess these people.

27

But the look on Reuben Stowbridge's face as Nathan pulled his buggy to a stop before the small group told him any kindly thoughts were not returned.

"Good morning. I'm Nathan Trent," Nathan said as he climbed down from the buggy.

"I know who you are," Reuben growled in reply. "If I had my way, I'd shoot you before I let Delilah set foot on your place." He didn't nod his head, touch his cap, or offer any kind of conventional greeting. He simply stared back at Nathan, his face set, his body rigid with the effort he was exerting to keep his temper under control.

"I hadn't expected a warm welcome," Nathan said, deciding to treat Reuben's words as a jest, "but neither did I expect to be threatened before my feet hit the ground."

"I will shoot you if anything happens to my sister." Reuben's expression didn't change, but Nathan could tell the man's hold on his temper was slipping. It wouldn't take much for this angry giant to explode into violent action.

"I'm Jane Stowbridge," the woman said, her expression no more encouraging than her husband's. "I agree with my husband about Delilah."

"I killed a lot of Redcoats in the war," Reuben said. "I wouldn't mind killing one more."

"Don't threaten me," Nathan warned, his anger beginning to rise. "I didn't make you borrow the money."

His impulse was to get back in the buggy and drive away as fast as he could. If he hadn't been certain Delilah wasn't anything like her brother, he'd have *given* them a pair of oxen before he'd let her inside his home. They were crazy. They had to be. Sane people didn't go around threatening to shoot other people the minute they set eyes on them.

Yet despite his own anger, Nathan knew he'd have shot just about anybody if it would have kept his father from losing everything. These people owed him only a pair of oxen, but they were probably no more able to handle their

28

debt than his father had been. Some of his anger died. He might as well try to be friendly.

"My uncle's illness kept me pretty close to home. I haven't had much chance to meet my neighbors."

"I'm not your neighbor, and I don't want you here," Reuben said.

It was clearly a waste of time to try to be friendly, so they might as well get down to business. "I looked over your loan this morning," Nathan said, still trying to keep his tone cordial. "It's been extended twice already."

"Ezra was happy enough to lend us money *and* extend our credit until we voted him in as justice of the peace," Reuben answered angrily. "The first thing he did after the election was show up with a bunch of writs giving him the right to steal our property."

"Then you should be relieved that your sister has come up with a way to pay off the debt."

Reuben reacted as if he'd been struck in the face.

Nathan hadn't meant to hurt his pride. Well, maybe he had. He didn't like Reuben. The man's blind anger and stiff-necked prejudice made him mad. He knew the type too well. Loud and aggressive and unwilling to listen to anyone who wasn't stronger or bigger than they were.

"If it wasn't for the babies, I wouldn't let Delilah within a mile of your place," Reuben lashed out, his anger now held in only by his wife's grip on his arm.

"Delilah is a good worker, but she's not a field hand," Jane put in. "You see, she's not worked too hard."

"What do you think I am, a white slaver?" Nathan asked, incredulous. The sooner he got Delilah and headed home, the happier he would be. "Where's your sister? I must be getting back."

"Afraid some debts will slip through your fingers while you're gone?" Reuben asked with a sneer.

"My aunt doesn't like to be left alone. Our situation is rather remote."

"You must have enough servants about the place to hold off an army."

29

Nathan gave up. Nothing he could say was going to make a friend of this man. "Call Miss Stowbridge, please. I'll send someone over for her trunk."

"I might bring it myself," Reuben said belligerently. "I might take it into my head to see how you're treating her."

"By all means, come any time," Nathan said. He hoped the angry young giant wouldn't accept his invitation, but it was ridiculous to think he would try to keep a man from visiting his own sister.

"Now, if you would call your sister."

"Delilah!" Reuben shouted over his shoulder loud enough to be heard halfway to the next county.

Nathan hoped she would hurry. With Reuben and his wife treating him like a blood brother to Lucifer, and the two boys staring wide-eyed as if he were the boogeyman, he almost wished he'd lingered after the funeral.

"Jane, you'd better bring her out. The sooner we get this man off our land, the sooner we can breathe deep again."

Chapter Three

Delilah drew back from the window. She couldn't spy on Nathan Trent.

She could have if he had been Ezra Buel. But the young man talking fearlessly to Reuben had nothing of his uncle about him, and the thought of betraying him filled her with self-loathing. True, he was handsome in a way that at any other time would have caused her to smile wistfully and dream of moonlight walks and whispered conversations, but it was the character evident in him rather than his looks that skewered Delilah's composure and impaled her resolve. His was an honest face, straightforward, seeking to hide nothing. Why couldn't he scowl as he had that morning at Maple Hill? She had been a fool to think she could be around him and remain unaffected.

The fact that she'd spent the last week thinking about him should have convinced her she was rapidly losing control of her emotions. But she had been so self-confident she hadn't realized she was in danger until she'd looked out the window. Watching Nathan do his best to endure Reuben's belligerent anger with a smile made it impossible not to admire his courage and to feel sympathy for him.

This man was full of contradictions, and that intrigued her.

Two nights ago it had seemed the right thing to agree

31

to Captain Shays's proposal. All she had to do was keep her ears open and report anything she overheard. That couldn't be called spying. It was more like gossiping. Everybody did that.

But then Reuben had explained that spying meant breaking into Nathan's desk, reading his private letters, telling him lies, and breaking her word to him. She'd never intended to do anything like that.

How could she tell Reuben and Captain Shays that her sense of right and wrong was more important than preventing her friends' families from being stripped of their worldly goods? How could she explain that it was essential she not betray the trust of a man they considered an enemy?

"What's keeping you?" Jane asked from the doorway. "Mr. Trent is impatient to be off, and I'm ready for him to be gone. I don't know how much longer Reuben can hold his temper."

"I can't do it," Delilah blurted out.

"You don't have to," Jane said, not the least upset. "Reuben and I disliked the idea from the start."

"It's him," Delilah said, impatient with her sister-in-law's lack of understanding. "I can't do it to him."

"For heaven's sakes, whatever do you mean?"

"The spying. I can't spy on him."

"Oh, that. I doubt he'll hurt you if he finds out, but you needn't worry. I'll tell Reuben you've changed your mind, and that'll be the end of it."

"You don't understand," Delilah said, taking hold of Jane's arm, hoping she could force her sister-in-law to understand why her feelings had changed. "He's different from Buel."

"I don't know how you can say that about a man who collects debts by taking another man's possessions."

How could she explain the signs of goodness she saw in Nathan Trent when she didn't entirely understand her own feelings? How could she ask Jane to separate the

32

man from his deeds when she couldn't do that either? "I can't explain it," she said lamely, "but I know he's different."

"I don't agree," Jane said, "but that doesn't matter. I'll speak to Reuben. He's bound to find some other girl willing to take your place."

"No!" Delilah said. Her tone stopped Jane whose hand was on the doorknob. "I'll go."

"Are you sure? Once you leave here, you can't very well change your mind again."

"I'm sure. I owe it to Captain Shays."

The admiration in Jane's eyes made Delilah even more miserable. How could she tell her sister-in-law she didn't want to go because she was attracted to Nathan Trent? Even worse, how could she admit she was going because she couldn't stand the thought of another woman going in her place?

When Delilah stepped out of the house, Nathan wondered if he had been asleep the morning she'd come to Maple Hill or if a completely different woman stood before him.

He shuffled his feet. His heart beat a little faster. She was wearing the same simple style of dress as her sister-in-law, but all similarities stopped there. Whereas Jane's face showed the strain of bearing three children, Delilah's was as flawless as that of a young woman being introduced to London society.

How could he have fooled himself into thinking he could remain indifferent to her presence at Maple Hill? His aunt and cousin certainly wouldn't be.

Even though he was powerfully affected by Delilah's physical allure, it was the look in her dark blue eyes that riveted his attention. Though she schooled her expression into impassivity, her eyes made him think of a wild creature coming face to face with its hunter. Did

33

she think he was going to ravish her the moment he got her to Maple Hill?

Maybe not, but he'd bet fifty guineas Reuben did. The big man stepped up so close their noses almost touched, his eyes glaring at Nathan, murder in their depths.

"I'll not have any man look at my sister that way," he thundered.

"Unless you plan to put blinders on every man in Massachusetts, you'd better keep her locked away," Nathan replied. "She's a lovely woman."

"I'll not have her taken lightly either. Touch her and I'll . . ."

"Stop it, Reuben," Delilah's voice was clear and firm. "Mr. Trent is new to Massachusetts," she said, shifting her gaze from her brother to Nathan. "Maybe he doesn't know it's rude to stare."

"I know it all right," Nathan confessed with a wry grin. "I just can't do much about it."

Delilah's cheeks flamed pink.

"You must promise not to mistreat my sister-in-law, Mr. Trent," Jane said. "I'd throw myself on public charity before I'll let her be dishonored."

Oh God, he hadn't latched on to one of those ranting Puritan families, had he? If Delilah started preaching at Aunt Serena, it would be easier to live in Bedlam than at Maple Hill.

He struggled to get his temper under control. "You are welcome to come by at any time to assure yourself she's not being mistreated. However," he added, hoping to forestall any intention Reuben might have of camping on his doorstep or Jane might entertain of making the trip a daily pilgrimage, "I hope you won't make your visits either so frequent or so long as to interfere with the performance of her duties."

"You just be careful what kind of *duties* you're talking about," Reuben warned. "My sister's a gently raised girl."

34

"We don't overwork our servants," Nathan snapped.

"She's not a servant!" Reuben roared. "Not to you or anybody else." He started forward aggressively, but Nathan held his ground.

Delilah wasn't listening. No one had ever called her a lovely woman. And to have this gorgeous man say it, as if it should be perfectly obvious to everyone, shocked her. Her heart beat faster, and a flush again stained her cheeks. But Reuben's menacing movement brought her out of her abstraction.

"Fetch my trunk, Reuben." The unexpected sharpness of her command caused her brother to turn back to her.

"What need can you have of so many clothes?"

"I'm promised for four months. It'll be winter before I get back. Hurry," Delilah urged when her brother seemed unwilling to move. "I'm sure Mr. Trent is anxious to reach home before dark."

Reuben's sons, silent the whole time, peering at Nathan from behind their mother's skirts, ran forward when Delilah knelt down and held out her arms. They buried their faces in her shoulders, and she held them tight, one arm around each child.

"You be good boys while I'm gone," she said, a catch in her throat. "Remember, Daniel, you promised to watch out for David when the baby comes. Your mama won't have much time with me not here to help. She's going to depend on you." She turned to David. "And you make sure you mind your brother." Nathan was certain the child couldn't be much more than a year old.

Reuben emerged from the house, carrying an enormous trunk Nathan guessed was made of solid oak and lined with cedar. The huge man easily lifted it into the back of the buggy and secured it into place with rapid, jerky movements, a clear sign of his still dangerous mood. The boys scampered for the safety of their mother's skirts at the sound of their father's angry voice.

"You can be off now without fear of the dark overtaking you," he said scornfully, "And if anything happens to my sister—"

"Rest easy, Reuben," Delilah interrupted. "I'll be home before Christmas. Then we can put this out of our minds."

Delilah tried not to look back as the buggy pulled out of the yard. She told herself four months wasn't a long time, but right now it stretched endlessly before her. Every turn of the buggy's wheels seemed to be carrying her irrevocably away from that small farmhouse. She couldn't quell the foreboding sense that, for her, there would be no way back.

She sat, staring straight ahead at the rough track they followed between fields and through woods. She didn't dare let herself look at the man seated beside her; she tried not to even think about him, but her body was so thoroughly alert to his presence she started to wonder if she might not be coming down with a fever. She had never felt so peculiar in all her life.

It had taken all her courage to step out of the house. She supposed she was still too upset to react normally. Young, rich, and handsome, Nathan Trent was the image of the man she had dreamed of all her life, and— she could admit it now even though the very thought shamed her—if he hadn't been a hated Englishman and a grasping, greedy landowner, she might have fallen head over heels in love with him the minute she'd clapped eyes on him.

His arm brushed her sleeve. It was an almost indiscernible pressure, but it felt like the rending of the heavens to Delilah. Her whole body tensed, and a shaft of heat buried itself deep in her abdomen.

The thought of having to sit next to him for a whole hour demolished her composure. It was mortifying that she, Delilah Stowbridge, who had always been considered such a sensible girl, one not likely to be overset by trifles, certainly nothing so insignificant as working in

36

the home of a perfect stranger and spying on him, should have her wits scattered by a mere touch.

The buggy lurched under them. With a pithy curse, Nathan jumped down to inspect the wheel that had bounced through a deep mudhole.

"I'm amazed it isn't broken," he said. "It seems to me this country is little more than a series of tiny farms joined by nearly impassable lanes."

"You don't have rutted lanes in England?" Delilah asked, her pride stung.

"Farms in England are part of a proper estate. The landlord sees the roads are kept up."

"I'm sure the General Session would be glad to put the roads in your care."

She was being sarcastic again. Why did she always have to take everything he said as a personal insult?

"I don't have time."

"Then I suppose you'll have to put up with the ruts." Delilah lapsed into stony silence, leaving Nathan irritated and perplexed.

He climbed back in the buggy, but he had hardly gotten under way when a horse and rider materialized out of the woods.

"Hey, you there, stop!"

Nathan didn't know the man on horseback, and he couldn't think of a reason for his pugnacious tone of voice, but he obligingly pulled his buggy to a halt.

"Colonel Lucius Clarke," Delilah hissed through motionless lips. "A big landowner and a bigger mouth." Nathan glanced at her in sharp surprise.

"I hear you've forgiven Stowbridge's debt," Clarke bellowed without so much as a glance at Delilah. "You can't do that."

Nathan was dumbfounded that a perfect stranger should know his business, no matter how imperfectly, but he was appalled that the man would attempt to interfere in it. Clarke didn't seem to be particularly ill bred, but Nathan sensed a kind of low cunning about him. There was also an aggressive sense of the self-righteousness.

"I'm Nathan Trent, Ezra Buel's nephew."

"I know who you are," the man said, chafing at the delay. "I'm Colonel Lucius Clarke, and I want to know what you mean to do about this Stowbridge business."

Nathan was tempted to say he'd be damned if he would explain his affairs to anyone, but that wouldn't win him any friends or give him the information he needed. "Why should what I do be any interest of yours?" he asked as nonchalantly as he could.

Colonel Clarke looked at Nathan as if he were a simpleton. "You hold twice as many loans as the rest of us. Anything you do, they'll expect the rest of us to do."

Nathan decided he disliked Colonel Lucius Clarke more than anybody he'd met since he'd come to Massachusetts. "But you don't *have* to follow me, do you?"

"Dammit, man, you may be nothing but a scurvy Redcoat, but you can't be that stupid. Surely you've heard what they're saying in the General Court. Things are so bad some of them want to pass a law forgiving all debts under five pounds."

The feeling of rage that surged through Nathan's body was so hot he couldn't think for a moment. In his mind's eye he pictured legions of nameless colonists conspiring to destroy him, and he made a silent oath that no matter what he had to do, he would never let that happen again.

"For God's sake man, don't sit there like you're deaf. Can't you understand what I'm telling you?"

"Of course I can," Nathan replied when he felt he could control his voice. "What can we do to prevent it?" Even the mutinous Colonel Clarke seemed surprised by the intensity of his response.

"We're gathering to decide."

38

"You're welcome to meet at Maple Hill." He could feel Delilah tense.

"Thanks." Clarke's stern face broke into an unexpected smile. "Glad to know you're with us."

"Where else would I be?"

"I wasn't sure, not with you letting Stowbridge off."

"I'm not. My aunt needs more help in the house, and his sister offered to work off the debt. I'm taking her to Maple Hill now."

Clarke ignored Delilah. "Don't do it. It'll cause trouble."

Nathan felt the hot tide of anger rise in him again. "Would you be willing to take my advice on how to handle your affairs?" he asked in a deceptively bland voice.

"Hell, I'd be crazy to listen to every fool who wanted to stick his nose in my business."

"Then you'll understand why I'll not be following yours. I shall expect to hear from you about the meeting. Good day."

Nathan slapped the reins, and the horse started off at a brisk trot. He had the pleasure of seeing Lucius Clarke's face suffuse with rage before he pulled away.

Nathan's apparent anger at Colonel Clarke was only a tithe of the rage Delilah felt. The colonel had ignored her, acted as though she wasn't there. Not even Nathan had done that. She and Clarke were Americans, they were supposed to stick together, and here he couldn't wait to get together with Nathan. She wouldn't mind spying on Clarke—or anybody else like him.

It did her soul good to see his face grow purple with fury as they drove off. It also pleased her that Nathan didn't agree with everything Clarke had said. He'd gone against advice to let her work off Reuben's debt. What else would he do, given the proper impetus?

Nathan couldn't help but realize the meeting with Clarke had made an adverse impression on Delilah. Just

39

offering a place to hold the meeting was probably enough to damn him forever in her eyes.

You can't afford to take a personal interest in everyone with a sad story to tell, especially not this girl. You get her settled at Maple Hill as quickly as possible, and then put her out of your mind. But telling himself he *ought* to have no interest in Delilah, and actually *having* none were two different things.

"How old are you?" That wasn't what he really wanted to know, but it seemed a good place to start.

"I'm turned nineteen," Delilah replied, wondering why he wanted to know her age.

"The same as my cousin. I hope you will become friends." If he was going to get her out of his system, he had to find a way to get her off his hands. If she made friends with Priscilla, maybe he could forget her. Yet he was reluctant to do that. It disturbed his conscience to think of setting her down in a strange situation and then ignoring her.

"I'll make every attempt to please your cousin," Delilah answered in an even voice, "but I thought the household was your aunt's responsibility."

"That's true," Nathan admitted, wondering if he should warn her about Serena. He decided to wait. Maybe things wouldn't be as bad as he feared.

They rode in silence for a while longer.

"Tell me about your family," Nathan asked. He wasn't particularly interested in her family history, but if he was to get his mind off her nearness, they had to talk about something.

"Reuben is all the close family I have."

Silence.

"You must have had a mother and father. It was my understanding everybody did." His attempt at lightness was not returned.

Her story came out in one angry spurt.

"My father was wounded at Saratoga fighting the Brit-

40

ish. Mother was never the same after he died. When the farm started to slip into debt, she didn't care. She died before they came to take everything away."

"I'm sorry. . . ."

"Reuben was a great hero," she continued, "but it didn't do him any good. They didn't pay him enough to make up for the time he spent away from home or the musket balls they dug out of him. All he could do was buy that pitiful farm."

"Surely he—"

"It wasn't enough people like you had to kill my father and mother and take their farm, you had to start in on Reuben," she said, turning to accuse him.

"Now wait a min—"

"Why can't you leave him alone?"

Nathan realized it was useless to try to explain that, even though he was English, he had had nothing to do with her father's death, her mother's decline, or the loss of their property. If he could keep her talking, maybe she would work off some of her anger toward him. He didn't relish having such hostility in his house.

"Tell me how Reuben got into trouble. Remember, I just got here," Nathan explained when he saw her well-stoked wrath about to explode. "There's a lot I don't understand just yet."

"Why should you want to understand? All you have to know is everybody owes you money. If they don't pay, you can take whatever you want."

"Indulge me," Nathan said, wondering how Delilah could show so much anger toward him and still be appealing. "Pretend I'm a friendly uncle you've gone to for help."

"You're hardly older than Reuben. And you're not the least friendly or you wouldn't have threatened to take Reuben's oxen. Besides, I wouldn't go to any Englishman alive."

"Okay, look at it this way," he said sharply, his patience wearing thin. "We've got to spend the next hour in this buggy. If we don't talk about something, I'll die of boredom. Then I'll probably take it out on the horse, or you." Delilah turned her startled gaze upon his face. "You're absolutely burning with reproaches you want to fling at my head. I give you permission to fling away."

"I don't know that I can *fling* them at you, not rightly," she admitted. Now that Nathan had given her permission to blame him for everything, she felt reluctant to do so.

"Don't worry about who is to blame," he said, his tone a little less harsh. "Just tell me what happened."

"It started before the war," Delilah began, "the War of Independence." She was unsure of what to say, even why she bothered to say it at all, but she felt a need to explain it to him, to have him understand it wasn't Reuben's fault.

"Everybody thought once we drove the British out, things would be all right." She looked down at her hands rather than at Nathan. It was hard to talk about the British, knowing he was one of them. "Instead, they got worse."

"Why?"

"King George wouldn't let us sell anything to England, only buy. Then the merchants demanded we pay with gold. Pretty soon we didn't have any left. So the states started printing paper money. They even paid their soldiers with it. Reuben thought he was being smart to turn his into land right off, but then the cost of everything started going up and the price of what he could grow went down. Nobody would take paper money anymore, and nobody had gold. The taxes got so high people could hardly pay them."

"Is that what happened to Reuben?"

Delilah fell silent a moment.

"Reuben's a good farmer, and Jane is a good manager, but, well you see, Reuben likes to do things for people.

Nothing much, just a few pennies once in a while, but money never stays in his pocket. When it came time to pay the taxes, he didn't have enough."

"So he borrowed what he needed from my uncle and couldn't pay him back."

Delilah nodded her head. She couldn't help but feel ashamed of her brother's debt. It was a blow to their pride.

"Whose idea was it that you work for me?"

Delilah's head jerked up. "Mine. Do you think Reuben or Jane would have suggested such a thing, even if they had thought of it? They'd starve first."

Nathan's head did a little jerking of its own. "Have you forgotten that until just a few years ago everyone in Massachusetts was English? Or do you think the mere act of crossing an ocean has transformed you into a different race? I can't see that this savage land has cleansed your souls of pride and covetousness, or any other sin. In fact, if my uncle's correspondence is any indication, greed and lust for power run unchecked throughout the colonies. England might not be the perfect society, but at least we are civilized."

They rode for a while longer without speaking, and Nathan was aware his anger was being drained away by a very different kind of feeling, one that was a direct consequence of Delilah's presence. He gripped the reins a little harder. His body grew stiff from leaning imperceptibly away from her. No woman had ever so affected him.

Her mere presence filled him with excitement. She was truly lovely, but she was unforgiving—and she probably cursed his very existence. What could be appealing in that? Yet he wouldn't have stepped down from the buggy if he had been given the chance.

Give up! Get your mind off Delilah. Think about your loans, Lucius Clarke, the General Court.

"I don't know what you're expecting, or maybe I

should say afraid of, but you'll be well cared for at Maple Hill. You won't be overworked, and you'll be returned to your family not a whit worse off than the day you left."

"I didn't expect you would hurt me." Her utter complacency caused Nathan's desire to flare. Shocked by the burning intensity of his feeling, he spoke harshly to hide the truth from her.

"Then what in the blazes did you expect? You and your family acted as if I were a first lieutenant of the devil come to cart you off to my private chamber of horrors."

Delilah couldn't help but laugh. It helped cover some of her embarrassment. "I guess we have acted pretty badly," she admitted. "I doubt if I could explain it to you."

"Try," Nathan said, a sharpness in his voice. "Since we are to live under the same roof, I should feel a good deal more comfortable if I didn't have to wonder whether your fondest wish might not be to sink the carving knife into my back rather than the Sunday roast."

Delilah felt herself blush.

"I don't want to do anything to harm you."

"That's a relief. For a while there I was wondering if I might not be better off trading you for someone a little safer." He felt Delilah looking at him, hard. "I don't yet know what it's like to live in the colonies, but in England we're not used to going to bed in fear of our servants."

"You needn't be sarcastic."

"I'm surprised you noticed," Nathan shot back. "What with holding me personally responsible for the war, the ruin of your family, and the loss of God only knows how many oxen, horses, cows, and pigs, I don't know how you found time to notice sarcasm."

"A deaf man could notice sarcasm in an Englishman,"

44

Delilah replied, nettled by the truth of his accusation as well as his ungentlemanly conduct in putting his feelings into words.

"You aren't going to try to convince me your treatment of me has been subtle, are you?" Nathan asked.

"Nothing about this situation is subtle. I hope you don't expect me to face the loss of everything I own without showing anger. I can't do it. Could you?"

Honesty made Nathan shake his head.

"It may not be fair to blame you, but you *are* an Englishman, and if England hadn't closed her markets to us, this might not have happened."

"And I just happen to be the one who holds your brother's debt, even though I'm not the one who lent him the money and it wasn't my fault he went into debt."

Delilah nodded.

"You can't imagine how much better it makes me feel to know you have no compunction in blaming me for everything that happens, regardless of where the blame should rightly be placed."

"How dare you imply I'm unfair."

"Aren't you?"

"You hold my brother's note," Delilah persevered. "You could forgive it."

"Then I would have to forgive all the other debts owed me."

Delilah looked uneasy. "Well . . ."

"Would you forgive them if it meant you had to sell your house, maybe even your farm?"

"But you're rich."

"Would you have all the landowners pauper themselves, or is it just me you're trying to ruin?"

Delilah didn't answer, but she seethed. He had no right to accuse her of trying to ruin anybody. *He* was the one causing all the trouble.

"And what are the farmers going to do when they run

out of money a second time and need a loan to pay their taxes, or to buy a new bull or have a few drinks?"

"You don't have to be insulting," Delilah said. "Nobody expects you to give away all your money . . ."

"I'm relieved to hear that."

". . . but there must be some way for people to pay back their loans without losing their property."

"Isn't that what you've done?"

"Y-yes."

"Then the other farmers can too. It's better than my giving everything I have to a lot of strangers. I daresay they wouldn't do it for me."

Delilah knew several farmers who would probably forgive a debt to a particular friend, but she was certain if they were in Nathan's place, every one of them would do exactly what he was doing. In fact, to be perfectly honest, several would have been even worse than Ezra Buel.

"Is that what you're hoping, that the farmers will all figure out new ways to pay their debts?"

"I'd much rather have my money than a lot of oxen. I haven't been here long enough to know all I should about my uncle's affairs, but he's got too much money tied up in small loans to suit me. I want some venture capital."

"What is that?" Delilah asked, bewildered.

"Money to invest," Nathan explained. "Some people can get rich farming, but a man has to go into business if he wants to become wealthy."

Delilah didn't know what he was talking about. Everyone she knew was a farmer, even rich Ezra Buel had been one.

"I don't understand," she said.

So Nathan explained how a farm was basically limited in the amount of goods it could produce. But when it came to manufacturing goods for sale, the only limit was the size of the market and the strength of the competition. He talked about bankers, shipowners, factors, and lawyers. He talked of rates of interest, margins of profit, costs of doing business, and the difficulty of finding cheap raw materials. He explained how a man could begin with just himself and end up with hundreds of people working for him.

"Everything depends on the cities," he finally explained. "There people can't grow or make all the things they need and want, so somebody has to do it for them. The more of something I sell, the more money I make."

Delilah wondered if Reuben had thought of that. Probably not. All he wanted was a chance to live out his days in the familiar ways. He would be lost in the world Nathan Trent wanted to create. Jane, too, though she would get along better. Jane could adapt. She doubted Reuben could.

But what about herself?

She knew the answer immediately. She hardly understood any of what Nathan had said, but it sounded like a challenge, possibly even a dangerous one. And that excited her. She liked challenges; she even looked forward to them.

A thought struck her. Had she agreed to spy on Nathan because it represented a challenge?

No. Spying was deceitful, and she hated dishonesty. She had agreed to spy on Nathan because she'd had no other choice. But she was aware of an uneasy feeling in the pit of her stomach, a feeling that had appeared sometime after she'd given her word that she would act as a spy.

What was it? It made her nervous and apprehensive but not uncomfortable, wary and distrustful but not afraid, excited and expectant but not pleasured. She couldn't put her finger on it, but she knew instinctively it was dangerous and it had something to do with Nathan. Something about him was a threat to her.

Delilah pulled her mind back from these thoughts.

There would be plenty of time for soul-searching later. They were approaching Maple Hill. She felt as though the bars of debtor's prison were about to close around her.

Chapter Four

"What's she doing here?" Serena Noyes stood squarely in the middle of the hall.

"She's here to help Lester," Nathan explained.

"Then take her back where she came from. I won't have her kind here."

Delilah resisted a desire to draw close to Nathan. Though she hadn't been willing to admit it, even to herself, the closer they had come to Maple Hill, the more apprehensive she'd become.

To be met by a shrill harpy the minute she stepped inside the dark hall was almost too much of a test of Delilah's courage. She remained rooted to the floor, unable to retreat or move forward to meet Nathan's aunt.

"She's doing it to pay off her brother's debt."

"I told you I won't have her in my house," Serena repeated. "She's poor, dirty, and probably stupid."

Delilah tensed, her gaze riveted on Serena's angry face. All thoughts of running away were forgotten. She might be poor—she had never expected to be anything else—but she wouldn't stand for anyone calling her dirty or stupid.

"I bathe regularly," she said, looking squarely into Serena Noyes's watery blue eyes. The challenge was unmistakable. "In fact, one of *my* requirements is that I have the use of a tub and hot water *every evening.*"

"The cheek of her," exclaimed Serena, but her voice betrayed a note of uncertainty.

"Neither am I stupid," Delilah continued. "My work will soon give you reason to know that."

"I doubt you'll find much scope for proving anything in the wash shed," retorted Serena spitefully.

"Miss Stowbridge will work with Lester," Nathan stated firmly. "Now that he's got someone to help him, you and Priscilla can entertain more frequently."

Serena directed a venomous look at her nephew. "I won't have that girl serving my friends."

"As you wish," Nathan replied, unperturbed. "We need to settle on sleeping quarters. Which room should she have?"

"The loft above the laundry."

"I thought one of the rooms on the third floor would be suitable," Nathan said. Delilah could see the tension in his jaw as he spoke.

"You mean to house a common servant under the same roof as your own family!" It was not a question. It was a screech of disbelief.

"It's only a temporary situation. She will return to her brother's home as soon as the debt is repaid."

"It would be better if you had taken his oxen."

"I have assured Reuben Stowbridge and his wife that his sister will be safe while she is here. I can only do that by keeping her under my own roof. Don't you agree?"

"No, I don't," Serena snapped. "And to think you're forcing this wretched girl on me the very day my beloved brother was laid in his grave. You have no consideration for my feelings, Nathan Trent, and no respect for your uncle's memory."

Delilah felt a twinge of sympathy as Serena dabbed ineffectually at her eyes.

"I'm not as gullible as your friends, so you can put away that handkerchief and stop pretending an affection you never felt," Nathan said with brutal frankness. "After what you said when you heard the conditions of his will, I'm surprised you didn't shovel the dirt over him yourself."

"I would have if it would have changed anything,"

Serena said, dropping all pretense. "Ezra was hard and cruel. I don't suppose you'll be any different."

"That will depend on your attitude toward me," Nathan stated. "Miss Stowbridge would like to know her duties."

Serena directed a hate-filled glare at Nathan before turning her cold gaze on Delilah. "You can help Lester clean up, keep the rooms dusted, lay the fires, and empty the grates. You ought to have some experience in that, even in a farmhouse."

"Is that agreeable?" Nathan asked.

Delilah nodded her head. She recognized deep-seated enmity in Serena Noyes's eyes, but she also saw fear. What hold could Nathan have over this embittered woman?

"Your uncle would never have settled for a servant girl in exchange for his money," Serena hissed, a look of scorn and triumph mingling in her eyes. "He'd have taken the oxen, the plow, and the farm if necessary, but he'd have had his money. That's how he built Maple Hill." She pointed an accusing finger at Delilah, a look of loathing on her distorted features. "She's how you're going to lose it."

"I don't intend to lose my inheritance," Nathan said.

Delilah could see him struggle to hold back the words balanced on the tip of his tongue.

"You're just like your father," Serena almost screamed. "There's no Buel in you. You're all Trent, soft and weak. If Ezra had left Maple Hill to me, I'd have thrown the wretches out months ago."

"Even Uncle Ezra believed in giving people a chance," Nathan said, dismissing the subject. "Now I think you ought to show Miss Stowbridge to her room."

"Put her where you want. I'll have nothing to do with it." Serena Noyes turned and stalked away.

Nathan forced himself to breathe deeply and slowly. He wanted to get out of the house before the wave of exasperation, which had been building inside him all day, swept away the last of his self-control. But after his aunt's disgraceful display of hostility, he couldn't leave Delilah without some explanation. He weighed his words carefully.

"Aunt Serena expected to inherit Maple Hill. She hates me so much she can hardly stand to set eyes on me."

"Then why doesn't she leave?" Delilah asked. They had started to climb the ornate staircase situated midway in the hall.

"Uncle Ezra left me everything, even the linen and china. I'm to provide a home for her until her daughter marries."

"Can't you give her an allowance and let her live somewhere else?" Delilah knew this was none of her business, but she couldn't imagine Nathan sharing a roof, even one as large as Maple Hill, with such a shrew.

"Another of Uncle Ezra's conditions prohibits me from allowing Serena to live anywhere except Maple Hill."

"Surely you can ignore that."

Nathan smiled, rather grimly Delilah thought. "Apparently he didn't trust me not to. He saddled me with a set of trustees for the next two years."

"No wonder the poor woman is eaten up with bitterness."

"I wouldn't mind her being bitter at Uncle Ezra," Nathan said. "It's her anger at me I find difficult to tolerate."

As they reached the upper landing, they paused before a double dormer window with a superb view of the maple-lined avenue leading up to the house. Those trees were all that remained of the stand of sugar maples that once covered the hillside and had given the estate its name.

"Why does she hate you?"

"I'm an Englishman."

Delilah felt a stab of shame. After seeing how ugly that attitude was in Serena, she was embarrassed to have felt the same way herself. "But you're her nephew."

"My uncle came to Massachusetts forty years ago to escape being impressed into the navy. After he became prosperous, he invited his sisters to join him. My mother stayed in London and had a son, and Aunt Serena came to Massachusetts and had a daughter. It's difficult for her

52

to see the cause of her ruined hopes staring her in the face day after day."

Delilah wondered why she felt no sympathy for Serena. They were actually in somewhat similar situations.

"I can see how you might sympathize with her," Nathan said, "but it's unfair to hold me responsible for everything that's happened in her entire life."

His words merely increased Delilah's feeling of guilt. Hadn't she done the same thing?

Nathan led her to the back of the hall, where he opened the door to a small but bright and cheerful room. The yellow-painted walls were plain, the woodwork was unadorned; but the bed, piled high with mattresses and pillows, was covered with a cotton print bedspread which matched the curtains at the single dormer window. A chair, washstand, and wardrobe were the only other pieces of furniture.

"It's not very large," Nathan apologized, "but I'm afraid you won't get to spend much time here. There really is a lot of work to be done."

It was to be her own. Delilah thought it was the most beautiful room she had ever seen. "It's perfect," she said, unconsciously comparing it to her own tiny loft at home.

"Talk to Aunt Serena if you want anything else."

Delilah looked up quickly, surprise in her eyes.

"She will calm down before long."

Delilah could have sworn she saw a trace of tolerant amusement in Nathan's eyes.

"She hates change, but she's been complaining more than Lester about needing help."

"Wouldn't it be better if I told you and you spoke to your aunt?" Delilah had already decided to stay as far away from Serena as possible, but as she spoke she realized the real reason for her suggestion was a desire to hold on to some contact with Nathan.

"I won't be around very much," he said. He had turned to leave the room, depriving Delilah of the chance to see his expression, but she thought there was a different sound to his voice. "I have a lot of property I've never seen. I can't be a good landlord until I know what I own. Now you must meet Lester. He'll be your real boss."

For the first time Delilah wondered about the wisdom of coming to Maple Hill. Serena Noyes obviously disliked her. Nathan Trent would be gone much of the time. And now she was being turned over to a third person, probably one whose only interest in her was getting as much work out of her as he could. Delilah felt abandoned.

Unlike the two upper halls, which had large windows at each end, the downstairs hall was lit only by the fanlight above the front door. Runners on the stairs and hallway deadened the sounds of their steps, and in the fading light of the late afternoon, Delilah felt like a ghost floating through the house.

"Most of the time you can find Lester in the butler's pantry or the dining room," Nathan said as he opened the door to a room at the back of the hall. The walls were lined from floor to ceiling with shelves loaded with china, crystal, and plate. A tall, gaunt, gray-haired black man sat at a low table, polishing a large silver serving spoon. "When he's not here, he's in the kitchen."

"You needn't be looking at me like you seen a spook," the man said, not unkindly, as he waved the large spoon at Delilah. "I get to tell you what to do." He lifted himself out of the chair. "Here, you finish with the polishing while I see to setting the table. Before you know it, Mrs. Stebbens will be hollering for me to fetch the first course, and me without the linens laid out yet. Don't stand about with your mouth open, gal. Ain't you never seen a black man before?"

"Of course I have," answered Delilah, quickly recovering her composure. "I can also set a table."

"What would the likes of you know about setting any table in this house?" Lester asked, condescension clearly written on his thin features. "You polish that silver nice and bright, and I'll see about teaching you to lay out a table the way proper folks do it. But not until you have

54

every piece shining so bright it'd put your eyes out to look at it in the sunlight."

"I was told I would help wait on the table," Delilah said with a certain hauteur of her own. She wasn't about to become a servant to a servant.

"And have you breaking up the china? I may let you hand around the dessert if you're careful, but you ain't getting your hands on the soup tureen or one of them serving dishes. Why, it'd take you five years to pay for them."

"I'll leave you two to get acquainted," Nathan said, turning toward the door. "Remember, let my aunt know if you need anything, but Lester will probably be able to take care of you."

"You'd best talk to old Lester," the black man said the minute the door closed behind Nathan. "Mrs. Noyes was born with a real nasty streak, and she's been improving on it ever since."

Delilah looked despairingly at the closed door through which Nathan had just disappeared.

"He ain't going to help you none," Lester said. "The only man that's going to stand between you and that screech owl is me, so you better get to work on that silver while I see to the table." He paused before he went through the door, turned back, and gave Delilah an appraising look. "Now that I think of it, it might be better if she don't see much of you for the next few days."

"She knows I'm here."

"Sure she does, but if she don't see you, it won't bother her so much."

"I don't understand."

"You will," said Lester as he turned and opened the door. "You most surely will."

Delilah seated herself at the table and picked up the spoon Lester had been working on. She had never seen anything so beautiful in her life. It had a double-line border and a heavily embellished initial — B — engraved on the handle. The only piece of silverware Delilah could remem-

55

ber seeing was a small cup someone had given Reuben when he was born. They had sold it during the war. She looked at the shelves around her. There was enough silverware in this one room to pay off half the debts in the county. What right did Nathan Trent have to own so much expensive tableware when hundreds of people around him were struggling just to put food on the table?

She felt an irrational urge to snatch up that big china serving dish and smash it on the floor. Why couldn't Nathan give up just one of these pieces for Reuben's debt? It wouldn't mean anything to him. He probably wouldn't even know it was missing.

But Delilah dismissed the idea almost as soon as it occurred to her. Nathan might forgive the debt, but that wouldn't cancel it. Only when she had paid back every shilling could she leave Maple Hill with her family pride fully restored.

Then she might smash a piece of his china.

She picked up a cloth and began to polish the spoon. She would turn her back on Nathan Trent just as quickly as he had closed the pantry door on her. Her only loyalty was to Reuben and to the others who were laboring under debts and struggling with high taxes. No, she didn't owe a single thing to Nathan Trent or his kind.

But Delilah couldn't dismiss Nathan that easily. She still felt a lingering excitement, a tantalizing remnant of what she'd experienced while sitting next to him during the buggy ride. She had never been around a man as attractive as Nathan Trent, and it was impossible for her to simply forget him. He was too tall, too handsome, too alive. But it wasn't just his looks. It was what he did to her that was so shocking.

He made her feel funny all over.

When she was close to him, an ache pervaded her whole body. If he smiled, she was light-headed; if he frowned, she felt she had no head at all. Her breath seemed shallow, her chest tight, and her voice a mere whisper. First she was too hot; then she felt cold. She couldn't remember ever feeling so strange.

Her mind was no better. Not only had she begun to question her reasons for coming to Maple Hill, she was starting to question Captain Shays as well. No sooner did she decide Reuben had a right to keep his oxen than she also decided Nathan had the right to collect the debts owed him. The moment she determined Nathan was the enemy and should be treated as one, she realized he was just as much a citizen of Massachusetts as she was.

She laid the spoon down, took up a large fork, and began rubbing it very hard. She didn't want to think about it. Everyone would be better served if she kept her mind on her work and off Nathan Trent.

Nathan mounted the steps two at a time and went quickly to his room. He knew it was callous to desert Delilah so abruptly, albeit it was better to leave her with Lester than his Aunt Serena, but he didn't want to be around her any more than necessary. She was too damned enchanting. As long as it was only a matter of physical attraction, there was a chance he could control his interest. He had known many beautiful women in London, some more beautiful than Delilah. Realizing they were beyond his reach had made it possible for him to think of them without uncontrollable longing and desire.

He pulled his clothes off and, in his haste to change and be gone, unceremoniously tossed the discarded garments on the floor. He wanted to be out of the house before Priscilla had a chance to corner him. That was one woman he *did* look upon with longing and desire—a longing to get away from her and a desire never to see her again. He reached into the cupboard for one of the two clean shirts left there.

For all practical purposes, Delilah was just as much out of his reach as any grand lady in London, but he had been thinking of her lustfully from the moment he had set

57

eyes on her. He didn't know how he was going to get through the next four months. He couldn't stay away from home all the time.

Maybe he could go to Boston and see what was happening in the General Court. No, he had to stay closer to Maple Hill and put his estate in order. And that meant putting Delilah out of his thoughts.

But he found himself bedazzled by a pair of dark blue eyes. There was nothing special about them. There must be thousands like them in Massachusetts. Still, something about this pair would not let him go. And, of course, her mouth was too wide. She had only smiled once, but instead of thinking her smile showed too many teeth for classic beauty, he had wanted only to know what had made her smile, and had wanted to see her smile again.

He thrust his arms into his coat. *She's a witch. She's one of these Puritan witches I've heard about. They can make you think anything they want.*

Of course he didn't believe that.

Priscilla Noyes was waiting for him at the bottom of the stairs. She was really quite attractive—she had a thin, fragile beauty, much as her mother must have had twenty years earlier; but lines of discontent were already visible on her face, and the hard, predatory look in her eyes made Nathan's skin feel cold and damp. His aunt made no secret of the fact that she planned on Nathan's marrying his cousin, but Nathan had no intention of sharing his name, his fortune, or his bed with Priscilla Noyes. To him, that would be practically the same as marrying Serena.

"Going out again?" Priscilla sighed with spurious sympathy. "It must be a great responsibility to be so rich."

"It's easy to *be* rich," Nathan said impatiently. "The hard part is to *keep on* being rich."

"That shouldn't be difficult. Mama says Uncle Ezra left you a simply huge amount of money."

Serena Noyes never missed an opportunity to use the supposed size of her brother's fortune as a weapon. When

58

she wanted something Nathan wouldn't buy, she didn't see how anyone so rich could be so stingy. When she offered him advice, she did so because even such a huge fortune wouldn't last long the way he was handling it.

"What Uncle Ezra left me," Nathan responded, too brusquely for courtesy, "is dozens of farms which need careful management so they won't *cost* money rather than make it, widely scattered investments in businesses suffering due to poor times, hundreds of uncollectible debts scattered the length and breadth of Massachusetts, a huge house that swallows money without making a shilling, and a few hundred pounds in cash. We could easily end up as poor as Delilah."

Priscilla tittered; it was a silly laugh, one intended to show she knew they were sharing a joke. "You don't have to pretend with me. I know you're just saying that because of mother."

Nathan swore aloud.

Priscilla drew closer. She was always trying to get close to him, to get her hands on him. It made Nathan's skin crawl. She whispered confidentially in his ear.

"She's still angry that Uncle Ezra left you his money. She says you're an Englishman, that you really aren't part of the family." She laughed. It was the same silly titter. "She says there ought to be a law against Englishmen inheriting our money."

"Just as there ought to be a law requiring all colonials to pay their English debts?"

Priscilla stared at him, her face blank. Nathan was exasperated with himself for letting his temper get the best of him. "All Uncle Ezra did to become an American was cross an ocean. I've done the same, so I guess I'm an American too."

"That's not what people are saying," Priscilla told him. She was leaning against him, their bodies touching from thigh to shoulder. "But they might look upon you differently if you married a *real* American."

"I'm not ready to think of marriage," Nathan said, carefully disengaging himself. "I have too much to do."

Priscilla put a hand on Nathan's arm and looked directly into his eyes with her vacuous gaze. "You need a wife who won't make demands on you, one who understands you, one who knows how to be the mistress of your house."

"I couldn't ask anyone to marry me. I may go back to England."

"A dutiful wife would follow her husband anywhere."

Not even the threat of returning to England seemed capable of driving Priscilla into retreat.

For the last two weeks Nathan hadn't let himself think about going back. He had come to Massachusetts with the intention of converting his inheritance into cash, but two things stopped him. First, the amount he could realize from the sale of his uncle's estate wasn't enough to enable him to reestablish the family business. Second, even if he could sell all his uncle's property and business interests, he wouldn't get half of what they were worth.

"Mother says you're going to lose everything Uncle Ezra left you," Priscilla continued. "She says you don't have his brains or his backbone."

She said that just as blithely as if she were telling him to expect company for dinner. If this was her idea of how to seduce a man, she would never get married.

"Let's hope your mother is in for a big surprise," he said, trying to control his temper. "It would be a shame if all of us had to leave Maple Hill."

"We can't. Where would we go?"

Nathan could see genuine fear at the back of Priscilla's eyes, and some of his impatience disappeared. She was selfish, vain, and maybe a little bit stupid. She could never adapt to poverty.

Delilah could go from being rich to poor without a pause, he thought. And without making her husband feel it was his fault. Not only that, she would find a way to help him get ahead again. With a woman like that, no man would be poor.

Damn! He had to get his mind off Delilah.

"Tell Aunt Serena I won't be back for dinner," Nathan said as he picked up his gloves and riding crop from a long, narrow table.

"You always work so hard. Don't you like to have fun?"

"I don't have time," Nathan replied impatiently. "I've got to see several people tonight. It'll be easier if I eat at the tavern."

"You must be tired of talking to men all the time. You need a change of company." Priscilla smiled sickeningly. She oozed over and leaned suggestively against Nathan.

"The more I move among the neighbors, the more quickly I will begin to understand them," Nathan said, disengaging himself once again. "And the quicker I understand them, the better I will manage my property. I want to start making money, not just to be trying to collect what's owed me."

"Uncle Ezra always said the easiest way to make money is to take what someone else already has."

"That's not my way," he said.

But now he understood his uncle better. It was a wonder the old bastard had been allowed to die in bed.

Chapter Five

Nathan had a choice. He could think about the cold and tasteless dinner served him at the tavern, he could brood over the fact that everyone seemed anxious to avoid his company, or he could ignore both disagreeable realities and let his mind dwell on Delilah.

He took the easiest alternative, despite knowing it was a waste of time to think about her. Or any woman. They could not be trusted. He had reason to know. He had made a fool of himself once already.

Nevertheless, thoughts of Delilah invaded his mind. He couldn't fool himself into thinking this weakness had its roots in a feeling of guilt over leaving Maple Hill before she'd had time to settle in. Delilah could take care of herself. He'd seldom seen a more self-sufficient woman.

No, he had run away because he couldn't control his response to her. Not admirable behavior, certainly not the kind he expected of himself. And he couldn't use Delilah's devastating effect on him as an excuse. Any self-respecting man ought to be in better control of his emotions. It was probably just as well he'd learned of his susceptibility. A few days more and it might have been too late.

If their first meetings had been battles, he would now be suffering from nearly mortal wounds. And as far as he could tell, he had yet to make any impression on her. She still hated everything he stood for, and her feelings for him consisted of equal parts of dislike and distrust.

A prudent man would recognize when the encounter was

lost. He would withdraw his forces and wait for a more propitious moment to fight. If the war could not be won, he would gather his forces and remove to a foreign land where he might begin over again.

Nathan knew he wasn't being prudent. He might never win the friendship of these silent, angry colonials—Americans they called themselves now—but he intended to win their respect. However, he wanted more than respect from Delilah.

He knew he couldn't treat her as he would another woman. As with the mute, somber men who directed angry gazes at him across mugs of rum or ale, too much stood between them. If he made a direct attack, she would repulse him without a second thought.

If he made a flanking maneuver . . . Well, one could never tell what might happen.

Nathan was back.

For a week the house had slumbered in a state of quiet waiting while he had traveled about the area to survey his holdings. Serena visited friends or spent the days in bed. Priscilla spent most of her time out riding. That left Delilah, Lester, and Mrs. Stebbens pretty much to themselves.

"It's almost like we own the place," Lester had observed after they had spent a quiet evening in the kitchen.

Delilah enjoyed Mrs. Stebbens's company, but she didn't feel the same way about Lester. She was certain he disliked her—she didn't like him much either—but he had already shielded her from Serena's vindictiveness.

"Don't think I do it for you, girl," he'd said when Delilah tried to thank him. "I was just looking out for myself. If that woman makes trouble for you, Mr. Trent will make trouble for me."

When Delilah asked him what he meant by that, Lester replied quite rudely, "When I wants you to know, I'll tell you."

After that Delilah pretty much ignored Lester, and life quickly settled into a dull routine.

Nathan's return to Maple Hill shattered that.

Serena got dressed and issued so many orders Lester turned from an affable despot into a moody tyrant. Mrs. Stebbens had to cook a dinner large enough to feed ten people, Delilah ran up and down the steps with cans of steaming bath water, Priscilla just puzzled over which gown to wear for dinner.

"Get yourself a pot and shell them peas," Lester told Delilah. "When you're done with that, pull a dozen ears of corn and shuck 'em. Mind you, I don't want them ears full of worms. I don't want silks left between the kernels neither."

"I'm not supposed to work in the garden," Delilah objected.

"You work where you's needed," Lester said. "Old Applegate's too laid up with the rheumatism to go fetching vegetables for dinner."

"I don't even know where the garden is."

"You can find it, girl. Ain't nobody trying to hide it."

"Why don't you give her a hand," Mrs. Stebbens suggested. "It's time for me to have dinner in the pot."

"It ain't no good being a butler if I has to go digging in the dirt while some green gal who ain't never been inside a house without dirt floors stays in the cool," Lester stated flatly. "Besides, Mrs. Noyes said she was to take over picking the vegetables. With all this rain, old Applegate can hardly get out of his bed."

"Come on," Mrs. Stebbens said. "I'll give you a hand."

"You supposed to be cooking supper, not gallivanting about no garden."

"There won't be any cooking without vegetables," Mrs. Stebbens grumbled as she searched in the cupboard for the particular bowl she wanted. "Wouldn't be any needed either if Mr. Trent would take a cold supper like civilized folks. When I agreed to cook for Mr. Buel, I never knew I'd be working for some foreigner who'd want hot food all hours of the day. You'd think that much to eat in the middle of the night would give the man nightmares."

"Sleeps like a baby from all I can tell," Lester said.

"I don't much care for that man," Mrs. Stebbens said to

Delilah as they made their way to a kitchen garden.

"These peas are cold," Serena said the moment Delilah set the bowl on the table. "I told Lester you were to bring the food to the table the minute it was done."

Delilah gaped at Serena. She could see the steam rising from the bowl.

Nathan raised his eyebrows in an unspoken question. "You should try eating your dinner in England," he said. "Half the time the grease is hard in the dish by the time it reaches the table."

"I wouldn't tolerate it," Serena stated emphatically.

"You'd get used to it," Nathan replied. "Or not eat."

He had done no more than glance at Delilah during the meal, but she thought she detected a note of sympathy in his voice. Serena must have heard it too because she unwisely decided to pursue the topic.

"I never admired the English," she stated, completely ignoring the fact that she had been born in England herself, "but I should hope they have better servants. This girl is useless."

"Why?"

"Just look at her."

Nathan sat forward in his chair and scrutinized Delilah intently. A flush rose in her cheeks.

"Speaking purely from a man's point of view, I find her appearance quite pleasing."

Delilah's cheeks flamed pink.

"Go wait for the next course," Serena snapped at her. "And make sure it arrives hot."

"The peas are hot, Mother," Priscilla said after Delilah had left the room. "They burned my tongue."

"What do you mean her appearance is pleasing?" Serena demanded of her nephew, ignoring her daughter. "She has no notion how to carry herself . . ."

Nathan's mind filled with the picture of Delilah's upright carriage and the way it thrust her young breasts well forward.

65

". . . her hair is too thick and long . . ."

He could imagine the clean scent of her luxuriant dark tresses as he buried his face in her neck.

". . . her skin is actually brown . . ."

He longed to touch her shoulders to see if they felt as soft and smooth as they looked.

". . . and that dress is an embarrassment."

Unburdened by thick layers of cloth and whalebone stays, the dress clung to Delilah's limbs, delineating every part of her body as she moved. Nathan's own body tightened in response to visualizing that.

"I would be embarrassed for her to serve any of my friends."

Nathan forced himself to focus on his aunt. "Then let Lester do all the serving or provide her with new clothes. Priscilla can teach her deportment. You can even offer to cut and style her hair," Nathan said, imps of mischief dancing in his eyes. "That way you can be sure it's just the way you like it."

"It's unthinkable I should personally tend a servant," Serena stated, aghast. "Not even your Uncle Ezra would have suggested that."

"He never provided you with a servant to tend," Nathan pointed out. "Lester tells me that until Uncle built this house, you did all the cooking and cleaning."

Unchivalrously forced from her position, Serena gave vent to the wrath burning inside her. "Ezra was a cruel, tightfisted man. It pleased him to see me work until I was ready to drop."

"Then be content you no longer have to," Nathan said. "Servants will do all the better for an occasional word of praise. As for making unfounded accusations . . ."

Nathan left the sentence unfinished, but his gaze settled unwaveringly on his aunt.

"I like Delilah," Priscilla said. "Don't you?"

Nathan felt sure Priscilla had asked that question for a particular reason, but her simple-minded stare obscured any thoughts that might be in her head.

"I hardly know Miss Stowbridge," Nathan replied, "certainly not well enough to have developed an emotional response to her."

"But you brought her here in the buggy. An hour is an awfully long time." There was definitely insinuation in her voice.

"Are you accusing your cousin of improper advances to a farmer's daughter?" Serena asked, aghast.

Priscilla pouted. "I just said I liked Delilah."

"Then I hope you will make friends with her," Nathan said. "She's bound to feel lonely."

"She'll do nothing of the kind," Serena said. "If that girl is lonely, she can go home."

Nathan steered the conversation into other channels for the remainder of dinner, but as Lester served the dessert, he said, "I'll be having quite a few people here on Thursday night. Ask Mrs. Stebbens to prepare some refreshments. You'll know what kinds they like better than I. We'll also need extra wine and ale."

"How many will there be?" Lester asked.

"Who's coming?" Serena demanded.

"I don't know, probably about twenty," Nathan said, answering both of them. "We'll need Delilah to help serve. Ask her to come in, Lester."

"That girl's not presentable," Serena protested even before the door closed behind Lester.

"The men won't care," Nathan told her. "They're coming to discuss what to do about the court closings. According to some of the people I talked to during this last week, the whole district is on the verge of rebellion."

"They should all be put in jail," Serena declared.

"Possibly, but there aren't enough jails to hold half the male population of western Massachusetts."

"Are there that many?" Serena asked, her color fading a little. "Will they fight?"

"I don't know, but they've chosen a war hero as a leader, someone by the name of Daniel Shays."

"Oh my God!" Serena moaned.

"There's also Luke Day—they tell me he's a huge man,

something of a bully—Adam Wheeler, Job Shattuck, and several others. Do you know any of these people?"

"Of course not," Serena snapped, "but I've heard your uncle talk about them. They're rough, lawless men. Are you sure there won't be any fighting?"

"I'm not sure of anything," Nathan replied.

Delilah came into the dining room during Nathan's remark. "You asked for me?" she said.

"I just wanted to let you know you are to help Lester with the serving this Thursday."

"Is that all?"

"It would be nice if you could wear something pretty."

Delilah bristled at the suggestion. "If I'm not good enough like I am, you can get someone else to carry around your wine and ale."

"Now see here, young woman, you're not to talk to us in that way." Serena was incensed.

"I'm here to work," Delilah replied, "not to be gawked at by a lot of drunken men."

"Our guests are never drunken," Serena insisted.

Nathan gave her a skeptical sidelong glance, but all he said was, "Wear anything you please. It's just that you're an attractive woman. That dress doesn't do you justice."

Nathan and Delilah stared at each other. How could she stay mad at a man who said she was attractive? Some of her anger evaporated. "It's the best I've got," she said more quietly.

"I'm sorry. I didn't mean to hurt your feelings," Nathan apologized.

Delilah's anger faded still more. "It's all right. You couldn't know."

The whole time Delilah helped Mrs. Stebbens with the washing up, she stewed and fumed and simmered. He had no right to expect her to dress up for a lot of his drunken friends to gawk at. And they would be drunk sooner or later. Her uncle owned a tavern, and it seemed that men weren't capable of going to bed unless they were tipsy.

And Nathan was no different. He drank brandy. A lot if the amount which disappeared every day was any indication. Delilah knew what happened when drunken men got around pretty females, and she made up her mind it wouldn't happen to her.

But she would love to have a pretty dress. Aside from a natural desire for beautiful clothes, she wanted to look pretty for Nathan even though he hadn't given her any reason to believe he thought about her any more frequently than he thought about the furniture.

Still he had called her attractive. Fortunately she had been able to keep from blushing. People had always told her she was pretty, but somehow it felt even better when Nathan said it.

She tried to tell herself not to be foolish, that Nathan only cared about how she would appear to other men, but she didn't want to admit that could be true. She had never been attracted to any man as she was to Nathan Trent. If it turned out he was totally disinterested in her . . . *You'd better keep your mind on your work and off that young man and pretty dresses. You're just asking for trouble.*

But two hours later, as she sat polishing the silver, Delilah hadn't been able to forget Nathan's request. In fact, it had become such an obsession that if she had had a dress at home, she would have walked back just to get it.

The opening of the dining-room door startled her. She was surprised to see Priscilla Noyes.

Priscilla paused as though uncertain of what to do. She walked over to where Delilah had laid out each shining utensil on a thick felt cloth.

"Do you have to polish the silver every time it's used?" she asked.

"Lester says your mother likes to see everything shining."

"I'm glad I don't have to do that. I'd bet it ruins your hands."

"No worse than washing dishes or scrubbing floors."

"I hadn't thought of it that way."

Priscilla moved around the table letting her finger trail along the edge. Clearly she had more on her mind than

69

polishing silver.

"Why did you get so angry when Nathan asked you to wear a pretty dress?" She didn't look up, just kept making invisible designs on the table with her finger.

"He had no business asking such a thing."

"He likes you."

"He hardly knows I'm around."

"He knows. His eyes follow you."

"Only to make sure I'm not late with the next dish," Delilah said. "I've never seen a man eat so much and stay so slim."

"He feels just the opposite about you. He told mother to see you had enough to eat. He seems to think you're underfed."

Delilah flushed in mortification. "I don't eat a lot because I don't want to," she said. "It's a waste to serve as much food as we did tonight. Most of it will be thrown out later."

Priscilla studied her for a moment, not with the stupid, vacant expression she employed with Nathan or her mother.

Finally she said, "I have a dress I can't wear anymore. I've grown too tall," she explained before Delilah could protest. "It's wrong for me — I never looked good in dark colors — but it would suit you just fine."

Delilah shook her head.

"It's blue," Priscilla added. "I heard Nathan tell mother he liked blue best of all."

"It's not proper for me to wear your clothes," Delilah protested.

"Why?"

"I'm only a servant. Your guests will think I'm getting above myself."

"Those men won't remember a thing except whether you're pretty or not."

"Thank you, but I can't."

"Are you sure? I've got more than one."

Delilah was more tempted than she wanted to admit. The chance to wear a real gown, even if it was only one tenth as nice as the pink gown Priscilla now wore, tempted her almost more than she could bear. But she thought of what

Reuben and Jane would say.

"Well, I guess I'll just have to give them to somebody else," Priscilla said. "Do you think Lucy Porter could wear them? Maybe they're closer to Hope Prentiss's size."

Priscilla might as well have stabbed Delilah with a pin.

Hope Prentiss and Lucy Porter, finding themselves unable to attract the attention of the very males Delilah was at pains to fend off, made it a point to constantly remind her of her poverty. When they had turned their poisonous barbs on Delilah's family, they had earned her perpetual enmity. She could no more think of either of them wearing Priscilla's blue dress than she could go on breathing.

"I guess I could take one," she said reluctantly. "But I won't wear it except when you have company."

Delilah was stunned to learn that Priscilla meant to give her six dresses.

"You can't have outgrown all these."

"Uncle Ezra bought up a lot of cloth. He said it was a waste if Mama didn't have it all made up."

"I can still take only one."

"I'll put the rest in the room next to yours," Priscilla said, having failed to talk Delilah into taking a second or third dress in case she spoiled the first. "I need the space," she explained when Delilah started to protest, "and this way you can take all the time you need to decide which one you really want."

Delilah felt guilty for even thinking about taking the dresses, but the certainty that otherwise they would go to Lucy or Hope was a wonderful salve to her conscience.

She decided on three.

Chapter Six

The kitchen was in a bustle. Even though Nathan had set supper forward an hour, they had barely finished cleaning up when the guests started to arrive. Lester had been absent for the last hour, taking cloaks and ushering the men into the drawing room where Nathan and Serena waited.

Serena insisted upon being present, even though Nathan had told her the men were there to discuss business. Priscilla took the opportunity to disappear.

"Didn't they eat before they came?" Delilah asked as Mrs. Stebbens took three meat pies out of the fire.

"It's Mr. Trent's orders," Mrs. Stebbens said, fanning herself from the heat. "Even Mrs. Noyes tried to tell him he was ordering too much food, but he wouldn't have less. I don't know what they do in London, but if this is how they eat, I'm surprised there's a one of them that can heave himself out of his chair."

"It's seems a sin to waste so much food," Delilah said looking at the plates piled high with hot biscuits filled with slices of baked ham, the custard cups, the blackberry pudding with sauce, the aged cheese, and the watermelon and fresh grapes. Every time she served a meal at Maple Hill it reminded her of the meager fare Jane set before her family.

"Where's that Lester?" Mrs. Stebbens fussed. "I need a tray for these pies."

"I'll get it," Delilah offered.

"What you doing up there, gal?" Lester asked when he found Delilah up on the ladder. "You know you ain't supposed to handle none of the dishes."

"I'm looking for a silver tray for Mrs. Stebbens," she said.

"You don't use a silver tray for hot pies. It'll burn your hands before you get it to the parlor. Here, git down and let me do it. You don't know nothing about which platter to use."

"Teach me," Delilah fired back. "Then you won't always have to do things for me."

"All in good time. Right now you stick to serving."

"Well, I can't do that if you won't allow me to handle the china, can I?"

"No, you can't," he said as he took a platter off the shelf and handed it down. "If you take this to the kitchen without breaking it, maybe I'll let you carry it into the dining room."

"It's about time," Mrs. Stebbens said when Delilah returned with the platter. "Mrs. Noyes will be complaining that the food is cold."

"Only if I serve it," Delilah said. "Lester could bring in coagulated grease and she wouldn't say a word."

Lester chuckled. "That woman's made up her mind not to like anything you do. I'd stay out of her sight if I was you."

"And how is a body to do that," asked Mrs. Stebbens, "with her dogging Mr. Nathan's heels like she was afraid he'd make off with the money box if she wasn't looking? You can't even ask the man what he wants for breakfast without her chiming in with her piece."

The bell for the drawing room rang.

"Probably wanting more wine," Lester said as he hurried away.

"You be careful you don't spill anything on that dress," Mrs. Stebbens warned as Delilah carried the last plate into the dining room. "It'll be a long time before you get another one like it."

Delilah blushed. She was wearing the blue gown Priscilla had given her. For the one hundredth time she wondered what Nathan would think when he saw her in it.

"I'm so jumpy it'll be a miracle if I don't spill something."

"And it's not because of those guests," Mrs. Stebbens said with twinkling eyes. "Maybe you can hide it from the others, but you can't hide it from me."

Delilah couldn't pretend she didn't know what Mrs. Stebbens was talking about, so she didn't try. "It's not that I have anything to hide. It's just that I'm not used to a man dressing like that."

"Fair sets your blood to boiling, doesn't it?" Mrs. Stebbens said with a wicked chuckle. "Indecent, I call it, but it makes me feel twenty years younger every time I set eyes on him."

"Please don't say anything to Lester."

"It's not him you've got to worry about. It's that Mrs. Noyes. If she thinks you're eyeing Mr. Nathan, she'll be on you like a cat on a mouse."

"I'm not eyeing him," Delilah said. "I merely said I couldn't be around him and remain unaffected."

"Could be he feels the same way about you."

"He never looks at me if he can help it," Delilah said, gripping the folds of her dress to hide her shaking hands.

"I know," Mrs. Stebbens said, "and it ain't natural for a healthy young man not to be looking at a pretty gal. Ought to be fair drooling every time you walk in the room. Instead he spends his time looking at his plate like he's never seen food before. Fair runs out of the room the rest of the time if you ask me. He didn't do that before you came."

If it hadn't been so ridiculous to think a man would hide in his own house, Delilah would have said Nathan was doing everything in his power to keep out of her sight. "He's got too much on his mind to be wasting time on a serving girl," she said as she picked up the plate of food.

"You're no serving girl."

"I am," Delilah said. "And it's best if none of us forgets it."

"How much money do you have tied up in outstanding debts?" Eli Beck asked Nathan.

"I can't say," Nathan replied, again surprised by the impertinence of these colonials. In spite of his efforts to be more genial, their intrusive prying had the effect of making him more distant. "I haven't had time to become fully conversant with my uncle's affairs."

"They're your affairs now, aren't they?"

"I guess they are."

"Then you'd better get conversant, or you may find yourself unable to go on living in this house."

The undertone of contempt in Eli's voice surprised Nathan more than his question had. Could it be Beck hoped that Nathan would lose Maple Hill? Did he mean to buy it in that case?

"What is your trade?" Eli asked. "I can't recall your uncle ever said."

Nathan didn't know what devil got into him. Maybe it was Eli's insistence on rooting out every bit of information he could. Maybe it was his antagonism toward men whose greed and insensitivity appalled him. Whatever the cause, the moment the words were out of his mouth he wished he hadn't said them.

"I was a painter."

Eli Beck looked at him as if he didn't understand the word, then hurried away to spread the news.

"It's bad enough you have to be an Englishman, but why did you tell him you were a painter?" hissed Serena. "In ten minutes there won't be one man in the room who'll respect you."

"They don't have to. I certainly don't respect most of them."

"Do you want to hold on to what you have?" Serena demanded furiously.

75

"Of course."

"Then you'd better stop acting so superior and listen. These men know what those farmers are up to."

"Why don't you open the doors to the dining room," Nathan suggested. "Maybe that will take their minds off my disgraceful profession."

Serena made a noise indicating supreme disgust with her nephew's attitude, then pinned a forced smile on her face and sailed away to preside over the refreshments.

But it wasn't the food that made them forget Nathan's background. Like a magnet, Delilah drew the gaze of every man in the room.

All week Nathan had been trying to keep his distance from her. He couldn't keep her out of his thoughts, but by staying away from the house most of the day and occupying his mind with business when he came home, he had gotten himself under some kind of control.

The sight of Delilah in that blue dress, wreathed in candlelight, destroyed all the progress he'd made. He still lusted after her, and if he wasn't careful, his state of mind would be plain to all.

Despite himself, he drew closer. She had been lovely, even in the drab, faded dress she always wore, but the blue satin gown transformed her. Her eyes danced with excitement; her whole body glowed with youthful vitality.

Nathan had never been so aware of her eyes. They were a deep blue, like dark lapis. The gown seemed to bring them alive. It was a simple muslin gown trimmed with ivory-colored lace at the sleeves and bodice. The neckline exposed her shoulders and the deep cleft between her bosom, while the cut of the gown emphasized her small waist and rounded hips.

Her lips, always full and inviting, parted in a smile to reveal a row of even, white teeth. Her hair was gathered at the back of her neck and topped by a cap which was at once too small and too pretty to be suitable for a serving wench.

Delilah had never looked like a serving wench, but tonight she looked like something out of one of his dreams. Considering the way some of the men were looking at her, he wished he could have kept her in them.

"How dare you dress like this in my house?" Serena demanded in a harsh whisper, struggling to keep the superficial smile on her face.

"Mr. Trent asked me to do so," Delilah hissed back.

"Why don't you bring me some of that ale?" one of the guests called out. "These greedy beggars won't let me pass."

"I want a look just as much as you," a second man replied.

"You should be thinking of your wife instead of this piece," another said.

"You think of her," came the reply. "I prefer to ogle this filly."

"Stop craning your neck, Silas. If I tell your missus, you won't be allowed out for a month." Raucous laughter greeted the little man's scowl of anger.

Delilah looked about her in dismay. She had been so concerned about making a good impression on Nathan, she had forgotten she might impress his guests even more.

Retreat was cut off. Several men stood between her and the door, all determined to hold their position. Instinctively she looked to Nathan.

He couldn't help but feel pleased when she did that. Unconsciously he stood a little taller, walked toward her a little more eagerly, approached her with a faint swagger.

"If you gentlemen will form a line to one side, not only will each of you be able to reach the table, Miss Stowbridge will be able to serve you in turn."

The men didn't move very fast, even when Serena seconded Nathan's suggestion. A second look at Nathan, however, made them reconsider. He seemed ready to move them himself if necessary.

"Where'd you find that gal?" Noah Hubbard asked him. "She one of your English lasses you brought along to keep you warm at night?"

Nathan's hands tightened into fists, and he had to resist an impulse to knock Noah's buck teeth down his scrawny throat.

"Her name is Delilah Stowbridge. Her brother owns a farm not far from here."

"Now I understand why you decided to let her work off his debt. Maybe she could work at my place after she's done here."

Nathan's hand snaked out, grabbed Noah by his shirt front, and pinned him against the wall. "Miss Stowbridge is in my aunt's charge while she's in this house," he said, his face a mask of contempt.

Noah's eyes gleamed with pleasure at having penetrated Nathan's air of cool detachment. "Is that why she's decked out in a dress her brother couldn't afford without selling half his farm?"

Nathan had to admit the little viper had guts even if he did have the sensibilities of a swine. "My aunt makes provision for our servants," he said in a voice frozen with disdain. "You should direct any questions about Miss Stowbridge's wardrobe to her."

But Delilah was magnificent, and Nathan's body responded to her. He released Noah and turned away, forcing himself to concentrate on the implications of Noah's words rather than on Delilah's breasts, which seemed to be struggling to free themselves from the too-tight bodice. As much as he would have liked to smash Noah's leering face, neither a fight nor his aroused state would convince anyone of his honorable intentions.

And his intentions were honorable. No matter how much he lusted after Delilah, he would not do anything to stain her reputation while she was at Maple Hill.

"I had no idea she would cause such a commotion," Nathan said to his aunt in a soft voice when he was able to attract her attention.

"She wouldn't have if she hadn't worn that indecent dress," his aunt hissed. "Where did she get it? Did you give it to her?"

78

"Where would I get a dress? Here she comes. I'll speak to her." Nathan waited until Delilah reached him. "I think you'd better go back to the kitchen."

"Did I do something wrong?" She looked upset.

"You wore that dress," Serena hissed.

Nathan placed himself between his aunt and Delilah. "The men appear to be having a little trouble keeping their minds on business."

A faint smile curved Delilah's lips. "Shall I return later to clear the table?"

"I think you should leave that to Lester."

"He'll be fit to be tied."

"Possibly, but I'd rather have one irate butler than a riot on my hands."

Delilah looked self-conscious, but she couldn't hide a tiny smile of pleasure. "I'll help Mrs. Stebbens."

"Fine. And Delilah," he said as she turned away.

She turned back.

"The men are right. You look magnificent tonight."

Delilah hurried out of the room before the heat which began to flood her cheeks gave the men the wrong idea about what Nathan had said.

Outside in the cool, dark hall, she leaned against the closed doors. Nathan had looked at her; he had said she looked magnificent. She needed only her body's reaction to know that was what she had been waiting for all evening.

Her muscles had gone weak, but there was a bone-cracking tension in her limbs. Nerve endings all through her body arced and sparked until she thought she was being pricked by hundreds of tiny pins. And her breasts felt tender. She had been aware of them all evening. Priscilla might be bigger and taller, but her bosom was not so ample. Now the gown seemed intolerably confining.

Too hot and disturbed to go back to the kitchen, too confused to answer Mrs. Stebbens's questions, Delilah needed a few minutes to calm herself. Nathan's voice carried from the parlor, and heat rose in her neck and face all over again.

Tonight he wore a black swallow-tailed coat and white satin breeches. If every man in London dressed like that, she didn't know how anybody there managed to sleep at night. His left profile had been visible to her when the doors had opened. In the few seconds before the men closed in on her, her brain had registered a picture of his body from ankle to powerful shoulder. But it was the recollection of his powerful thighs which would invade her sleep for several nights to come. She had been concerned that her dress fitted too tightly, that her bosoms might be thought to be too boldly displayed, but the effect could not compare to what those breeches did to Nathan's body.

The more Delilah thought about it, the hotter she got. She couldn't go to the kitchen, but she was too restless to go to her room, her muscles too taut, her body too warm. She decided to go outside for a short walk, knowing if she stayed within, she would melt from her own heat.

When she moved, her body was dead weight. She could hardly lift her feet. She had reached the end of the hall when the door to the parlor opened and she heard Serena's voice.

Delilah threw open the outer door and fled into the night.

Nathan caught a glimpse of Delilah's gown before the door closed behind her. Why had she gone outside? Had the men's behavior upset her? Should he check on her?

"Find out what's become of Priscilla," Serena called to him from the drawing room. "She should have come down before now."

Serena always tried to make sure her daughter was present when Nathan was home. He wasn't sure how Priscilla felt about her mother's plan for them to marry. His cousin's response to him followed one of two patterns. She was either simpering and suggestive or unaware of his presence. He had no idea which approach represented her true feelings, and he wasn't interested enough to find out.

But Priscilla's arrival spared him from having to look for her. She descended the stairs, dressed in a rose-colored silk gown which became her admirably. Her hair was bound up under a cap that seemed to be composed entirely of ribbons and flowers. It wasn't to Nathan's taste, but he imagined the men inside would like it well enough.

Maybe Priscilla would take their minds off Delilah.

He was still angry over the way they had bunched around her as if she were a tavern wench in heat. Because Delilah's family was not as well off as they were, was she fair game for their lusts? And by what stretch of the code governing decent behavior did they have the effrontery to tell him he must be sleeping with her or planning to do so?

That inference made him feel guilty for the thoughts he had harbored the last several days. True, he wanted Delilah more than any woman he'd ever met, but he hadn't insulted her by assuming that because he wanted her she would yield. In fact, from the little bit he knew of Delilah, she would do just the opposite.

Priscilla sidled up to Nathan, a simpering grin detracting from her prettiness.

"Your mother's been asking for you," he said. "She's trying to turn this into a social occasion, and I think she wants your help."

"Are you running away? Do you want me to come with you?" She gave him a provocative look.

Nathan didn't voice the reply which came to mind. Instead he said, "And have your mother looking for both of us?"

"She wouldn't bother if she knew I was with you."

There was that witless I'll-do-anything-you-want look. It made Nathan feel like the quarry in a fox hunt. "I'll be back in a few minutes."

"Where're you going?"

Nosy female. "There are some things a man has to do in private."

Priscilla giggled, but no answering smile found its way to Nathan's lips. The minute she entered the parlor, he slipped out the front door.

To the east of the house lay the stables and the home farm. To the west lay the garden and the river.

Nathan went west.

He hadn't gone very far before he stopped. He had never been in the garden, he had only looked at it from his room, and he suddenly felt out of place. The soft murmuring of the river formed a backdrop for the sounds of tree frogs and the crunching of Nathan's boots on the gravel of the carriage drive. It was dark under the trees. He had to wait until he could see where to step. Tripping over the stones that lined the path and finding himself in the rose bed or the fish pond didn't appeal to him at all.

The river was closer now, the gurgling its waters made while swirling around rocks, limbs, and tree roots louder. He became aware of the soft whisper of rustling leaves. On silent wings, a bat floated by his head, causing Nathan to start.

This was nothing like London at night.

Then he saw her, leaning against a picket fence, staring out at the reflection of the moon on the river. She had never looked more lovely, like a goddess, all pale and beautiful, almost too perfect. The only touch of color was the deep red of her generous mouth. Nathan longed to kiss those lips, to taste their sweetness, to feel them respond to his touch and part in invitation.

He had to stop thinking of them, or he wouldn't be in a decent state to approach her.

Should he go to her now? They weren't on very good terms, and he had no idea what had made her leave the house. He might say something that would make her run from him.

He didn't want to do that.

The sound of boots on the coarse, river-bottom sand of the garden pathway warned Delilah that she wasn't alone. Her breath caught in her throat as she saw Nathan approaching. In the moonlight, he looked quite astonishing. His coat and boots faded into the night while his breeches and waistcoat shone ghostly white. He looked like a beautiful statue, perfect in every way.

"Is anything wrong?" he asked as he drew near.

Delilah wanted to shout out that his presence kept her silent, his nearness upset her calm, and the sight of his slim body caused her heart to beat painfully in her chest. She tried to speak, but no sound passed her throat. Uncomfortable, she wanted him to leave, but she was glad he had come.

"I hope you didn't let their remarks upset you," Nathan said when she didn't reply.

He'd think her an idiot if she told him she hardly remembered a word, that she had barely been aware of anyone else from the minute she'd seen him.

She lied. "A little bit."

"You don't have to go back."

"It's all right. My uncle has a tavern. I know what men are like when they drink."

"Nevertheless, you don't have to see them again."

"I must. I mean, I will." She couldn't tell him she had fled because he'd driven her out of control any more than she could tell him she had to go back because she had to spy on him. "You didn't hire me to run away every time you have guests. It's partly my fault anyway. I shouldn't have worn this dress."

"I'm glad you did. You look particularly lovely." He wanted to tell her that her eyes were full of starlight, that her lips tempted him almost beyond bearing, but he could see she was poised to run away. He didn't dare touch her, though his whole body ached with wanting to.

"Servants aren't supposed to look lovely."

Nathan started to tell her that she could never be a servant, but he stopped short. She had asked to be a servant, and only by being one could she eradicate the black cloud—Reuben's debt—which always seemed to hang between them.

"Why did you wear that dress? You said you wouldn't."

Delilah sidestepped his question. "Shouldn't you get back? They might start wondering where you've gotten to."

Nathan experienced a pang of disappointment. She wanted him to go. Was she afraid of him, or did she merely dislike him? He couldn't blame her in either case. He had given her little reason to think he was different from his uncle.

"I can't leave you here. I'll wait and walk with you."

"No."

"Why not?"

"Can you imagine what those men would say?"

"I don't care," Nathan said, realizing with a bit of surprise that he really didn't.

"I do. What they think now is pure conjecture, but if they were to see us walk into the house together, they would announce it as fact."

"No one will see us. The doors to both the drawing room and the dining room are closed."

"But Lester will know. And he'll tell your aunt."

"I'll see that no one bothers you."

"You can't. I mean, you can try, but you can't."

The trace of arrogant aristocrat buried deep within Nathan spoke up. "I'm not accustomed to having my orders disobeyed."

When he acted like that, Delilah could see why Jane said he wasn't any different from his uncle. He had an unbending, autocratic streak. What good was it for him to be wonderfully handsome outside when he was mean and ugly inside?

But was he? Maybe he just didn't understand Americans. Maybe she didn't understand Englishmen. Either way, this was no time to try to figure it out. If they didn't return to the house soon, there'd be lots of questions to answer regardless of whether they went back separately or together.

"If you're really interested in what's best for me, you'll go back now."

84

"You don't believe I can protect you?"

"People can sometimes control their own thoughts, but they can never control those of others. Look at your country," she hurried on when he started to protest. "England wasn't able to change the Americans' opinions of its laws no matter what the reasons were for enacting them."

Delilah's mention of the war caused some of Nathan's eagerness to comfort her to fade. Even though he had begun to think of her as separate from everyone else, she was still associated with the rebels who had caused all the trouble in his life.

"Don't stay long."

"I won't."

There was more he wanted to say, but the moment had passed. Even now, Delilah was drawing away from him.

He turned and walked back toward the house.

Delilah watched him go, for once barely aware of the sensuous movement of his hips.

He was worried about her. He had actually left the gathering to make certain she was all right. He had been willing to risk censure to escort her back to the house. He thought she looked lovely in her new dress.

Her heart soared.

For the moment it didn't matter that it was unlikely he could have more than a passing interest in her, that he represented people who had brought tragedy and suffering into her life, that in part he might be ugly, possibly even cruel. He was a gorgeous man and he was interested in her.

For the moment that was enough.

Chapter Seven

"It's time we got started," Lucius Clarke said when Nathan returned to the drawing room.

"Who's going to moderate?" Eli asked.

"It ought to be Lucius," Noah Hubbard said. "He knows the most about what's going on, and he's got the best connections in Boston."

"It's Nathan's house," Eli said. "And he's owed more money then all of us put together," he added when both Lucius and Noah looked at him as if he had lost his mind.

"My nephew doesn't understand the way we do things," Serena said, aligning herself against Nathan. "If he did, he'd have Reuben Stowbridge's oxen in his barn rather than the man's sister under his roof."

"We're not here to discuss the manner in which debts are collected," Nathan informed his aunt, "rather, the situation in general."

"It won't do a bit of good to make up a whole lot of rules if you do something different when the situation gets specific," Serena retorted.

The men eyed each other uneasily.

"We'll keep your warning in mind," Nathan said.

"Nonsense. You mean to ignore it altogether," Serena snapped. "Priscilla and I will occupy the sofa." She seated herself. "You may sit or stand as you please."

Priscilla remained standing. The men became increasingly restless.

"Wouldn't you be more comfortable in the sitting room?" Nathan asked.

"No. Sit down, Priscilla," his aunt said.

"I think I'll go to bed, Mama. I'm rather tired."

"All right, but I shall remain." Her words were a challenge to Nathan.

"You insist upon remaining on the sofa?" he asked, his gaze cold and calm.

"I do." Serena felt uncomfortable, but she took assurance from the presence of the other men.

"I would never ask you to give up your seat," Nathan said, his eyes now gleaming like agate. "Eli, would you open the doors into the hall. Colonel Clarke, if you would take the other end of the sofa."

At first mystified, Lucius grinned broadly the moment he understood what Nathan had in mind. He strode to his end of the sofa.

Nathan and Lucius lifted the heavy piece of furniture simultaneously. Serena clutched at the arm rest to keep her balance as they carried her out and deposited her in the hallway.

"Would you like Lester to bring you a branch of candles?"

Hearty laughter convinced Serena that the men sympathized with Nathan. As furious as she was, she had no alternative but to accept her exclusion.

"Don't disturb yourself," she said, trying to salvage as much of her dignity as possible. "I should have thought you, of all people, would have wanted my advice."

"You've given it so unstintingly during these last weeks, I'm sure I have enough to last the night."

"I shall not come down once I'm in my room."

"I would not expect it of you."

Convinced she wasn't going to circumvent Nathan, Serena marched upstairs.

"I liked the way you handled that," Asa Warner said. "Simple and effective."

"I'd have clouted my old woman if she'd defied me like that," Noah said.

"Serena Noyes is not my *old woman*," Nathan replied.

"I still say a good whack on the head saves a lot of trouble."

"And destroys any chance your wife will be anything more than a servant in her own house."

Nathan hadn't intended to sound so supercilious, but he disagreed violently with Noah. He couldn't help but act as though he were talking to an idiot.

"No man worth his salt needs help from a woman to run his affairs," Noah said, anger turning his countenance red. "I don't put up with any lip neither."

"We're not here to discuss domestic arrangements." Asa Warner was attempting to head off a dispute that could divide the gathering before those present got to the subject which brought them together.

"We still haven't decided on a moderator," Eli reminded them.

"I yield any claims my hospitality might give me," Nathan said.

As soon as it was decided the moderator could not speak, Colonel Clarke stood aside. Asa Warner was finally chosen.

Delilah entered the back of the hall just in time to overhear Nathan's remark about a wife being a slave in her own home. It shocked her to realize he was right. Even though her father had loved her mother dearly, she had never questioned any of his actions. Jane could sometimes talk Reuben into the course of action she thought best, but she would never think of going against any decision he made.

Would my husband expect me to do the same? Would I? Never! Delilah had always argued for the right to do what she thought best. Otherwise she wouldn't be at Maple Hill. She couldn't imagine giving up the right to make decisions which concerned her. But it was a shock to learn that Nathan, a man she had previously considered autocratic, would not expect her to do so.

Delilah turned her thoughts to a more pressing problem. How could she find out what the River Gods were planning when she was banished from the drawing room? She had overplayed her hand when she'd chosen that dress. She had to find some way to get back inside, and she didn't have very long to do it.

"Where have you been?" Lester demanded, stepping out of the butler's pantry as Delilah emerged from her hiding place under the staircase. "You should be helping Mrs. Stebbens."

An idea flashed into Delilah's mind as she preceded him into the dining room.

"Mr. Trent said I was to take in the ale. You're to help Mrs. Stebbens."

"You're lying, girl," Lester replied, outraged. "Mrs. Noyes would never hear of it."

"Mrs. Noyes was just moved out into the hall, sofa and all." The sofa still rested in the center of the shadowy hall, mute evidence of the truth of her statement.

Lester's eyes grew big. "Whatever for?"

"You'll have to ask Mr. Trent."

Delilah smiled inwardly when Lester recoiled at her suggestion.

"But that's always been my job," he protested.

"It's mine tonight. If you don't believe me, ask Mr. Trent."

As Delilah hoped, Lester decided not to challenge her.

"Now I see why you wore that dress," he said spitefully. "It won't do you any good. None of those gentlemen are interested in the likes of you, at least not for a wife."

"I'm not interested in them either."

"Does that include Mr. Trent?" Lester demanded. "Don't seem to me servants ought to be wearing fancy dresses. Not unless something's been promised that ought not've been."

Hot anger flooded Delilah in an instant. Coming on top of the men's accusations, it was too much. She picked up the heavy silver tray bearing the last of Mrs. Stebbens's

89

custards and brought it down over Lester's head with a dull thud. The blow stunned Lester and scattered custards all about the room. The tray fell to the floor with a ringing crash.

The doors to the parlor were thrown open. "What the hell's going on!" one of the men exclaimed. Several heads poked through the door.

"Lester just dropped a tray," Delilah said sweetly. Then she calmly closed the doors on the men's curiosity.

"I'll get you for lying," Lester growled.

"You say anything like that about me again and you'll be dead."

As angry as Lester was, he didn't have the makings of a genuine bully. "It ain't natural for Mr. Nathan to be so easy on you," he said, aggrieved.

"He promised Reuben I wouldn't be treated like a common servant," Delilah explained. "Reuben threatened to shoot him if he went back on his word. He'd shoot you, too, if I told him what you just said."

Like everybody who lived near Springfield, Lester knew of Reuben's explosive temper.

"You'd better pick up those custards and bring some ale up from the cellars. With the kind of talk they're having tonight, they'll be ready to drink the cellars dry."

"Me! It was you who tossed them all over."

"Pick them up, or I'll tell Reuben what you said."

Lester glared at her malevolently, but he picked up the custards.

"Nasty bitch," he muttered to himself after Delilah had gone into the kitchen. "You wait. Mrs. Noyes'll put you in your place, and I'll make sure you stay there."

Delilah took care to avoid meeting Nathan's gaze when she brought in the ale. The men had less attention to spare. Colonel Clarke was holding forth on a subject dear to their hearts. Money.

"We have to stop them from closing the courts," he was saying. "I can't get my money unless I can sell what I confiscate. I can't sell anything without a court order, but I can't get that order unless the courts sit."

"I've got a dozen head of livestock on my place right now eating their heads off," Noah Hubbard said.

"I've got a barn full of furniture and linens I don't know what to do with," Eli added.

"The worms and moths will take care of it for you," someone said with a chuckle.

"If you can't sell it, can't use it, and it might die or be eaten up by insects, why did you take it?" Nathan asked.

Every man in the room turned to him as though he'd spoken heresy.

"Hell, you can't let people keep owing you money."

"You've got to collect sometime."

"The man's an idiot."

"What do you expect from a Redcoat?"

"You mean to let yours go?"

"Of course not," Nathan answered, seemingly unaffected by the contempt that greeted his question. "I merely wondered why you bothered to take anything that wasn't to your advantage."

"It was owed to me, and I was damned well going to take it," Noah said pugnaciously.

"We didn't have any trouble selling it until they started closing the courts."

"But we never got a decent price, even then."

"You can't just do nothing."

"I don't mean that you should," Nathan explained patiently, "but they'll have a hard time paying their debts without their livestock and tools. They certainly can't do it from inside a debtor's prison. Speaking for myself, I'd rather they fed their own livestock."

"Me, too," Asa said, but voices clamored for immediate action to stop the Shaysites and protect the courts so what had been confiscated could be sold.

Delilah was furious. She didn't dare allow herself to look up. Even her surprise at Nathan's words wasn't sufficient to subdue her fury. She kept her gaze focused on

91

the empty mugs held out to her. She was embarrassed, too, that an Englishman, rather than her own country-men, should be the only one to show some humanity and common sense.

"Most of these people are subsistence farmers," Colonel Clarke explained. "They don't clear any more ground than they have to, and they don't plant any more crops than they must to keep going from year to year."

"We'd all be better off if they moved west. Let them run off the Indians and open up the new land."

"It's about all they're good for."

"Deceitful, shiftless lot. That's what I say," added Noah. "I can't think why we ever fought a war for them."

"So they can go on having daughters like this lass," one man said, making a futile attempt to pat Delilah's behind.

That was too much. Caught in the process of filling a mug, Delilah spun around so quickly she spilled half the ale over the offending speaker and the rest over two other men, a chair, and a large part of an Aubusson rug. She slammed the empty pitcher down on a Queen Anne drop-leaf table.

"Most of you didn't lift a finger in the war," she said, in-cluding the whole room in one all-encompassing gesture. "You stayed safely in your store, Noah Hubbard. You made sure you extracted the full price for everything you sold to the soldiers, but you never so much as lifted a musket yourself."

"I suppose I didn't fight?" asked Colonel Clarke.

"Your company fought bravely, but you made sure you were well away from the hottest action. *I know everything you did,*" Delilah declared when Clarke tried to interrupt. "My father fought in your company. He had little else to talk about while he lay dying of his wounds."

Clarke's face suffused with blood.

"But your uncle was the worst of all," Delilah said, turn-ing on Nathan. "He sold anything he could to both sides—spoiled food, stolen medical supplies, weapons, clothes, boots, anything he could lay his hands on. He

92

didn't care who needed it, only who could pay the most.

"All the while these *deceitful, shiftless* farmers you're so afraid of gave their lives, and their sons' lives, so we could all live free. And what did they get? Reuben got three hundred dollars in script which was only worth ninety dollars when he tried to buy some land. My father got two wounds which killed him. What did the rest of us get out of it?" she swept on relentlessly. "Higher taxes to pay the interest on your bonds. Debts when we couldn't pay the taxes. Our property taken away when we couldn't pay the debts. You won't be content until you have everything."

"I warned you not to come back," Nathan whispered over the hubbub which greeted Delilah's angry tirade.

"I didn't want your guests to get thirsty," she said loud enough for everyone to hear. "I would hate them to be chilled during their ride home."

"Is that why you spilled the pitcher over Mr. Pickering, Mr. Clinton, and Mr. Howe? I believe Mr. Prentiss escaped only because the pitcher was empty."

"I did that?" she asked. She stared in surprise at Nathan. She could hardly believe her eyes. His lips twitched, and his eyes danced with suppressed merriment.

"I believe you were upset over something Mr. Pickering said."

"Did he make a remark about daughters?"

"I'm afraid he did."

Delilah was looking at Nathan now. It was almost as though he were talking only to her.

Then she swung around to face Otis Pickering, and the man visibly shrank from her. "Then I'm not sorry."

"I didn't think you would be. But Mr. Pickering does need to dry off."

"I'll bring some towels."

"Maybe you should ask Lester to do that. He knows where they are kept."

"But—"

"I'm certain Mrs. Stebbens needs your help. You know, Lester's not very good with crockery."

Lester had never dropped anything in his life, and Nathan was aware of that.

"You don't wish me to bring more ale?"

"My needs are quite adequately provided for, but why don't you ask Mr. Pickering?"

"You think he would like more?"

"No, but it would be polite to ask."

"Sir, you're making a mockery of us!" Colonel Clarke suddenly exclaimed.

"On the contrary," Nathan said, the sparkle vanishing from his eyes. "I'm attempting to treat you with exactly the same degree of consideration you have accorded Miss Stowbridge."

Delilah was pleased to see that several of the men looked abashed. One even turned red in his embarrassment.

"You may retire," Nathan said to Delilah. "Tell Lester I require him immediately."

A smile lightened Delilah's features the minute the doors closed behind her, but her lightheartedness didn't last long. It had been exhilarating to tell those posturing faint-hearts they weren't fooling anybody. It was wonderful to share a joke with Nathan. It was even more wonderful to know he was much more understanding than she had guessed, but she had gotten herself thrown out of the drawing room again and she hadn't learned a thing for Captain Shays. She didn't even know what they were talking about.

Delilah spent the next hour helping Mrs. Stebbens finish up in the kitchen, enduring a long harangue from Lester on her behavior—with more emphasis on his being required to clean up the ale than on her pouring it over the guests—and trying to figure out how she could get back inside the parlor.

As soon as her work was finished, she bade Lester and Mrs. Stebbens good night and went upstairs. A thin rib-

94

bon of light shone under Serena's door. Priscilla's room was dark.

Delilah changed into a dark brown gown without frills and hurried back downstairs. She tiptoed to the drawing-room door and put an ear to the keyhole. She could hear people talking, but she couldn't understand their words. She'd have to think of something else. Just as well. She couldn't think of any acceptable explanation for her actions if someone found her.

She would have to go outside and see if she could listen at one of the windows. The weather had turned cool, but with the heat of so many bodies and candles in the drawing room, she doubted all the windows would be closed.

She started to go toward the back of the house, but heard Lester moving around in the pantry, so she tiptoed back down the hall and carefully turned the handle of the front door. It opened without a creak.

The full moon made it impossible to hide. She crouched down, keeping her body close to the house, and moved toward the first window. It was closed. So was the second. Her only hope now was the window at the side of the house, but a large thornbush stood at the corner.

Deciding that if she was going to be caught, she'd better be on her feet, Delilah walked around the bush as if she were just wandering around outside after eleven o'clock, then dropped to a crouch again.

Light poured from the open window. The speaker stood so near she could hear every word.

"What we've got to do is get somebody inside their organization," Lucius Clarke was saying. "In addition to knowing their plans, we need the names of their leaders, the people they listen to."

"Do we know any of them yet?" someone asked.

"I've got a list here," Lucius said, holding up a piece of paper, "but I doubt I've got everyone. Pass it around. If you know of anybody, add his name to the list."

"It's all well and good to know the leaders," someone else put in, "but what can we do to them?"

"If they owe a debt they can't settle, we can put them in jail. Trent here holds a note on Stowbridge."

"His sister's working it off now," Nathan pointed out.

"You can find a reason to get rid of her if you want to," Clarke said impatiently. "Say she's lax or you caught her stealing. Hell, you could even say she tried to crawl into your bed."

Delilah gasped. Her first impulse was to climb through the window and punch Lucius Clarke in the face. Was there nothing these men wouldn't do to collect their money?

"If any man made such a statement," Nathan said in a dangerously quiet voice, "I should feel compelled to knock him down."

Delilah could hardly believe her ears. This was the third time this evening that Nathan had come to her defense. If he defended her, would he defend her family as well? She doubted it, especially if he discovered Reuben was one of the leaders. He'd be more likely to be angry because Reuben had repaid him by turning against him. She knew he was determined to collect all the money owed him—he had told her so several times—but maybe he wouldn't go to the same lengths as the others.

Still, all this was supposition, a waste of time. She needed to know who was on that list. She also needed to know what they were planning to do. More importantly, if Lucius Clarke found out Reuben was one of Shays's most trusted lieutenants, could he force Nathan to put him in jail?

"What's the governor going to do?" Asa Warner asked.

"Governor Bowdoin has written to all the sheriffs ordering them to call out the militia," Lucius said.

"That won't be any good," Noah Hubbard declared. "Every time they come face to face with the regulators, they turn their backs and go away."

"Got too many relatives among them," someone pointed out.

96

"The militia captains are scared of their own shadows," said another.

"He's ordered them to shoot if they have to," Lucius said.

His words brought silence. So far no one on either side had fired a shot. Firing on the regulators would mean war.

"He's preparing a riot act to be read to them before anything happens," Lucius continued. "That ought to make some of them back down."

"But if they don't?"

"Then we shoot."

"Has anyone met with the farmers to listen to their grievances?" Nathan asked.

Everyone stared at him.

"They wrote the governor, but he didn't waste time replying."

"Why not?"

"You don't talk with rabble like that," Clarke exploded. "They're too stupid to understand anything beyond their farms. Hell, they wouldn't be in this mess if they could learn to live more economically."

Delilah's fingers curled into claws. If she ever got her hands on Colonel Lucius Clarke, she would . . .

"It's possible their complaints are reasonable," Nathan persisted in a cool, controlled way that was apparently beginning to irritate the men in the room as much as it heartened Delilah. "You really can't say, can you, until you know what they are?"

"You ought to keep quiet and listen," Noah exploded. "You don't know anything about these people. Damn, you can't even talk right."

"In England everybody knows where he belongs," Lucius Clarke said, almost in the manner of an exasperated teacher explaining a problem to a witless student. "It's not the same over here. These people think they have a right to do anything they want."

"I have noticed that," Nathan replied. He grinned

to himself; he was thinking of Delilah.

"We've wandered from the point," Asa Warner said when he saw both Lucius and Noah turn angry eyes on Nathan. "Our question is what to do now. We can work on a cure after we have things under control."

"I say the courts meet a day before the announced date," Tom Oliver suggested.

"It's worth a try," Lucius admitted.

"But we've got to keep after those leaders," Noah insisted. "If we can get them in jail, maybe even hang a few, this revolt will disappear like it never was."

"Somebody's got to keep the list," Lucius said. "I'm on my way to Boston and then Newport and Providence."

"I'll keep it," Noah volunteered.

"We need someone closer to Springfield," Asa Warner said. "We can't always be running fifty miles just to add a name to the list."

"How about Trent?" asked Tom Oliver. "He's close enough, and we all know where he lives."

"We know too little about Nathan to trust him," one man said.

Another contradicted him. "It's foolish to think he would join the rebels and rob himself."

Everyone had some family connection with the insurgents, and the others weren't sure who could be relied on to put down every name turned in. Nathan had no reason to withhold any name.

"Can you guarantee its security?" Noah demanded. He wanted the list, but no one trusted him to do anything not directly related to making more money for himself.

"I'll keep it locked in my desk," Nathan offered. "If I'm not here, you can leave a message with my aunt. No one can doubt her willingness to remember every name you give her."

"If we're done, I've got to be going," Noah said, his disappointment obvious. "I've got a long ride ahead."

The other men quickly excused themselves, and within

minutes Nathan was at the door bidding Asa Warner goodbye.

"We've got to do our best to keep anybody from shooting," Nathan was saying. "This isn't another revolution. It's an economic crisis. Nobody's going to win unless we all win. And it won't happen overnight."

"They're not going to wait for their money," Asa said. "Don't know that I can either. Your damned bloody British merchants are squeezing me dry. If they would just let us trade with the West Indies—"

"That's beyond our control," Nathan said. "We'd better concentrate on getting through the next few weeks with as few scars as possible. We all have to live together."

"I'll keep that in mind." Asa regarded Nathan speculatively. "You're mighty calm about this. They don't want sensible advice, you know."

"Then we'll have to give them a reason to take it."

"I'll think on it. Good night."

Delilah hid in the shadow of the thornbush as Asa Warner mounted his horse and rode off. She tried to reconcile all the aspects of Nathan Trent she had seen over the last several days. He was in turn arrogant and insufferable, as unsettled by her physical presence as she was by his, silent and distant, ready to defend her from his family and his friends, and a blunt, efficient businessman. Somewhere in this combination of behaviors and attributes was the real Nathan Trent. Or was there someone inside him she hadn't yet discovered.

She started out of her trance at hearing a bolt shot home and a key turning in the lock.

She was locked out.

Chapter Eight

Delilah stared at the locked doors in dismay. She hurried back around the corner of the house, but the window was shut. She was just in time to see Lester close the drawing-room door behind him. It was out of the question that she bang on the door and have to explain to Nathan why she was outside again at this hour of the night.

Mrs. Stebbens! Did she have a key to the back door? If an explanation had to be made to anyone, Delilah would rather it be to that kindly woman. As she passed along the side of the house toward the wash-shed loft where Mrs. Stebbens slept, Delilah's attention was caught by a light in the butler's pantry. As much as she didn't want to have to explain anything to Lester, he was still better than Nathan.

Delilah could just reach the lowest pane. She gave it a sharp rap and was amused to see Lester practically jump out of his skin. When he saw her face pressed to the pane, he turned so white she thought he would faint.

"It's me, Delilah," she called as loudly as she dared. "Let me in."

Lester peered through the pane before he opened the window. "What are you doing outside?" he demanded.

"I was taking a walk," Delilah explained. "Mr. Trent closed the door before I could get inside."

"What's wrong with knocking?"

"Just let me in," Delilah said, impatiently. "You can question me later."

"I ain't used to the help running about in the dark,"

Lester complained as he let Delilah in the back door. "I don't approve of it neither."

"I won't do it again," Delilah said. "I wasn't thinking."

"Don't seem to me like you ever think," Lester protested. "I never saw anybody stir up people like you do." He gave her a sharp look. "You ain't doing nothing bad, are you? And don't give me that insulted look you give Mr. Nathan. I ain't no fool. Better gals than you have got themselves in trouble."

"What could I be up to?" Delilah asked. "Everybody's in bed."

"I don't know, but never bring a poor man into a rich man's house is what I say. Causes trouble every time."

"I'm not a man."

"That brings me to the next thing I mean to say."

"Don't tell me. I can guess," Delilah said, forestalling him. "Now I'm going to bed."

"Ain't you going to tell me why you was outside?"

"No," Delilah said with an impish grin as she slipped off to bed.

"That gal is up to something," Lester said to the empty room.

An hour later Delilah's door opened on silent hinges. Moonlight pouring in through the window at the front of the hall turned the landing into a study in black and silver. The dark brown of the floor had become a carpet of silver crisscrossed by a lattice of thin black strips. Chairs, tables, and the spokes in the bannister cast elongated shadows whose ghostly forms strained toward Delilah as she headed down the stairs.

She paused on the second floor long enough to make sure no light came from under Nathan's door. The steps creaked in faint protest under her weight, but keeping close to the wall, she went down the main staircase quickly. Retreating into the darkened recess of the library door, she paused to listen.

She heard nothing.

101

Using great care, Delilah turned the knob and pressed in gently. Again a faint protest. She stepped into the room and closed the door behind her.

Leaning against the door frame, she took a deep breath. Her heart beat so hard it actually hurt her chest. If anybody caught her, what could she say to explain her presence in the library at this hour of the night?

She would get a book. It wouldn't convince Serena, but maybe Nathan would believe her. She had twice seen him reading. Delilah pulled a book from the shelf—she didn't even bother to read the title—and hurried over to Nathan's desk.

Locked! She should have expected that. She didn't know any more about desks than she did about tea.

She smiled at that memory as she racked her brain for a way to get into the desk. She had to see that list. And she had to learn the names added to it in the weeks to come. But how? She had no reason to need Nathan's key. She would just have to think of something. Reuben's life might depend on it.

Delilah woke out of a deep sleep. She'd been dreaming about depraved English lords stalking her. She smiled to herself, turned over, readjusted her pillow so her cheek would rest on a cool spot, and started to drift off again.

Then she heard the footsteps again. Only this time she wasn't dreaming. They came from outside her door. Someone was pacing the hall. Who? Why? She might have been frightened if it hadn't been clear the footsteps went back and forth without pausing when they passed her door.

Then she heard a sound like a faint moan. Or maybe it was a whimper. Whoever it was stopped walking and halted in front of the entrance to her room. Delilah jumped out of the bed, grabbed a robe, and hurried to the door. She eased it open and peeped out.

Serena Noyes stood in the hall, pulling at a few loose

strands of hair and crying silently. She had lost her night-cap, and her gown sagged so far off her left shoulder it nearly exposed one sagging breast.

Delilah stepped out into the hall, but Serena seemed to be in a trance, as if someone had hypnotized her. She stared into the space before her, seeing something Delilah couldn't make out, mouthing words Delilah couldn't hear, fearing something Delilah couldn't identify. Tears rolled down a face that looked twenty years older than it had just hours earlier.

"You shouldn't be out of bed," Delilah said gently, draping her own wrap around Serena's shoulders. "You'll get chilled." She tried to turn Serena toward the stairs. There seemed to be no tension in the older woman's body, yet she was as immovable as if she had been carved from stone.

From the stench of Serena's breath, she had been drinking heavily, but Delilah doubted she was drunk. "You can't remain in the hall," she said, trying to coax her to move. "At least come sit in my room."

But Serena wouldn't budge. Then, without warning, she started to moan, much louder this time. Delilah couldn't understand any of the words Serena spoke, but it was clear she was frightened.

"No." The word was quite clear. Now she looked straight at Delilah. "No!" she cried once more and began to back away. The more Delilah tried to help her, the more frightened she became. Then, quite unexpectedly, she extended one hand in front of her as though to ward off a blow, drew the other across her face, and uttered a sharp cry.

Delilah thought she heard two doors open on the floor below.

Serena stumbled, and as Delilah rushed forward to catch her, Priscilla came running up the stairs. It took both of them to help Serena to her feet. Even though Serena appeared thin and frail, Delilah had difficulty keeping her balance when Serena pushed her away.

"I'll take care of her now," Priscilla said with none of the coyness she used around Nathan. It was clear she didn't want Delilah there.

"I found her standing in front of my door," Delilah said, trying to explain. "I tried to get her to go back to her room, but she wouldn't move. She seemed to think I was going to hurt her. That's when she cried out."

"It's all right," Priscilla said, turning Serena in the direction of the stairs. "She's not fully awake. She doesn't recognize you."

"Are you sure you don't need some help?"

"No, thank you. I'll return your robe in a few moments."

"Don't bother. I only wore it to be decent."

Priscilla didn't respond to the friendly overture. Still talking softly and soothingly, she helped Serena down the stairs and back to her room. Delilah remained standing in the hall, completely mystified. What nightmare terrified Serena? What had caused the difference in Priscilla?

Delilah looked down toward Nathan's room. No light shone under the door, but she could have sworn she'd heard a second door open. Was she mistaken? If not, why had he closed it again?

Only Priscilla came down to breakfast the next morning. She wore her usual pastel-colored gown, overloaded with white lace trimming at the bodice and the sleeves. She had carefully curled and dressed her hair, decorating it with a profusion of ribbons, and the perpetual smile was on her lips. But there was a tightness about her eyes. She looked tired. And unhappy. No, worried.

"Is your mother feeling better?" Delilah asked as she set a plate before Priscilla.

"Yes, but she's too unwell to come down for breakfast." She spoke in the same breathy voice but without the archness or coyness Delilah had come to expect from her.

"Shall I take something up to her room?"

"No. I'll bring her something later. There's no need for

anyone to worry about Mother today."

In other words, don't go near her.

"Shall I tell Lester to take his orders from you?"

"Good Lord, no," Priscilla said, lapsing back into her familiar personality. "What would I know about running a house? He ought to ask Nathan. Nathan owns Maple Hill."

Delilah reeled. Would she ever be able to tell how Priscilla was going to act? It was like talking to two people and never knowing which one was going to answer.

"Nathan left before breakfast," Delilah said. "He told Lester he wouldn't be back until late in the day."

Priscilla blinked for a moment, as though an unwelcome thought had crossed her mind, but her expression didn't change. "Then let Lester decide," she said with a flip of her lace-covered shoulders. She ate in silence, but when Delilah came in with the coffee, she asked, "Have you decided about the dresses?"

"I picked out three," Delilah replied, ashamed to admit she'd yielded to her own vanity.

"You'll be tired of three dresses before the week's out. Besides, Nathan will like seeing you dressed up." Priscilla giggled. Positively giggled. "Don't you just tremble and quake when he's around?" Without waiting for Delilah to answer, she went on. "Even Mother's a little scared of him. Whenever he turns that awful gaze on me, I feel he could murder me. When he gets mad, he's worse than Uncle Ezra."

"I don't—"

"You should see him after he's been studying Uncle Ezra's books." Priscilla shuddered. "Mama wants me to marry him, but sometimes he frightens me to death."

Delilah couldn't imagine anyone being scared of Nathan. After growing up with Reuben's uncontrolled rages, Nathan's tightly controlled anger was a welcome relief. She supposed that came from being English. He was formal, maybe even haughty, but she couldn't find any fault with

105

that.

Of course she didn't trust him when he started to smile in a certain way. She could tell he was about to do something unexpected.

"He probably feels surrounded by enemies," Delilah said, realizing for the first time what it must be like for Nathan. "Your aunt loathes him for inheriting Maple Hill, the other River Gods despise him for being English, and the others hate him because they owe him money."

"Then I think you ought to be nice to him and wear all my dresses."

"I hardly think that will make up for his being treated like he has the plague," Delilah replied rather astringently.

"I won't have a servant in my house dress like that," Serena told Nathan the next morning. "It's not proper."

"She did look awfully pretty." Priscilla smiled idiotically at Nathan. "Did she look as pretty as me?"

Nathan didn't look up from his plate. His cousin's simpering grated on his nerves so badly he couldn't make a civil response.

"She could never look as pretty as you, darling," Serena said. "Not that you should have to be worried about being better dressed than a servant. Whatever possessed you to give her that dress?"

"You said it made me look all washed out, and Nathan said he wanted Delilah to wear something pretty. She didn't have anything, so I thought I'd give her that old dress. She did look nice in it. Did I do something wrong?"

Nathan watched, fascinated, as a great big tear began to form in each blue eye.

"No, darling, it was sweet. It's just that you shouldn't give servants things that are too nice. It encourages them to get above themselves."

The words had hardly left Serena's mouth when Delilah entered the dining room. The green dress she wore had clearly come from Priscilla's wardrobe.

"Where did you get that?" Serena demanded, in such a dramatic tone that Delilah had to struggle to keep from spilling the contents of the bowl she carried to Nathan.

"Priscilla gave it to me."

"How many dresses did you give her?" Serena demanded, rounding on her hapless daughter. "Do you think I spent all that money on clothing you just so your gowns would end up on some servant's back?"

Priscilla started to cry, but that didn't slow Serena for an instant.

"Take it off," Serena demanded turning to Delilah.

"If Priscilla can't wear it—" Nathan began.

"I'll not have *her* wear it," Serena said vindictively. "Take it off. Now!"

Delilah eyed Serena with a look Nathan had never seen before. It wasn't rage. In fact, she didn't seem angry at all. It wasn't hatred, though it was fairly obvious Delilah held his aunt in contempt. It was more like a call to battle.

Instinctively he became alert.

Delilah whipped off her apron and swiftly began to undo the buttons running down the front of the dress. The moment Nathan realized what she meant to do, he started to speak. One look at Serena stilled him.

Serena's jaw dropped, and her eyes seemed to start out of her head. "Not now . . . I didn't mean . . ."

"You said *now*," Delilah said coolly as she allowed the dress to drop to the floor. She stooped, retrieved the garment, and tossed it at Serena.

She stood before them in her petticoats. Pink colored her cheeks, sword points flashed from her eyes, but not the slightest hint of embarrassment could be found in her stance. She actually defied Serena to rebuke her.

Nathan couldn't help but admire her. He didn't know any respectable woman with the courage to undress before a man, but judging from the look on Delilah's face, she wasn't even aware she had committed a breach of decorum. She looked as proud and defiant as Athena.

Quite unexpectedly Nathan had an idea.

"Don't we have a great deal of leftover cloth in the attic?" he asked Serena.

"Bolts of the stuff, and most of it completely unsuitable," Serena said, apparently relieved not to have to deal with Delilah's state of undress. "I can't think what to do with it."

"I'm glad you said that," Nathan replied. "Miss Stowbridge, since my aunt doesn't want it, you may have it. Your coloring is so very different from my aunt's and cousin's you may find quite a lot of that material useful."

Nathan winked at Delilah. No doubt about it. She was so stunned she couldn't reply at once. Serena, on the other hand, could.

"You did say you didn't want it, didn't you, Aunt?" Nathan asked just as Serena opened her mouth to protest.

"I-I don't," Serena said, her tongue stumbling over the words at the shocking thought of Delilah being given so much expensive material, "but Priscilla may."

"You said you'd die before you'd let me be seen in a single piece of it," Priscilla whimpered. "I remember because I especially liked the blue dress I gave Delilah."

"Naturally it's difficult for a girl of your complexion to wear strong colors," Serena said, trying to find a way out of the situation she had created for herself, "but something may be contrived. In any event, Delilah can't have all that cloth. Half of my acquaintances aren't so well provided for."

"I wouldn't think of embarrassing your friends by offering them our castoffs," Nathan said in mock horror. "And I wouldn't even attempt to divide it among the farmers' wives. It would take more than Solomon's wisdom to do that."

"Burn it."

"What?" Nathan and Delilah asked in unison.

"Burn it," Serena repeated. "That's what we do with everything else we have no use for."

108

Nathan hadn't realized until now the depth of Serena's animosity toward Delilah. He looked straight at his aunt so there would be no mistaking his meaning.

"Miss Stowbridge shall have as much of the cloth as she desires. When she's properly dressed, maybe you won't be ashamed for her to serve your friends. Do you sew?" Nathan asked, directing his gaze to Delilah.

"Adequately."

"Are you quick?"

"I guess so," she replied, at a loss to understand his meaning.

"Good. I would prefer that you serve lunch in something other than your shift."

Only now did Delilah realize what she had done and become embarrassed. "I have other clothes."

"But I have developed a particular abhorrence for that brown dress."

"I have other dresses."

"All brown, no doubt," he said. Then he smiled.

Delilah didn't know why she had never noticed his smile. It quite turned her knees to rubber. What it did to her resolution was even more calamitous. That collapsed entirely. She'd had no intention of accepting the material. Now she couldn't turn it down.

"I couldn't possibly sew up a dress and get my work done," she said, hardly knowing why these words were coming out of her mouth. Was she so anxious for his attention she would simper and fawn like Priscilla?

"Who sews for you?" Nathan asked Serena.

"Amelia Cushing, but I don't see—"

"See that a message is sent to her at once. I want her to start on Miss Stowbridge's dresses today."

"I will not—" Serena started to say, chagrin and fury distorting her features.

"What a good idea," Priscilla chimed in before her mother could quite swallow the angry denunciation trembling on her lips. She seemed to be the same old Priscilla this morning, but there was an unfamiliar quality to her

109

voice as she looked straight into her mother's eyes. "I don't see why she shouldn't have something nice, Mama." She cast her mother a particularly penetrating look and said, "She has been very helpful. And if Nathan wants it . . ." The thought was left unfinished, but the simpering smile was back full strength.

"I'd rather make my own dresses," Delilah told Nathan.

"What will you wear until then? I really won't have you in that brown dress."

Delilah's eyes went inadvertently to the green gown still in Serena's grasp.

"She can wear my dresses, can't she, Mama?" Priscilla asked. Only it sounded more like an order than a request.

"It's certainly better than having her dresses made by my own dressmaker," Serena said, still obviously staggered by the morning's events. "I could never hold my head up in Springfield again."

"Then it's decided," Nathan stated. "Miss Stowbridge will sew her own dresses. In the meantime, she will borrow some from Priscilla."

"She can use my patterns, too," Priscilla offered.

"She can not," Serena contradicted. "She may be dressed in a style totally unsuitable for a servant, but she will not wear a dress of the same pattern as my daughter."

"I don't want to," Delilah said. "I prefer a more simple style."

"I'll leave it to you," Nathan said, clearly dismissing the subject. "I will be having several people to dinner on Thursday."

Serena dominated the conversation from that point, asking about the guests, attempting to add her friends to the list, and being firmly refused by Nathan.

Delilah, buoyed by the knowledge that Nathan not only cared how she looked, but that he had defied his aunt to provide her with some new clothes, was too happy to care about being cut out of the conversation.

"What's got you dancing all over this kitchen?" Lester demanded, suspiciously.

"Nothing," Delilah said.

"When a gal says nothing with that look in her eyes, you'd better believe it's something," Mrs. Stebbens observed. "Now come on child, tell us what's got you so head over heels."

"I'm to have some new dresses."

"Is that all?" Lester said, disgusted.

"No, it is not all," Delilah said, piqued.

"There are a lot of bolts of very expensive cloth in the attic, and Mr. Trent said I'm to have every bit of it if I want."

"You won't get it," Lester said. "Mrs. Noyes will see to that."

"She already tried, but Nathan said I could have it anyway. He even asked her to call her seamstress to sew for me. Priscilla offered me some of her patterns."

"Gawd!" Mrs. Stebbens said.

"I don't believe it," Lester exclaimed. "Mrs. Noyes would die rather than allow that."

"It doesn't matter what you believe," Delilah replied with a rather unladylike hunch of her shoulders. "I said I wanted to do my own sewing and make my own patterns."

"That'll be a waste of material," Lester said as he left the room, a fresh pot of coffee in hand.

"Nasty man," Mrs. Stebbens said, but she quickly forgot Lester in her excitement. "Do you know how to sew?"

"Well enough."

"Would you like some help? I'm wondrous fine with a needle. Mrs. Noyes precious Amelia Cushing can't do no better."

Delilah jumped at the offer. The only dresses she'd ever made were the plain brown ones Nathan disliked.

"Are you sure? You've got your work here."

"There is a mortal lot of cooking to be done," Mrs. Stebbens said with a sigh, "especially with him wanting all kinds of English dishes I never heard of for this party."

"I know how to prepare English food," Delilah said. "My father liked Mother to fix dishes out of a cookbook she'd inherited from her mother. I can help you if Lester will allow it."

"He won't have any say," Mrs. Stebbens said. "If I leave, Mrs. Noyes will have to take over the cooking again. She'd do just about anything before she'd let that happen."

Later, when they were able to take a few minutes to go to the attic and look over the bolts of cloth, Mrs. Stebbens went into raptures.

"I've never seen anything like it," she said in awed tones. "There must be twenty bolts here. And he said you could have it all?"

"Every bit."

"We'll start with this," Mrs. Stebbens said, picking out a bolt of white muslin decorated with tiny sprigs of dark blue flowers and one of a green- and red-striped taffeta. "We can save the velvet and brocade for when it gets cold."

"How about this?" Delilah asked. She held up a piece of crimson-colored silk.

"Oow, that is lovely. I doubt you could wear it without giving Mrs. Noyes palpitations."

Delilah laughed. "Maybe I'll save it until she's away."

"What a lot of doodahs," Mrs. Stebbens commented, digging among the ells of ribbon, pieces of lace, and bolts of gauze. "This will be ever so pretty."

"I want it to be prettier than anything Priscilla gave me," Delilah said.

"I thought you wanted a dress for day use."

"It would be a waste of this material to keep it for spilling coffee and splashing grease. Besides, I can wear my old gowns in the kitchen."

"Mrs. Noyes will have a fit."

"I don't care. I've never had anything really nice, and I'm not going to let Mrs. Noyes ruin it for me."

"Atta girl," Mrs. Stebbens said, and she reached for the silk.

112

They were cutting out the muslin on the kitchen table when Nathan came in. Delilah was glad the scissors were in Mrs. Stebbens's hands. She'd have ruined the piece of cloth the minute she set eyes on those breeches.

Why did he have to wear them? They were stretched so tight there wasn't a wrinkle anywhere. Today they were a pale yellow, a perfect match for his gold waistcoat and tan coat, but Delilah couldn't think of anything except those breeches. She could almost feel the muscles in her arm straining to reach out and touch his tempting buttocks. She hid her hands behind her back so Nathan could not see her fingers clench and relax.

Delilah despised herself for thinking like a trollop. A decent girl wouldn't be so powerfully affected by a man's body. Anybody could tell you that. It only made it worse that this man was an Englishman and her enemy. She felt like a traitoress.

"I want a few words with you about the food for Thursday evening," he said. He watched, fascinated, as Mrs. Stebbens continued to cut the material, following lines only she could see.

"Tell me," Delilah said. "She's concentrating."

"I want a round of beef and a saddle of mutton."

"We don't have any beef or mutton in the smokehouse," Delilah told him.

"Then slaughter some," Nathan said as though the solution was obvious. "Of course there'll be fish, and I've been promised a dozen quail."

Delilah was staggered by the amount of food he seemed to think should be served at an ordinary meal.

"I suppose you'd best choose the vegetables. Six ought to be enough. And a pie, a cake, and some pudding for dessert. Or maybe they would prefer a sillabub. Lester's taking care of the wines. I hope he can find at least three to go with the meal, but I'm afraid we may have to settle for two."

"Are you meaning to serve all that at the same meal?"

Mrs. Stebbens asked. The recital had finally distracted her attention from the cutting, and she stood poised over the table, her gaze fixed on Nathan's trim body. "And at eight o'clock in the night."

"This is a small dinner by my mother's standards," Nathan said. "I can remember many evenings when we spent more than a few hours at table."

"How do you ever keep your figure?"

"By not spending the whole time eating," he replied with a smile that caused Delilah's heart to turn upside down.

"But it's still hot," Delilah said.

"What's that got to do with it?"

"People shouldn't eat heavy food in the summer. Besides, most of it will be left over. With the little bit this house eats, it'll spoil."

She knew she should hold her tongue. It was none of her business what Nathan chose to eat or do with the food he couldn't use, but the thought of so much going to waste when so many went hungry made her angry. She didn't dare think of her own family. She wouldn't be able to limit what she said.

"I take it you disapprove?" Delilah knew Nathan didn't like having his decisions questioned.

"People here eat their big meal at midday and then have a little something cold in the evening."

"But this is a party."

"We don't have parties at night, not with all that food and drink. People have to get up early the next morning to go to work."

"We get up in the morning and go to work in England, too."

"I don't see how, not if you eat like that every night," Mrs. Stebbens said, sparing Delilah the onus of making all the objections.

Nathan looked thunderous, as if he were ready to bite off somebody's head. Delilah felt guilty. He didn't need her and Mrs. Stebbens coming down on him, not when everybody he came into contact with seemed to be aligned

114

against him.

"I'm sorry," Delilah said. "We shouldn't have said any-thing. It's just that we're not used to doing things your way. " Nathan's expression was still formidable, but Delilah thought she detected a change in his eyes. "I don't suppose it would do us any harm to try your way. You seem to get along in spite of it."

Now there was a definite twinkle in Nathan's eyes.

"You think we'd get along even better if we ate and drank less?"

"Well, of course I do. Anybody who . . ." She caught herself. "How could I know, not until I've tried your way . . . or you've tried ours?"

"Well, I know," Mrs. Stebbens stated defiantly, "and I say you're lucky you don't have gout and have to keep to your bed. Anybody who eats like you must be full of the flux near 'bout all the time."

Nathan's gravity nearly deserted him.

"Then I suppose the only solution is to let you choose a meal for me. Let me see, I believe my aunt has already ordered tonight's supper. I will be away Wednesday. How about Friday? Would you be so kind as to choose my din-ner for Friday?"

He was clearly looking at Delilah.

"Of course she would," Mrs. Stebbens answered when Delilah blushed with embarrassment.

"If you're sure," Delilah said.

"Of course I am. How else will I find out whether I'm full of the flux?"

Delilah's lips twitched. She couldn't resist looking at him. She adored his smile.

"I'm sure you don't have the flux. You look too healthy." Why had she brought up his looks? Now she couldn't stop staring at his body, and she was becoming embarrassed.

"I'm glad to learn you're concerned for my well-being. There was a time when I thought it might be the other way 'round."

The desire to laugh left Delilah. "I never felt that way,"

115

she said. "I didn't like you at first, and I still don't like what you're doing, but I never wanted any harm to come to you. Even if I did, I don't any longer. How could I when you've been so kind?"

Nathan looked a little surprised. "Kind?"

"I'd have been a lot less comfortable here but for your intervention. I meant to thank you at a suitable time."

Now Nathan looked embarrassed. "Your continued interest in my health is more then enough thanks. If you look as nice in that dress as I expect, I'll be suitably rewarded."

He departed, leaving Delilah speechless.

"Don't know when I've seen a man like him bowled over by a gal who didn't even like him," Mrs. Stebbens observed. "You'd think he'd have them climbing all over him."

"He's not bowled over by me," Delilah protested. "He's just kind."

"And my aunt Jessie loves children," Mrs. Stebbens said about Springfield's infamous child-hater. "That man stiffens up like he's got starch in his drawers every time he's around you. What's wrong with him? He afraid he'll do something you'll dislike?"

"I have no idea what you're talking about," Delilah said.

"I'm talking about a man who defends you against his own kin and gives you a fortune in cloth to do with as you like."

"You think he really does like me?" Delilah asked, realizing that she was almost breathless with hope.

"I think he's nutty on you. He's just afraid you're going to treat him like everybody else has since he got here."

"They'll not do it for long," Delilah said. "I'll see to that."

Chapter Nine

Delilah hummed while she polished the silverware. She had a light soprano voice, a little too thin for true beauty. Being particularly happy, and since Nathan had left before breakfast and Serena and Priscilla were still in bed, she occasionally broke into song.

"Make sure you get into all the crevasses," Lester said. "I don't want any of those women saying we can't set a proper table. Times may be rough, but I'll not put up with dirty silver."

"I'll bet I'd do a better job than you on the glasses," Delilah challenged. Lester still did the crystal himself. Delilah saw his shoulders slump every time he looked at the triple row of wine glasses. It was evident that his resolution not to allow her to touch anything breakable was weakening.

"You keep a civil tongue in your head, missy, or I'll be forced to tell Mrs. Noyes you're getting above yourself."

Delilah knew he wouldn't accept her challenge because he wouldn't spend half the time on the glasses she would spend on the silver. She smiled and let Lester depart with his dignity. She didn't care. She was too happy this morning to care about anything Serena or Lester could do.

Nathan cared about her, and that was all that mattered. He had sent her out of the room when the men

117

had ogled her. He wanted her to look nice just for him.

And Delilah was determined she would. She and Mrs. Stebbens had stayed up until after midnight cutting and fitting the figured muslin. She had looked longingly at the crimson silk, but Mrs. Stebbens had advised her to wait.

"You'd best begin slow, or Mrs. Noyes will kick up such a fuss we'll never get the rest of them dresses made."

Delilah knew the kindly woman was right. Still she spent the night dreaming about how she would look in a rose silk gown. But if she didn't get her work finished soon, she wouldn't have time to sew the dress before Nathan's party.

So she polished harder. The dress had to be ready. Lucy Porter would be one of the guests, and Delilah was determined that for once she would not be outshone by that jealous, sharp-tongued female.

But the harder she worked, the louder she sang. She was giving the last touches to a serving spoon when Serena Noyes jerked open the pantry door.

"Is that you caterwauling?" Serena demanded, peevish annoyance writ large across her face.

"I was singing a popular ditty if that's what you were referring to," Delilah replied, arching her eyebrows. *Caterwauling indeed!*

"You sound like a cat with a scalded tail," Serena said. "I'm surprised you don't know such noise is unacceptable in a house like this."

Delilah felt too full of herself to take that without a response. "I do know you're unable to appreciate it."

Her sarcasm went right by Serena.

"I have very sensitive nerves," the older woman said. "I find all but the most beautiful singing utterly intolerable."

"I won't disturb you again."

"You would do well to remember what I've said. Your

future employers may not be so well disposed as to over-look your faults."

"It's kind of you to warn me," Delilah got out through clenched teeth, "but I won't have any future employers."

Serena readjusted her shawl and started to leave, but she stopped at the door. "Someone named Jane came to see you. Please make it plain to this woman that anyone calling for a servant should go to the back door."

"Where is she?"

"How should I know? I sent her around to the kitchen," Serena said and floated out of the room.

Delilah bit her tongue to keep from uttering a sharp answer. She jumped up to put away the silverware. It was cold this morning. She hoped Mrs. Stebbens hadn't made Jane wait outside.

When Delilah reached the kitchen, Jane was trying to refuse the cup of coffee and hot buttered bun Mrs. Stebbens was urging on her.

"Eat it," Delilah said. "They'll only throw it out if you don't."

"I've already eaten two thick slices of bread," Jane protested.

"It's a long walk. You'll need something to keep you warm."

When Jane continued to stare at her, Delilah realized she had noticed her dress, Priscilla's dress.

"I didn't walk," Jane said. "Reuben had to deliver some lumber to Jonas Selleck." She bit into the bun, her eyes still on Delilah's dress. "I'll have to walk back, though. He's doing some work for Gad Clark."

"And the boys?" Delilah asked anxiously.

"They're with my sister, Polly."

"And how're you doing?"

"Okay, but we miss you. I didn't realize how much work you did. I confess I'm more tired than I've ever been."

Delilah felt guilty. It must be difficult taking care of

119

Reuben and the boys and doing all the work alone.

"Polly comes over nearly every day. She's still too young to be left unsupervised, but at least she can take care of the boys."

"And Reuben?"

Jane was silent while she took a swallow of coffee and a bite of her bun. "He figures he has to keep the oxen busy every minute you're here or he's letting you down. That's why he's working for Clark. We'll have the money for the taxes this year."

But not enough to pay off the debt as well. Delilah would have to stay at Maple Hill for the full four months. Jane didn't say that, but Delilah understood.

They talked of unimportant things until Jane got ready to leave.

"I'll walk a little way with you," Delilah offered.

"Do you think you ought?" Jane asked, glancing at Mrs. Stebbens.

"You go on," Mrs. Stebbens said. "There's not much to do around here this morning."

"Reuben's name may be on their list," Delilah said the moment the back door closed behind them.

"What list?" Jane demanded, anxiety creasing her brow.

"The list Lucius Clarke gave Nathan."

"Nathan who?"

"I mean Mr. Trent." Delilah's cheeks flushed. "We all call him Nathan behind his back. Mrs. Stebbens says he's too young to be a mister."

"Why is the list important?" asked Jane, not the least interested in Nathan or what anybody called him.

"They're trying to get a list of the insurgent leaders. Reuben is one of them, isn't he?"

"He's practically Shays's right-hand man. What do they mean to do with the list?"

"I don't know, but they said if they could get these people, they could stop the rebellion in its tracks."

"You've got to find out if Reuben's on the list."

"Nathan keeps it locked up in his desk."

"Then distract him when he's working on his accounts or something."

"He's gone most of the time, and Lester's taken to keeping the library door locked."

"You've got to think of something. I won't have Reuben hurt just because he's on some list."

"He may not be on it."

"If he's not, he soon will be. Reuben never could keep a still tongue in his head, not when he gets mad. And he's been mad all the time since you came to work here. You are being treated all right, aren't you? He'll box my ears if I don't ask you."

"I'm fine. In fact, I think they're all in league to protect me from Mrs. Noyes. She's truly detestable, but Nathan is careful she doesn't mistreat me."

Jane's gaze narrowed. "I don't think I like the sound of that."

"Well, you should," Delilah fired back. She had to convince Jane that nothing was wrong, or Reuben would be upset and the fat would be in the fire. "Nathan told Mrs. Noyes he promised Reuben I'd be treated like a lady, and if she didn't do that, he'd know the reason why."

"As long as he doesn't start getting ideas about you."

"He's almost never here. If you stood by the road, you'd probably see more of him than I do. Besides, why should he be interested in me?"

"I've seen the way men look at you, some of them well above your station. They have lust in their hearts."

"He can't do much lusting with his aunt and cousin dogging his heels every step. Serena Noyes is determined he'll marry her daughter. They don't let him out of their sight for as much as a minute."

"Then why are you wearing that dress?"

The dress.

"It's one of Priscilla's castoffs. She told me she'd give it to Lucy Porter or Hope Prentiss if I didn't want it."

"You mean Lucy could be wearing that dress right now if you hadn't taken it?" Jane asked, merriment springing into her eyes.

Delilah nodded.

"Does she know?" Jane's lips quivered.

Delilah shook her head.

"Are you going to tell her?" Jane put a hand over her mouth.

"Maybe, if she makes me angry. She's coming to a party here Thursday night."

Jane sputtered with laughter.

"I wish I could see it. A more mean-spirited, spiteful girl I've yet to meet. You realize she'll preen herself on being a guest while you're a servant."

"That's all right," Delilah said, thinking of the dress she would wear that night.

Delilah could hardly credit the image she saw in the mirror. It was difficult to believe that young woman was herself. She wore a white sprigged muslin gown, with deep ruffles trimmed with wide pieces of deep-blue velvet ribbon. Her nearly black hair fell loose from a purely decorative lace cap. The deep cut of the neckline only escaped being scandalous by the judicious addition of a small sprig of blue flowers.

But it was the smile on her face that transformed Delilah into a beauty. The girl in the mirror was obviously a lighthearted creature used to being the most beautiful female around, not a poor farmer's daughter playing dress-up in the house of a rich merchant.

No, it wasn't just the dress, the hair, the cap, or even the wide smile of happiness. It was the feeling of anticipation, as though this girl thought something wonderful was about to happen to her.

"She thinks she's a moth turned into a butterfly," Delilah said to Mrs. Stebbens.

"She sure looks like it," agreed Mrs. Stebbens, delighted with the success of her efforts.

"Little does she know that women like Serena Noyes love to pluck the wings off butterflies."

"He'll protect you."

Maybe, thought Delilah, but if she wore this dress tonight, she would be moving beyond the scope of a serving girl being protected from a cruel mistress by a compassionate young master. She would be declaring herself to be part of their world, expecting them to accept her on an equal footing.

And that was foolish. Even though Serena and Priscilla might have trouble steering clear of her in the egalitarian atmosphere of Springfield, she would never be part of their social class. They would expect Nathan to agree. After all, he was English and distantly related to an earl if Serena Noyes was to be believed. It was inconceivable he would have anything to do with a serving girl.

"He won't be able to take his eyes off you," Mrs. Stebbens said, as delighted for Delilah as she would have been for her own daughter. "Mrs. Noyes couldn't hold a candle to you, not even when she was an innocent young girl."

"Was Serena pretty?" Delilah asked. It was difficult to image Serena beautiful, impossible to envision her as young and innocent.

"She was the spit of Miss Priscilla, only prettier," Mrs. Stebbens assured her, "but she was nothing compared to you. Now, put an apron over that dress. It'd be a shame to ruin it with gravy spots."

"Maybe I shouldn't wear it," Delilah said. Now that the time had come, she wasn't certain she wanted to take this step.

"You can't be saving it for anything else. Mrs. Noyes

123

ain't never going to let you out of the kitchen, not unless Mr. Nathan orders it. And how is he going to know he *wants* to order it unless you show him what you look like when you're wearing something pretty? You wear that dress, keep a smile on your face no matter what anybody says, and see if you don't end up a parlor-maid before the night's out."

"And backed into some dark corner for a stolen kiss with one of the male guests. No, thank you," Delilah said with a rueful laugh. "I'll stay in the kitchen. At least that way I'll be able to leave here with an unsullied reputation."

"Nobody's asking you to sully your reputation," Mrs. Stebbens said, rather disgusted with Delilah's lack of vision. "I'm just asking you not to hide yourself under a bushel when a little candlelight would work wonders."

"I won't hide," Delilah said with a warm smile, "but I won't expect miracles either."

One glance at Nathan's face, and Delilah knew Mrs. Stebbens was right. She ceased to feel the weight of the nearly sleepless nights she had spent sewing or the ache in her fingers from pulling the needle through the material countless times. Nathan's look was intimate; it ignored everybody else. If she'd ever had any doubt about his interest in her, she had none now. The man couldn't keep his eyes off her.

Serena was outraged. The shock and fury on her face when she fully understood the effect of Delilah's dress on Nathan almost made Delilah laugh aloud. She knew she would suffer for this later, but she would ignore Serena for the time being.

Though aware that it didn't speak well of her, Delilah was certain she would cherish the look on Lucy Porter's face for years to come. Shock, chagrin, envy, and rage combined. Lucy knew Delilah worked at Maple Hill, and she had probably looked forward to flaunting her position as a guest. For a girl who had spent her entire life eaten up with jealousy of Delilah's looks and popularity, it was too unsettling to see the one she envied in a more beautiful gown.

"Why bless my bones and knock me over," Lucy said, "if that isn't little Delilah Stowbridge. I hardly recognized you the way you've got yourself all tarted up. Look, Mama, it's Delilah. She must be one of Mrs. Noyes's servants now."

The other guests were shocked by Lucy's outburst. Even Serena, thinking how she would have loved to flay the skin off Delilah, looked at Lucy with disapproval.

Delilah didn't even pause in her work.

"Miss Stowbridge is not here as a servant," Nathan said, directing a look at Lucy which momentarily stilled her tongue and caused thought to desert her. "She was engaged to nurse my uncle. She stayed to help until the household has recovered from the shock of his death. She thought it inappropriate to have dinner with us, but I have insisted she join us in the drawing room later."

Delilah didn't know where to look. He hadn't said a word about that. She would have refused if he had. Did he really mean it, or was he just giving Lucy the setdown of her life?

Serena's jaw dropped nearly as low as Lucy's. "Would you see if the next course is ready?" she asked Delilah, desperate to get her out of the room. "And tell Lester we need more wine."

As reluctant as Delilah was to leave Nathan's admiring gaze, she was relieved to be out of the range of Lucy's tongue. No matter how badly Lucy behaved, she was still a guest and Delilah a servant. That put them on different planes. Nothing either one of them did could change that.

"What'd he say when he saw you?" Mrs. Stebbens asked the minute she returned to the kitchen.

"He said I wasn't a servant and I was to join the guests in the drawing room after dinner."

"I told you so." Mrs. Stebbens did a little quickstep to show her delight.

"But I can't."

"Not unless you have a hankering to be dead before tomorrow morning," said Lester, coming in with the dirty wine glasses. "Mrs. Noyes would murder you for sure."

"You're not going to turn down his invitation?" Mrs. Stebbens asked, incredulous.

"I can't serve dinner one minute and then sit down to talk with the guests the next," Delilah explained, "any more than you could go sit next to Mrs. Noyes after you finish up the washing."

"Well of course *I* wouldn't, but when I was your age I'd have set next to the devil himself to get close to a man like Nathan Trent."

"I've been telling Lucius he has nothing to worry about," Mrs. Porter was saying to Nathan. She had buttonholed him the minute they'd entered the drawing room. "Anyone who owns such a house as this has to be anxious the General Session doesn't pass any laws making it more difficult to collect our money."

"Are they considering such laws?" Nathan asked, his eyes on the door.

"Why surely Lucius told you that dreadful Captain Shays has been trying to get Governor Bowdoin and the General Session to issue paper money and let the insurgents use it to pay their debts."

"Why would that be such a problem?" Nathan asked. He didn't care about paper money or Mrs. Porter's opinions on the situation. He wanted to know what was keeping Delilah. Ever since she had appeared at dinner, looking like a young woman being introduced to society

126

at a London ball, he had been waiting for the chance to be near her, to talk to her for a few minutes.

He didn't know why he had invited her to join them. It went against every precept he had been taught. He could tell from Serena's face it was equally shocking on this side of the Atlantic, but he didn't regret having done it. He would do it again. He had to talk to her. Since he couldn't trust himself alone with her, this was his only chance and he didn't want to miss it.

". . . British merchants will accept only gold for their debts. What good is paper when . . ."

He had been fighting a losing battle with himself for several days. He had known it from the first, but he'd thought he could control himself.

". . . ordered too much. With the West Indies markets closed to us, they can't pay their own debts unless . . ."

But after spending whole days forcing himself to concentrate on business, he no sooner fell asleep than Delilah occupied his mind to the exclusion of all else. He used to have nightmares about being reduced to eating rats to stay alive. Not anymore. He dreamed of losing Delilah.

Absurd. How could he lose her when she didn't even like him?

". . . to shoot if they don't disperse. Governor Bowdoin has declared their actions to be treason. He's ordered . . ."

Nathan stood up when Serena entered the drawing room. "I'll make sure I remember that," he said. "Excuse me. I have to speak to my aunt."

"Did you see her?" he asked Serena the moment he reached her side. "Is she coming?"

"Of course I didn't. Naturally she isn't," Serena replied. "I don't doubt you've been living in fear she would accept your extremely rash invitation," Serena added, misinterpreting Nathan's eagerness, "but fortunately she's not lost to all common sense."

"What are you talking about?" Nathan demanded.

"I sympathize with you," Serena said, putting a hand on Nathan's arm in a way that made him feel like a fly being enticed into a spider's web. "Lucy Porter needed a good reprimand. The child has always been rude and presumptuous. I won't invite her here again. Forcing her to spend an evening in Delilah's company would be a perfect punishment if it were to take place anywhere but in my drawing room."

"Are you telling me Delilah won't come because she thinks I issued the invitation only to punish Miss Porter?"

"What other reason could you have had?" demanded his aunt.

"I thought everyone was equal in America."

Serena snatched her hand from his arm. "Servants are still servants," she hissed. "I won't allow that woman in my drawing room."

"May I remind you that this is my drawing room, Aunt, and I will invite anyone I please." He turned to leave the room.

Serena ran after him.

"You wouldn't mortify me by inviting that woman in here."

"I already have. And I'm going to find out what's keeping her."

Chapter Ten

They were standing at the wash tub, Mrs. Stebbens handing Delilah the plates to dry as she rinsed them off, when Nathan entered the kitchen.

"You're supposed to be in the drawing room," he said.

"I have to help Mrs. Stebbens," Delilah replied.

"Lester can do it. Here, put that plate down and come with me."

Delilah knew if she really looked at Nathan she would never have the strength of mind to do what she must. He wore a blue broadcloth coat, a white silk waistcoat worked with royal blue thread, white hose embroidered with blue clocks, black shoes with silver buckles, and breeches of pure white cashmere, soft, clinging, and more provocative than anything she had ever seen.

She kept her eyes on the plate she was drying.

"Thank you for your invitation, but I can't accept it."

"Why?"

"It's not suitable."

"Why?"

"Surely you know."

"No. Tell me."

He's being obstinate, Delilah thought. A glance at his set chin confirmed her suspicion. Well, he wouldn't bully her into going into the drawing room and being stared at like a two-headed calf.

"You know you can't ask servants to sit down with company. It'll only upset everybody."

129

"I thought only the English were committed to preserving the class system."

"You needn't be sarcastic," Delilah snapped, no longer looking at the plate but looking him squarely in the face. "It only takes common sense to see that—"

"Then why did you wear that dress?"

Delilah hadn't expected that question. She knew the answer, but she wasn't ready for Nathan Trent to know it.

"I shouldn't have. My vanity was stronger than my common sense. I never had anything this pretty, and I wanted to show off, especially for Lucy. She's never seen me in anything but the brown dresses you hate so much. I know it wasn't wise of me. Nobody can blame you if it led you to think I meant something more than I did."

Now Nathan felt guilty. He had practically forced her to take the material and make the dress. If she had done anything inappropriate, she had done it at his bidding.

His invitation to join them in the dining room had been prompted by Lucy's remark. Though made with good intentions, it shouldn't have been made it at all, but he never could keep his head around Delilah.

Even now, seeing her, being near to her, having her within reach caused him to have difficulty concentrating on his words. He wanted to touch her. He literally ached to let his fingertips brush her lips, to feel the softness of her cheeks, her hair.

More than that, he wanted her to look at him. Really look at him. Every day he talked to people who wouldn't meet his gaze or who glared at him in anger, suspicion, hate, distrust, or envy. He wanted somebody to look at him with acceptance, and he wanted that person to be Delilah.

The stirring in his groin riveted his attention. In a few seconds his state of mind would be obvious to both women.

It took concentration, some imagining that Priscilla was in his arms rather than Delilah, for his body to subside, but he managed to control it.

"You must not blame yourself for my mistake," Nathan said. "Neither should you assume my only reason for wanting to enjoy your company was to thwart Miss Porter, though even my aunt was appalled by her behavior."

"Not enough to want me in the drawing room," Delilah said before she could stop herself.

"No, but then my aunt and I disagree on many things."

Delilah glanced at his face. There was no mocking smile in his eyes, no scornful twist to his lips. He seemed to mean every word.

But could she afford to let herself believe that? It was all right to think he enjoyed looking at her. She was pretty enough to interest any man. But if he became interested in her, if he really sought her company, then that . . . that scared Delilah.

It also threatened her way of relating to Nathan, to Reuben's debt, to Serena, to Lucius Clarke, to everything. It would force her to ask questions she was not only unable to answer but didn't want to pose.

Delilah looked up at Nathan. "Please don't insist I go. My presence would make your guests uncomfortable, and I would be miserable."

How could he force her to do anything she didn't want to do, especially when she looked at him as though he held her fate in the palm of his hand? If only she could understand that everything he had done, including letting her come to work at Maple Hill, had been for her. But, considering the power she had over him now, maybe it was better she didn't know.

"I let my anger cause me to act impulsively. I never meant to distress you."

"I know," Delilah said, blushing furiously as she realized Mrs. Stebbens was a rapt auditor to every word he spoke. "Now you'd better hurry back before your guests think you prefer the servants' company to theirs."

"I do," Nathan said. Then he turned on his heel and left.

Mrs. Stebbens let out her pent-up breath in a noisy

whoosh. "Well, I never! He practically begged for your company, then begged your forgiveness for wanting it. The man must be besotted."

"It's nothing of the kind," Delilah said, hoping to convince herself more than Mrs. Stebbens. "He's just kind. I'll bet he's glad to be out of it."

"He looked downright miserable to me."

"You'd be miserable, too, if you had Priscilla and Lucy gushing over you. It's enough to turn a man off marriage."

"I can't say what he might be thinking," Mrs. Stebbens said, looking vastly pleased with herself. "But if it's marriage he's considering, it's not Lucy or Priscilla he's got in mind."

Delilah was descending the stairs when she heard the horse gallop up. No one raced a horse over a country lane unless an urgent situation demanded haste. It was too dangerous.

Delilah didn't move to answer the loud, insistent knocking. That was Lester's job, and he wouldn't thank her for overstepping herself. Then she remembered Serena had sent him on an errand. She hurried to open the door, only to find Tom Oliver, a young and fairly attractive man, in the clutch of great excitement.

"Where's Nathan?" Oliver demanded brushing roughly against her as he strode into the hall. "I've got to talk to him at once."

"He went out early this morning."

"Where'd he go?"

"I don't know."

"Why don't you?"

"It's not Mr. Trent's habit to inform the servants of his whereabouts," Delilah said. She probably shouldn't speak to a guest that way, but Tom Oliver shouldn't have brushed by her as if she weren't there.

As Tom's gaze traveled over Delilah, the irritation in his

eyes changed. He had looked at her lustfully many a time during the last three years, and he found that her attractiveness had not diminished.

"Why don't you be a good girl and show me to the library?" he said.

From his expression, Delilah suspected that talking to Nathan was no longer uppermost in his mind. She was tempted to tell him to come back later. She didn't like him and never had.

"I'll tell Mrs. Noyes you're here."

"I don't want to see that bitch," Oliver said sharply.

"You keep a decent tongue in your head, Tom Oliver, or you'll go right back out the door."

"You going to chuck me out?" he asked, an insolent smile showing a mouth full of straight, strong teeth.

"There are half a dozen men within the sound of my voice."

"Just take me to the library," Oliver growled.

"Follow me," Delilah said, feeling rather pleased with the way she'd handled him.

She opened the library door, walked inside, then stepped aside to allow Tom to enter.

The room was completely paneled in honey-colored pine adorned with fluted pilasters and rosetted capitals. Eight bookcases were set into the wall and fronted with glass. A Chippendale slant-front desk and corner chair sat between the fireplace and the two windows which looked out over the garden and down to the river. Two tall-backed Windsor chairs were set against the far wall with a butterfly drop-leaf table between them, and a high-backed settle stood against the near wall. Between the two windows was a tilt-top table.

Before Delilah could guess Oliver's intentions, he pulled the door out of her hands and kicked it shut. Then he trapped her in the corner, his large physique between her and the rest of the room.

"Now, my pretty, scream all you want and see who'll hear you."

Delilah wasn't afraid of him, but she didn't like the situation.

"Don't be foolish," she said, hoping her face revealed none of the apprehension in her heart. "If you're trying to show me you're bigger than I am, you've made your point."

"You always were a haughty female," Oliver retorted, remembering past rebuffs. "Always thinking you were too good for most people."

"Not too good. Just not interested."

"Not interested?" Tom asked. His eyes gleamed lecherously. "I bet you'd change your mind for the right person."

"Not interested, period," Delilah insisted.

"I find that hard to believe. A good-looking gal like you ought to be wanting a man."

"A man, perhaps. It's overgrown boys I have no time for."

"I'm a man now." Oliver pushed his body up against Delilah until she could feel the swelling at his groin.

"If you were a man, you wouldn't think of attempting to trap me in a corner and steal a kiss," Delilah said contemptuously. "Now get out of my way. I've got work to do." She tried to get past him on one side and then the other, but he blocked her.

"Always trying to run away."

"That's been part of your trouble from the beginning," Delilah said, placing her hands on her hips and facing him squarely. "You never could tell the difference between a girl who was running away and one who was turning her back on you."

Oliver turned dark red with anger. "You won't turn your back on me this time."

He spun her around to face him as she tried to move past, grabbing her shoulders and burying his fingers in the soft muscle between Delilah's neck and shoulder. The pain was intense.

She raised her arms to push him aside. At the same

time she shrugged her shoulders, breaking his hold.

"I'll always turn my back on the likes of you."

Tom grabbed her arms and pulled her up against him. "Not until I find out whether you're worth half what you think you are."

Delilah's head spun. Surely he couldn't have meant what that sounded like. No man would think of forcing himself on her in another man's house.

"I've been wondering if it's you filling out that dress or cotton wadding."

The worst of her fears receded. Anger took their place. "There's nothing false about me, Tom Oliver."

Delilah feinted to her right. When his grip held, she kicked him in the shins as hard as she could. He yelled in pain and lost his grip, but he was able to block the door.

"You'll pay for that, you little bitch," he growled. He dashed toward the Windsor chair she was hiding behind and sent it spinning across the floor out of his way. When Delilah hid behind a second chair, Oliver threw it aside as well.

"I'll kick you again if you touch me," she said between pants.

"Bitch," Oliver roared. He came after her again. This time he overturned the table between them. "When I get my hands on you I'll—"

"You won't do anything because you're not man enough."

That was too much for Oliver, and he came at Delilah over the upended table. She screamed and dived behind the desk. As she scrambled out the other side, the door burst open and Serena Noyes's horrified gaze took in the upheaval.

"What is the meaning of this?" she demanded.

"That bitch threw herself at me," Oliver said before Delilah could get to her feet. "When I told her I'd have none of her, she kicked me. She upset the room to keep me from getting my hands on her."

135

Delilah brushed the dust off her dress and straightened her clothing.

"I did nothing of the kind," she said with a calm dignity Serena couldn't help but respect. "I wouldn't have anything to do with Tom Oliver before he married. I certainly wouldn't tempt him to be indiscreet when he's about to become a father."

"You can't believe a farm bitch," Oliver said to Serena. "They'll do anything to attract the attention of a man with a little bit of money."

Serena looked confused. She found it hard to believe that Delilah would attempt to seduce Tom Oliver. It wasn't like her. On the other hand, Oliver was a man of her own station. How could she not believe him? Besides, he was married, about to become a father. Such a man wouldn't waste his time on the sister of a poor yeoman farmer. Still, Serena didn't really believe Tom. But she had been looking for a chance to get rid of Delilah. She couldn't pass up this one.

"I never wanted you here," she said, turning on Delilah. "I told my nephew you would cause trouble, but I never dreamed of this, not even from one of your kind."

"You say 'one of your kind' like that again, Serena Noyes, and the bruise on Tom's shin won't be anything to what I do to your face," Delilah announced. She was utterly furious, madder than she had ever thought possible. Oddly enough she wasn't that angry at Tom. She had expected something crude from him. She wasn't even too upset that Serena had sided with him. She had expected that, too.

What *did* make her so mad she was ready to fight them both with her bare hands was that she would be considered guilty of something she hadn't done, especially such a sordid act. It made her even madder to know she was defenseless. No one had seen it. No one in the house would take her side.

"I want you out of this house in half an hour," Serena decreed. "And don't leave anything behind."

136

Delilah started to object, but realized she had no ground to stand on. She faced Serena squarely, her eyes looking directly into the older woman's, and for a long moment did not speak, the silence of the room becoming heavier the longer it lasted. Serena squirmed uncomfortably, but didn't turn away.

"I always knew you disliked me," Delilah said at last, "but I gave you credit for common decency. You know Tom Oliver's lying, but you choose to accept his obscene accusation because it suits your convenience. It doesn't matter to you that my reputation may be ruined or my family may lose their only means of making a living. You're a sick, twisted woman, Serena Noyes. I pity you."

Serena shrank back as if she had been struck.

"You stop talking to Mrs. Noyes like that, or I'll take a whip to you," Oliver threatened.

"You so much as lay a finger on me, Tom Oliver, and I'll leave a set of scratches down your cheek you'll not see the end of for a month. How will you explain that to your wife?" Delilah was so furious her whole body shook.

Oliver drew back in some confusion.

"I'll pack my things and leave immediately."

"What's going on?" Nathan demanded from the door. "Why are you packing?"

No one had heard him come in. Delilah looked up to see confusion on his face. Even in the midst of the most all-consuming rage she had ever experienced, she was affected by his physical presence. The two powerful emotions battled briefly within her, and her physical response to Nathan won. Her rage at Tom and Serena started to subside with astonishing speed. Within seconds, it might never have existed.

"I thought you wanted to stay until you'd paid off your brother's debt."

Delilah couldn't answer. How could she accuse one of his friends of lewd behavior, his aunt of using a lie to get rid of her?

"I'm waiting for an answer." He might have been speak-

137

ing to all three of them, but he was looking at Delilah.

She shook her head helplessly.

"You can't just shake your head. I want to know why you're leaving." When Delilah didn't answer, he turned to Serena. "Can you tell me?" His aunt opened her mouth to speak, but Delilah sent her a look so filled with rage that her mouth slammed shut. "Have you also fallen dumb?" Nathan asked Oliver.

"Hell, no," Tom said, as he shot Delilah a look of triumph. "The little whore made a pass at me, and Serena told her to get out."

The last word had barely escaped his mouth when a powerful blow from Nathan's fist sent him crashing to the floor between an overturned chair and a broken table.

He lay still.

"Now," Nathan said, turning to the two women, "will one of you tell me the truth."

Serena looked from Tom to Nathan and back to Tom, horrorstruck. Then she sank into a chair, one hand at her throat, the other at her breast. Speechless, she stared at Nathan.

"Well," he said, looking to Delilah.

He hadn't turned a hair. He wasn't even breathing hard, yet Tom Oliver lay unconscious in the middle of the library floor.

"Tom . . . he . . . I can't . . . I really didn't . . ."

"Don't try to explain that nonsense," Nathan said impatiently. "Whatever happened, I know you didn't make a pass at Tom Oliver."

Delilah looked at him in amazement, a great weight lifting from her chest. "How could you know that?"

"I haven't been around you this long without coming to a fair estimation of your character. I wouldn't put it past you to stick a knife between my shoulder blades or to tell your brother and his friends everything that goes on here, but you wouldn't steal so much as a crumb even if you were starving—and you wouldn't make a pass at any man under any conditions."

138

Delilah's world turned upside down.

She had known for days her feeling for Nathan had become more than a mere physical attraction. So many things had happened to show her he wasn't the man she had first believed him to be, but it had never occurred to her he would concern himself with her character. She had certainly never imagined he'd believe her rather than Serena or one of his friends.

Yet he had. Without hesitation.

The realization of what this meant made her so weak she wanted to sink down onto a chair as Serena had. But she didn't. She stood facing him.

"Tom Oliver brought a message for you. When you weren't here, he got fresh. It made him angry when I rebuffed him."

She stopped. She didn't want to say any more.

"Is that all? I don't see how that accounts for the state of the library."

Delilah looked down at Oliver. He was a weak man, but she really didn't dislike him.

"That was all," Delilah said. She sneaked a glance at Serena, who hadn't moved.

"Then I suppose I shall have to have him arrested."

"Why?"

"He must be drunk. He broke up my house. He could have become violent."

Delilah knew what Nathan was doing. "You would really have him arrested?"

"Certainly."

"Even though you know that's not true?"

"How could I know that? No one has told me the truth."

Delilah didn't see how learning the truth was going to help anybody, but she couldn't allow Tom Oliver to be arrested.

"I made Tom mad."

"How?"

"Some things I said."

"What things?"

"I told him he wasn't very attractive."

"Why?"

"Isn't that enough?"

"No. Why did you tell him? You don't make a habit of being rude."

"He always resented me because I wasn't attracted to him."

"And?"

"He threatened me."

"How?"

"He didn't say."

"But you were able to keep away from him?"

"If I hadn't, he wouldn't have been on his feet for you to knock down."

Delilah's spurt of temper made Nathan grin. "Now tell me why you were getting ready to leave."

Again Delilah fidgeted. She knew she had to tell him this time. She was just trying to decide how much to tell.

"Mrs. Noyes came in on us. Oliver told her I had made advances, kicked him when he'd turned me down."

"So why were you leaving?"

"It's impossible to keep a servant such as Tom said I was. Mrs. Noyes had no choice but to tell me to leave."

"But he was lying."

"How could she know that?"

"I did."

That was unanswerable.

"I promised your brother you'd be safe. I obviously haven't done a good job." He looked down at Oliver, who had begun to moan. "Get up," Nathan ordered. When Tom didn't move, Nathan roughly hauled him to his feet. "You're not to come to this house—ever again." The fires of deep anger flamed in his eyes once more. "If you have a message for me, send it by someone else."

"But—" Tom began.

"Bother Delilah again, and I'll horsewhip you." A single push of powerful arms sent Oliver stumbling through the still-open door. Seconds later Nathan had thrown him out of the house and slammed the door behind him.

"Now," Nathan said to his aunt when he returned to the library, "why did you believe any of this nonsense?"

"I didn't know. I couldn't . . . it's impossible to . . . Tom would have told everybody that she—"

"I don't intend to mold my behavior to fit what Tom Oliver or anyone else says. When you know a person of character, no matter what their station, it's your responsibility to stand up for them. You can't believe Oliver just because he has money. You can't be afraid of him for that reason either."

Both women stared at Nathan. He had said more in the last five minutes than he'd said in the last two weeks. He had defended all people of integrity, had attacked the honor of the wealthy merchants, and had backed a servant's actions rather than his aunt's.

"You may want to consult Mrs. Stebbens about dinner," Nathan said to Serena. It was a dismissal, however politely worded, and they all knew it.

Serena fled in haste.

"Now tell me what really happened," Nathan said, turning to Delilah. He came closer, so close she could hardly breathe.

"I told you. . . ."

"Only in part. What did he do?"

"He did exactly what I said. He got angry when I said some unkind things about him. He wanted to punish me."

"Punish you! How?"

Fury blazed in Nathan's eyes, and Delilah knew right away she had used the wrong word.

"I don't mean punish. I suppose he only wanted to scare me, to bolster his vanity by proving he was bigger and stronger than I am."

"Did he touch you?"

"No."

"Is that the truth?"

"Yes."

Nathan stared hard at her. Delilah didn't let her gaze waver.

"Why are you trying to protect him? Why won't you tell me what happened?" He advanced a step toward her.

"I have." She stepped back.

"No, you haven't." She saw his eyes flicker from her face, hold, and then grow vivid with fiery anger. "How do you explain the bruises on your shoulders?"

She had forgotten them.

His right hand reached out and touched the bruised spot on her left shoulder. As Delilah stood transfixed, his left hand reached out to the right. Delilah hardly knew what was happening to her. She could barely think.

"He didn't mean to do that. I said he was vulgar and crude, and that made him mad."

"You shouldn't have let him touch you. You should have called out."

She felt she would jump out of her skin as an incredible amount of energy surged through her; then she was sure she would faint from the weakness that invaded her limbs.

"I've known Tom all my life. He's nothing but a braggart. He can't stand it when a woman doesn't find him attractive."

She wanted to run away because she couldn't control the way he was affecting her; she wanted to stay rooted to the spot and let him touch her again and again. She wanted to tell him how happy she was that he cared about her; she was afraid to say a word lest it break the spell.

"If you knew what he was like, why didn't you stay away from him?"

Delilah stepped back, breaking contact with Nathan's fingertips.

"Why are you getting mad at me?" she demanded. "I had no idea anything would happen, or I wouldn't have opened the door. And if you believe I did anything to suggest I would welcome his advances, I'll leave this house immediately."

"I don't believe anything of the sort," Nathan said, the

fire in his eyes cooling. "I suppose I'm feeling guilty for not protecting you, and I'm taking it out on you."

He stepped forward and allowed his fingers to caress her skin from the arch of her shoulder to the curve of her neck.

"It's not your fault," she said.

"Yes, it is. This is my house."

Nathan stroked her cheek with the back of his hand, gently, tenderly.

"None of this would have happened if I had been home. I've been a fool to think I could accomplish anything by running away. It won't happen again."

Delilah sensed that he was talking to himself more than to her, but she didn't care. Her whole being seemed to become focused on the hand that moved down the side of her neck, brushing her skin ever so slightly, burning like fire, causing her muscles to go weak.

"I want you to feel safe here."

"I do."

"If anything happens, anything at all, you're to come to me. You understand?"

Delilah nodded. His touch had rendered her helpless. Her whole body shivered uncontrollably.

Nathan didn't move. He seemed almost as transfixed as Delilah. His fingertips continued to travel over her skin, sending shivers through her. His face came closer to hers until she was burningly aware of his lips.

Nathan's body stiffened with desire. The feel of Delilah's skin was like an aphrodisiac. He was consumed with an uncontrollable craving to do more than touch its softness and gaze longingly at her parted lips. He wanted to experience the intoxication of being alone with her, to take her in his arms and smother her with kisses.

Their lips touched. Briefly. Gently.

They drew apart. Each gazed at the other with new eyes.

"You're beautiful," Nathan whispered. He cradled her face in his hands. "Very, very beautiful."

"You're beautiful, too," Delilah replied. "I've thought so from the moment you opened the door to me. You confused me so much I asked for tea. I didn't even know how to serve it."

"I wanted you here so much I invented something for you to do."

"Reuben almost didn't let me come."

"I would have found a way."

Nathan kissed her again. He could feel Delilah's lips quiver under his, then tense in response. The tension left his body, and his kiss became more insistent, more hungry. But a kiss wasn't enough. He wanted to caress her, hold her, crush her to his chest.

They broke apart, each aware of what they had done, each aware of how much more they wanted to do.

Just as Nathan was about to yield to the tide sweeping over them both, the door opened and Mrs. Stebbens entered the room.

"Her brother's come," she said. "He's waiting for her down by the river." She disappeared as silently as she had come.

Nathan stepped back. "He'll see those bruises. He won't let you stay."

"Do you want me to go?" Delilah said, her voice sounding as weak as she felt.

"No," Nathan said softly.

"I'd better see Reuben. He's not very good at waiting." *Neither am I.*

144

Chapter Eleven

Delilah fled to her room. She needed time to calm her racing pulse and cool her flushed cheeks. She needed time to sort through the jumble of thoughts in her mind, to analyze the tangle of emotions in her heart.

She also needed something to cover her shoulders. She was completely incapable of answering another question about her bruises.

The hope that Nathan would become interested in her was no longer a daydream. No man touched a woman in that way unless she was very special to him. She could still feel his kiss. He'd kissed her like a man making a wondrous discovery, like a man kissing a woman for the first time — no, like a man who kisses the *woman he cares for*, for the first time. If Mrs. Stebbens hadn't interrupted them, he might be kissing her still.

She might be touching him.

That thought sent shivers all through her.

From the first, he had held an unexpected fascination for her. And it wasn't just his handsome face. It was the sheer impact of his physical presence on every part of her anatomy. That made her feel she was about to explode. She had never responded to anyone that way before. Now he had touched her, and she knew she wanted to touch him. Nathan wanted her just as much as she wanted him.

What was she prepared to do about it?

Delilah didn't know. The differences caused by a war, an ocean, an entirely different way of living, and several thousand pounds had kept her from giving serious thought to anything more than that he was attractive and she wanted him to notice her.

His understanding and sympathy for people like her was more sincere and more profound than the feelings of many of her countrymen. Could she have found her greatest ally in this most unlikely man?

She would have to think about that. After she thought about Reuben.

His arrival served to point up the fact that she hadn't done any of the things she'd been sent to do. She had never wanted to spy on Nathan, but it would be even more difficult now. How could she spy on a man who constantly concerned himself with her comfort and happiness? Who gave more attention to her than his own family? Who looked at her as if he'd never seen a woman before?

It would be a betrayal.

But wouldn't going back on her word be a betrayal of her family and Captain Shays? Who had the greatest claim on her loyalty — a handsome, seductive stranger, who had every reason to support her enemies, or the family and friends who loved her and had supported her through the most trying hours of her life?

They hadn't asked her to hurt Nathan or deprive him of anything. They were merely asking for a chance to hold on to their property so they could pay their debts. Wasn't that a good enough reason to spy on him?

It might have been at one time, but not now. He had reached out to her as his only friend in the midst of enemies, and her feelings had changed. She didn't know exactly how much, but she could no more think of betraying Nathan than she could Reuben.

And what of Nathan's feelings for her? His trust? She could never look him in the face if she used his vulnerability to betray him.

But could she live with herself if she did nothing to help her brother and the other poor farmers who were fighting for the little that was left to them?

Delilah couldn't see any way to reconcile her feelings, at

least not now. Firmly putting the question out of her mind, she pulled a light shawl over her shoulders and went down to the river to meet Reuben.

"I was beginning to think that Noyes woman wouldn't let you out," Reuben said when she reached him. He was standing at the river's edge, skimming stones across the smooth surface. The early frosts and dry summer had already begun to turn the leaves to red, gold, and brown. The stalks, topped by dying flowers, crackled in the wind, and hard seeds rattled in their pods.

"I had something to finish up."

Reuben looked his sister over carefully. "You look all right. I guess they're treating you nice."

"Mrs. Noyes doesn't want me here, and Lester would prefer someone who didn't argue with him, but Mrs. Stebbens is very good to me. She's the cook. And I like old Applegate. You'd like him, too. He's responsible for that garden."

"I looked it over," Reuben said, his mouth pulled down at the corners. "We could have a garden like that if we had bottom land and unlimited water."

"Is the well holding out?"

"It's a little sluggish, but it'll last."

That was a relief. As long as they had water, they could go on. Without it . . .

"How are the boys?"

"Getting out of hand. Jane doesn't have the time to keep after them."

"I wish I—"

"You're doing more than you ought," Reuben said, turning his head away so he looked out over the river. "Don't go wishing you could do more."

"How're you getting along?"

"I got the best price ever for the flax. From him," he said as he motioned toward the house. "And I've got more work offered for the oxen than I can do."

"I'm glad. I was worried."

"You shouldn't be. I'm going to have the money for taxes

and maybe a little extra. We'll be all right." Reuben paused, uncomfortable. "I couldn't have done it without you." He still didn't look at her.

Delilah felt embarrassed. Reuben usually found it impossible to thank anybody for anything. It wasn't that he was selfish or ungrateful. Saying thanks just didn't come easily for him.

"Have you decided on a name for the baby?" she asked, changing the subject.

"We'll call him Johnny if he's a boy, Delilah if she's a girl."

Delilah thought she was going to cry. "You said you were going to call her Margaret?" Margaret was their mother's name.

"Jane said Mother wasn't strong enough to stand up to the hard times after the war. She just gave up and died. You didn't. She would rather our daughter be like you."

Delilah cried. How could her devotion to these two dear people ever waver? Why did she have so much trouble even remembering it when she was with Nathan?

They talked of other things, mostly the insignificant concerns that filled their days, and they were soon talking as though she had never left home.

Until they saw Nathan coming toward them. Delilah could feel Reuben tense, even without looking at him. She heard it in his voice.

"How's *he* been treating you?" her brother queried.

"Why do you ask?"

"He's acting peculiar. I don't understand him."

"How do you mean?"

"People owe him twice as much money as anybody else, but he hasn't taken property from more than half a dozen people."

"Maybe he doesn't know enough about things yet."

"He knows. They weren't intending to pay him."

Reuben fell silent. Nathan had reached them, and the two men stared at each other for a moment.

"I hear Captain Shays has been rather busy lately," Nathan said finally. "You with him?"

Reuben's body became even more rigid.

148

"You can't ask him that," Delilah protested. "It's the same as asking him to incriminate himself."

"I don't care whether Reuben is with the regulators or not," Nathan said. "And I certainly don't intend to tell the sheriff if he is."

"But what about . . ." It was on the tip of Delilah's tongue to ask about the list in his desk.

"What about Colonel Clarke and the others?" Nathan asked, supplying the question for her.

Delilah nodded.

"I can't speak for them. While I don't approve of their methods, I don't approve of closing the courts either."

"What's wrong with that?" Delilah asked before Reuben had a chance to open his mouth.

"It's illegal for one thing. It appears to sanction anarchy for another. It also stops due process of law and encourages people to believe they can refuse to pay their lawful debts if enough of them agree to it."

"That's not what we're trying to do," Reuben burst out. "We're only trying to find a way to save ourselves so we *can* pay our debts."

"That may be true for some of you, but not for all," Nathan insisted. "There are men with you who are calling for civil war."

"We only want the General Session to give us some relief."

"Then find a better way to go about it. Governor Bowdoin has just declared your actions treason and has ordered the militia to shoot."

"They won't," Reuben declared confidently. "Too many have brothers among us."

"General Shepard doesn't. And he's the one who will give the order to fire."

"Why?" Reuben asked. "There's been no fighting."

"There will be if you don't stop closing courts."

"And let your kind take everything we've got," Reuben exploded. "I'll see you in hell first."

"I didn't say you were to give up," Nathan said, "just find another way."

149

"What other way is there?" Delilah asked. "We've held town meetings, sent petitions to the court, talked to every delegate who'll listen, and still the General Session refuses to vote for paper money. Closing the courts is the only thing they've been able to do that's made anybody listen."

"The government is getting the wrong message," Nathan said. "They're preparing to fight."

"Let 'm," Reuben shouted. "We'll be ready." He stalked away without even saying goodbye to Delilah.

"Why did you come out here?" Delilah asked. "Just to make him angry?"

"I wanted to talk some sense into him."

"Talk sense! All you did was ask him to stop doing something that hasn't hurt a single person."

"It will if they continue. It will harden the opposition against them as well."

"What are they supposed to do, roll over and die?"

"No, they're supposed to look for other ways to pay their debts. Like you did."

"Not everybody can work as a servant."

"There's more than one way to do anything."

"Like what?"

"I don't know."

"Then don't go around saying there're solutions until you find a few."

"Why should it be up to me? They're not my debts."

"Somebody has to."

"Then you do it."

"Me!"

"Yes. You grew up here. You know these people and what they can do."

"You're serious, aren't you?"

"Of course. I don't like confrontation. I like war even less. If I can find a way to get my money and help somebody else at the same time, I will be happy to do it. When do we start?"

Delilah was nonplussed. "I'll need some time to think."

"How much?"

"We ought to start with the families in the worst situation.

Give me a list, and I'll let you know when I have some ideas."

"Suppose I make up a list today, and we go over it together tomorrow morning."

"Agreed." Delilah was feeling a little breathless. When Nathan decided to do something, he didn't waste time.

"I'll go to the library and start on that list. Oh, I almost forgot. My aunt has invited you to eat dinner with us this evening."

Delilah stopped dead in her tracks.

"She thought it might serve as an apology for this morning."

Delilah knew Serena Noyes hadn't sent that invitation. Nathan wanted her to have dinner with him. If she said no, she would be refusing him.

But she should refuse. How could she go back to being a servant after sitting down at the table as an equal? How would Mrs. Stebbens and Lester react? Serena's hatred of her would be raised to fever pitch, but she doubted Priscilla would object. She didn't know much about her, but she did know that under those silly affectations there existed a very different woman.

Yesterday she'd have turned down the invitation without hesitation, but after this morning, it wasn't enough to see Nathan at meals on the days he was at home. She wanted to be near him all the time. If she was a fool for letting her feelings run away with her, she didn't care.

Tomorrow she would be sensible. Tonight she was going to have dinner with Nathan Trent.

Nathan cursed. There was a tear in his shirt. The second one this week. At this rate he wouldn't have a decent shirt left by Christmas. He'd have to sew it up when he had time; he didn't have a minute to spare now. Nor a thought.

He had to dress for dinner, and he wanted his appearance to be perfect. All his life he'd been taught that one's appearance counted for more than one's personality, even one's abilities. He didn't think Delilah believed that, but so much stood against him he didn't want to overlook any possible advantage.

He tossed the torn shirt aside and took another off the shelf. He couldn't help but smile to himself when he turned to inspect himself in the mirror. He knew his physique had a powerful affect on Delilah, and he intended to use that weapon.

Nathan took pride in his body, and worked to keep it trim and fit. He had patronized the best tailors so his clothing would show off his assets to advantage, but now he had nothing in his wardrobe less than four years old. The velvet looked worn, the wool shiny and thin, the silk permanently creased, the cotton yellow with age and repeated washing.

He hoped the candlelight would hide these faults, but he also hoped Delilah would be more interested in him than in his clothing.

He admitted he had first been attracted by her beauty. To state the matter plainly, he had lusted after her. It was impossible for a red-blooded man to be around Delilah and not feel the tug of her physical appeal. She was designed to drive a man crazy. Her shoulders were flawless. He had ached to touch them from the moment he'd set eyes on her. If Mrs. Stebbens hadn't walked in, he might still be standing in the library caressing her skin.

He told himself to control his thoughts, or he would betray his state of mind. When his lusts were inflamed, his body swelled with passion. He was afraid Delilah would be frightened or repulsed by such an obvious display of desire.

Too bad Lady Sarah Mendlow hadn't been repulsed.

Nathan pushed aside the hateful memory. Judged against the pleasure of being with Delilah for an entire evening, even that nightmare didn't have the power to hold his attention.

But he would have to proceed slowly. He didn't yet know where his heart would lead him, and Delilah had become unaccountably precious to him. Being in the same house with her had done nothing to abate his desire to claim her body. It had, however, given him an opportunity to realize she wasn't merely a good-looking woman. She had courage, principles, and daring. Maybe she was trustworthy as well, able to value him above the world's counterfeit riches.

But a nagging voice, the voice of doubt, would not be silenced. Or was it mistrust? He had only loved two women, and both had attempted to use him for their own advantage.

What did Delilah want?

Delilah didn't bother to look in the mirror. She tried to chastise herself for being so concerned with her looks, but failed entirely. She knew she looked lovely, and she was glad.

She thought of Nathan and his tight breeches, and her body grew taut. She felt a tingling sensation in her breasts. Curious, she touched one and found the nipple hard and tender. Even her skin was sensitive to her touch.

Think about the *man,* you dolt, not just his body. But in trying to take her own advice, Delilah realized she didn't know much about Nathan. He had never told her about his life in England, and she had been so certain he was like all the rest of the greedy merchants.

He's kind, she told herself. At least he's been kind to you. He's taken your part on several occasions when it hasn't been to his advantage. And he has taken extraordinary care to make sure you're comfortable. And there's the material for the dresses.

She wasn't sure about his advising Reuben and Shays to find another way to pursue their protests. Delilah thought they had found the best way possible, but now she wasn't sure. Nathan's understanding of things continued to surprise her.

The list of names in his desk came to mind. What did he plan to do with it? Would she find Reuben's name on it? Surely, after their conversation by the river this morning, he knew Reuben followed Shays.

But he had advised the merchants to alter their tactics as well. Did his being a foreigner mean he had no understanding of what was going on, or did it mean he had ideas the locals hadn't even thought of yet?

The longer Serena looked at Delilah, the more furious she became. Not only had Nathan forced her to sit at table with a servant who was being served by her own butler, she had had to swallow the humiliation of knowing Delilah looked more beautiful than Priscilla. How was she going to convince Nathan to marry his cousin when Delilah was more alluring?

And Delilah was more interesting as well. Priscilla giggled and simpered and deferred to Nathan on every point. Delilah stated her opinions and defended them intelligently. Serena had never valued brains in a female, but she had to admit that Priscilla's idiotic giggle was enough to drive a man into another woman's arms, especially when those arms looked like Delilah's.

It galled her to have been forced to provide Delilah with the means to dress so stunningly. Obviously the girl and Mrs. Stebbens could do better work than Amelia Cushing. The needlework was gorgeous, though it had taken them only three days to make the gown. Serena knew because she had made it her business to find out.

"Shall we retire to the drawing room?" Serena asked, rising abruptly after Priscilla had capped one of Delilah's more intelligent observations with one of her most irritating titters. "I'm sure Mrs. Stebbens is expecting you in the kitchen," she added when Delilah rose to her feet.

Serena had waited all evening to say that.

"I've engaged Mrs. Pobodie to help Mrs. Stebbens. Miss Stowbridge is free to spend the entire evening with us," Nathan told his aunt.

Angry spots flamed on Serena's pale cheeks. "Hepsa Pobodie is a laundress."

"Who more suitable to help with the washing up," Nathan replied. He winked at Delilah.

Delilah turned pink.

Serena turned red.

"I won't have you altering the housekeeping arrangements without consulting me," Serena announced.

"You are free to make any objections you wish, but as

long as this is my house, I will make changes as I see fit." Nathan's gaze had grown hard, so reminiscent of his uncle's that Serena immediately began to give ground.

"Who cares who washes the dishes?" Priscilla said, leading the way to the drawing room. "I think having Delilah join us will be great fun."

"But what will she do?" Serena asked. "Raised as she has been, she can't possibly have any accomplishments."

"Then we shall talk," Nathan said.

"I hope you don't mean to discuss the political situation," Serena cautioned. "I think that would be most unwise as long as Delilah's present."

"Would you tell on us?" Priscilla asked in her most foolish manner.

"I certainly would," Delilah said, deciding the best way to handle the question would be to make a joke of it. "I would hurry up to my room and write down everything you said. Then I would sit up all night copying it out in cipher so no one else could read it."

"Wouldn't it be easier to tell your brother or sister when they come to visit you?" Nathan inquired.

"That would take away all the fun, don't you think?"

"I think you ought to put the message in a jar and let it float down the river," Priscilla said.

"But then anyone might find it," Delilah objected.

"There's no need to make light of a very serious question," Serena interposed.

"What would you really do?" Nathan asked.

"I don't know. I thought of writing on the ruffle of my petticoat. It sounds wonderfully clever, but I can't think how it would do the least good."

Priscilla giggled. "Can't have men reading your petticoats. Most improper."

"I'm astonished at you!" exclaimed Serena.

"I said it was improper," Priscilla answered, pouting.

"I suppose that eliminates hiding a note in your bosom?" asked Nathan.

Priscilla giggled again, but Delilah said, "I would imagine so."

"You could put it in your mouth," Priscilla suggested. "Then when you kiss a gentleman friend, you could pass it to him."

"Priscilla Noyes, how could you think of such a loathsome thing?" Serena demanded, aghast. "What do you know about kissing men?"

"Lucy and Hope tell me what it's like," Priscilla replied defiantly. "Their mamas don't keep them locked away."

"I don't lock you up, darling. I'm merely very careful about the men you see. I want you to meet only the right kind."

"I don't suppose the *right kind* would pass a note in a kiss," Priscilla said, still sulky.

Delilah could have sworn she saw a light of devilment flare in Priscilla's eyes, but she couldn't be sure.

"He most certainly would not. I think we have exhausted this most unsuitable subject. What do you wish to do now?"

Nathan thought about and discarded several ideas for games. Cards would ordinarily have been acceptable, but he had already learned that Serena cheated and Priscilla became hopelessly muddled when expected to recall the play of more than three hands.

"It's a shame we have no one to fiddle," said Priscilla. "I would dearly love to dance."

"If Miss Stowbridge would agree to play the pianoforte, I see no reason why you and Nathan shouldn't dance as much as you like," Serena said.

From the smug look on Serena's face, Delilah could guess the next question.

"Would you play for us, Miss Stowbridge?"

"I don't play," Delilah answered.

"It's not necessary that you play well."

"I don't play at all."

"But you do sing," Nathan said. "I've heard you."

"Singing gives me a headache," Serena moaned, "especially female voices."

"We can sing quietly," Nathan said.

"I only know folk songs," Delilah said.

156

"That's all I know," Nathan replied. "Why don't we each sing a song in turn."

"I don't sing," Serena announced. "I never cared for it."

"I can't sing either," declared Priscilla, "but I can play for you." She hopped up and seated herself at the pianoforte before her mother could object. "What are you going to sing, Nathan?"

"Do you know 'Little Musgrave'?" Priscilla began to play the refrain.

"I don't have much of a voice," Nathan warned them.

"Men's voices are always more pleasant than women's," Serena said.

Nathan sang well enough to earn the praise of his aunt, who was careful to praise her daughter even more. But Serena's attitude turned sour when Delilah's turn came.

"I won't be responsible for myself if I am overtaken by one of my sick headaches," she warned.

"Would you like some cotton for your ears?" Nathan asked.

Priscilla giggled. "Like I had when I was a little girl and had the earache."

"No," said Serena as she visibly prepared herself to suffer in silence.

Delilah sang a popular song called "Brambletown." Over Serena's protests, she and Nathan continued to sing, one after the other. Sometimes an English tune had been given different words in the colonies, and they had fun singing first one version and then the other.

Delilah had a very difficult time keeping her eyes off Serena when Nathan sang "The Farmer's 'Curst Wife," especially when the devil sent the wife back because she was too mean to stay in hell, but the mood turned more serious when he followed that by "Barbara Allen." The tale of a young man dying of love for a hard-hearted woman made Delilah wonder if Nathan had chosen the song intentionally.

"Do you know 'The Lass of Glenshee'?" he asked Delilah.

"I don't think so."

"I've never heard of it," Priscilla said.

"Surely we've had enough singing," Serena complained.

157

"My head aches from it."

"I can sing it without accompaniment," Nathan said, and he began to do so before his aunt could voice another protest.

> "As I was a-walking one morning for pleasure,
> Just as the dawning broke over the sea,
> Upon my returning I spied a fair damsel,
> She was tending her flocks on the Hills of
>   Glenshee."

Delilah smiled inwardly. Did he imagine she had ever tended sheep, or did he like the mental image of her in a pastoral setting? Maybe he thought if he got her alone, with only sheep for chaperons, he might not have his kisses interrupted.

> "I said, 'Pretty fair maid, will you come along with
>   me?
> I'll take you over my friends for to see,
> And I'll dress you up in pure silks and fine satins,
> And you'll have a footman to wait upon thee.' "

Delilah felt embarrassed when she thought of the bolts of cloth he had given her, the favorable treatment, the embraces in his office. She had always doubted the propriety of such favored treatment, but she couldn't help herself. She wanted his attention. She knew Englishmen treated women differently, expected different things from them, but surely he didn't think she would give herself to him for a dress and a few kisses.

A hissing noise made her wrench her gaze away from Nathan. To Serena, at least, the meaning appeared to be clear. She appeared to believe Nathan was planning to make Delilah the mistress of Maple Hill, right in front of his aunt and cousin.

> "She said, 'I don't want your silks nor your
>   satins,

Neither your footmen to wait upon me;
I'd rather stay home in my own homespun
   clothing,
And tend my flocks on the Hills of Glenshee.' "

Delilah felt a great sense of relief arc through her. Silly to attach so much importance to the words of a folk song, but she felt reassured to know Nathan didn't think she was likely to trade her honor for a few baubles.

"I said, 'Pretty fair maid, you misunderstand me;
I'll take you over my bride for to be,' "

Delilah couldn't help it. In answer to the warmth that glowed in Nathan's eyes, she broke into a self-conscious smile. Did he mean he loved her, wanted to marry her?

" 'And on that very night in my arms I will hold you.' "

Nathan's gaze bored into Delilah's, making her painfully aware of his presence, reminding her of his kiss, the feel of his hands on her skin. When she thought of what it would mean for him to take her in his arms on their marriage night . . .

"She then gave consent and she came along with me."

Delilah's body betrayed her utterly, and she blushed. Her muscles tensed, were shaken by spasms, and let go altogether. That was only the tip of the physical response which washed through her. To think of being with Nathan always, to be able to reach out and touch him whenever she wanted!

"There's seven long years since we've been united,
Seasons have changed but there's no change in me,
But if God spares my health and I keep my right
   senses,
I'll never prove false to the girl of Glenshee."

Promises of love, faithfulness. Delilah felt as though Nathan had just proposed to her.

"I've never heard a more unseemly song," Serena said, irritation and condemnation in her voice. "Most unsuitable outside the confines of one's family."

"I think it's sweet," Priscilla said. "I'd like some man to say that to me."

"They don't mean it, my dear," Serena said bitterly, "none of them."

"Do you agree with my aunt?" Nathan asked Delilah.

She didn't know what to say. His eyes, his expression, his whole demeanor told her the question had nothing to do with Serena. He was asking if she trusted him, if she believed he would remain faithful to his vows. The tension in his body, the stiffness of his limbs said her answer was important.

Delilah spoke slowly, carefully weighing each word before she spoke. "Love is almost never what we hope it will be. Too many other constraints twist and bend it out of shape. But I would like to believe that once in a great while two people fall so deeply in love they can never be false to one another, that they would face death rather than dishonor the vows they share."

"I never heard anything so ridiculous in my life," Serena stated.

For Delilah, the look of wonder, of awe, in Nathan's eyes drowned out Serena's words.

"If that sort of thing did happen," Serena said rather more quietly than usual, "it would be between people who could never hope to live happily together. One would already be married or of a completely different station in life. It could only cause pain."

But Delilah thought only of the unending happiness of being loved her whole life by the most wonderful man in the world. Could previous alliances or differences of station matter to two people so in love? Would they matter to her or Nathan?

"What do you think, Nathan?" Priscilla asked.

An undecipherable shadow crossed Nathan's face. "The weight of experience tells me Aunt Serena is correct. But like Delilah, I prefer to think that for a man and woman who can believe in each other, believe without question, for two who are willing to risk everything, and to give everything, for those special people such a love is possible."

"Do you think it's possible for you, for any of us?" Delilah asked.

"As long as we hope, anything is possible."

"It's time to retire," Serena said, rising to her feet. "We've talked enough nonsense for one evening."

"But it's just after ten o'clock," Nathan pointed out. "In England we stay up past midnight."

"We don't keep such late hours in America," his aunt said. "Besides," she added, following the direction of his gaze, "Delilah's duties require her to be up at five."

"Why don't you have dinner with us every evening?" he asked.

"I don't think that would be a good idea," Delilah replied. Dreams were wonderful, but it was time to wake up to reality.

"Why not? You had a good time, didn't you?"

"Of course, but it's not suitable for anyone in my position to try to go back and forth between the kitchen and the parlor."

"She's right," Serena said. "If this became common knowledge, it would be to her detriment."

Her words made Nathan realize Delilah couldn't do as she pleased, no matter what he might like, as long as she remained a servant in his house.

"Then I shall say good night. Don't forget our appointment tomorrow."

"I won't," Delilah replied. She was aware the moment she heard her reply that her tone was not that of someone setting up a business appointment.

"What is this?" demanded Serena, after Delilah had left.

"She's going to think of ways the farmers can pay their debts."

"Either they pay in cash or you take their property,"

161

Serena declared flatly. "That's all you need to know."

"But she doesn't agree with you," Nathan said. "I don't either. Nor do I want to be known as a man who puts women and children out on the road."

"Then you'll die a pauper," Serena snapped.

"Don't you mean to say you don't want me to make a pauper out of you?"

"Of course I don't," Serena snapped.

"Then support me in this. I don't intend to be poor again."

Chapter Twelve

Delilah couldn't go to sleep even though she knew she would be tired the next morning. Nathan was smitten with her. He really liked her; he didn't just want to get her in his bed. And that realization sent her heart soaring.

Because she liked him, too.

More than she would have thought possible. She had become obsessed with him. She thought of him all the time, and now she wanted to be with him. She had eagerly accepted the invitation to dinner and then had compounded her mistake by spending the rest of the evening in the drawing room. It might not have any serious repercussions in the kitchen, but it could only lead to disaster everywhere else.

The society which had shaped Nathan perpetuated the belief that she would never be good enough for him. He might be overwhelmed by her beauty now, but little things he'd hardly noticed would build a wall between them in time.

And what about her? The people she had grown up with, had known all her life, would turn against her if she were to marry him. Worst of all, Reuben and Jane would never understand. They were all the family she had. Could anything be worth the risk of losing them?

No, she would have to rein in her emotions while she still could.

Besides, she had never thought of marriage, not really. An Englishman or an American merchant didn't marry to his disadvantage, certainly not to a foolish little serving girl who would bring him nothing but ridicule.

Nathan would probably look for a wife in Boston, or Providence or Newport. He might even look as far afield as New York or Philadelphia. With his looks, she doubted there would be many girls who would mind marrying him, even if they did happen to be wealthier than he was. All the money in the world couldn't make a man grow up to look like Nathan.

He would probably seek out a beautiful woman who would feel at home in London society, someone who could play the pianoforte and sing all the English ballads he knew. Plenty of Tory sympathizers in America would jump at the chance to marry an Englishman. They would be only too willing to build enormous houses for him, give him lots of money, buy tight breeches for him.

"This is stupid," Delilah said aloud, trying to combat the depression these visions were bringing on. *His choice of wife can't possibly concern you. You'll leave here before Christmas and probably never see him again.*

But that thought brought no comfort. The only thing worse than Nathan's marrying some rich, hard-hearted female who would take him away from her would be never to see him again.

Nathan managed to keep his speculation on the evening at bay until he was in bed, but once he put out the lamp, Delilah occupied his thoughts to the exclusion of all else.

She was the most fascinating woman he had ever met. She had an intelligence and self-assurance which not only allowed her to be a servant in his house without apology but enabled her to be his guest without feeling out of place or ill at ease.

He had no way to judge whether she was genuine or he was just confused by the different standards of behavior which operated in America. And they were different. He still hadn't become accustomed to the fact that Priscilla could go off for hours without anyone knowing where she went, yet her reputation did not suffer. In England five minutes beyond the sight of a chaperon could ruin even the most carefully brought-up young woman.

Maybe that was the reason Delilah felt at ease in his company whether they were in the garden or the house. If so, he was thankful. Though she disapproved of him and what he wanted to do, the only happy moments he had spent in this country had been with her.

Maybe happy didn't accurately describe his mental or emotional state when he was with her. There was the perpetual attraction which, at any moment and completely without warning, could cause his groin to swell with embarrassing rapidity. He had even considered purchasing some of the loose clothing preferred by Lucius Clarke and Asa Warner, but he could not yet convince himself to look so . . . so . . . He wasn't sure what he thought he would look like, but he doubted he could ever become accustomed to such ill-fitting clothes.

If you don't do something, you'll embarrass yourself beyond redemption one of these days. You get worse about that woman with each passing day. And she hasn't given you any encouragement.

But she hadn't run away either.

She'd done what he'd asked and no more. Well, maybe she had done a little more than was absolutely necessary, but he couldn't pride himself on it being very much.

Don't act like a fool. And stop trying to bend and twist everything she says or does to make it look as though she's falling in love with you. She came here for a purpose, and when she's done she'll leave. You'll probably never see her again.

"Nathan."

Nathan sat up in bed as quickly as if he'd been stung by a hornet.

"Nathan."

He wasn't mistaken. The hissed whisper came from outside his door.

"Who is it?" he called out.

"Let me in."

He hesitated to get out of bed. He was naked under the covers.

"Quick, let me in."

It had to be Delilah. No one else needed to whisper, but what could she want with him at this hour? Whatever it was, it must be important. Despite his body's response, he was certain that *wasn't* what she had come for. Nevertheless, once the thought had taken hold in his mind it would not be dislodged. The stored-up desire, frustrating dreams, and hours of imaginings concentrated themselves in his groin until he was uncomfortably hard. And absolutely unpresentable.

He trembled with excitement. If she *had* come to him . . . He couldn't keep himself from imagining her in his arms, her craving for him as strong as his for her. His body ached with hunger, his limbs grew taut with desire. No matter how strongly his conscience warned him that he would feel differently in the cold light of day, he couldn't vanquish the hope she would invite him to satisfy his need in the warmth of her body.

He couldn't get out of bed in this state, but he couldn't leave her standing in the hall either. If Serena or Priscilla woke and found her outside his door, her reputation would be ruined.

"Just a minute," he called out. He wrapped the sheet loosely about his body. Then after making sure the extra material was bunched in front of him, he climbed out of bed and tiptoed across the room. He turned the key in the lock and opened the door a crack. It flew open; someone rushed in and promptly closed the door.

Priscilla!

Nathan reacted as if he'd been dosed with a barrel of cold water. Priscilla's reaction was just the opposite. She had no sooner taken in the fact that he stood wrapped in nothing but a sheet, her eyes glistened in the near dark of the room, and a smile curved her lips. She advanced on him, hands outstretched. Whether merely to touch him or to pull away the protective sheet, Nathan didn't know, but

166

he was of no mind to find out. With a leap which would have done justice to an antelope, he bounded up onto the middle of the bed.

"What are you doing here?" he demanded in a tortured hiss. "Your mother will kill us both if she discovers you in my room."

"She wouldn't care," Priscilla said, preparing to climb onto the bed with Nathan. Her hand had fallen away from her bosom allowing her gaping robe to reveal a nightgown perilously transparent. "She wants me to marry you. She wants us to get married right now."

Even as she lifted her leg to climb onto Nathan's bed, he lowered his foot to slip off the other side.

"I'm not interested in getting married."

"You don't like women?" Priscilla paused, a confused look on her face.

"Now," Nathan amended. "I'm not interested in getting married now."

"But I need a husband," Priscilla said, reassured. She climbed across the bed, and Nathan moved around to the other side. "I want gowns. I want money of my own. I want a house of my own. I want all kinds of things I can't have unless I'm married." She giggled. "Do you ever have urges, Nathan?"

"What kind of urges?" he asked, pulling the sheet more tightly around him.

"*Urges*. Sometimes they keep me awake. I feel that my body is burning up."

She stalked Nathan.

"I feel I've got to touch secret places, and I can't even stand clothing next to my skin."

Nathan climbed back on the bed. Priscilla followed without hesitation.

"Mama says those urges disappear when a girl gets married. Mama says a man makes them go away."

Priscilla tumbled off the bed right behind Nathan. He took refuge behind a high-backed Windsor chair.

"Please marry me, Nathan. I don't think I can stand it much longer."

Nathan forced himself to be calm, though he kept imagining Serena bursting into the room with Lester and Delilah in tow and announcing to everyone in the western half of Massachusetts that he must marry her daughter because he had ruined her.

And if she and he were found in this compromising position, he would have ruined her, even if he'd never touched her. Bitch. Why couldn't she find someone else to stalk?

"Pull your robe together and stop this nonsense," he said as sternly as he could in a whisper. "I'm not marrying you or anyone else."

"Then let me sleep with you," Priscilla pleaded, reaching for him across the chair. "Mama says that works just as well."

"I can't believe your mother said any such thing," Nathan said, certain in his own mind Serena would have in order to incite Priscilla to just such an exhibition as this.

"Mama said men like to have women sleep with them. She says men are terrible that way." Priscilla giggled. "Lucy says the same thing, only she says some women like to sleep with men." She giggled again. "Do you think I would like it? With you, I mean?"

"I doubt it very much," said Nathan, feeling exceptionally hot in his sheet. "You should only marry someone you love a great deal."

"But I like you a lot."

"Like is not enough. It is very important in a marriage for two people to be in love."

"If I can like you this much already, maybe I could love you after we got married."

"I will bet if you were to go away tomorrow, you would forget me in a week."

"I can't go away. Mama has no money."

An idea popped into Nathan's head. It was a coward's way out, but he didn't feel he had many choices just then.

168

"I can give you some. Would you like to go on a visit?"

"I'll have to ask Mama. I can't go anywhere without her permission."

"You can ask her first thing tomorrow. Maybe I'll send both of you to Boston. Would you like that?"

"I don't know. I'll ask Mother."

Empty-headed bitch. Why does she have to be my cousin?

"Go back to your room. If you don't, you won't be able to go to Boston."

Priscilla seemed to be thinking it over. Nathan could only hope the offer of going to Boston was more attractive than sleeping with him so she could get rid of her urges.

"You promise I can go to Boston?"

"I promise."

"Very well," she said, but Nathan thought she still looked doubtful. He held his breath as she turned and walked toward the door.

"Are you sure I wouldn't prefer to sleep in your bed?" she asked as Nathan started to open the door for her.

"Positive." Nathan held back a sigh of relief. "You will enjoy Boston much more. You might even find someone you would rather fall in love with than me."

"I don't know." Priscilla did look doubtful. "Mama says you may be a bloody fool, but you sure can fill out a pair of breeches."

Nathan almost burst out laughing.

"Well, I don't have them on now, and if I'm caught with you in this state, there'll be hell to pay. You hurry back to your room and dream about Boston. We'll talk in the morning." He turned her around and pushed her out the door. As he turned the key in the lock, he made a silent vow never to open the door again except in full daylight.

He had already decided Priscilla lacked common sense, but he'd never thought she lacked sense altogether. If Serena thought he would marry her, she had better think again. No intelligent woman would have come to his room on such an errand. He only hoped she would forget what had occurred by tomorrow.

But if Nathan had seen Priscilla a few moments later, he would have seen the episode in a different light. She scampered to her room as quickly and quietly as she could. Once inside, she dashed to her bed, buried her face in the pillow, and laughed until her entire body shook. It was ten minutes before she grew calm enough to consider going to sleep.

"Are you sure you feel well enough to be up this morning?" Nathan asked his aunt. Serena didn't look well. Her eyelids drooped, and she looked as though she had a bad headache. "You can go back to bed if you like."

He had been making a concerted effort to engage her in conversation, but Serena made only minimal responses. Priscilla had said nothing about the past night—indeed, she seemed to have forgotten all about it—and he avoided her eyes. He didn't want to do anything to jog her memory.

"I feel it's my responsibility to be up when you are here," Serena said in response to Nathan's solicitude. "I never missed a morning for my husband or Ezra. They would have thought it very odd if I had."

"Well, I don't. You can stay in bed any morning you don't feel well."

An uncomfortable silence fell over the group. Priscilla ate her breakfast in a desultory style—actually she played with her food rather than ate it—her mind apparently far away from the table or the people seated about it.

Nathan felt his best first thing in the morning. He enjoyed breakfast, and he liked being up early. But apparently no one else did today. Except for Delilah. She had come in only moments before, looking brighter than spring sunshine. Somehow it seemed inappropriate to feel the stirrings of desire at this early hour, but one look at her and his body responded as it always did.

Nathan placed his napkin in a strategic place.

Delilah entered the dining room again. "Mrs. Stebbens wants to know if you would like any more batter cakes.

There's also more fried apples and veal croquettes."

Neither Priscilla nor Serena responded. "I'd like some apples," Nathan said. "And coffee."

Delilah disappeared through the door. She reappeared a moment later with a small bowl of apples and a blue speckled pot of steaming coffee.

"This is the last of the winter's supply," she said as she set the bowl of apples next to Nathan's plate. "There won't be any more until picking time."

Nathan handed his cup to Delilah. She poured the coffee and handed it back. He had a brief intimation of how it might be to have breakfast with her every morning, her pouring his coffee, both of them sharing plans for the day, then his looking forward to seeing her again in the evening.

Nathan shook his head to get rid of the daydream. She was not sitting at the table with him, so there was no use teasing himself.

"Did you know the Supreme Court met at Worcester two days ago?" Nathan asked.

Delilah stiffened. For the first time that morning Serena showed interest in the conversation.

"They indicted Luke Day and ten others in the group that closed the court at Northampton last month."

"It's about time they did something," Serena said, a smile of satisfaction on her thin lips.

"Was Reuben with that group?" Nathan asked Delilah.

"Of course he was," Serena stated. "He's probably hand in glove with half the rebels in this part of the state."

"Reuben wouldn't follow Luke Day anywhere," Delilah said. "Luke's got a terrible temper and uses his size to bully his men."

"Sounds a lot like your brother," Serena commented.

"They don't get along," Delilah explained, ignoring Serena. "They never have."

"Probably both wanting to be the leader." Serena apparently wasn't going to pass up any opportunity to annoy Delilah.

171

"Captain Shays doesn't trust Luke Day either," Delilah said.

"Heaven help us," Serena exclaimed. "We have a servant in the house who's intimately acquainted with half the rebels in the state. She'll tell them everything she knows."

"She could tell *us* everything she knows," Nathan pointed out.

Surprised, Delilah looked squarely at him. What she saw reassured her. "But you won't ask me."

"No, I won't."

"Why not?" demanded Serena. "You could force her to tell you."

"I know more about the insurgents than she does. You didn't know about Luke Day or the Supreme Court, did you?"

"No."

"That's fine in the ordinary way," Serena said, "but someone may let a vital piece of information slip."

"If someone did such a thing, would you tell your brother?"

Delilah had never expected Nathan to put this question to her. For one wild moment she thought he must know she was a spy and was about to expose her. Then she remembered the extent of her spying had been looking in the window. The existence of the list was the only thing she knew that he hadn't told her. And her mentioning it to Jane probably didn't matter. Shays had to assume they had such a list.

But that wasn't what Nathan asked her. He wanted to know if she would give Reuben any information she uncovered. I ought to lie, she told herself. She knew she was more likely to learn something if he didn't suspect her. But she couldn't lie to him, even though that didn't make sense when he was opposed to what Shays and Reuben were trying to do.

"Yes, if I thought it would keep him out of danger."

"I told you," Serena said. "Get rid of her."

"Would you tell the rest of your friends?" Nathan asked.

Delilah's hand fiddled with the hem of her apron. She didn't want to answer this question because she wasn't sure of the answer. She would do almost anything for Reuben, but for the others?

"I don't know," she finally answered. "I don't want anybody to get hurt. I guess I would do just about anything if I thought it would prevent a battle."

"Pack your things and be out of this house within the hour," Serena ordered. "I won't have a traitor staying under my roof."

"I don't know why I must continually remind you that it is *my* roof." Nathan's voice was quiet, the deadly quiet Delilah had learned to distrust.

"But she admitted she would spy on us."

"No, just pass on information. It's only reasonable to expect her to protect her brother. If I were part of her family, I hope she would feel the same way about me."

Delilah didn't dare look at Nathan, not under Serena's eagle-eyed glare. She didn't know what he meant by those words. Maybe she placed too much hope in things spoken as an ordinary part of conversation. But something in Nathan's voice had sounded new, unfamiliar. She couldn't identify it just yet.

"You'll never learn anything about taking care of your own, will you?" Serena asked, spots of rage on her sallow cheeks. "Let a female smile at you, and you invite her to sit down with us for dinner. Let her tell you she plans to carry information to the enemy, and you say it's only natural she should want to protect her family. What are you going to say when they come in here demanding we empty our storehouses for them?"

"No one is going to threaten Maple Hill. If you feel unsafe here, maybe you and Priscilla would like to go to Boston for a visit."

"And leave you here to be preyed upon by this brazen hussy?"

"If you refer to Miss Stowbridge as a hussy again, you will leave this house whether you have anywhere to go or

173

not. As for Boston, Priscilla and I talked about it last night. She would like a chance to visit her friends. She feels confined here."

"Priscilla will feel as I tell her to feel," Serena declared. "We're not moving a foot from Maple Hill. Any friends she wants to see will have to come here."

"Why don't you make up a list of those you wish to invite?" Nathan said. "I'll be in the library if you wish to discuss it. Delilah, don't forget our appointment at ten."

"Appointment?" Serena demanded, apparently having forgotten about the past night's occurrences. "If it's about the household, she should go to Lester and he will come to me."

"It has nothing to do with the house," Nathan told his aunt, "so you need not put yourself about."

Serena continued to protest, but as Nathan left the room without answering her and Delilah made her escape while she could, she was left with no one to listen to her except Priscilla.

"What do you mean by telling Nathan you'd like to go to Boston?" her mother demanded. "If I were to leave now, there's no telling what that girl would get up to. Your cousin is no more able to take care of himself than a young colt."

Priscilla came out of her abstraction with a snap. "The sooner you get over the idea Nathan is impressionable, or that you have any influence over what he does, the quicker you'll see what's really going on around here." Her voice was still wispy, but the hard glint in her eyes gave the lie to the fiction that she was a silly, half-witted female.

Serena looked startled. "If you would only marry him, everything would be all right."

"Nathan doesn't want to marry me."

"But he's not clever. Surely you could entice him into—"

"When will you realize Nathan is as strong minded and astute as Uncle Ezra was. Maybe more so. No one is going to *entice* him into anything, except maybe Delilah."

"That female! If I had my way—"

"You'd do something stupid and Nathan would throw us out. No matter what happens, leave her alone. I'm working on getting what I can for both of us. Don't get in my way." Priscilla threw down her napkin and stood up.

"But I don't understand . . ." Serena no longer looked like a virago. She seemed confused and frightened.

Priscilla's eyes softened. "You never did, Mother. Not your husband or your brother. You never understood men at all."

Nathan stopped to consider whether he should light a fire, but the autumn days had remained much warmer than in England. Too, he had discovered that a wood house wasn't so cold as one made of stone. He resisted the temptation to open the windows and allow the crisp, refreshing breeze to blow through the library, but he positioned his chair so he could see the changing fall panorama as he sat at his desk. After spending nearly every day of his life in London, he found himself fascinated by the limitless space, the pervasive quiet, and the unequaled beauty of the changing hillsides. It might not be such a terrible thing if he couldn't return to London. He might be able to get used to living in Massachusetts.

As long as Delilah is with me.

The thought had not been in his head before, but here it was, just like that. What more proof could he want that her hold over him had become more than a painful longing to claim her body. He had developed a strong interest in her, and that meant he wouldn't be satisfied with a few tumbles in the hay.

But then he had always known Delilah wouldn't accept that kind of relationship. It might be common practice in England, especially when the man was a wealthy aristocrat and the woman a servant, but both his aunt and uncle had been at pains to inform his parents, frequently and at great length, of the differences between the colonists' morals and those of decadent, sinful, merry old England. In

175

Massachusetts, a servant girl could be ruined just as surely as a lord's daughter.

A healthy young man naturally desired a beautiful young woman. It was natural he should think of her often when she worked in his household. But it was also natural for him to realize that if he had any real feelings for the girl, he couldn't use her and discard her afterward. Nathan had begun to think about a different kind of relationship. He found himself looking for a way to keep Delilah with him.

He was standing at the window overlooking the garden when Delilah entered the library. The light blinded her to his features, but the perfection of his silhouette hit her like a broadside. *If I start thinking about his body, I'll never make any sense,* Delilah told herself. *He's asked me to offer advice. If I can't come up with anything that makes sense, everything I've said loses its value.*

"I'm glad to see you remembered," Nathan said as he turned toward her.

"I almost didn't come," Delilah replied, a tiny smile on her lips. "Your aunt is on the stairs, looking so fierce I nearly backed out."

"Really?" Nathan said, pulling one of the Windsor chairs near his desk.

"I was tempted. It's never pleasant to have your employer angry at you."

"I'm your employer, and I'm not angry."

Delilah swallowed. "You know what I mean."

"I do, but I think it is time I rectified a mistake I made at the very beginning."

"That's for you to settle with your aunt," Delilah said, dropping her gaze to the papers Nathan handed her. "You asked me here to discuss a different matter."

"Quite so," Nathan said, smiling at her determination to stick to business. It was good that one of them could. His thoughts kept getting sidetracked by her lips. He didn't know why he hadn't noticed them before. He should have. They were the most inviting, kissable lips he had ever

176

seen. They could almost make him forget the inviting mound of her bosom. Almost, but not quite. Nothing could do that when he was standing above her and his line of vision included more of her tempting flesh than he'd ever seen before.

"This is a list of the farmers, merchants, and townspeople who owe me the most money. I want your advice, most particularly about the farmers. I included the others in case you had any thoughts that might be of help."

"What's Hector Clayhart's name doing on this list?" Delilah asked, surprised. "His inheritance ought to make him one of the biggest of the River Gods."

Nathan didn't blink at her unconscious use of the derogatory phrase. "His father let everything go during the war. Then he had to borrow money from my uncle to keep up his style of living. His debts will keep Hector poor for years."

Delilah shrugged fatalistically. "He'll hate that. I'm surprised he hasn't abandoned the whole thing." She turned back to the list. "I see George Morton's on here, too," she said with a slight sniff. When Nathan raised his eyebrows in a questioning look, she added, "If he could keep his wife from spending twice her allowance every month and his son from gambling away a fortune while he's at Cambridge, he could pay you back within two or three years. He's the most sought-after lawyer in Springfield."

"I thought you wanted to help the farmers."

"I do," Delilah said with a quick, guilty smile. "I guess I was just being nosy. Anyway, it's not going to be as easy for them. They don't have much they can do without. And don't say I already told you so."

"Take your time. I've got plenty of work to do."

Nathan seated himself at his desk, his profile easily in the range of Delilah's peripheral vision. This would never work. As long as she could see him, she couldn't keep her mind on the list. She fidgeted in her chair.

"Is anything wrong?" he asked.

"I need more light." She got up and went over to the

177

window. "This is better." She had her back to him. It was much better.

But that didn't help as much as she had hoped. Nathan's presence was so pervasive she could only see things as they related to him. The view to the river was gorgeous because it was one she shared with him each day. The library on the first floor, his bedroom on the second, and her room on the third, all looked out over the same piece of lawn, the same stretch of river, the same distant hillside resplendent with fall colors.

She forced her mind back to the list. Henry Wheaton's name came first. His debt must be the equivalent of the whole farm. Poor Henry. He seemed to be perpetually dogged by bad luck. His only good luck had come when he'd married Emma.

Ebenezer Gardner was just plain lazy. Delilah doubted she could suggest anything to help him.

Isaac Yates, Andrew Russell, Gilbert Eells, all good men who'd fought in the War of Independence, all with so little to show for years of hard work. Where was the inheritance they had fought to hand down to their sons and daughters? They faced perpetual debt, the disgrace of prison, the hardship of selling up and going to the western lands to start all over again. It wasn't right, not after they'd given years of their lives to win the war. Delilah had finally admitted Nathan couldn't be held responsible for their plight; still, somebody ought to be.

But what could she do? What could Nathan do? They were only two people. And she couldn't help wondering about him.

He intended to keep what was his, but he resisted the tyrannical suggestions of those who had much less at stake. He had gathered the reins of his household and properties into his own hands, but he hadn't let this power blind him to the rights of those with less of the world's goods.

He wasn't like anybody she had ever known.

Chapter Thirteen

"Are you ready?" Nathan's question brought Delilah out of her abstraction.

"I don't know," she said, turning away from the window. "I don't have any suggestions for half of these people."

"Then we can begin with the other half."

If he was going to smile at her like that, she would forget the few ideas she did have. She seated herself on the chair and concentrated on her list.

"You'll never get any money out of Henry Wheaton, but you might get some from his wife."

"How?"

"You buy a lot of flax, and Emma Wheaton is the best spinner in Springfield. She might spin for you if you ask. And she has three daughters at home who can help."

"It'll take quite a while. The debt is rather large."

"Emma will do steady work. It's Henry you can't count on. When you talk to them, you'll have to talk to Henry. Emma won't disgrace her husband by assuming his place, but make sure she's there when you make the arrangements. Henry won't know if she can do one spindle a week or a dozen."

Nathan made some notes in one of his ledgers. "Who's next?"

"Ebenezer Gardner's so lazy he probably wouldn't lift a finger to feed himself."

"Then how can I get anything from him?"

"Through his wife, Anna. If she can talk Ebenezer into letting their son Jonas take over the farm, you'll get your money."

"And if he won't agree?"

"Foreclose and hire Jonas to work the farm with the understanding it reverts to him as soon as the debt's paid off."

"Isn't that a little hard on Ebenezer?"

"Jonas would take care of his parents. Besides, I don't have patience with people who are too lazy to try. Anyway, Jonas has been wanting to marry Dorothy Price for more than a year now. He could do it if he had a farm."

"What about Andrew Russell?"

"I don't know. Did Gilbert Eells have any surplus crops this year?"

"Yes."

"He always grows more than he needs and then runs up a credit with Noah Hubbard. You could take some of his credit and force Noah to give you hard money for it."

"I already thought of that," Nathan said with a grin which almost made Delilah lose her train of thought.

"It might help if people see that you're not totally against the farmers."

"I'm not against anybody," Nathan said. "I just want what's mine."

"That may be, but as long as you're collecting debts, you'll be lumped with all the other debt collectors."

"I'm depending on you to see that doesn't happen."

"How?"

"By helping me find alternatives. If they see I'll only confiscate their property as a last resort, that I'll even help them get ahead if it will help me at the same time, maybe it'll stop some of this trouble."

"Why should you care what happens here? I thought you were going back to London."

"I may not. Several of my family found they preferred

180

Massachusetts to London. Maybe I'm finding the same thing."

His gaze was so penetrating, so unwavering, it made Delilah feel warm.

"But it's decidedly unpleasant to have your neighbors gaping at you as if you're some sort of executioner. Even less pleasant when you're trying to be just the opposite."

His words went straight to her heart. His intentions were exactly the same as they had been the day she'd come to Maple Hill, only he seemed to be looking for more sensible, useful, humane ways to handle his affairs. That didn't mean he was no longer a danger to her friends, but it certainly took the sharp edge off the sword.

"Things might change if you give them time," she said.

"How?"

"Lots of people have relatives in England," she replied, thinking rapidly. "They don't hold them responsible for the war."

"Just me."

"There're still plenty of tories in Massachusetts. If they can be forgiven, you can eventually be accepted."

"It's been my experience that people forgive their friends and relatives virtually anything. They never forgive strangers."

"If you married someone from around here, you'd have lots of friends and relatives."

The shock of hearing the words that escaped her lips turned Delilah crimson.

"Who are you offering as the sacrificial lamb?"

"It's not a sacrifice. I m-mean it w-wouldn't be a sacrifice," Delilah stammered, mortified, "if I were to marry you. I-I m-mean it wouldn't be for the woman you asked to m-marry you."

"But it might be very difficult for you, or any other young woman from Springfield, who married me."

"People wouldn't understand at first," Delilah said,

181

making sure to keep her gaze on the floor, "but they'd get used to it." She looked up. "It'd probably be a lot harder on you."

"Why?"

"This can't be the kind of life you're used to. Coming from London you're bound to want grand parties and clever people. Just the way you dress shouts that you don't belong here."

"Don't you like the way I dress?"

"It doesn't matter whether I like it or not. It's just different. Like the kind of dinners you eat at night."

"Are these all my reprehensible habits, or am I totally irreclaimable?"

"They're not reprehensible. . . . You've got me all confused," Delilah said. She paused and took a deep breath. "And you're not irreclaimable. I imagine there'd be dozens of girls in Boston and Providence, even Newport, who'd be glad to have you."

"None in Springfield?"

"You wouldn't marry anyone from Springfield."

"Why not?"

"Except for Priscilla, we're nothing but farmers around here. Even Lucy Porter."

"I've never known any farmers before, but I might find I prefer them to London aristocrats."

"What would you do with Lucy or Hope in London? They'd be blushing one minute and giggling the next. And no telling what they'd say."

"I didn't mean I would like all farm girls. One would be enough. Besides, farm girls can be quite enchanting," Nathan continued.

"With brown skin and strong shoulders? They look down on us in Boston. I don't imagine your precious lords would even speak to us in London."

"Apparently my aunt has been using my *exalted relatives* to impress her friends," Nathan said. "She's notorious for stretching the truth."

182

"You don't have to explain anything to me."

"I want to. I don't want you believing I think I'm better than you. My mother was Uncle Ezra's sister. On her side of the family my relatives are London merchants. My father's family were also merchants, but his oldest sister married the fourth son of a poor earl. It meant I would sometimes be invited into the homes of the aristocrats, but I never belonged there."

Delilah saw a spasm of anger distort his features, but he controlled it quickly. She could see hurt as well. She wondered if this had anything to do with his leaving England.

"I never considered not going back until I met you."

"Me! Why?"

"I'd like to say it was your spirit, it sounds more admirable, but knowing me, it was probably the fact that you're the loveliest woman I've seen in America."

Delilah had always known she was pretty. Massachusetts farmers had an outspoken appreciation for an attractive woman—but the loveliest woman he'd seen in America! Either the man hadn't put his nose outside the door while he was in Boston, or he was besotted with her.

"You look surprised."

"Of course I am. Next you'll be telling me I'm prettier than all the women you knew in London."

"No, there's one who's absolutely without parallel. Everything about her is perfection, but you're much nicer."

Again the fleeting impression of remembered pain, but Delilah was too shocked and surprised by the enormity of his compliment to do more than notice it in passing.

Nathan laughed softly. "Hasn't anyone ever told you you're absolutely beautiful?"

Delilah shook her head. "Pretty, but not absolutely beautiful."

"That he lies awake at night thinking about you?"

She shook her head again.

"Then I'm certain no one ever told you what wonderfully expressive eyes you have."

"No."

Nathan moved closer. "Or that to have you within reach and not be able to caress your skin is a temptation almost greater than a mortal man can endure."

"No."

He moved closer still. "That your lips are an irresistible invitation to kiss you?"

"No." Her response was a little breathless.

"That I've spent days thinking of ways to get you out of the kitchen so I can see you as much as possible. Every beautiful woman should know she's appreciated." He reached out and touched her cheek.

"How would you do that?"

"It's very simple." He drew so close she could almost feel the heat of his body. "You let her know what you like about her."

Delilah felt paralyzed. She had never had a man court her this way.

"I particularly like your lips," Nathan murmured. Their lips were now so close they almost touched. "They are so full and red and wanting to be kissed." His fingertip traced the outline of her mouth.

"I don't think they are."

"You just don't realize it," Nathan said.

Then, leaning even closer, he let his lips brush Delilah's. She felt as if she'd been struck a blow. Before she could decide what to do, he kissed her, this time pressing his mouth fully against hers.

"Can you tell now?"

Delilah's breath caught in her lungs. Her whole being felt suspended, disembodied. How could a simple kiss affect her so profoundly?

"Tell what?" she murmured.

"That your lips are longing to be kissed."

How could he ask her to think? She felt as though she would jump out of her skin. Her whole body cried out to be kissed, touched, caressed, held close. Some primitive instinct told her that the only remedy was prolonged contact with the cause of this delicious ache.

"Yes."

He took her face in his hands, drew her closer, and kissed her again.

Delilah felt claimed.

Nobody had ever kissed her like this. She wouldn't have let them, yet she didn't want Nathan to stop. The gentle movement of his lips against hers caused her whole body to lean in his direction, drawn by the nectar of this sweet honeycomb from which she longed to drink deeply.

"Can you feel it now?" Nathan's lips never left hers.

"All over," she murmured. "Everywhere."

Nathan drew her closer until her body pressed against his. He kissed the corner of her mouth, then used the tip of his tongue to delicately trace the outline of her lips.

Delilah shivered in ecstasy. Never had the touch of a man so nearly destroyed her ability to function, reduced her to such a spineless puddle of desire.

Nathan kissed the top of her nose and planted a pair of kisses on her chin before turning his attention to her parted, expectant lips. Delilah's lips moved with his, touching briefly, enjoying the delicate softness, moving, seeking before Nathan claimed her in a deep, strength-sapping embrace.

"Can you feel my desire now?"

"Mmmmmm." Her need to be close to him, the wish to concentrate her whole attention on the pleasure of his kisses overwhelmed her.

Footsteps on the stairs intruded. Before she could shut them out of her mind, the angry *rat-a-tat* of heels sounded on the wide heart-of-pine floor in the hall. Delilah barely had time to step back from Nathan before the

185

library door burst open and Serena Noyes entered, two leather-bound volumes in her hand, the light of battle in her eyes.

"Thief!" she exclaimed, pointing an accusing finger at Delilah. "I found these in your room." She waved the offending volumes under Delilah's nose.

"What were you doing in my room?" Delilah demanded, a flood of anger instantly transforming her rapture to outrage.

Serena turned to Nathan. "Maybe this will open your eyes to the kind of person you've nurtured in our bosom."

"Answer Delilah's question," Nathan ordered.

His angry scowl stopped Serena so abruptly, it took her a few seconds to adjust. "What question?" she asked.

"What were you doing in her room?"

"I was looking for these," she said, showing him the books.

"Am I to assume you wanted to read those particular volumes and being unable to find them on the shelves, decided Delilah must have them?"

"I'd never read this stuff," Serena said, scornful of the two rather thick histories of the ancient world. "I can't think what she wanted them for—"

"Why don't you ask her?"

"—except to sell them."

"That's insulting," Delilah cried. "I know I shouldn't have taken them without asking, but they looked interesting."

"What were you doing in here?" demanded Serena.

"My job," Delilah snapped. "Cleaning out the grate."

"Cleaning the grate doesn't include looking through Nathan's books."

"I've already said I shouldn't have borrowed them, but I won't have you saying I stole them to sell. Who could buy them?"

"Do you really want to read these books?" Nathan asked.

Delilah felt poor and insignificant, and that made her angry.

"Yes," she responded, trying hard to keep her wounded pride from making her say something she'd regret later, "but not if it means she has the right to search my room. I promise never to touch a single thing in this house again, but I won't have anybody going in my room whenever they like."

"I'll search any room in this house as often as I wish," stated Serena.

"Does that include mine?" Nathan asked. He was speaking softly again, with the look Serena hated so much in his eyes.

"N-naturally I didn't mean yours."

"Do you intend to search Priscilla's room?"

"There's no need to—"

"Or Lester's?"

"I wouldn't think of it!" Serena said, outraged.

"Or Mrs. Stebbens?"

"I . . ."

"Nor will you search Delilah's room again."

Serena opened her mouth to speak, but Nathan cut her off.

"Not you. Not me. Not anyone. Furthermore, she can use the library as much as she likes."

Serena closed her mouth, slowly, stunned surprise fighting bottled-up anger for control of her features.

"Unless you have something else you need to say to me, Delilah and I still have work to do."

"You're a fool, Nathan Trent," Serena burst out, her fear of what Nathan might do to her insufficient to hold back her anger. "There's nothing to stop her from lying to you and going behind your back to those rebels."

"Nothing but her own integrity."

"You're even more foolish than I thought." Serena's face turned ugly with fury. "Her brother's out there right now closing the courts. They meet at her uncle's tavern to

187

make their plans. Do you think she's going to put you before her own kin?"

"No. I wouldn't do that myself." Nathan's calm acceptance increased his aunt's fury.

"But you give her free rein to search the house, even your library. That list of traitors is in here. Are you going to let her find that?"

Nathan opened one of the small drawers and took out a piece of folded paper. "Tell me if there's anybody on this list the whole county doesn't know about."

Serena almost snatched the paper from Nathan's hand. This was the first time she'd been allowed to see the conspirators' names, and she almost trembled with excitement.

"I don't see Reuben Stowbridge's name here." She looked vengefully at Delilah. "That's one we can add to the list."

"The governor asked for leaders, Serena, not followers. If he isn't one of Luke Day's cohorts, he had nothing to do with any of the court closings."

"We don't know that," Serena said.

"I do," Delilah said. "If Captain Shays hasn't closed any courts, Reuben hasn't either."

Serena looked from one to the other, her fury mounting. "You'll rue the day you listened to that hus—to her," she said between clenched teeth. "You'll leave here just as poor as you came," she snapped at Delilah.

Turning and stalking out of the room, Serena slammed the door so hard Delilah thought it would break loose from the wall.

"My aunt is certain I'll lose my inheritance and she'll be turned out without a penny," Nathan explained. "It causes her to become hysterical sometimes."

"I can understand that," Delilah said, feeling a surprising surge of sympathy for Serena.

"I have another list you might like to see." Nathan looked at Delilah with what seemed a calculating glance before handing her a second list taken from the same drawer. "These are people who are suspected of being potential leaders. Do you know anything about them?"

Reuben's name was at the head of the list.

"I doubt John Skelly and Abel Judkins are leaders," she said. "They didn't fight in the War of Independence, so they've never been particularly looked up to. I don't know the rest."

"And Reuben?"

"I told you, Reuben only follows Shays. If you don't see Shays, you won't see Reuben."

"And if we do see Shays?"

"I don't live at home anymore," she said after a pause. "I don't know what my brother plans to do."

Delilah felt uncomfortable under Nathan's scrutiny, but she resolutely faced his challenging gaze. Whatever her suspicions, regardless of how certain she might be Reuben was involved, she didn't *know* what he was doing.

Nathan reached out for the list. She gave it back to him.

"I won't hold you responsible for it, whatever it might be. Now, do you have any more suggestions?"

Delilah gave Nathan a blank stare, not realizing at first that he was referring to the debts. It took her a moment to reorganize her thoughts.

"I have no idea what to do about Hector or Andrew Russell, but Isaac Yates and his son spend more time on their boat than they ever do on land. I'd hire him to take everything you can sell down the river to Windsor and Hartford. Yates can handle the boat, and young Samuel is a natural salesman."

"Why hasn't he started a business of his own?"

"Noah Hubbard controls everything around here. A body can't do anything if Noah doesn't like him."

"I should have talked to you earlier. It would have saved me weeks of riding over the countryside and seeing

189

people who didn't want to talk to me. How do you know so much about everybody?"

"I've lived in Springfield my whole life. My father sold housewares. The wives used to gather in the shop when they came into town. After being alone on a farm all week, they loved to talk. I heard a lot. What I didn't hear there, I learned playing with their children."

"I appreciate your advice. If it works out, I'll take something off Reuben's debt."

Delilah's expression lost its warmth. She didn't know why Nathan's offer should offend her so much, but it took the pleasure out of the morning and reduced their time together to a business arrangement.

"I did this because you asked—and for them." She pointed to the list of names. "If you want to give a consideration, take it off what they owe."

She stood up just as the door opened without a warning knock.

"Her sister-in-law is out in the kitchen," Serena said. "Probably come to collect as much information as she can."

Nathan was conscious of a strong desire to strangle his aunt and leave her body under a bush.

"I'll come right away," Delilah said. She left without looking at Nathan.

Serena remained standing in the doorway.

"Well?" Nathan asked.

"That girl's trying to trap you."

"What?" Couldn't Serena tell Delilah was angry at him.

"She wants to get you into her bed, so she can force you to marry her."

"You're crazy."

"You don't understand how it is here in America. Men aren't allowed to take a mistress. When you get a girl in trouble, you have to marry her. If she is gotten with child and turned off, her brother will kill you. And the

190

county will be behind him, even Lucius Clarke and Noah Hubbard."

"I'm not trying to bed her, and I won't let myself be seduced."

"I've been married. I know men have different needs than women, needs they sometimes can't control." An odd expression came into Serena's eyes, an expression of anguish Nathan had not seen in them before. "You ought to marry Priscilla. She's a pretty girl. Obedient, too. Then you wouldn't need to go sneaking about with the servants."

"I'm not sneaking around with Delilah, and I'm not interested in getting married," Nathan said. "Besides, I don't think Priscilla wants to marry me any more than I want to marry her."

"She likes you. She'd do everything you'd want her to do."

"I'm not going to marry Priscilla," Nathan repeated.

Serena's face turned hard. "That girl's going to catch you. People will laugh. They'll say you were trapped neat as a beaver."

"I have no plans to marry anyone at the moment, but I will not allow you or anybody else to choose my wife."

"They'll blame me," Serena almost screamed. "They'll say I ought to have warned you, that I ought to have turned the girl off."

"Console yourself with the fact that you have warned me on an almost hourly basis."

He turned back to his desk. Serena fled the room, uttering a muffled cry of frustration.

"Tell me about Reuben," Delilah said as soon as she got Jane settled in a sunny corner of the garden. A brisk wind blew across the river from the northwest, but a thick arborvitae hedge shielded the bench where they sat.

"He's still getting more work than he can accept. He's turned the keeping of the money over to me."

That relieved part of Delilah's worry. It also told her how seriously Reuben was taking her working off his debt. Before this his pride would never have allowed him to hand his money over to any female.

"I mean what's he doing with Captain Shays?" Delilah asked. "Nathan says the Supreme Court indicted all the leaders at Northampton. They're supposed to meet in Springfield next, and he says they'll indict everybody who was at Worcester."

"Reuben wasn't at those places," Jane assured her. "He and Shays are still hoping the governor will act on our petition."

"If he doesn't?"

"I don't know. I don't listen to their plans. It's best for a woman not to know."

"Why?"

"Politics and fighting are a man's business."

"But it's a woman's home that's burned over her head, her kinfolks who are killed."

"Men don't like for a woman to ask too many questions or to tell them what to do."

Delilah thought of Nathan. He was more than willing to listen to her and act on her advice. True, she knew more about the residents of Springfield than he did, but so did Serena and Priscilla and he hadn't asked them.

Delilah thought of the many times her mother had tried to make suggestions to her father. He'd always pretended he didn't hear them. Delilah had never understood why her mother accepted such a situation. She had always thought Jane, who was so strong and so full of common sense, could control Reuben. Now she realized Jane had no more influence over her brother than her mother had had over her father.

That wasn't going to happen to her. She couldn't imagine letting someone like Noah Hubbard or Lucius Clarke make all her decisions. Nathan treated her better than that, and she worked for him as a household servant.

"You tell Reuben to stay away from Day, Wheeler, Gates, and all the rest," Delilah warned Jane. "Governor Bowdoin has declared that closing the courts is treason. They can be hanged."

"For a little thing like keeping a judge from behind his bench?"

"He's also ordered the militia to shoot anybody who refuses to disperse."

"Captain Shays says the militia won't fire on them. Reuben told me so himself."

"Are they planning something?"

"I don't know, but they've been meeting every night for the last week."

"You tell Reuben not to be a fool. Tell him I said to stay home. He won't help you or his babies with a minnie ball in him or dangling from the end of a rope."

"How did you learn all this?" Jane asked.

"Nathan. He gets regular information from Lucius Clarke and Noah Hubbard."

"I don't think you can trust him."

"Why should he lie to me? I can't do anything to hurt him."

"People don't trust him. Not even the men on his side."

"Why not?"

"I don't know, but I heard it from Agnes Porter herself."

"You can't believe a word Lucy's mama says," Delilah said, disgusted that Jane should be so gullible. "She's just put out because Nathan didn't show any partiality for Lucy."

"How do you know that?"

"She got real uppity when she saw me serving. Even Serena got angry at her. Makes Serena look bad to have friends like that, and Serena doesn't want to look bad in Nathan's eyes, for all she would cut his heart out if it would get her Maple Hill."

193

"Who does it go to if something happens to Mr. Trent?"

"I don't know. I never thought about it. Nathan's father is dead, and he has no brothers and sisters."

Jane seemed to be struck by a very unwelcome thought, and she subjected her sister-in-law to a very hard look.

"How do you know so much about him?"

Delilah laughed. "What do you think servants talk about all day? Nathan—what we know about him or what we suppose."

"You shouldn't be listening to gossip."

"Captain Shays told me to."

Jane looked unconvinced. "I don't like it."

"I didn't like it from the beginning, but nobody listened to me. Not even you."

"That was before you got to know him. Now it doesn't seem right."

"It never seemed right," Delilah said, "but I doubt it matters anymore. He knows I would tell Reuben anything I could."

"How?"

"I told him."

"What!"

"He asked me. Do you think he'd have believed me if I'd said I wouldn't breathe a word?"

"I guess not."

"I like it better now. At least I don't feel like I'm doing anything underhanded. If I learn something, he already knows what to expect."

Chapter Fourteen

"They closed the Supreme Court," Lucius Clarke shouted the minute he burst into Nathan's library. "That fool Shepard let them march up and down the street until the judges were scared silly."

"You'd better tell me from the beginning," Nathan said, sprinkling sand over his letter. "I've been too busy to go into Springfield."

"What can you have to do here that's more important than keeping the courts open?" demanded Clarke. "We can't do a damned thing until those judges give us the go-ahead."

"Let's just say I'm trying to manage my holdings."

"If you don't get up from that desk and find out what's going on, you won't have any holdings to manage."

Nathan realized Lucius was too upset to listen to any viewpoint but his own. "What happened?" he asked.

"Shepard was so busy keeping his eye on the arsenal, Shays had a free hand with the court."

"You're sure it was Shays?"

"No doubt. He spoke directly with Shepard and Chief Justice Sewall several times. And that girl you have working here, what's-her-name . . ."

"Delilah?"

"Yeah, her brother was right behind Shays. You can add his name to the list."

"It's already there," Nathan said reluctantly.

"Not one man in the militia would fire on the regula-

195

tors. I don't think Shepard ordered it even though he got permission from the secretary of war to take a small cannon and four hundred muskets from the arsenal. He had over two hundred armed men."

"How many did Shays have?"

"Reports say he had seven hundred when he reached Springfield. Hundreds more joined him today, but only one out of four had muskets. The rest had clubs or ax handles."

"And you expected General Shepard to order his militia to fire on virtually unarmed men?"

"It was the best time to get them. Next time they may all have muskets."

Before Nathan was able to give expression to his building rage, Lester ushered Tom Oliver and Eli Warner into the room. Minutes later Asa Warner and Noah Hubbard entered, leading an angry gaggle of merchants and landowners.

"Something has to be done soon," said Silas Bennett, "or I'm going to have to slaughter my livestock. I can't afford to feed them any longer."

"Turn them out in your fields," Nathan suggested.

"That's fine for you, surrounded by thousands of acres. I have less than ten."

"You'd have been better off letting the farmers feed the stock and taking it when you could sell it."

"I thought I could," Silas replied, anger making his face turn dark red. "Then they started closing the courts."

"Can't we stop them?" someone asked.

"Not when they have over a thousand men and the government has only two hundred."

"They should have used that cannon," Lucius said.

"They damned well can't," someone in the back spoke up. "My brother is with Shays. And misguided though he may be, I'll not have him shot." There was a murmur of approval.

"Then you'd better tell him to keep his head down," Silas Bennett shouted. "I intend to demand that Governor Bowdoin force the militia to fire. And I've got two cousins with Shays."

"They're committing treason," Lucius said. "They should be hanged."

While all the men wanted something done, Nathan could see they weren't likely to agree on what to do. Much more and they'd be ready to shoot each other. He hurried to the butler's pantry.

"Get several tankards of ale from the cellar as quick as you can," he told Lester. "And tell Delilah I want to see her immediately."

Delilah came running, her face a study in surprise, worry, and curiosity.

"I need your help," Nathan said, "but I won't ask it if you don't want to cooperate."

"How?" asked Delilah. It never occurred to her to refuse Nathan.

"Shays closed the Supreme Court in Springfield today, and I've got an angry mob in my library—about to tear each other apart. I want you to bring in the ale."

"What good will that do?"

"None of them are so drunk or so angry a beautiful woman won't distract them a little, at least enough to calm them down a bit. But I can't promise they'll be polite. Your brother was with Shays."

Delilah didn't have to think about it. She would help Nathan. Even now she could hear angry voices coming through the two closed doors.

"I'll serve it in the hall," she said beginning to take pewter mugs off the shelf and put them on a large wooden tray. "Spreading them out ought to help."

Nathan started filling a second tray.

"You don't have to do this. I have no right to ask you to let yourself be ogled by a lot of angry men."

"It won't be any different from serving the same men

197

at my uncle's tavern. Besides, they won't say anything with you here."

"You have a lot of faith in my ability to control these people."

"They look to you for leadership whether they admit it or not. It's just natural, I guess."

"Because I'm richer than they are?"

"No, because you know what you want to do and won't let anyone talk you out of it. People respect that even if they don't agree with you."

Lester returned with four large pitchers brimming with cool ale.

"As soon as you bring in the second tray, open the doors to the parlor and the drawing room," Nathan said to Lester as he held the door for Lester and Delilah to pass through before him. "I want to give them as much space as possible."

The argument had become so strident by the time Nathan opened the library door, he thought he wouldn't be heard over the hubbub. But after a long dusty ride from town and a hot dispute, the call for refreshments penetrated even the most heated brain. Within a matter of minutes everyone had left the library to seek out the ale being served in the hall.

And a chance to feast their eyes on Delilah.

She wore a hunter green gown trimmed with cream lace. The cap on her head didn't cover the abundant hair cascading unhindered around her shoulders, a view of which was enhanced by the very low neckline of the gown.

Nothing hindered the men from looking their fill. Not even the arrival of Serena Noyes.

By the time Lucius and Noah had filled Serena's head with the threat posed by the regulators and their inability to understand why Nathan didn't seem to be concerned about the safety of his property, she had worked herself into a rage. Feeling like a woman wronged, she rounded on Nathan.

"You're not going to do anything, are you?" She didn't even wait for Nathan to answer. "I told you from the beginning what would happen, and you didn't listen to a word I said."

"I've heard everything you said. Many times over," Nathan said wearily, but Serena swept on.

"And you brought that woman into the house, knowing she would tell her brother every blessed thing she knew."

"What does she know, Serena?" Nathan demanded. "What can she tell anyone that everyone doesn't already know?"

"She could go through your papers, listen at keyholes, look in your room. Anything. You've given her the run of the house."

"My desk is always locked, there's nothing of importance to overhear at keyholes or elsewhere, and she couldn't very well clean out the grates if she couldn't go into my room, could she?"

One of the men snickered. Serena, rightly deciding he was laughing at her, lost all ability to reason. She saw Nathan as the man who had taken the wealth which should have been hers and was about to lose it, thereby casting her into eternal poverty.

"He's not one of us," she said, addressing the men in the room. "I've tried to tell him what to do, but he won't listen. I think he's in league with the regulators."

"Don't be daft, Serena," Lucius Clarke said. "He has more to lose than any of us."

"He doesn't care," she said. "He plans to go back to England. He thinks you're all fools, imbeciles. I'll prove it to you," she shouted when she saw none of them believed her. "I'll show you what he really thinks of you."

She rushed up the stairs.

"You sure she's not suffering from brain fever?" Asa Warner asked Nathan in a half-whisper.

"She's never gotten over my uncle leaving his money to

me. And she can't understand why I don't do everything the same way my uncle did."

"Why don't you?" Asa asked.

"I'm looking for a better way."

"Have you found it?"

"In some cases."

Serena came running down the steps, her skirt billowing behind her.

"Look at these," she said, flinging a handful of caricatures into the air to flutter to the floor at the feet of the nearly twenty men gathered there. "Now tell me I'm a silly old woman who doesn't know what she's talking about."

"Where did you get those?" Nathan demanded.

His voice was quieter and more deadly than Serena had ever heard it. It terrified her. She desperately wanted to run away, but she had gone too far. Besides, these men would be on her side when they saw what he thought of them. They wouldn't let him hurt her.

"I found them in your room," Serena flung at him, but she literally shrank before the fury that blazed from his eyes. A fury so hot she felt scorched.

There were seven drawings, each of one of the men present, and each fiendishly clever. They were so telling, no one had to ask for names.

"By God, I'll kill you for this," Noah Hubbard shouted when he saw how Nathan had drawn him.

Lucius Clarke made a sound which could only be described as a cry of extreme anguish.

"I think this one of me is rather funny," Asa Warner said.

"You wouldn't say that if you'd been made to look like some kind of strange goat," Tom Oliver cried.

"That's a satyr," Delilah said.

In their anger at Nathan, they had forgotten her.

"What is that?"

"A Greek woodland deity known for its riotous and lascivious behavior," she explained.

"You drew this of me?" Tom snarled, turning to Nathan.

"I drew it," Delilah announced. "I think you know why."

Tom blushed. It would be impossible for him to explain to anyone what had happened in the library a few days earlier.

"You're a liar!" Serena screamed. "Nathan drew those. I found them in his room in one of his drawers."

"I don't know where you found them," Delilah said coolly, "but Nathan came upon me when I was drawing them. He took them away and made me promise not to do any more."

"I don't believe you," Serena said.

"Why should you draw pictures like this?" Lucius asked.

"Because I despise you for what you're doing," Delilah burst out. "Every one of you has more money than you'll ever need, yet you're doing everything you can to squeeze more out of men who are so poor they can barely feed their families. Then you turn around and whine like whipped dogs when they close a court so you can't sell your booty. You're contemptible."

The men were speechless. No one had ever had the courage to lay their sins before them so clearly. Certainly not a woman who looked more like their favorite daydream than a ranting revolutionary

"Return to the kitchen," Nathan said. "Lester will serve my guests. I shall speak to you when I'm done here."

Delilah didn't mind going. She didn't know why she'd defended Nathan. It hadn't been thought out. She had simply realized he was in trouble, and before she'd been consciously aware of what she intended to do, she'd heard herself say she had drawn the caricatures. She didn't know how he had reacted. She had looked only at the others. She had to convince them Nathan was inno-

201

cent of creating those malicious pictures.

"I don't believe you did these drawings," Serena protested. "I don't think you can draw."

"Nevertheless, I did."

"Prove it. Draw another one. Right now."

Delilah felt uncomfortable. She could draw; she'd always fiddled during odd moments, and she had often been complimented on her designs for quilts, embroidery, weaving, anything else she made herself. But she saw true artistry in Nathan's work. His drawings were brilliant. She couldn't do anything nearly that good.

"I'd rather not."

"I knew you were lying," Serena exclaimed triumphantly.

"It's one thing to draw a picture of someone when you're alone and angry," Delilah explained. "It's quite another to do it with someone staring over your shoulder."

"They won't care about anything the likes of you can do. Draw."

"If you insist, but I'll need pen and ink."

"And a fresh piece of paper," Noah said.

"There's plenty in my desk," Nathan offered. "Have you chosen your subject?"

"Yes."

"Would you like him to pose?"

"No. I can remember the features quite easily." A few simple lines quickly drawn and a picture began to emerge. It was something she'd done often over the last few weeks, sometimes in flour on the kitchen counter, much to Mrs. Stebbens's amusement, sometimes in the soft garden dirt. Once in a sandy spot by the river. It took her less than a minute to complete.

She handed it to Nathan. A muscle at the corner of his mouth twitched, but he managed to keep his face composed.

"Let me see it," Serena demanded.

"I don't think you should."

"I will see it," she cried.

Nathan handed it to her without comment.

Serena's face registered total incomprehension at first. Then, in quick succession, shock and horror and fury.

"You vile creature," she moaned. "You cruel, wicked girl." The picture slipped from her weakened grasp and fell to the floor. Noah picked it up.

"It's you," he said to Serena. "She's knocked you off clean as a whistle."

The men passed the picture around, to their considerable enjoyment. None of them could see the difference in the strokes, the detail, or the incisiveness of the characterization. They saw only that Delilah had created a wickedly funny caricature of Serena.

"Return to the kitchen," Nathan said to her, but his eyes remained on his drooping aunt. "I trust you're satisfied?"

"Satisfied!" Serena cried, indignation giving her strength. "You let her make fun of me and then ask if I'm satisfied?"

"You insisted she draw another picture."

"She drew only one," Serena screeched. "You drew the others."

But clearly no one believed her.

"I'll prove it," she said to the nervous and embarrassed men. "And I'll prove he's consorting with those people behind your backs."

"Listen to me, and listen well," Nathan said to his aunt.

That look was back in his eyes. Serena tried to back away, but there was nowhere for her to go.

"I have borne with your unending lamentations over Uncle's leaving me his fortune. I've suffered your castigations against my character and my family, but I will endure no more. If you ever enter my room or search it, if you accuse me before my friends of perfidy and treason, I shall turn you out of this house *within the hour.*"

"You can't mean it," Serena gasped.

Several of the guests murmured in protest.

"The hour you put it to the test will be your last under this roof."

Serena crumpled up and sank to the floor in a dead faint.

Nathan looked down at her in disgust. He longed to turn his back on her, but he couldn't. Even if he hadn't had guests, he wouldn't have done it.

"I'll take her upstairs," he informed his guests. "Go on with your discussion."

He lifted Serena easily. More frail than she looked, she weighed very little. He carried her to her room and deposited her on the bed. She showed no sign of reviving, so he went to Priscilla's room and knocked on the door. No answer. After knocking once more without receiving a reply, he opened the door and looked in.

The room was empty.

Not one to waste time with idle speculation, Nathan rang the bell. Delilah came in answer to the summons. She stopped in the doorway when she saw Nathan bending over his aunt.

"I need someone to stay with her. Priscilla's gone, and I have to go back downstairs." Delilah didn't move. "I'll ask Mrs. Stebbens if you like. After what she said about you, I wouldn't blame you if you refused."

"It's all right."

"Just one more thing I have to thank you for."

Delilah slowly approached Serena's bedside.

"Why did you defend me?" Nathan asked.

Delilah thought of pretending she didn't know what he was talking about. She thought of trying to say something clever. She even thought of running away.

But she did none of these.

"They would expect something like that from me. But if they thought you had done it . . ." Words failed her. She couldn't think of a single consequence that didn't make her cringe inwardly.

Nathan finished for her. "On top of being a Redcoat and not approved of by them, it might have been the straw that broke the camel's back. Would they have shot me?"

"I don't know what they would have done, but you don't need any more enemies. And if Noah Hubbard thought you had done that drawing of him, he would have hated you for the rest of his life. Lucius Clarke might have challenged you to a duel. He did challenge a man once. And killed him."

"So you decided to sacrifice yourself."

"It wasn't a sacrifice. I just confirmed what they already thought."

"You more than confirmed what I thought of you."

Delilah was embarrassed by the undisguised admiration in his voice. But she heard something else as well—it had nothing to do with admiration—and that excited her.

"What made you do those drawings?" she asked, an amused twinkle in her eyes. "They were the most wicked things I've ever seen."

"You never told me you could draw," he countered. "That was an adept picture you did of Serena."

"It could not compare to yours. They are brilliant. You ought to be an artist."

There was that same flash of pain again. Clearly she had pricked some old wound, a deep one which still had the power to abrade him.

"But you haven't told me why you drew them."

"Because of you."

"You can't blame that on me."

"I was angry about the way they'd treated you that first night. I knew I couldn't fight them all, so I did the next best thing. I drew the most abominable sketches I could."

"People don't appreciate being mocked."

"Why should you protect me? You don't even like me."

"That's not so." Delilah realized too late that the speed

and vehemence of her denial told Nathan far more than she wanted him to know about her feelings. The warm look in his eyes was positively burning now. And he was no longer standing still. He was moving toward her.

"I wanted to protect you, but I haven't."

"You've always protected me," Delilah contradicted. "I've felt perfectly safe from the moment I climbed into your buggy."

"You're wrong," Nathan said, so close now she could feel the heat of his body. "You were always in more danger from me than anyone else."

"What do you mean?" she asked, but she knew.

"I wasn't brought up among men in the habit of denying themselves pleasure. From the minute I saw you standing on the doorsteps, I wanted you. I think somewhere in the back of my mind I even laid plans to seduce you, but something always kept me from attempting it."

"What?"

"You weren't the kind of woman who would be seduced. By the time I figured that out, I knew I didn't want just a few minutes or hours with you. I wanted to be with you all the time."

"That's impossible. Your friends would be certain you'd taken up with the enemy if you were more than friendly with me." But she sounded like a woman hoping to be convinced she was wrong.

"I don't care what that lot downstairs thinks."

He had possessed himself of both her hands, and the strength of his grasp made it difficult for her to continue to protest.

"You don't understand," Delilah said. "You can't be neutral. They won't let you. Some people tried it during the war. If one side didn't burn them out, the other did."

"I'm tired of everything we say being colored by my being English or by Reuben's debt or Serena's fury or Shays's closing of the courts." There was an emotional in-

YES! ☐

Sign me up for the **Historical Romance Book Club** and send my TWO FREE BOOKS! If I choose to stay in the club, I will pay only $8.50* each month, a savings of $5.48!

YES! ☐

Sign me up for the **Love Spell Book Club** and send my TWO FREE BOOKS! If I choose to stay in the club, I will pay only $8.50* each month, a savings of $5.48!

NAME: _____

ADDRESS: _____

_____

TELEPHONE: _____

E-MAIL: _____

☐ I WANT TO PAY BY CREDIT CARD.

☐ VISA   ☐ MasterCard.   ☐ DISCOVER

ACCOUNT #: _____

EXPIRATION DATE: _____

SIGNATURE: _____

Send this card along with $2.00 shipping & handling for each club you wish to join, to:

**Romance Book Clubs
20 Academy Street
Norwalk, CT 06850-4032**

Or fax (must include credit card information!) to: 610.995.9274. You can also sign up online at www.dorchesterpub.com.

*Plus $2.00 for shipping. Offer open to residents of the U.S. and Canada only. Canadian residents please call 1.800.481.9191 for pricing information.

If under 18, a parent or guardian must sign. Terms, prices and conditions subject to change. Subscription subject to acceptance. Dorchester Publishing reserves the right to reject any order or cancel any subscription.

JOIN NOW!

tensity in Nathan's voice that thrilled Delilah, partly because it was so unexpected.

Partly because it so perfectly matched her own passion.

She had long known she was interested, more than a little, in Nathan, but his declaration tore the roof off her restraint. The magnitude of her feeling for him surprised her almost as much as his feeling for her. She struggled hard to keep a cool head, but it was nearly impossible with Nathan holding her as no man ever had.

"I've wanted to do this almost from the moment I saw you," he said. "Do you know how hard it is to sit at the table, have you constantly going in and out of the room, and not reach out and touch you? Can you guess how often I've wondered what goes on in that beautiful head of yours? When you think of me," he added, "not your brother or Shays or some equally worthy Massachusetts farmer."

"Maybe I don't think about you."

"I know you do. Lester says you and Mrs. Stebbens gossip about me all the time."

Delilah blushed. "And what else do you wonder about?"

"I wonder what you look like when you first wake up in the morning."

Delilah blushed at the implication of his words.

"There is an innocence, an easy quiet about the early morning you can't find at any other time of day. You remind me of that—calm, serene, and innocent."

"Me?" It sounded so unlike Delilah's picture of herself she wasn't entirely sure Nathan wasn't making fun of her.

"You can be fiery, too," Nathan added. "And honest and fair and compassionate."

"Is my character all you think about?"

"No, but I thought that would make you like me more."

Delilah laughed. "You don't know much about women, do you?"

207

Nathan looked a trifle startled. "I thought I did."

"If you want to impress a girl's parents, tell them about her virtues. If you want to impress the girl, tell her about her eyes and skin and hair and clothes, all the little vanities we're not supposed to care about."

Nathan grinned. "If I told you what I have been thinking along those lines, you'd slap my face."

Delilah gave him an answering grin. "Talk about my eyes."

"Can I start a little lower?"

"You can't see much lower. You've got me pressed up against you." She had meant this to be a light response, but all the ease went out of it when she realized that her nearness had aroused Nathan and her body was responding. She could feel the tension in her limbs, the hardening and sensitivity of her nipples, the heavy warmth in her abdomen. She had never been so intensely aware of her body.

A burst of laughter reminded them of the men downstairs.

Reluctantly, they moved apart. Nathan's aroused state was easy to see. Delilah knew she ought to turn her eyes away, but for a few seconds her gaze lingered on his groin. She knew something of what she could do to his mind and his emotions. Now she knew that she could inflame his body as well. It gave her a feeling of power.

"We shouldn't be doing this. Not here."

"We could go to my room."

"No, we couldn't," Delilah stated emphatically. "Serena might wake up at any minute, or Priscilla could come back. And you have guests downstairs."

"I don't care about any of them," Nathan said.

"Well, I do. I'll not have my name smeared, even for the pleasure of kissing you."

"You enjoyed it?"

"Of course. But it's too dangerous."

Serena groaned and opened her eyes. She put a hand

208

over them. "What happened?" she asked.

"You just had a little dizzy spell," Delilah told her. "Go before she sees you," she whispered to Nathan. "Maybe I can get her to sleep before she remembers everything that happened."

"I haven't finished what I want to say."

"Not now," Delilah said, pushing him toward the door.

"After breakfast, in the library. We can go over the list again."

"Out," Delilah hissed. She pushed him through the door just as Serena sat up.

"Who're you talking to?"

"It was just Colonel Clarke asking about you, but he's gone now."

"Dear Lucius, always so thoughtful, and tied to a wife who only accepts him in her bed out of duty. It's a shame we can't pair ourselves up better."

Chapter Fifteen

The noise woke Delilah out of a sound sleep. There was someone in the house. She could hear movement downstairs. She heard a low moan. Serena again. Quickly she swung her feet out of the bed, searched for her worn slippers, and reached for the thick robe that lay across a ladder-back chair.

Serena was walking very unsteadily across the second-story hall. Holding her robe so she wouldn't trip on it, Delilah hurried down the stairs. She reached Serena in the same moment Nathan's bedroom door opened.

He had only removed his coat and tie, but his shirt, open at the throat, allowed Delilah a glimpse of the smooth skin of his chest. The sight affected her like a physical blow. Her stomach lurched and odd sensations began to radiate to all parts of her body. Then came the almost overwhelming, compelling need to reach out and touch him — and she ached with immediate, throbbing desire. If she had been powerfully affected by his body before, the effect was doubly powerful now.

She struggled to refocus her mind on Serena.

"Get Priscilla," she said as she approached the older woman.

Serena allowed herself to be guided toward her own room, all the while moaning and talking. Sometimes she raised her voice to a near shout, but Delilah couldn't understand any of the words.

"Priscilla's not here," Nathan said, flabbergasted. "Where could she be at this time of night?"

"Maybe she's staying with one of her friends," Delilah suggested.

Serena fought free of Delilah and staggered two steps before she fainted. Nathan caught her.

"Open her door. I'll carry her to the bed."

Serena continued to fight, but she was no match for Nathan's muscular arms. Delilah looked at his powerful shoulders from the back, let her gaze wander down to his narrow waist, then pause for a time at his firm buttocks before taking in powerfully muscled thighs. Her stomach lurched once again, and a hot, heavy feeling began to burn in her belly.

With a visible effort, she wrenched her gaze away from his body. "I'll get her robe. She's liable to catch a chill with nothing on but that gown."

Delilah opened the door of a large wardrobe. She had actually reached in and taken hold of the robe before she saw the empty brandy bottles at the bottom of the closet.

So this is what happens. For a moment she stared at the two dozen or so bottles.

Then Nathan helped her get Serena into the robe. It wasn't difficult with two of them. It would have been nearly impossible to do alone.

"I'll stay with her," Delilah volunteered.

"She's not your responsibility. You can't be expected to sit up with her."

"Maybe not, but you can't do it. I don't know what makes her go off like this, but I think it has something to do with a man. If she were to wake up and find you here, she might get worse."

"You are an astute young woman."

"I just do what has to be done. Most women are like that, and we don't expect any praise for it."

"You'll get plenty from me. And permission to neglect your duties tomorrow."

After they had settled Serena between the sheets,

Nathan walked around the bed until he faced Delilah.

"One of these days I'm going to find a way to repay you. But until then . . ." He took her hands and put them on his waist. Delilah trembled when she felt the warmth of his flesh through his shirt.

Nathan put his arms around Delilah's waist and drew her toward him until their bodies touched.

"Nathan, please . . ."

The pressure of his body increased until she wasn't aware of anything except the points where their bodies touched. Her breasts pushed up against Nathan's chest so hard they ached. His thin shirt was no barrier at all. Despite the thickness of her robe, she felt naked in his arms, as though he had stripped away her defenses.

Nothing protected her from the effect of his limbs pressed tightly against her own. This was a new experience for her, and she didn't know how to handle what was happening to her body.

Then Nathan kissed her, and she forgot all the rest.

There was nothing quick or tentative about this kiss. Holding her in an iron embrace, his mouth came down on hers in a hungry, possessive, demanding, hard kiss that bruised her lips and ignited her senses. He neither asked nor implored. He took. She felt limp in his arms, completely helpless to do anything but return his kiss.

As Nathan pressed himself against her with no regard for the electric response in her breasts or the churning sensation deep in her belly, his mouth became more insistent. His tongue insinuated itself into her mouth. When she parted her teeth, it touched her tongue, exploring her mouth.

Delilah broke away with a sharp intake of breath.

"We've got to stop," she said when she finally managed to push Nathan away.

"Why?"

"We can't go on kissing in Serena's bedroom. It's . . . it's . . . I don't know what it is, but we shouldn't be doing it."

212

"Kissing you can't be wrong no matter where I do it."

"You try it in front of Reuben and you'll discover your mistake quick enough."

Nathan laughed. "Are you always so practical? Do you ever throw caution to the winds and do what you want?"

"I've never had that luxury. Most of the time people use that as an excuse to do something wrong."

"Is what we just did wrong?"

"No, extremely unwise." He looked so disappointed she couldn't help adding, "At least here."

"Then I shall start to build a kissing room first thing tomorrow, and we shall always have a suitable place."

"Don't be foolish," Delilah said severely. "People would swear you're crazy." But she couldn't help but be touched by the thought.

"You make me crazy."

"You have to leave."

"I'll go, but only if you promise to see me tomorrow."

"I will."

"Alone"

"Yes."

"Miles away from the house."

"Maybe."

Nathan sat down on the edge of the bed. "Maybe nearly always means *no*. I'm staying right here until you make up your mind."

"Very well, I'll meet you down by the river, but only if you leave this minute."

"Are you sure you don't need any help?"

"Positive."

"Maybe she'll start screaming at you."

"She won't."

"Maybe I ought to remain, just in case."

"You ought to go to bed. Serena won't thank you for seeing her like this. I don't think Priscilla will either."

He still seemed reluctant to leave.

"You haven't been well treated here, not even after the kind things you've done for all of us."

213

"We can talk about that tomorrow. Now leave."

Delilah breathed a sigh of relief when the door closed behind Nathan. As much as she feared Serena might wake up, she was more afraid of herself. Things had moved too quickly. She liked being with Nathan, but she needed time to decide what she wanted to do about the feeling developing between them.

At present she had two questions, one dependent on the other. Did she want the mutual attraction to develop into something permanent? If so, how could she resolve her conflicting loyalties, specifically how could she give her heart to Nathan and remain true to Reuben?

Delilah had never felt so happy as when she was with Nathan. Even her fears for Reuben and the regulators couldn't vanquish the joy she found in his company. Nor could Serena's bitter enmity make her unhappy. She didn't know why Nathan's regard should be so vital to her, how it could so quickly induce a bliss and a contentment her family could not give her.

That had to be due to the indefinable something which happens between two people when they're falling in love. But whatever the cause, this feeling was too powerful to be ignored just because it couldn't be explained logically.

Delilah gave herself a mental shake. She'd be better off trying to deal with Serena. That she could explain.

But there was very little she could do, not as long as Serena remained unconscious, whether from sleep or brandy. The older woman's breathing was heavy but unlabored. The breathing of a drunk, Delilah thought, remembering some of the men who had passed out at her uncle's tavern.

She wondered what could drive a woman like Serena to drink.

About an hour later, Delilah heard footsteps in the hall downstairs. Serena was still sleeping peacefully, so she went to the door and opened it a crack. In a few moments, she saw Priscilla coming up the stairway with extreme care so the treads didn't squeak. Just as Priscilla

214

was about to pass her mother's room, Delilah opened the door and stepped out.

Priscilla couldn't stifle a gasp.

"You scared me half to death jumping out at me like that," she said, her voice tinged with anger. "What are you doing in Mother's room?"

"Step inside," Delilah said. "I don't want to wake Nathan."

"I want to know what you are doing here?" All pretense of friendliness had left Priscilla. If Delilah had ever had any doubt that Nathan's cousin had been playing a role most of her life, she had it no longer. Priscilla was a very angry, dangerous woman.

"She had another sleepwalking spell tonight. She seems all right now, but Nathan had a struggle getting her in here."

Priscilla rushed over to the bed. She tenderly felt her mother's brow and readjusted the covers over Serena, but when she turned back to Delilah, there was a harsh, antagonistic look on her face.

"What did you do to her?" she demanded. "She never has a spell unless something upsets her."

"I didn't do anything to her," Delilah said, unable to hide her resentment at Priscilla's automatic assumption.

"If it wasn't you, it must have been Nathan."

Delilah felt an almost overmastering desire to tell Priscilla just exactly where the fault lay, but she decided such a tactic would achieve nothing.

"Shays closed the Supreme Court today," Delilah began, trying to keep the exasperation out of her voice, "and everybody came here. Serena tried to turn them against Nathan by showing them some sketches she said he'd done. She got very upset when I said I did them."

"Did you?"

Delilah's gaze didn't waver. "I proved it by doing a sketch of your mother."

"I don't imagine it was very nice."

"She hasn't been very nice to me. She was particularly

215

unkind tonight. She got upset when the men didn't believe her, but I think what upset her most was Nathan's saying he would cut her off without a penny if she did anything like that again."

"The bastard." Priscilla let out a furious hiss. "The bloody, stinking bastard."

Delilah had decided that Priscilla was not nearly so sweet and helpless as she tried to appear, but the chiseled look of rage on the young woman's face shocked her.

"Why can't he just bloody well leave her alone?"

"Serena attacked him in front of his friends. She tried to turn them against him by showing them those pictures."

"Where did she find them?"

"In Nathan's room."

"You mean she . . ." She turned back to her mother.

"Nathan was livid."

"I suppose he was."

"Why does she hate him so much? She's always saying something cruel or trying to discredit him. She even said something about his mother one time. I thought he was going to strike her then."

"There's a lot you don't know," Priscilla said.

"Would it explain why the bottom of her wardrobe is filled with empty brandy bottles?"

"By God, you've been snooping."

"I was looking for her robe."

"Does Nathan know about the bottles?"

"No."

"Do you plan to tell him?"

"That depends on your explanation."

"And if I don't explain?"

"Your mother's growing more out of control every day. Whether I tell him in a way that will protect Serena or he learns it in a way that will put her in a very bad light is up to you."

"Why are you doing this?"

This was no time to dissemble. Priscilla knew Delilah had a personal interest in protecting Nathan, but maybe

216

they could work together instead of against each other.

"I doubt you'll believe this, but I feel sorry for your mother. She's obviously miserable. I've had enough unhappiness in my own life not to wish it on anyone."

"And Nathan?"

"That's not so easy to answer."

"Try. I imagine it'll be interesting if nothing else."

Delilah didn't like exposing her most private thoughts to anyone, especially Priscilla, but she decided only candor would serve at this point.

"Part of it is guilt. When I came here, I disliked and distrusted him as much as anyone. And I made no effort to hide it. I blush to think of some of the things I said. I even meant to spy on him. Nathan knew all this, and he still shielded me from your mother's ill treatment. He even tried to ease the shame of my position by providing me with nice clothes and inviting me to dine with you occasionally."

"So much for your conscience." Priscilla's tone was bitingly cynical. "Now why are you *really* doing this?"

"Because I admire him very much." Delilah took a deep breath. "And I like him even more than that."

"Now we get to the crux of the matter. The little serving girl wants to play Cinderella, to move from cleaning the grates to being mistress of the castle."

"Of course I would like to marry someone rich and handsome like Nathan, what girl doesn't dream of something like that happening to her, but I'm no fool. I don't know anything about London or the kind of life he's used to leading. I could make a fool of myself and not know why."

"Do you think he's interested in you?"

"Yes, but partly because most of the people here won't have anything to do with him. I know I'm pretty, but there are prettier girls in Boston and Providence, especially London. And that's where he's likely to go when all this is over and he gets his money."

"Are you in love with him?"

Delilah was not too taken up with her own thoughts to hear that Priscilla's tone of voice had become halfway sympathetic.

"I don't know. I'm so bewildered I hardly know what I feel. I never thought anything like this would happen to me. I dreamed of a Prince Charming, but Nathan is real." She shivered. "Then tonight, when your mother was wandering about the hall, he came out of his room in nothing but a thin shirt. Open at the throat. I nearly forgot about your mother."

Priscilla frowned. "Nathan saw Mother?"

"He carried her in here. I couldn't control her. She fought me."

"Did he say anything?"

Quite a lot, but nothing I'm going to tell you. "He wondered why you weren't home."

Now it was Priscilla's turn to feel uncomfortable, but she didn't seem very concerned about what Delilah might think of her.

"I was visiting a friend."

"I don't think Nathan realizes how often you visit this friend."

"I don't care whether he knows or not." Priscilla was defiant.

Go slowly. There's something here you can't see just yet.

"But I will tell you why my mother acts the way she does. I don't think it would change how Nathan feels about her, but you may feel differently."

"Don't judge him before you give him a chance. I did that, and I was very wrong."

Priscilla didn't look convinced, but she let the statement pass.

"My mother married Abner Noyes when she thought she was too old to attract a man any longer."

"But your mother must have been very pretty when she was younger."

"I don't know why she felt like that; she just did," Priscilla continued. "Mother didn't want to marry him—he was an older man and he made her a little uncomfortable—but Uncle Ezra told her to marry Noyes or leave his house. Mother had nowhere to go, so she did as she was bid. She met my father almost immediately after that."

Priscilla glared across the bed, but Delilah kept her face impassive.

"He was a young boatman on the Connecticut River. I don't know anything about him—Mother refuses to speak of him—but they fell in love and met as often as they could. A week after he was killed in an accident on the river, Mother learned she was pregnant. When I grew up to look nothing at all like him, Noyes must have suspected I wasn't his daughter. He started to mistreat Mother.

"He had always been awful to her in private, but now he started to be cruel in public. He embarrassed and ridiculed her. But what he did behind closed doors was worse. As he grew older, he found it more difficult to perform in bed. But he soon discovered if he had an argument with Mother, things were better. She could always tell when he wanted to be amorous by the ferocity of his abuse.

"It got worse when things started to go badly for his business. He hit her. He was always careful to avoid hitting her where anyone could see the bruises, but I can remember seeing her with marks all over her shoulders and sides.

"She became petrified of him. One night he came home drunk and mean, and headed straight for Mother. She screamed at him from the top of the stairs not to come up, but he paid no heed.

"I don't know what happened. Mother turned and ran when he reached the top of the steps. Whether she caused the rug to slip under his feet or he was too drunk to keep his balance, I don't know. He fell down the staircase and broke his neck.

"We were left penniless. It turned out he had lost everything on speculation with a slaver that went down in a hurricane. We would have been thrown out into the streets if Uncle Ezra hadn't taken us in. But it might have been

219

better if he hadn't. He made Mother a slave in his house, made her beg for everything she got from him. Mother lived for the day she would have some funds of her own.

"Uncle Ezra made a lot of money during the war, so he built this house and hired servants because he wanted to look good in the eyes of the community. All the time he promised my mother she would have his fortune when he died."

"And he left everything to Nathan."

"Mother nearly went mad. She used to drink before Noyes came home so it would be easier to stand his abuse. When we moved in with Uncle Ezra, she drank when he was cruel to her. Now she drinks whenever she feels threatened."

"Has she always wandered about in a stupor?"

"No, that just started."

"She might hurt herself."

"I know she'd be all right if she would leave here," Priscilla said. "Maybe go to Boston. She has friends there. But she won't budge. She's afraid Nathan will go broke if she's not here to watch him."

"Maybe if you explained this to Nathan . . ."

"I don't want anyone to know. I wouldn't have told you if you hadn't pressed me."

"He may figure it out for himself. He's not a stupid man."

Priscilla laughed. "I'm not afraid of him. I still have a trick or two up my sleeve."

"Maybe, but the trickster can be tricked, and I have a feeling Nathan Trent is a bad man to cross."

"What makes you say that?"

"He seems so quiet and easygoing, people make the mistake of thinking they can talk him into doing what they want, but you'll notice he gets his way every time."

"How will that help my mother?"

"I have a strong feeling there's some trouble in his past. He knows what it's like to be stepped on, to be the one to suffer. I don't know what he'll do if you talk to him, but I think you ought to trust him."

"No." It was emphatic.

"Before you do anything desperate, please reconsider."

"Why are you so high on Nathan all of a sudden?"

"Because he's the only person in this whole snarled tangle who's been able to take advantage of the situation rather than letting conditions dictate how he responds."

Nathan was waiting when Delilah entered the garden. She could see him down by the river, watching the leaves flutter from the trees and float off on the sluggish current, their scarlet and gold deserting the landscape, leaving it brown and barren. Even the grass had begun to lose its color. A few more nights of frost and it would turn as brown as the leaves.

Only some late carrots and a few bedraggled turnips remained in the garden. Old Applegate had cleared away the debris and had cleaned up the rows in preparation for next year's planting. His only remaining task was to wrap the roses and mulch the flowering shrubs to protect them through the deep cold of the winter ahead.

Everything looked forlorn compared to the day she had arrived. At variance with the way she felt then and now. That August day had been one of the most miserable of her life. Today she looked at Nathan and knew a happiness she had never before experienced. She walked toward him.

You had best make up your mind what you think about him. He's clearly got some course in view, so unless you want to find yourself agreeing to something you'll regret later, you'd better know what you mean to do before he tells you what he wants you to do.

But she had already tried to do that. She had never felt this way before, and she wasn't sure what it meant. Worse, she couldn't even talk to Reuben or Jane about it. They would never understand. No matter what happened, they wouldn't accept the fact that Nathan could be anything but the enemy they perceived him to be. And she

221

guessed she couldn't blame them. Even though they would be out of danger when Delilah completed her four months, Nathan and his like would still be the reason the regulators were pushing to close the courts.

And she didn't know if Nathan's attempts to find ways for people to pay their debts without ruining themselves would make much difference. So many people owed him money, yet he could only offer such a chance to a few. And no matter what he did, it wouldn't stop men like Noah Hubbard and Lucius Clarke from abusing those indebted to them.

"I was beginning to wonder if you would come," Nathan said as she stepped through the hedge that separated the formal garden from the more natural area along the edge of the river.

"It's not easy for me to leave the house without being noticed. With just three servants, everything I do is observed."

"I'll start hiring tomorrow. By the end of the week they won't be able to find you in the crush."

Delilah laughed. "You could hire a boy to help in the kitchen. You'd be surprised what a lot of fetching and carrying has to be done."

"Especially with me making you stay up half the night."

"That's part of it," Delilah agreed. Then, before she could say another word, Nathan drew her into an arbor formed by two willow trees and a towering elm. He gathered her in his arms and kissed her fiercely. She started to protest, but the sweetness of his lips and the excitement of their nearness destroyed any desire to pretend he wasn't doing exactly what she wanted. She put her arms about his neck and returned his kiss with equal fervor.

The moment Nathan's tongue dipped into her mouth, Delilah's own tongue responded. It stirred, quivered, and then roused itself to pirouette around Nathan's tongue. As Nathan's excitement increased, Delilah's tongue darted under his and entered his mouth. She quivered with excitement. Success made her bold, and she explored his mouth as he had hers.

She didn't resist when he slipped his knee between her legs. She wanted to touch him. She wanted her whole body alive with the excitement of being in his embrace, of being virtually entangled with this man she had watched from afar for so long. She longed to touch his buttocks, but she didn't have the courage. It seemed brazen enough that she should have her arms wrapped tightly around his neck.

She became aware that one of Nathan's hands was no longer at the small of her back. It moved down her side and then across her abdomen, making her stomach flutter in a way that unsettled her. She trembled as Nathan backed her up against a tree. His effect on her was so weakening, the task of supporting herself so far beyond her, she felt thankful for the support.

Nathan caressed her breasts with the back of his hand, and it nearly set her on fire. Who would have believed the mere touch of his hand could turn her nipples hard? Delilah became embarrassed, certain he could feel her stiffening nipples through her dress. She was only too aware of how sensitive they were to the pressure of his chest.

Then she became conscious of another pressure, this time in her abdomen. She knew immediately what caused it. Her breath caught in her throat. It was almost as though he didn't have any clothes on, as though nothing shielded from her the effect she was having on his body.

She told herself she should move away, escape before this powerful response destroyed her ability to think. But desire urged her to press herself to him, to strive to become one with him. The heat of his swelling manhood unleashed a response in her as basic, primitive, and powerful as his more obvious arousal. Instinctively she knew only Nathan could cool the heat in her loins.

Yet when his hand slipped into her dress and cupped her bosom, she was unable to stand any more. With a startled gasp, Delilah pushed him away. She darted away when he tried to recapture her.

223

"I think it's best if you stay over there and I stay over here," she said, fighting hard for breath and for control over her emotions, wanting on the one hand to save herself and on the other to throw herself back into his arms.

"Are you frightened of me?"

She nodded. "Of me, too."

"You know I wouldn't hurt you."

"Not intentionally, but neither one of us is in a state to decide what's best right now."

"I want you, Delilah. I want you so badly I can't stand it."

"I can tell you do," she said, her eyes falling to the proof of his statement. Though amazed at her own brazenness, she was somehow unafraid. "I'm afraid I want you, too."

Nathan started toward her, and she skipped out of his way once more.

"But that's not what we ought to be thinking about."

"Why?"

"There are consequences to everything a person does, and I don't think you'd be too keen on some of the consequences of what you've got in mind just now."

"I love you, Delilah."

"You want me: that's not the same."

"I know the difference. I love you."

"Maybe. At least the way you think of love. But I don't know whether I love you, not the way I think of love."

"What's your way?"

"It starts with marriage and includes a home and babies. That's not what you had in mind, is it?"

"What do you think I want, Delilah?"

"I'm not sure. I think you want someone to like you. I think you want someone you can talk to and enjoy being around. I also think you want someone you can bed as often as your body demands it."

"Is there anything wrong with that?"

"Not if it doesn't stop there. If I were to love you, I'd have to be willing to live with your aunt and cousin. I'd have to be ready to face the anger of the women who wanted you for themselves and the contempt of my friends who'd think I had sold myself for your riches. I'd also have to be willing to leave Massachusetts, to accustom myself to English society, to love your mother even though I've never met her.

"If you loved me, you'd have to be ready to take Reuben and Jane as deeply into your heart as they are in mine. You'd have to try to understand the anger of poor people caught between forces they can't control and doing what they see as the only way to save their families. And you'd have to be willing to help them, even if it costs you dearly."

"You don't make it easy, do you?"

"It's not my doing. If it were just you and me, it could be the way you want. There'd be nobody to consider, no consequences. But it can't be like that for us. I don't know if it can be like that for anyone."

"Does that mean you won't meet me again?"

"I'll meet you as often as I can," she said, gazing straight into his eyes.

"But it means you can't give your body until we're both ready to accept everything that gift implies. Is that right?"

"Yes."

"And if I said I was ready now?"

"My heart would beat even faster than it's beating," Delilah said, "but I would tell you to think about it for a while. I would say you had to make certain you weren't mistaken. I would say loving me may be the most difficult thing you've ever done."

"And what would you say to yourself?"

"Pretty much the same thing. I've come to like and respect you, maybe even love you" — Nathan tried to sweep her up in his embrace, but she forestalled him — "still, it's happened so fast I can't be sure yet."

"I won't let you go this easily," Nathan said. "I've waited too long for someone like you to let you get away because things are a little complicated."

Delilah couldn't help but smile at this understatement

of their situation.

"It happened quickly for me as well," he went on, "but I'm not confused. And I know all about accepting relatives and friends, and about community disapproval. I won't pretend to like it, but if I can't have you any other way, I'll do it."

"It's sweet of you to say that . . ."

"Sweet be damned," Nathan exploded. "I mean it."

"I know you do, now, but what about tomorrow? And the next day? This is not a matter of social acceptance or cold disapproval. The people of Springfield have just finished fighting one war, and they're ready to fight another one. You're in firing range of both sides. Marrying me would be just about the worst thing you could do for yourself."

"I don't care."

"Well, I do. I have a brother who wouldn't understand. How do you think I'd feel if I had to choose between my family and my husband? I don't think I could do it. We have to take a little time, make sure what we feel for each other is lasting. Then we have to decide whether we're willing to pay the price."

"I never thought I'd hear a woman preach caution in love," Nathan said ruefully. "If anything, I'd have thought you'd be ready to tie the knot and worry about the consequences afterward."

"Then I guess you don't know me as well as you think. Maybe it's a good idea if you take the time to better acquaint yourself with me."

"Very well. I'll make a deal with you. For one week we'll go on as we always have."

"Two weeks."

Nathan wanted to argue, but he gave in. "Okay, two weeks."

"But?"

"But we'll meet in the library every morning. We'll tell Serena you're advising me."

"Won't I be?"

226

"Yes, but that won't be all."

"I hope not. I want to learn everything there is to know about you. Will you tell me about yourself?"

"Yes."

But his response was neither as quick nor as eager as it should have been. A chill swept through Delilah. Was Nathan hiding a secret? Did it have the power to destroy their love before that was fully born?

Chapter Sixteen

The next ten days were a beautiful, wonderful, happy time for Delilah. The few times Serena came downstairs she barely spoke to anyone but Priscilla and Nathan. Priscilla continued to act the bubble-headed fool around Nathan, but dropped the role with Delilah. This didn't bring about any change in their relationship, but the change made Delilah more comfortable.

Nathan hired Tommy Perkins, the thirteen-year-old son of one of his debtors, to help in the kitchen. Mrs. Stebbens was no longer so tired, and Lester had someone to boss around. Now that she had some extra time, Mrs. Stebbens insisted that every piece of material from the attic be turned into a dress.

"You'll be going home at Christmas. I know you won't take a bolt of cloth, but you can take a few dresses."

So every day Delilah and Mrs. Stebbens spent several hours working on the gowns. Delilah guessed she'd own at least half a dozen new outfits when she left. She didn't know what Reuben and Jane would say about such a wardrobe. She'd half made up her mind to leave everything behind when she went home, but right now she didn't know what to do.

The best thing about the last ten days was that Nathan hadn't been away from home.

"He hasn't missed a single meal," Mrs. Stebbens said. Then she winked at Delilah. "Doesn't seem like he can stand to take his eyes off you."

"It's a good thing you come into the kitchen every once

228

in a while to fetch something to eat," Lester observed caustically. "Otherwise he'd starve to death with food sitting right under his nose."

"It's not that bad," Delilah said, but she didn't mind having Nathan look at her as if she were the only woman in the world. It gave her a wonderful feeling, one she would never get enough of.

She looked forward to Nathan's increasingly frequent invitations to join the family members in the drawing room, but she never accepted when guests were expected.

"My presence will make everybody uncomfortable," she had explained.

Serena soon figured out what Delilah was doing, and she began to issue open-ended invitations to everyone she met.

Nathan quietly rescinded them.

The time Delilah spent with Nathan in the library became the focus of her day. There, behind the closed door, with a view of the gardens and the river, she could forget they were separated by so much, that people and forces were at work to keep them apart forever. She could almost believe no one else existed but Nathan and herself.

One thing hadn't changed. She still couldn't control her response to his tightly clad body. She had only to look at him and her nipples became hard. He had only to touch her and his body became stiff with desire. That meant a quick parting and a stern effort to return their attention to the long list of names.

This morning started off no differently from the rest. Nathan engulfed her in a crushing embrace the minute the door was closed.

"Do you think Serena knows how you feel about me?" she asked when she came up for breath.

"She can't," Nathan responded, lightheartedly. "She hasn't been carried off by a fit."

He tried to kiss her again, but she held him at arm's length. He pulled her onto his lap, but she didn't feel any safer there. She was falling more and more in love with him, and he was becoming more and more necessary to her everyday existence. She couldn't imagine how she could live without him.

The library door burst open and Serena rushed into the room, followed by Colonel Lucius Clarke. Serena stopped dead in her tracks when she saw Delilah sitting on Nathan's lap.

Delilah leaped to her feet.

"Nathan Trent," she exclaimed, "I can't believe what I'm seeing."

"If you hadn't burst in unannounced, you needn't have seen it," Nathan replied with brutal frankness.

"I don't care if he wants to canoodle with the servants," Lucius said, moving past Serena. "Have you seen this letter? It's from Shays."

As angry as she was with Serena, Delilah grew even more angry with herself for the guilty flush warming her cheeks. While she hadn't been doing anything wrong, her mortification would make it seem that she had. Serena wouldn't miss the blush. She was bound to think the worst.

"I haven't heard of any letter from Shays," Nathan said.

"Well, read it, man," Clarke said, then proceeded to read it aloud.

"And listen to this part," he said after he'd covered several paragraphs. He grew more indignant with each word. "I told you that man intended to start a revolution. 'Assemble your men together. See that they are well armed and equipped, and ready to turn out at a minute's warning properly organized under officers.' He wrote that to the selectmen of all the towns in Berkshire and Hampshire counties. They could have twenty-five thousand men ready to march within a month."

"There aren't twenty-five thousand muskets in the whole of Massachusetts," Nathan pointed out. "It won't do them any good to leave their own firesides."

"Don't you understand anything yet?" Lucius demanded. "This is a call to war."

"I don't believe Captain Shays would do that," Delilah said. "He never wanted war."

Nathan looked at the paper again. "It's got his signature at the bottom."

"It could have been forged. He knows how everybody suffered in the last war."

"It doesn't matter what he wants any longer," Lucius said. "Governor Bowdoin has called a special session of the General Court. They've already talked about suspending habeas corpus and confiscating property. We're going to see if he'll add a year's imprisonment. At the very least we want public whippings."

"Who's *we?*" Nathan asked.

"Tom Oliver, Noah Hubbard, and myself. We're going to Northampton to talk with the merchants and property owners there. It's about time the legislature did something. I mean to see as many people as possible across the state start sending them the message. You willing to come with us?"

Nathan looked at Delilah and his aunt. Their expressions could hardly have been more different, more telling. Delilah looked horrified, shocked that her peaceful world threatened to explode and destroy them all. She was probably imagining Reuben jailed, beaten unmercifully, his small farm taken away. No matter what role Nathan took in the conflict, he feared that he and she would be forced farther and farther apart.

Serena's face was wreathed in triumph. She'd been telling Nathan this would happen. Now she would be proven right, and he would have to listen to her advice in the future. Neither he nor men like Lucius Clarke could ignore her any longer. No one would ever laugh at her again.

Nathan saw himself as caught between two forces moving irrevocably toward conflict, a conflict that could cost him everything he wanted—Delilah and Maple Hill—unless he did something to keep the situation from exploding.

"When are you leaving?"

231

"This afternoon. We figure once the legislature sees Shays's letter, they'll move quickly. We want a chance to have our say before they decide what to do."

Nathan looked at Delilah once more. She appeared frightened and confused. He longed to take her in his arms and comfort her, but he knew even his embrace couldn't provide the kind of reassurance she needed now.

"Serena, you'll be in charge while I'm gone."

Serena flashed Delilah a look of triumph too obvious for anyone to miss.

"But I don't want any of my arrangements changed *under any circumstances*," Nathan stressed. "Now if you and Lucius will leave me alone with Miss Stowbridge, I'll be with you shortly."

"What can you have to say to a servant your own aunt can't hear?"

"I'm not prepared to tell you that."

Serena, feeling she had Nathan over a barrel, proceeded to go too far. "I won't move from this spot."

Nathan gave her a look which indicated he understood what she was doing and would not be bullied. "Do you wish me to leave Delilah in charge during my absence?"

"You wouldn't dare!"

"If you're not outside that door in half a minute, you'll find out exactly how much I will dare."

"We'll wait for you in the drawing room," Lucius said, and tactfully withdrew. Serena waited a moment longer, but she'd already seen too many examples of Nathan's determination to believe he'd let himself be thwarted this time.

"I consider your conduct unseemly," she announced, then spun on her heel and left. Observing that the door was not entirely closed, Nathan kicked it shut with his foot.

"Officious shrew," he said, half hoping Serena had her ear to the keyhole.

"What are you going to do?" Delilah asked the minute he turned back to her.

"I don't know, but there has to be somebody there to counter these hotheads."

"You're not going to ask for all those things Lucius wants?"

Nathan looked a little surprised. "Of course not. I wish I had time to talk to Shays myself, to find out what he's really after, but I don't suppose that's possible, not with all this talk of guns and imprisonment and public whippings. Do you suppose Reuben could arrange it?"

"Jane told me they don't trust you. She said neither side trusts you."

"Just shows what you get for trying to look for a different solution," Nathan said bitterly.

"Don't give up," Delilah begged. "I don't know what will happen to Reuben if Lucius and Noah get their way."

Nathan felt a stab of anger. He was jealous of Delilah's never-flagging loyalty to Reuben. No matter what happened, no matter who was concerned, Reuben came to Delilah's mind before all else. He had thought he was making headway, but only in times of crisis is it clear how people really feel, and it was evident that Delilah's deepest feelings were still reserved for the people she had known all her life.

But Nathan did not despair. Instead he became doubly determined to prove he was as worthy of her affections as Reuben or anyone else. He took her in his arms, held her tight, and kissed her firmly.

"I'll do my best for Reuben and your friends, but I keep wishing it could be my name that sprang first to your mind and made your heart beat faster. I know he's family and he took you in when your mother died," Nathan said when she started to protest, "but I want to be family as well. I don't want to ever let you go. I know that brings up another set of problems, but I do want you to know how I feel. I love you, Delilah Stowbridge, more than ever. And I don't intend to stop trying to prove it to you."

Reuben did come first, but how could she reassure Nathan that she thought of him even more often than Reuben?

"I think I love you, too."

"But not enough to put me first in your heart."

There he was again, asking her to do the impossible.

"I . . ."

"I know, Reuben comes first. I'm giving you clear warning. I intend to change that. Now, give me a kiss."

Delilah couldn't have been given an order she was more happy to obey.

She was no longer shocked when his tongue delved into her mouth. It had taken her only a short time to realize it was terribly exciting. Even now, as she opened her mouth to accept his tongue, her body tensed with expectation. This was a kind of intimacy she had never shared with anyone else, had never wanted to share, and it bound her even more closely to Nathan.

"How long will you be gone?" she asked when he deserted her lips for the side of her throat.

"I don't know," he replied without interrupting the nest of kisses he was planting in the crook of her neck. "It will depend on whether we have any success."

"Don't stay too long. I might forget all I've learned from you."

"Then I would have the pleasure of teaching you all over again."

Delilah took Nathan's face in her hands and drew his lips down to her own. This time it was her tongue which darted eagerly into his mouth. After a tiny pause of surprise, Nathan responded with a growl of desire. His tongue probed even more deeply. Then it wrapped itself around Delilah's with a sinuousness that destroyed her last reluctance to match his boldness.

Nathan's kiss was hungry, insistent. His lips moved with urgent haste as though they were trying to taste all of her at once, asking, demanding, pleading that she share her innermost self with him. He seemed to be asking her lips for the promise her heart could not give him.

Delilah knew she could make no such promise, but she could give him hope. She wanted very much for him to keep on hoping.

It had been the longest seven days in Delilah's life. Serena received two letters from Nathan, the first on his reaching Northampton, the second on his departure from Northampton for Worcester. He didn't know how long he would be gone, but he wrote that he would let Serena know his plans as soon as they were made.

Delilah cared about only one plan, his plan to come back to her. After seven days of not seeing him, of aching for his touch, for the taste of his lips, the sound of his voice, she felt starved, cut off from everything that made her life more than drudgery. Nathan couldn't have done anything more calculated to prove to her that she was in love with him.

Delilah went to the wash house to supervise Hepsa Pobodie's work. Hepsa was a good laundress, but she was inclined to take an extraordinarily long time about her work. With all the ironing and mending Delilah had to do, this threw her behind in her work. Serena had decided that was unacceptable, so Delilah had been assigned the job of supervising Hepsa.

It was just one of the new duties Delilah had acquired since Nathan's departure.

"There's no use your standing about watching me," Hepsa said. "I can't do me work no faster than I'm doing it already."

"That's not what Mrs. Noyes thinks," Delilah said. But honesty prompted her to add, "At least that's what she says. Maybe she's more inclined to want me out of the house than to hurry you along."

"Don't make no difference to me what she wants," Hepsa replied. "I does my work and that's all that matters."

"Perhaps you'd like to explain that to Mrs. Noyes."

"I don't want to explain nothing to her. She don't listen to anything except what she wants to hear."

"A common enough problem," Delilah said, wondering how to fill the next few hours. There was only so much entertainment value to be gained from talking to Hepsa.

"Mrs. Stebbens tells me you're handy with a needle."

"Better than most."

"Why don't you busy yourself sewing up them tears in Mr. Trent's shirts. It shames me to see what he does to 'em."

"Nathan sews his own shirts?"

"I don't know nothing about no Nathan," Hepsa said, her tone and expression a severe reprimand, "but Mr. Trent doesn't have a shirt that doesn't need mending. That man's clothes were mighty fine once, but he seems to have fallen on hard times since then. I suppose those as live in the big house knows all about that."

You suppose no such thing, you nosy old bird. Delilah was not going to let Hepsa know that she herself was equally ignorant.

"Are they in the work basket?"

"I told you Mr. Trent darned them himself. Why would I put them in the work basket?"

"If they're already darned, what am I supposed to do?"

"Pick out the mess he made and fix it so the females on this place won't be ashamed to have him take off his coat."

"I don't suppose he left many shirts when he went to Northampton."

"You won't never know until you look, will you?"

Irrefutable logic. Delilah longed to say something rude, but she bit her tongue as she made her way to the house. *If you ever do marry Nathan, you'd better learn how to manage people like Hepsa Pobodie. You can't treat everybody the way Serena does.*

So now she was thinking of marrying him. It was more than a hastily conceived idea. She had considered it so much it had popped into her head without warning. And until Shays's letter there had been no reason she shouldn't consider it. The trouble had been settling down. She had hoped Nathan's helping so many farmers would cause Reuben to accept him as a brother-in-law.

Of course there had been other problems, but if Reuben and Jane accepted Nathan, the other ones wouldn't have mattered much.

Then Shays's letter had appeared and thrown everything into a tangle.

There was nobody in the hall when Delilah entered. Nor was there anyone on the stairs when she came back from her room with her sewing basket.

She paused a moment at Nathan's door, uneasy about going into his room. It wasn't that she had been forbidden to go in or that no other servants entered it. Mrs. Pobodie went in every time there was laundry to be changed or clothes to be put away. And, of course, Mrs. Anderson went in when she came to sweep. But Delilah had never been in his room; Nathan never lighted a fire in the grate.

Fearing Serena would see her if she waited any longer, Delilah turned the knob and slipped quickly inside, closing the door behind her.

The room, decorated in blue and white, was dominated by a large, canopied Hepplewhite bed flanked on either side by piecrust candle stands. A stenciled walnut chest rested at the foot of the bed. A magnificent cherry chest-on-chest shared the far wall with an even larger walnut wardrobe. A marble-topped walnut stand bearing a pewter basin and ewer stood next to the fireplace, which was faced with Dutch tiles. A large portrait of Ezra Buel hung above the carved mantel. The walls were papered in a blue and white Chinese pattern, and hooked rugs covered most of the wide-planked floor.

As with the rest of the house, nothing about the room reflected Nathan's personality. It was almost as though he had never occupied this space. Odd that a man who affected the people around him so powerfully should have so little interest in his surroundings. One could easily get the impression he didn't plan to stay.

Delilah shrugged off an uneasy feeling.

It wasn't difficult to find the shirts. There were a half dozen in the chest, and every one had been darned. It made Delilah's heart swell with tenderness to see Nathan's efforts. The poor man knew nothing about using a needle. He had just bunched the cloth up and sewn the rent together. This resulted in a bump in the shirt and a slight pull when the fabric couldn't lie flat. Delilah settled herself in the chair and began picking out the repairs. It shouldn't take long to fix them. Then she'd take the shirts down, have Mrs. Pobodie launder them again, and Nathan would never know.

An hour and a half later Delilah had finished her work. As she stood up, she noticed a door on the wall toward the front of the house. She hadn't noticed it when she'd entered, but now that she thought about it, the bedchamber was too small to take up all the space in this corner of the house. There must be another room, a private office or maybe a dressing room.

She opened the door. This room contained no furniture, and the carpet had been rolled up and set against one wall. An easel stood in the middle of the room. It held a canvas which faced the light pouring in from three windows. Tubes of paint, rags, and brushes in jars were everywhere. Nathan had been painting, and he had done it in this room so no one would know.

She walked around to look at his work and suffered a severe shock. The painting was of her, and it was utterly beautiful. A work of excellent quality, it proved to her as nothing else had that Nathan had spent much time thinking of her.

As she looked at the painting, she realized it wasn't just a faithful rendering of his impression of a beautiful woman. He had painted a woman of character and integrity, a woman who expected more of herself than she expected of others.

This was what Nathan thought of her? Maybe he did love her. Maybe he was ready to face all the responsibili-

238

ties and difficulties of making her his wife. He might be ready to put her above everything else in his life. He had told her he was, but she hadn't quite believed him.

Now she did.

But what about herself? She couldn't ask a man to do what she had asked of Nathan without knowing he was more important to her than anybody else in the world. If she married him, she had to be willing to heed the Biblical injunction to leave her family and cleave only unto him. Could she?

The answer came with surprising quickness.

Yes.

"Do you know the whereabouts of a Queen Anne cream server?" Delilah asked Mrs. Stebbens.

"I can't tell one cream pot from another, lass," Mrs. Stebbens said without taking her attention off the bread dough she kneaded. "Is Mrs. Noyes calling for that dratted thing again?"

"You'd think it was the only cream server in the house instead of one of a dozen," Delilah complained. "I don't know where it could have gotten to."

"Maybe the same place as those little biscuit plates she asked about the other day. Lost in her imagination. She wouldn't be needing any such fa-la's if she wasn't trying to impress everybody with her importance. Ever since that letter came, she's taken to parading herself about as some kind of fortuneteller. You'd think she'd be afraid of being taken for a witch."

"All the same, she ought to be able to remember the silver in the house. She was Mr. Buel's housekeeper for all those years."

"Ask Lester."

"He said much the same as you."

"There you have it. Now don't worry me anymore. If I don't get this bread to rise proper, I'll be fit to bust."

"If you want me to help . . ."

239

"You've been a blessing, child, teaching me to cook a dozen things I didn't know nothing about. Don't know what I would have done without you, but I got to learn to do it myself. If I can't do all the dishes you been helping me with, when Christmas comes Mr. Trent's going to know it was you all along. I may complain about Mrs. Noyes, but this is the best situation I ever had. I can't afford to give it up to anybody else."

"I don't know what's getting into servants these days," Serena was saying to her guest. "When I first came to Springfield, I had no trouble at all."

"It's because of the war," Agnes Porter said, "and all that foolishness the politicians talked, about equality and such."

"That was just to get them to fight," Serena said.

"Maybe, but now they think they're just as good as anybody else."

"Don't I know it. The things I have to put up with from that Stowbridge girl. She won't even put herself out to find the serving pieces I ask for. Of course I put the blame entirely on Nathan's shoulders. And I've told him so."

"Is he still encouraging her?" Agnes asked.

"Worse than that. If I told you the things I saw . . . Well, I won't. I couldn't. Suffice it to say Miss Stowbridge is in for a shock unless she's more clever than I give her credit for."

"You ought to have more servants," Agnes commiserated. "You shouldn't have to run a house of this size without at least three more. It must keep you worn to the bone."

"It would if Priscilla weren't such a dear. She takes a lot off my shoulders. I couldn't go on otherwise. And now with Nathan gone for I don't know how long . . ."

"Didn't he give you any idea when to expect him back?"

"It wouldn't surprise me if he's away for another three weeks. A man of his importance must be in great demand in Boston."

"Peggy Oliver despairs of ever having Tom at home again. She declares she almost wishes they were still poor. At least she saw her husband then."

"Peggy Oliver is an underbred woman." Serena lowered her voice to a confidential whisper. "Do you know she told me she finds pleasure in her husband's arms. I never thought to hear a respectable female make such a statement."

"You won't hear it from my Lucy," Mrs. Porter said. "I've made sure she knows what's her due."

"And I've done the same with Priscilla. Nathan will find that she will steadfastly eschew the marriage bed except under the impress of duty."

"I didn't know she and Nathan were engaged."

"They're not—officially. I thought Nathan ought to have some time to settle in before being thrown into a whirl of nuptial celebrations."

"When are you going to announce the happy event?"

"Priscilla hasn't quite made up her mind. I think she should wait until Christmas, but the girl is so deliriously happy I doubt she'll be able to keep it quiet beyond Thanksgiving."

"I doubt they'll be back by then, not with this spying business to settle."

"Spying?"

"Haven't you heard?" Mrs. Porter asked, glad to find something Serena didn't know.

"Nathan is a very sparing correspondent," Serena said through compressed lips.

"Someone on our side is giving Shays information. He knows our plans almost before they're made."

"Delilah," Serena expostulated with satisfaction.

"I know how much you'd love to place the blame on her, but almost anyone could have done it. All of us have friends or relatives associated with the regulators."

"But none more conveniently placed than Delilah."

"How would Nathan feel about that?"

Serena responded as if she'd been shot. "About what?"

"Your accusing Delilah of spying. I hear tell he promised her brother he'd take a special interest in her. And
from what I saw the night we came to dinner, he's fulfilling his promise."

"Nathan cares for no one but Priscilla," Serena stated
with all the hauteur she could muster. "But he's most determined that Reuben Stowbridge shall have no cause to
complain of our treatment of his sister."

"But that wouldn't extend to her being a spy."

"It most certainly would not," Serena snapped. "If such
proves to be the case, I shall drive the girl from the house
myself."

Delilah walked disconsolately along the river's edge. The
sharp breeze coming off the water made her pull her collar
closer around her cheeks, but she hardly felt the cold.
She'd hardly felt anything since Nathan had left two weeks
ago. Serena had said his two letters mentioned no date for
his return. Delilah longed to read them, but she knew
Serena would never allow it. Not wishing to give Serena
the pleasure of refusing her, she hadn't asked.

The days dragged endlessly by. With little work to do,
time hung heavily on Delilah's hands. She was about to sit
down on the bench in her favorite arbor when she caught
sight of Applegate trudging along the path behind her.
She waved and waited for him to catch up.

"Got a letter for you. From Boston."

Delilah's heart nearly jumped into her throat.

"One of Asa Warner's boys brought it over. Said I was
to put it in no hands but yours."

Delilah thanked the old man and took the letter with a
shaking hand. She suffered while Applegate finished his
chat and then turned away and headed back down the
path. Feverish to open the letter, she waited until she was
absolutely alone. Then she ripped it open and her gaze
flew to the signature.

It was from Nathan.

Her heart fluttered, and she smiled.

Dearest Delilah,

Forgive me for not having written sooner, but I confess that only now have I thought of this simple way of telling you how much I miss you. If I ever had any doubts about the genuineness of my love for you, this separation has removed them. I spend sleepless nights thinking only of the moment when I can hold you in my arms once again. The hours we shared are like beacons to guide me through this weary business.

And it is a weary business indeed. Everyone is determined to punish the regulators with severity. It is difficult for any voice of reason to be heard in this chorus of self-interest. Even Asa Warner has trouble remembering the truth. Pray God I, too, don't lose sight of it.

There is one concern which casts a cloud over our proceedings. Colonel Clarke and the others have become convinced there is a spy in our midst. I only mention it because I fear it will delay my return for some days.

I send you this letter because I'm sure Serena will not let you see the ones I've written her. Take heart. There is nothing of interest in either of them. I'm saving it all up to lay at your feet the moment I return.

I can't say when that will be, but I pray it will be soon. I can't bear to be away from you much longer. Remembering you with love,

Nathan

Tears poured down Delilah's cheeks as she pressed the letter to her bosom. Never could she have imagined that mere words on a piece of paper could have such power to move her, but she felt as though she could sob her heart out.

With relief.

Nathan had not forgotten her. He still loved her.

As long as she was sure of that, she could wait as long as necessary.

Chapter Seventeen

Two weeks later, near the end of dinner, Nathan returned home. Delilah's first impulse was to throw herself into his arms. But even if this urge had not been quickly suppressed, it would have been thwarted.

Serena insinuated herself between them.

"You should have warned us, so we could prepare a proper welcome," she said as she rose to her feet. "Priscilla darling, poor Nathan must be exhausted from his long ride. We must take very good care of him this evening. Delilah, set a place for him immediately, and make sure Mrs. Stebbens reheats everything at once."

"I'm not hungry," Nathan objected. "I just want to get out of these clothes."

Serena brushed his objections aside. "While I don't normally dine with men in riding dress, Priscilla would think her Mama a hard-hearted soul indeed not to make an exception on this evening. She would never forgive me if I were to deny you the comfort of your own home."

Overwhelmed by this gratification at his safe return, Nathan allowed himself to be ushered to his usual position at the head of the table—Delilah had had time to move Serena's plate to the opposite end—and he accepted a glass of ale from Lester.

"Drink it down at once," Serena instructed. "You must be dying of thirst after such a long ride."

Nathan was unwise enough to respond, "I suffer from little other than the cold."

"Lester, I want a fire laid at once," Serena ordered.

In his eagerness to comply, Lester almost bumped into Delilah as she brought the reheated food from the kitchen.

"You must be famished," Serena told Nathan. "Sit down and eat your dinner before it grows cold."

Delilah was kept busy bringing in the many dishes—most of which Nathan refused—and taking them away again, clearing away the plates, and finally setting dessert on the table. It was hard for her not to laugh. Nathan was so angry that once she thought he was going to tell Serena to shut up. She smiled at him, gave her head a tiny shake, and promptly left the room. It was her intention to stay away until they removed to the drawing room, but Nathan foiled her by following her into the kitchen.

"I want to speak to Miss Stowbridge alone," he announced.

Mrs. Stebbens took herself off to the pantry, where she regaled Lester with her notion of what Mr. Trent must be saying to Delilah.

But Nathan didn't waste time talking. He swept Delilah into his arms—apron, drying towel, wet plate and all—and covered her with hungry kisses. It was several minutes before she was able to take a deep breath.

"I thought I would go crazy with missing you," he whispered as he nuzzled her ear.

"I missed you, too. But it wasn't so bad once you started to write." She laughed happily. "I never expected you to write at all, but two letters in one day!"

Nathan smiled. "It was a bad day. Asa must think I'm a poor hand at business. I told him you were managing some of my affairs. I insisted I had to give you the most minute instructions."

Nathan showed every sign of settling back into kissing her, but Delilah stopped him.

"You can't stand here kissing me in the kitchen like I'm some common wench."

246

"It's my kitchen and I'll do what I choose in it, as long as you'll let me."

"That's all well and good, but I'm still a servant in this house. If Serena finds out what you're up to, it would set the cat amongst the pigeons."

"Then let's tell her now," Nathan said. He took Delilah's hand, intending to lead her from the kitchen, but she didn't move.

"Tell her what?"

"That you're going to marry me."

"But I'm not."

"Why?"

"You haven't asked me for one thing. And even if you had and I had said yes," Delilah added when Nathan tried to contradict her, "I'd have to talk to Reuben first."

"Why do I get the feeling Reuben will always be looking over my shoulder?"

"Reuben's my family. He has to know. And there's more."

"I knew there would be. Tell me," Nathan said and prepared to sit down.

"Not now," Delilah said. "We can talk tomorrow, in the library, after breakfast."

"I can't wait that long."

"Yes, you can. Now go back to Serena before she comes looking for you. I'm going to have enough on my hands with Lester and Mrs. Stebbens. I can't deal with her, too."

"I love you, Delilah Stowbridge, and I don't intend to let Reuben or Serena or anyone else keep us apart."

"Go."

Nathan left, but the glow of happiness he'd brought remained. Delilah brushed her lips with her fingertips, amazed that something as simple as a kiss could affect her so deeply. Her body hummed with so much energy she could hardly stand still. She wanted to shout and dance and make impossible leaps through the air. Nathan loved her, *really* loved her, and nothing Serena or the rebellion could do would change that. Not even the sounds of Lester's and Mrs. Stebbens's return had the power to dull her happiness.

"I'll bet Mrs. Noyes wouldn't be grinning like a cat at a milk can if she knew what had just passed in this room," Mrs. Stebbens said the minute she got a good look at Delilah. "She don't know yet you took all the cream."

Delilah blushed.

"Don't you try and tell me Mr. Trent shooed Lester and me out just so he could ask you how your brother's been getting along. Maybe I can't read, but I ain't stupid."

"You know exactly what he came for," Delilah said, deciding it was time to have done with pretense, "but you can also guess what a lot of trouble this is likely to cause."

"Lord, yes. There'll be dozens of people ready to put your eyes out for catching a man like that."

"It hasn't come to a question of *catching* him."

"You mean he's been nosing around like you was a bitch in heat and he ain't even asked you to be his wife?" Mrs. Stebbens looked so indignant Delilah wouldn't have put it past her to confront Nathan in the drawing room right in front of Serena.

"He has asked me, but I haven't agreed yet."

"Why, girl? You trying to play fast and loose? Men don't like a tease."

"It's not that. This may sound foolish to you, but there's going to be a lot of trouble when people find out. Maybe the worst of it will come from my own brother."

"More like that Mrs. Noyes. She'll screech loud enough to be heard from here to Boston."

"I don't care about Serena. But it won't be just her or my brother. It'll be everybody. And if there's fighting, it'll only make it worse. I'm on one side and Nathan is on the other, and nothing is going to change that. If there's killing, there'll be bitter hatred. I'll be looked on as a traitor. Do you know what it's like to have the whole town turn against you, to have the people you thought loved you the most persecute you? I saw it during the last war. People couldn't take it. Some went crazy. Others moved away. To be perfectly frank, I don't know that I love him enough to endure that. I'm not sure he loves me enough either."

"Have you told him this?"

"No, but I plan to in the morning."

"I think I'll go upstairs," Nathan said, interrupting one of Serena's endless sentences. He had the look of a man who has made a sudden decision which pleases him very much.

Serena looked at him in startled surprise. Nathan was never rude. His perfect English manners were nearly the only thing about him she liked. The look in his eyes worried her. Experience had taught her to distrust Nathan when he looked pleased. His ideas of fun rarely coincided with her own.

"I suppose we have been inconsiderate to keep you from your bed, but Priscilla and I are starved for your company. Why just yesterday she was saying she didn't know how much longer she could stand your being away. She has come to rely on you so much, you see."

Priscilla made a halfhearted attempt to support her mother's statement, but Nathan could tell something preyed on her mind. He had no intention of asking what it might be. As long as it kept her out of his bedroom, she could keep her secrets.

He took pains to make enough noise for Serena to know he had gone to his room. Then, taking care to make absolutely no sound, Nathan opened his door, stepped out into the hall, and listened intently. He could barely make out the murmur of voices—Serena's and Priscilla's—in the drawing room. Taking the stairs two at a time, he reached the top floor in a matter of seconds. He went straight to Delilah's room, went in, and closed the door.

Breathing a sigh of relief, he lay down on the bed to wait.

* * *

The house was quiet when Delilah finally climbed the stairs. Mrs. Stebbens had been in bed for at least an hour. Even Lester had given up his late hours in the pantry and had gone to bed. There were no lights in the drawing room either. She was the only person left awake.

She didn't mind that. She had a lot of thinking to do, and she could do it better alone. Odd, as long as even one person was up, she felt restless. But the minute everybody was asleep, she felt perfectly relaxed and free of all the day's pressures.

Her feet dragged up the stairs, not because she was tired, but because her mind was in a turmoil, her emotions too chaotic to allow her physical energy. Nathan's coming to her in the kitchen had brought home the reality of their situation and the inescapable fact that something had to be done soon. Their feelings for each other wouldn't remain a secret much longer. They'd better be prepared for the avalanche of anger and bitterness when it came.

As she reached the second floor she thought of the unfinished painting in Nathan's dressing room. That ought to be sufficient proof he loved her, but did he love her enough? His love had come so quickly, so unexpectedly, so easily. Could it go the same way?

She climbed to the top floor, thoughts tumbling about in her head. What about her love? Would she have come to love him if he'd worn the loose-fitting breeches common in America? But more important, what did she know about him and his life before he'd arrived at Maple Hill?

Nothing.

Not that she doubted he was everything he set himself up to be. His treatment of her proved that. And it had really brought about her change of heart. It was why she had come to love him.

Delilah paused at the top of the steps. Was their love strong enough to withstand the storm that would break

250

over them once everybody knew? She didn't know. She guessed she wouldn't until the opposition had to be faced.

What a chilling thought. Suppose they were wrong. They would be subjected to a lifetime of misery. She moved toward the door of her room. She didn't know what to do, but she would have to think of something before Nathan swept her off her feet and into something unwise.

She smiled to herself. For a man able to be cool and calculating in every other area of his life, even ruthless when the occasion demanded, he was remarkably impulsive when it came to her. Protecting her from Serena and asking her to help him with his business were unusual, but not impossible to justify. Giving her material for dresses and following her to the kitchen were . . . well, she hoped nobody in Springfield ever found out. These situations would be impossible to explain.

The moment Delilah closed the door she knew someone was in her room. She was about to scream when a hand clamped over her mouth and her arms were pinned to her sides. Her body tensed and was about to explode into furious action when a voice whispered in her ear, "I couldn't wait until tomorrow."

"Nathan!" she exclaimed.

Nathan crushed her in an embrace before she could tell him he had no business in her room. Delilah liked being hugged so much she decided to wait a few minutes before telling him to leave. After all, the damage had been done. He was already in her room.

"You shouldn't be here," she said when she could finally breathe. "Do you know what Serena would say we were doing if she found us here?"

Nathan kissed the hollow of her throat. "Nothing that hasn't already crossed my mind."

"Maybe," Delilah said, blushing crimson, "but it's a far cry from crossing your mind to doing it."

Nathan kissed Delilah's warm flesh below the neckline of her dress. "Don't I know it," he groaned.

"But Serena won't." Delilah tried unsuccessfully to

redirect Nathan's lips. "She'll assume the worst."

"I don't think we ought to disappoint her."

"Nathan Trent, don't you try to fool me with that innocent act. You'd be upset if I disgraced myself with you." The feel of his lips on her flesh made her wonder if she had misjudged him. Her words were for herself as much as Nathan. Did she really want him to stop?

"Surprised," Nathan admitted, "but I would get over it."

Delilah tried to break his hold on her, but he would have no part of that. She tried to hold his head against her bosom, but he wouldn't allow that either.

"You know there's still a lot between us we haven't talked about."

"Talking would be a waste of time," Nathan said.

He nibbled at her earlobe, traced the shell of her ear with the tip of his tongue. She couldn't understand why her mother always said there was no feeling in the ear. He was driving her crazy.

"I say we dash headlong and tell people about it afterward."

"I couldn't get married without telling Reuben," Delilah said, trying to keep her mind on the argument rather than his lips.

But the kisses on her ear were as nothing compared to her body's electric response to his kissing the back of her neck. The fine hairs on her nape sent fiery sparkles exploding through her until she was nearly incapable of thought.

"You'll have . . . to tell . . . Serena. Can't have it said the . . . surprise of her nephew marrying the kitchen . . . maid caused her to fall down dead in a fit."

"I'll tell Serena," Nathan mumbled. He was kissing her eyelids now. Delilah had never heard of anybody doing such a thing, but she liked it.

"You'll do what every man does," Delilah said, trying not to think about what the feel of his hands was doing to her. "You'll wait until it's too late, and that horrible Lucy Porter's mother will tell her."

Nathan didn't answer. Apparently he found he liked

letting his lips trail down Delilah's neck and along her shoulders much better than answering questions about his aunt. In fact, he seemed to like that better than talking.

"You'll need to . . . find somewhere else for . . . Serena and . . . Priscilla to live," Delilah said. Between Nathan's lips on her shoulders and his fingertips caressing the undersides of her breasts, she found it hard to keep to the thread of her conversation. "I don't think they'll . . . be happy with . . . us."

Apparently Nathan seemed happy enough with what he was doing to let the future take care of itself.

"Nathan, are you listening to me?"

She received a groan in reply, but Delilah wasn't sure whether it came from her or Nathan, for at that moment his hands cupped her breasts. Her body reacted as if it had been charged with electricity.

"No," she whispered. But immediately she wondered if that was what she meant. Her body certainly didn't seem to agree with her mind. She arched herself against Nathan only to be brought into contact with unmistakable proof that his blood was just as heated as hers. Delilah pulled back, but Nathan pursued her until she was backed up against the wall.

His hands continued to caress her breasts through her dress, his lips to lay trails of searing kisses across the top of her bosom, his body to scald her with the heat of his passion. The more she tried to summon the strength to push him away, the more her flesh cried out to hold him close.

Delilah thought she would pass out from the pleasure. How could she have survived all these years with no inkling of the intense gratification to be derived from the touch of the man she loved?

When his hands dipped inside her dress and lifted out one breast, she realized there was still more she had to learn. As he took her throbbing nipple between his lips and sucked it gently, she decided she couldn't stand any more. Her every nerve felt white-hot, her every muscle tense and expectant. Even her breathing accelerated in anticipation. She was conscious of nothing but the sweet agony of his lips on her breast.

"Nathan, stop. Please. You're driving me insane."

But apparently he was beyond control. He cupped her other breast and gently massaged its almost painfully sensitive nipple with his fingertip.

Delilah was certain she was going to faint. It was no longer a matter of the propriety of what Nathan was doing to her. The pleasure was so intense, the agony so unbearable, she doubted she could stand it one minute longer without calling out his name in a long, shuddering moan of desire. It was now a question of whether she could overpower her own fierce longing to satisfy her need.

Using all the strength and willpower she possessed, Delilah broke from Nathan's embrace. He reached for her again.

"Don't come any closer," she said, retreating around the corner of the bed. "I don't think you've given what you're doing enough thought."

"I've thought about it until it's nearly driven me mad," Nathan said. He moved forward, intending to trap her in the corner. She leaped up on the bed and rolled off the other side.

Her action stopped Nathan in his tracks. He had done the same thing the night Priscilla had come uninvited to his room. Could he do this to Delilah? She loved him, he was certain of that, but did he have the right to force himself on her before she was ready? He did not question the answer, only his ability to do what he knew he should.

It took a staggering amount of effort, but he reined in his rampaging desires.

"I don't know what came over me. I guess spending every night thinking about you was too much of a strain."

"I spent every night thinking about you, too."

"And you didn't feel compelled to try to seduce me, is that what you're saying?"

"No, just that I've spent a lot of time thinking about us, trying to decide if we could have a future together."

"And . . ."

"I found out I love you"—she had to hold Nathan off so she could finish the sentence—"but I don't know if I love you enough. I don't know if you love me enough either."

"I love you enough for anything."

"That's what you say now, when your blood is pounding in your ears and your body demands satisfaction." Delilah was delighted to see a tinge of color creep up Nathan's collar. She was glad to see that he, too, could feel self-conscious about his physical condition. "You said you wanted me from the time you first saw me."

"I still do."

"I shouldn't tell you—I don't think nice girls say this to men—but I wanted you, too. I didn't quite understand it then—I still don't fully understand all the things that happen to my body when you're around—but ever since I first saw you, I've hardly been able to think of anything else. If I didn't know I was a well-brought-up girl, I'd swear I was a tavern doxy."

"Who taught you to think that?"

"Never mind. I know now that it's natural. Mrs. Stebbens explained it to me one day. But there's more to it than that, Nathan. Even more than our wanting the same things. We're on opposite sides. If the regulators and the government start fighting, it'll be even worse."

"If you really love me, none of that matters."

"It will, regardless of how much I love you. I can't expect you to change the way you think, give up all your money just for me."

"And I can't expect you to give up your family, everything you've ever known for me."

"I couldn't do that if it were my choice. I couldn't stand it if they turned their backs on me and cut me off. They are my family and my friends. They're who I am."

"And me? What am I, Delilah?"

"The most wonderful man I'll ever meet, the man

I fell in love with, the man I want to marry."

"Isn't that enough?"

"I just answered that."

"I'll make you a promise," Nathan said. He took her by the hands, led her to the side of the bed, and they both sat down on it. "I'll give you till Christmas. I won't pressure you to make any decisions. I just want you to think about one thing."

"What?"

"If you could have only Reuben or me, who would it be? Don't tell me anything now; don't even think about it just now. But remember this. I love you more than anything else in the world, but I don't want just your body. I want all of you. Your intelligence, your curiosity, your loyalty, your friendship, your trust, your time, everything. Or I want nothing. If it should ever come to the point where I'm pitted against your brother and his friends, or anybody else with a claim on your loyalty, I want you to know I will do everything I can to be fair. Everything. But I must know I have your loyalty."

"I don't know if I can offer you that."

"I'm going to do everything in my power to convince you I'm the most important thing in your life. I'll shower you with gifts and grovel at your feet."

"You'll do nothing of the sort. I'd never be able to endure the gossip."

"God, the woman is never satisfied." Nathan groaned. "What do you want, my heart on a platter?"

"If you don't keep your voice down, Serena's going to have my head on one."

"Serena be damned."

"A lovely thought, but not entirely Christian."

"Be serious."

"I am. You've got to go before someone discovers us. You may be immune to gossip, but I'm not."

"I'd marry you."

"Then none of us, the townsfolk included, would ever know if we really loved each other."

"Do you doubt me?"

"No, but if I forced you into it, I would never know if you'd have made that last step on your own."

"Do you have so little faith in my integrity?"

"No, Nathan. In myself. Why should you marry me? What can you gain? I have no dowry, not even a decent wardrobe. My family is poor and sides with your opposition. My friends don't like you. The people I've grown up with don't trust you. I know nothing about living in a house like this, having servants, wearing beautiful clothes, meeting important people. I don't know how to do anything except be a farmer's wife. And in a few months I'll be twenty."

"You're beautiful."

"Okay, I'm beautiful," said Delilah, willing to concede him at least one point. "What good is that? You can't put me in a cabinet with the best crystal or lock me away with the silver."

"You're not meant to be locked away," Nathan said, a tender warmth coming into his eyes. "You're meant to be loved and cared for each day, to be prized above rubies but to be enjoyed as easily as stone."

"That's sweet, it really is, but you haven't given me an answer because you can't."

"You want to know what I love about you, what I need that I can't find anywhere else? I need your honesty. When I came here, I thought all colonials were out only for what they could get for themselves. Everybody I met here was like that. Except you. You didn't want anything for yourself, only for Reuben. I want your caring. I've never met anyone who cared so much about the people she loved. I've heard you mention Reuben and Jane, their boys, your friends until I almost want to banish them from the face of the earth. I wish you would care about me like that. I need your loyalty. I need someone who will always think of me first, someone I can trust enough to reveal my weaknesses. I need your strength. You don't know what it is to stand alone. You may think you do, but you've got your family, your community, the kind of life you've led—you've got all that to support you.

"I love you because it makes me feel good to love you. Just being in the same room with you is better than being able to collect on a dozen loans. And there are a hundred more reasons. I've never met anyone like you, and I know if I let you go, no matter the reasons why, I'll never meet anyone like you again. I give you fair warning, I don't mean to play fair."

Suddenly Delilah thought of the painting in his closet, and she understood the character of the person he had painted. He looked upon her as someone bigger than life, bigger than any human. He had put her on a pedestal, and she had the dreadful suspicion she might end up staying there for the rest of her life.

Delilah knew instinctively that would ultimately destroy what they had together. She wanted him to admire and respect her, but she wanted to be his partner, his *human* partner. As he saw her now, how could he come to her for help, admit a failure or a weakness? He would ultimately go to someone like himself, someone imperfect, and she would be left to her pedestal, alone.

She didn't like that.

She had to decide who was most important to her, but he had to decide whether he wanted a very human wife or a saint.

Nathan had overslept. If he didn't hurry, he'd be late for his appointment with Delilah. He jumped out of bed and began to get dressed. The cold in the room encouraged him not to linger over his shaving water. A boy he didn't remember brought it up piping hot.

"I'm Tommy Perkins," the lad informed him, "the one as was hired to help in the kitchen."

"How are you getting along?"

"Famous. Mrs. Stebbens says I needs some fattening up."

He does look too thin Nathan thought. I wonder if his family has enough to eat.

"And Miss Delilah sees to it that old Lester don't plague me too much."

"Does he plague her?" Nathan asked.

"Naw, but there's them that do."

Nathan was shaving under his chin. He paused and looked at the boy. "What do you mean?"

The boy struggled momentarily with his conscience. "I shouldn't be saying nothing, but I can't stay quiet, especially after she stood up for me."

Tommy was talking about Delilah. Even before he heard a word of explanation, Nathan felt a wave of anger start to build within him. His hands started to shake.

"You really going to wear them breeches?" Tommy asked, diverted by the sight of Nathan naked from the waist up.

"You think I shouldn't?" Nathan asked, rather startled.

"Looks like your long underwear."

Nathan's lips twitched. "You think they look immodest?"

"I don't know what 'immodest' means, but you sure do get talked about when you go into Springfield. My ma says you English are a sinful lot, always getting up to devilish things with young maids and the like. The mamas be fair pulling their daughters off the street when you come by looking like that."

Tommy's ingenuous words stunned Nathan. Having grown up in London where every man dressed similarly, he'd taken the American manner of dress as a sign of indifference to style. Now he began to wonder. This might also explain, at least in part, people's reaction to him.

"I'll keep that in mind. Now what was it you wanted to tell me?"

"It's the things they're making Miss Delilah do." He was clearly reluctant to explain further. "I ain't never lived in a big house before, but they don't seem right to me."

"If they don't seem right to you, I'm sure they will seem the same way to me. Please, go on."

With that kind of encouragement, Tommy hesitated no

259

longer. "They told her she was to do the laundry, but Miz Pobodie wouldn't let her help none. Said it wasn't proper, so they set her to doing the ironing. When she did that, they emptied out the chests and made her polish every piece of silver till it shined like new. Miz Noyes didn't like half what she did and made her stay up at night, doing it over again."

"Is that all?" It was enough. Nathan could feel his entire body shaking with rage.

"Yesterday they set her to oiling the floors. Now that ain't right, sir. Miss Delilah is a lady, even if she is as poor as a parson. Messing about with coal oil ain't a fit job for her."

"Thank you, Tommy. Now you'd better get back to your work. Is Mrs. Noyes up?"

" 'Course she is. Sitting in that parlor of hers, calling me to get something from the kitchen every fifteen minutes. Mrs. Stebbens is fair boiling mad."

An idea sprang full-blown into Nathan's head. "Go find Jacob Pobodie. Tell him to round up every man on the place and meet me downstairs in fifteen minutes. Tell him I said to hurry."

It had to be Serena. Lester wouldn't have ventured anything without Serena's backing. He had been a fool to leave her in control of the house and think she wouldn't take every opportunity to punish Delilah for his attentions. He supposed it was his fault as much as Serena's, but he had to do something about it now. Either that, or Serena was going to have to find somewhere else to live.

He was in the process of putting on a shirt when the repair of a small tear caught his eye. A cursory glance told him someone else had sewn up that one. He couldn't possibly have done any work that fine. He went through the pile of shirts in his drawer. Every darn had been picked out and redone.

Delilah. It had to be. But when had she found the time, what with ironing, polishing silver, and oiling the floors? His anger rose up all over again. It boiled over when he reached the main hall and found

Delilah on her knees, working oil into the floorboards.

Nathan knelt down, took the brush out of her hands, and pulled her to her feet. "You're done with this," he said, holding his voice as steady as possible.

"But I haven't finished the hall."

"Tommy will finish it when he can find time. You're not to touch that brush again, or to do ironing or polish silver."

"Who told you?"

"It doesn't matter. I would have found out the minute I saw you on your knees."

"What are you going to do?"

"Something I should have done in the beginning."

"She can't help herself. She hates me so much she can't see reason."

"I realize that now. If I hadn't been so wrapped up in my own worries, I'd have seen it before. Go change your clothes. I'm going to find my aunt."

But he was spared the effort. "I thought I heard your voice," Serena said as she emerged from her sitting room at the back of the house. "Priscilla and I were just trying to decide whether to wake you or let you sleep until midday." She stopped when she noticed Delilah and the can of oil. "You don't have to do that now," she said nervously. "I told Lester." All of her buoyancy and confidence evaporated as she looked at Nathan out of the corner of her eye.

"I don't like to have an unfinished task hanging over my head," Delilah said.

"Nor do I," Nathan put in.

The sound of his voice made Delilah look at him.

Serena glanced desperately about as though seeking some means of escape.

"It had to be done," she said. "Somebody had to do it."

"I asked you to change none of my orders, but I had hardly left when you began seeing how many burdensome tasks you could give Delilah."

"If she told you that, she's—"

"She never said a word."

261

"I told Lester she could take as long as she needed."

"How was she supposed to finish the floors between re-doing every scrap of ironing and polishing the silver as well as carrying out her other duties? And knowing how well she sews, I imagine you've set her to work on one of your dresses." It was a random shot, but it hit center target.

"Amelia Cushing can't do half as well."

"You pay Mrs. Cushing. Are you paying Delilah?"

"But she's a servant."

"Anything outside her assigned duties deserves extra compensation."

They were interrupted by the entrance of several men into the hall from the back of the house. When Serena saw they were tracking in the dirt on their boots, she positively swelled with fury.

"How dare you enter this house," she screeched. "Get out before you ruin the carpets!"

"I sent for them," Nathan said. "How else are we going to remove your furniture?"

"My furniture?" Serena repeated, totally uncomprehending.

"Your bed, tables, and wardrobes. I suppose you will want the chairs from your sitting room as well. You and your men can begin with the sitting room, Mr. Pobodie. Rear of the hall on the left."

"What's to go?"

"Everything."

"And when you finish with the sitting room, start on the bedroom. You'll need to ask Mrs. Noyes to help you with that."

"What are you doing?" Serena shrieked.

"I'm moving you to the overseer's cottage."

"Nothing, *absolutely nothing*, will induce me to set foot in that place."

"If you can't walk, you will be carried."

"B-but why?"

"You seem unable to live in my house without trying to order its running. I'm equally unable to live in a house where my orders are countermanded the minute I turn my back. This way we won't interfere with each other."

"But I can't move to that place. It's damp and the plaster is falling. How could I entertain my friends?"

"However you like."

Priscilla emerged from the sitting room. "Mother, have you gone mad? Jacob Pobodie says you're moving to the overseer's cottage."

"Nathan is forcing me to go."

"You can't do that," Priscilla said.

"I can," Nathan stated.

"But in the name of Christian charity and common decency—"

"Your mother exhibits neither. She has consistently scorned me and flouted my decisions."

"I was only trying to make you understand—"

"She didn't mean to. . . ."

Chapter Eighteen

"Nathan, may I speak with you a moment?" Delilah asked.

"I hope you won't try to dissuade me."

"There's something you need to consider."

"Jacob," Nathan called when he saw Mr. Pobodie enter the back hall.

Pobodie ambled toward him at a majestic adagio. "Yes, sir?" he said.

"When you finish with the sitting room, get one of the ladies to help you with the bedroom."

"I'll go with Mother if she leaves," Priscilla threatened.

"I expect you'll need more men," Nathan told Pobodie. "I want everything finished before noon."

Serena sent forth a long, drawn-out sigh and fainted in a dramatic heap.

"Your mother needs you," Nathan said to Priscilla. Then he turned on his heel to follow Delilah into the library.

"You can't move her into an overseer's cottage," Delilah hissed even before the door closed.

"You know, you're beautiful when your eyes flash like sapphires. You should always wear blue. It deepens the color of your eyes."

"Everybody will turn against you when the word gets around. Even Asa Warner."

"I saw some blue velvet in a shop in Boston. I was tempted to buy it for you."

"Everybody knows Serena is difficult, but no one will countenance your throwing her out."

"I also saw a necklace made out of some blue stones. They probably weren't valuable, but they match your eyes."

"Listen to me!" Delilah practically shouted. "I can't stay in this house if Serena and Priscilla leave."

That got Nathan's attention. "Why?"

"I'd be alone with you. Reuben wouldn't allow it even if I wanted to."

"Don't you want to stay?"

"We're not talking about what I want. We're talking about a scandal because you ousted your own aunt and cousin because of me. A worse scandal if I stay here."

"I'll ask you again. Do you want to stay here with me?"

"Not like that. I'll come to you with honor or not at all."

Nathan didn't look wholly displeased with her answer. "I don't mean to remove her permanently. If she promises to do what I ask, she can return in a day or two."

"Tonight."

"That won't be long enough."

"Even one night would be too much."

"I don't understand Americans," Nathan said, exasperated. "Last year Lord Ethelston banished his mother to the dower house. He even cut off her allowance for a month and allowed her just one maid. Everyone praised him for it. I attempt to chastise my aunt by a couple of nights in an overseer's cottage and you say the townspeople will be ready to stone me."

"I don't know anything about England, but here we feel your family is your responsibility, no matter how bothersome that might be."

"Serena is more than *bothersome*," Nathan replied.

"It doesn't make any difference."

"Does it make any difference that she is determined to

265

make our lives miserable? Does it make any difference that every time she does something to you, I want to choke the life out of her?"

"Only to me," Delilah said, her gaze softening. "To everyone in Springfield, you owe her more than me."

"The hell I do," Nathan exploded. "If she can't stay here without always clawing and biting at you, she'll have to go. And I don't mean somewhere close by like the overseer's cottage. Priscilla, too."

Delilah found it difficult to be angry at Nathan when he talked like that, but she had to remind herself she was acting in everybody's best interest, hers included.

"Maybe that's part of why America is different from England. We don't have a class of people who can treat others as they want and not care what ordinary people think. We have to work together. If somebody in the community needs something, others lend a hand whether it's providing food, building a barn, taking in crops, or fighting a war."

"That's all very laudable."

"But this kind of involvement requires everybody to act according to the community's idea of proper behavior. If you were married and Serena refused to get along with your wife, you'd be justified in putting her out. But you'd have to make decent provision for her."

"That's why I—"

"But you can't do such a thing before you're married. And to mention my name would ruin me."

"We could move to Boston."

"We're not talking about what *we* would do. We're talking about you and Serena. As far as Springfield is involved, I don't come into it at all."

"But you're at the center of it."

"I can't be."

Nathan continued to look at her with a tender concern that nearly melted her resistance. Why couldn't falling in love be easy?

"I'll let her come back in a few days if she promises to

leave you alone, but I'm putting you in charge of the house."

"You can't do that either."

"Is there anything this *community* of yours is going to allow me to do? And in my own home, I would like to point out. It's more of a tyrant than Serena."

"As long as I'm a servant in your house, you can't do these things."

"Then marry me now."

"You promised to give me a month."

"That was before you put my household at the mercy of every female within a hundred miles."

Delilah smiled sympathetically. "It's not that bad. You can do just about anything to control your own household, and the men will take your part."

Nathan grabbed Delilah and drew her to him. "I don't care about the good people of Springfield, and I don't care about Serena. I just care about you. I love you, Delilah, more than I ever thought I could love anybody. It's all I can do to see you in this house day in and day out and not touch you."

"Reuben—"

"To hell with Reuben! I'm sick of hearing his name. I don't keep my hands off you because of Reuben. I'd shoot him if that were the only way I could have you. I'm sorry. When it comes to you, I don't have any of your finer feelings for my fellow man. I want Serena out of the house, because if she continues to hurt you, I'm afraid I'll kill her."

Delilah's eyes were so misty she couldn't see Nathan's face. The adorable idiot. Did he think she was so fragile she couldn't stand a little hard work? Didn't he know as long as he continued to be so fiercely protective of her there was nothing Serena Noyes or anybody else could do that had any power to touch her?

Delilah smiled at his lack of understanding. "Don't you understand that Serena can't hurt me? You're the only one with that power. As long as you love me, I won't care if I have to oil every floor between here and Boston."

Nathan held her close to his heart. "I won't let you work on your knees, not for Serena, not for anyone."

"It doesn't matter. It won't last."

"Don't you understand? I want to do things for you. I want to give you gowns, jewels, houses, servants. I want to lay the whole world at your feet."

Delilah laughed with happiness. "I don't want the world. I think it would soon become a great burden. I want only you. If we wait, if we're patient—"

"Wait! Be patient! God, how I hate those words. Once I waited, I was patient, and what happened? Lady Sarah Mendlow completely and utterly destroyed me."

"I don't know what occurred," Delilah said, correctly divining Nathan's meaning, "but maybe she did you a better turn than you know."

Nathan gave her a hard look.

"You were never meant to be a suppliant in another man's house. If you come asking for something on your knees, and it's granted, you can never stand upright afterward. That would destroy you."

Nathan held Delilah close and buried his head in the crook of her neck. "I wish I'd met you long ago," he said softly. "I might not be so bitter now."

"Think of Serena in the same way. She's frightened and she's confused."

"Will she ever understand?"

"No, but as much as you would like to, you can't throw her out of your house."

"I'll think about it. In the meantime, as much as it pains me, I'll stay in Springfield."

"But that would be worse. You can't—"

"I've spent enough time thinking about Serena for one morning," Nathan said, banishing his aunt from his mind. He slipped an arm around Delilah and guided her over to the window. The garden was bare, the hillside long stripped of its color, but the raw majesty of the

268

landscape never failed to lift his spirits. "How is Mrs. Wheaton doing with her flax? While I was in Boston I found an English agent who will pay gold if I can deliver top quality thread."

Delilah had finally convinced Nathan to try the American custom of having a big hot meal at midday and a simpler, cold meal in the evening. Serena chose to eat her dinner in the cottage, but Priscilla came to the table.

"I've noticed a change in you over the last few days, Priscilla," Nathan observed. "Somehow you seem less submissive — or would you prefer accommodating? — than before."

"I've never wanted to be submissive or accommodating to you," said Priscilla, her soft voice in stark contrast to the angry glitter in her eyes. "I'm only here tonight because of Mother."

"How about the night you came to my bedroom?" Nathan asked. "I got the impression you were more than willing to be *accommodating* then."

Delilah was shocked to see Priscilla blush. Nathan had asked her to eat with him, but she insisted upon continuing with her duties until Reuben's debt was paid.

"You weren't interested in me, were you? Just how much money you might be able to scare out of me? You would have succeeded, too, if your mother hadn't been so afraid of what Delilah might do behind her back."

"I've never been interested in you," Priscilla replied, fury underlining her words. "I wouldn't marry you if you begged me on bended knee, not even for Mother's sake."

"Calm yourself. I won't ask for your hand, and certainly not on my knees." They stared at each other like circling combatants.

"And Mother?"

"I think that rests with you."

"How do you mean?"

"She's obviously unable to control herself. Even without

269

the brandy, I doubt she could keep to any resolution she made."

Priscilla looked mortified at the mention of the brandy, but she didn't appear to be ready to back down. "Are you saying she can move back into the house?"

"On two conditions, one of which applies to you."

Priscilla's body stiffened. "What are they?"

"Serena must agree to relinquish all control of the household. She's free to let everyone else believe things are as they always were, but I want it clearly understood that I make all decisions."

"And your condition for me?"

Delilah thought Priscilla looked unusually nervous. Could she possibly believe that after virtually fighting her off for months, Nathan intended to make physical demands on her?

"You must stay home to make sure she keeps her promise."

Priscilla flushed again, but she was clearly relieved.

"I don't wish to know where you go or what you do—that's between you and your mother—but she clearly can't control herself."

"Is that all?"

"Should there be more?"

"I thought you might make some announcement." She glanced significantly at Delilah who stood by the sideboard. "After all, it's unusual to keep servants in the room when discussing family business. Unless they've already become part of the family."

Nathan couldn't see Delilah's body stiffen at Priscilla's words, but he could feel it.

"I think your mother should be present for any further discussion. Ask her to join *us* in the drawing room next evening."

Both Delilah and Priscilla looked questioningly at him, but he resumed eating and soon directed the conversation into different channels.

270

"I don't think I should be present," Delilah said as soon as Priscilla left. "There's nothing to tell them about me."

"On the contrary, there's quite a lot."

On that enigmatic note, Nathan got up from the table, leaving Delilah to wonder what he meant to say. Her abstraction was so pronounced that both Lester and Mrs. Stebbens noticed it.

"Give me that," Lester said when Mrs. Stebbens started to hand Delilah a beautifully crafted serving dish. "The way she's mooning about, she wouldn't know it wasn't a tin cup."

"You do seem a bit befuddled," Mrs. Stebbens said. "You sure you're feeling all right?"

"How can anybody be feeling right with Mrs. Noyes put out of the house," Lester complained, "and Miss Priscilla running about like a weasel robbed of its dinner. Here, Tommy, watch where you're going, or you'll end up in the wood box with the kindling."

Lester took his precious serving dish to the pantry, and Tommy went out to split more wood for the breakfast cooking.

"If you ask me, he should have thrown her out long ago," Mrs. Stebbens said. "If he hadn't come home when he did, I was about to quit. Not that it would make any difference, you being able to cook better than me anyway."

"You could take over the sewing, and I could do the cooking," suggested Delilah.

"Never in your life. Mr. Nathan wouldn't give up your serving him." Delilah blushed, which Mrs. Stebbens didn't miss. "I swear that man would eat sawdust and not know any better as long as you served it to him. Is he going to ask you to marry him?"

"I . . . he . . ."

"Don't you let him go making any indecent propositions, not that I think he would, him being nutty on you like he is, but you never can tell about them English gentlemen. They don't act like regular folks."

271

"He's asked me," Delilah admitted reluctantly, "but there's so much to consider."

"Now don't you go letting other people's carryings-on keep you from looking out for yourself," Mrs. Stebbens advised. "If he wants to throw himself at you, along with this house and all his money, who are you to tell him he'd be better off with some Boston socialite with corn-silk hair and pale blue eyes? No reason you shouldn't have it."

"It's not his money I'm thinking of."

"Considering what he's got stuffed in them breeches, I should think not," Mrs. Stebbens said with a wicked chuckle. "But you can't stay in bed all the time. When you get up, it's nice to be able to put on silks and have somebody else do the cooking and cleaning."

"He said he'd give me a month to make up my mind."

"Don't you take no month. Men are terrible about changing their minds. Just like children, they are. They see something new and they got to have it. Don't matter they got something better back home."

"I wouldn't want a husband like that."

"Lord help us, child, they can't help it. They don't mean to be so wishy-washy, it's just how they're made. Why do you think us womenfolk have any control over them at all? It's because deep down they know they're foolish creatures. Oh, they wouldn't tell you for the life of them, but they listens. I know they do. There's not a man in the state, no matter how stupid, who will listen to a word a woman has to say about the law or how to run his business. But you show me one, even that nasty Silas Bennett, who doesn't listen to what his wife has to say when it comes to things having to do with family and community."

Delilah doubted Nathan could be counted among that number, but she decided against trying to convince Mrs. Stebbens. "I still don't know. He's so different from us."

"He's a man, ain't he?"

"Certainly."

"Then he's like every other man. The good Lord didn't make them deep, just full of sin and so nice looking in breeches even old prunes like Mrs. Porter can't help noticing your Nathan."

"Don't call him *my* Nathan. He may say he dotes on me and would give me the world if he could, but he always seems to end up doing things his way."

"It's all that conniving bitch's fault," Serena said to Priscilla as they walked up to the house two nights later. "She's the one who's put him up to it."

"I don't know," Priscilla answered. "I don't say she wouldn't like to marry him. It would hardly seem possible for anyone that poor to refuse anybody as rich as Nathan, even if he was ugly as sin, which you have to admit Nathan is not."

"I always thought he wore those breeches just to get women to do things they oughtn't," her mother complained. "Thank God I'm beyond the age of being attracted to things like that, but I don't know why you can't like him. He would be the ideal husband for you, and marrying him would be the perfect solution to our problems. Maple Hill should be mine, but if I can't have it, I'd rather see it belong to you."

"You've got to understand that Maple Hill belongs to Nathan, regardless of whether I marry him or not. It's not ours, Mother, and it's never going to be. Put it out of your mind."

"I can't," Serena agonized. "It's so unfair. I deserve it. I earned it. That man did nothing."

"Except be a man. To Uncle Ezra, that was all that was important."

"Bastards, both of them," Serena cursed. "And he's stupid. He'll lose everything."

"I don't know about that," Priscilla hedged. "I thought so at first, or at least I thought he was so pigheadedly English he wouldn't see what was in front of his face, but

273

I don't think that anymore. And now he's got Delilah helping him."

"What does she know? She's only looking for a chance to entrap him."

"Maybe, but since she's been working with him, he's got more than a dozen people, whole families in some cases, working for him."

"I have no patience with this foolish sentiment about helping the poor help themselves," Serena snapped. "I say if they owe a debt, get your money any way you have to."

Serena was so angry, her sense of injury so strong, she continued berating Nathan without noticing Priscilla's altered expression or realizing that she got no response to her accusations.

"I just hope that girl doesn't show her face in the drawing room. I doubt I shall be able to control myself."

Priscilla rounded on her mother with a ferocity even Serena's mantle of self-imposed martyrdom couldn't ignore. "You'll control yourself tonight—and all the rest of the time."

"I will not sit by silently while that girl insinuates herself into my house," Serena stated, outraged.

Priscilla turned her mother toward her before she could ascend the steps. "You'll keep your mouth closed no matter what she does, if I have to gag you myself."

"Are you mad. You can't mean to let Nathan—"

"When are you going to realize that neither of us has any power over what Nathan decides to do." Priscilla's voice had lost only a fraction of its seductive breathiness, but it displayed a sharp cutting edge. "He can marry Delilah, Lucy Porter, even Mrs. Stebbens if he wants, and there's nothing we can do about it."

"But as long as I live in this house—"

"You don't live in this house anymore, and you're not likely to ever again unless you realize we're here only as long as he allows us to remain."

"That's insufferable. I don't see why I should be expected to tolerate it."

"I don't see how you can call it tolerating," declared Priscilla, thoroughly exasperated by her mother's inability to face reality. "He's willing to give you a place to live, food, servants to care for you. All he asks is that you recognize the fact it's his house, his money, his servants."

"If only Ezra hadn't left him everything."

"Will you forget about Uncle Ezra," Priscilla practically screamed. "He's dead. Nothing can be changed."

"I'll do the best I can, but I can't promise—"

"Do you ever want another drop of brandy?" Priscilla had stopped trying to reason with her mother.

"W-what do you mean by that extremely impertinent remark?" Serena stammered, trying unsuccessfully to retain her dignity.

"If you do anything, speak so much as one word, to keep Nathan from letting us move back into that house, I'll see that not another drop passes your lips."

Priscilla stormed into the hall, leaving a greatly astonished Serena to follow in her wake.

Nathan heard the hoofbeats long before the first riders burst from the woods. By the time they reached the house, nearly all those at Maple Hill had paused at their various tasks. So many riders had never ridden up to the house at a gallop. Something terrible must have happened.

"They knew our men were coming," Lucius Clarke told Nathan only minutes later. "They were warned."

"How do you know?" Nathan asked. "It wasn't hard to guess we meant to stop them from closing the court."

"It wasn't that," Asa Warner said. "It was how it was all managed."

"They led our men on a wild-goose chase," Noah Hubbard explained. "They drew us off in all directions while the main body gathered in Worcester. By the time we realized what was happening, there were too many of them."

"I tell you, someone warned Shays," Noah insisted, "and that someone lives in this house."

Stunned silence. Lucius and the others may have had their suspicions, but no one had been ready to place the blame on anybody at Maple Hill.

"Do you suspect me?" Nathan asked.

"Good God, no."

"Then who?"

"I don't know, precisely," Noah admitted, "but you got the place swarming with regulators or their sympathizers." Noah pointed directly at Delilah as she bore a tray of mugs into the room. "Her brother is one of the ring-leaders."

"If it will make you feel any better, Miss Stowbridge hasn't left Maple Hill since she arrived."

"It makes no difference," Noah said, taking the silence behind him to be support. "She has the run of the house. She can gather the information and send it out with her brother."

"Reuben hasn't been here in weeks," Delilah said. "You can ask any of the men."

"Isaac Yates and his boy are in and out of this place like it belonged to them. Don't tell me you don't see them."

"I won't, since you're obviously unwilling to believe anything I say," Delilah snapped.

The men might not credit her words, but they were impressed with her demeanor. She didn't look like a woman with something to hide. She exuded the confidence of complete innocence.

"Miss Stowbridge is no spy," Nathan said. "Nor is anyone else at Maple Hill. No one comes here without a specific purpose."

"But how do you know someone ain't also spying?" Noah insisted.

"I don't suppose I can," Nathan replied, "but no one

comes up to the house except to see me. Since none of these folk are ever here when we meet, it's impossible for them to learn anything."

Noah's gaze shifted to Delilah.

"Foreseeing such a situation as this, I have made it a point to see that Miss Stowbridge couldn't possibly have access to any information," Nathan stated coolly.

"It's got to be coming from this house," Noah insisted.

"Surely you can't mean you suspect Priscilla or myself," stated Serena. She had come into the room just after Delilah.

"Certainly not, Mrs. Noyes," Lucius said. "Nobody was more relentless than your uncle in taking what was owed him."

"Shays's information comes from here. I know it," Noah insisted. "I say you send her back to her brother. Then if the leaks stop, we'll know who it was."

"And if they don't?"

"I say they will."

"You may not have noticed, but I'm not in the least bit interested in what you say," Nathan said in the same quiet, deadly voice Delilah had come to be wary of. "I consider your accusations offensive, your reasoning idiotic, and your integrity roughly equivalent to that of an egg-stealing snake's. Now if you don't leave my house immediately, I'll throw you out."

An unexpected step forward accompanied the threat, and Noah involuntarily jumped back. Several men laughed at this show of cowardice, and that broke the tension.

Noah looked around him with malice in his eyes. "I'll prove it's you," he said to Delilah as he retreated toward the door.

"You'll have a difficult time proving what exists only in your mind," Nathan said. "Now, if you're finished . . ."

"I'm going, but I'll be back."

"Miss Stowbridge, would you show him out?" Nathan grinned maliciously at the rage which suffused Noah's

277

countenance when Delilah opened the door for him. He grinned even more broadly when he heard the front door slam.

"Now, gentlemen," Nathan said, turning back to the others, "I want to say two things. First, I will state on my honor that no one I have brought to Maple Hill has ever stolen information for the regulators. I have even refrained from sharing information with my aunt and cousin."

There was a polite murmur of approval.

"However, since some doubt does exist in your minds, I suggest you neither hold your discussions as to your next move at Maple Hill nor invite me to be a party to them. Then if information is passed, you can be certain it didn't come from Maple Hill."

"There's no secret about what we plan to do next," Asa Warner said. "The next court sitting is at—"

Nathan held up his hand. "You're welcome to enjoy my hospitality as long as you wish, but not a word about your plans."

Much to everyone's surprise, once prohibited from discussing the insurrection, those gathered had an enjoyable time drinking Nathan's ale and talking about ordinary concerns which had been pushed aside. When the last of the men left, nearly an hour later, all were in a better humor.

"You didn't want them to tell you what they were going to do because you wanted no part of it," Delilah whispered as she cleared away the last of the mugs.

"I daresay you're right," Serena said, coming up in time to overhear. "He's shown all along he doesn't have the backbone to do what's necessary. Instead he coddles those lazy good-for-nothings and encourages them to continue being lax."

"On the contrary, he's encouraging them to be productive," Delilah contradicted her. "For every dollar Isaac Yates makes for himself, he makes two for Nathan. Now Isaac has hired two people who owe Nathan money, and

278

Emma Wheaton is offering work to any woman who can spin top grade flax yarn," Delilah added.

"I've earned more from Delilah's ideas than Lucius or Noah have gained by confiscation," Nathan disclosed.

"It won't do you any good in the end," Serena stated. "None of our people trust you, and I hear the farmers think you're only giving them work so you can get information."

"Mother," Priscilla hissed, "this is none of your concern."

"I'm not saying this for my benefit," Serena said piously. "I'd be remiss in my duty if I didn't recommend to Nathan most strongly that Miss Stowbridge return to her home. If she must meddle in his affairs, I don't see why she can't do it from there."

"Delilah's not leaving Maple Hill because I don't want her to."

"It's all fine and good to stand up for principle, Nathan, but what's the good of insisting that she isn't spying when nobody believes you? You would save her and yourself a lot of trouble if—"

"I love Delilah. I have asked her to marry me."

Priscilla looked only mildly surprised, but Serena appeared to have been turned to stone. For a few moments she sat immobile and stared at Nathan out of wide eyes.

"You couldn't possibly be guilty of such insanity," she finally managed to say.

"The only insanity I'm guilty of is thinking for all of one hour that Priscilla might make me a good wife. We would have soon come to hate each other."

"But Priscilla adores you. She always has."

"I've never liked Nathan, not even for one day," Priscilla said. "I would not have married him."

"But you said you would. And I saw you making up to him all the time."

"Uncle Ezra treated you better when I made up to him," Priscilla explained. "I figured it would work on Nathan as well."

"But—"

"I lied to you, Mother," Priscilla said in exasperation. "You wouldn't listen to anything I said, so I lied."

Serena looked crushed. "When will the wedding take place?"

"There isn't going to be a wedding, Mrs. Noyes," Delilah said. "I haven't agreed to marry him."

"You haven't agreed! Why you stupid girl! Do you think you'll ever again have a chance to marry such a rich husband?"

Nathan chuckled at his aunt's unexpected reaction.

"I haven't given up. I've given her until Christmas to change her mind."

"And then?"

"I'll kidnap her and marry her anyway."

"You really turned him down?" Priscilla asked, unable to believe what she had heard.

"With Reuben hating Nathan and your mother hating me, the community not trusting an Englishman, the regulators setting everybody against their neighbors, and the differences between our stations, what else could I do?"

"You're a more intelligent girl than I thought," Serena said, grasping at the only hope she saw. "It takes a noble person to give up a man for his own good."

"I'm not giving him up," Delilah said. "I don't think I could ever do that."

"None of those things matter," Nathan said, speaking to Delilah rather than his aunt and cousin. "You'll have your month, but after that you're going to be mine."

"But—"

"If Maple Hill and all those debts stand in my way, I'll give it away. I won't let anything as stupid as a house stand between us."

"Are you insane?" Serena shrieked.

"You'd do that for me?" Delilah asked, moved beyond words.

"Do you know what that would mean to me?" Serena demanded.

"I told you I wouldn't let you go," Nathan said to Delilah as he ignored Serena entirely. "Besides, I've already been poor. I'm not afraid of it."

"Where would I go? How would I live?" Serena inquired, frantic. "And there's Priscilla to think of. How would she ever find a husband?"

"You said you'd never give up Maple Hill, no matter what," Delilah reminded him.

"I didn't have a reason before."

"You're mad." It was the only explanation Serena could think of. "The strain has driven you insane."

"My answer still won't be ready until Christmas," Delilah added.

"I'll wait until then—but not a minute longer."

"Maybe he should go to Newport for the winter," Serena said to Priscilla. "I could go with him while you and Delilah look after Maple Hill."

"I don't think I could live in England," Delilah said.

"I won't care where we live as long as you're my wife."

Delilah couldn't answer. How could she be expected to do anything as commonplace as speak when the man she loved had just offered to give up everything he had for her?

"Nathan, listen to me," Serena begged, but Nathan didn't take his gaze off Delilah.

"Come on, Mother. Let's go to bed."

"I can't leave now. He doesn't know what he's doing. I've got to make him understand."

"He's not listening. I don't think he even knows we're here."

Chapter Nineteen

Delilah couldn't sleep. Every time she closed her eyes, she dreamed something horrible was happening to Nathan. And all because Noah Hubbard had accused her of spying. She felt a few pangs of guilt over her earlier intention to spy on Nathan, but that was soon replaced by her real fear that someone at Maple Hill was gathering information for Shays. But who could it be?

She quickly discounted Jacob Pobodie and his men. They might sympathize with Shays, but they depended on Nathan for their living. Besides, they had no opportunity. If someone was spying, it had to be someone inside the house.

It couldn't be any of the servants. Mrs. Stebbens never left the kitchen, Lester never left the dining room or pantry, and Tommy never went into the house if he could help it. Serena petrified the lad. One of them might overhear something once in a while, but none of them could be giving Shays a steady stream of information. Besides, as far as Delilah knew, no servant had received a visitor or had left Maple Hill since she'd arrived.

Obviously it wasn't Nathan. It made no sense for him to be helping people determined to deprive him of his property.

That left Serena and Priscilla.

Serena would do anything she could to discredit Nathan, but Delilah couldn't believe she would give information to the regulators. Daniel Shays was about the only human she disliked more than Nathan and Delilah. Besides, if the regulators won, Nathan would lose his money, and Serena feared poverty more than anything in the world.

That left Priscilla. If it hadn't been for Priscilla's frequent absences, Delilah would have dismissed her for the same reasons she had eliminated Serena. Where did she go, and what did she do? Delilah knew she didn't visit Lucy Porter or Hope Prentiss, but why would Priscilla do anything to hurt herself and her family?

Delilah cursed silently. Was she imagining things? Maybe there wasn't anyone at Maple Hill who wanted to hurt Nathan. Why should there be? After Ezra Buel, Nathan was a godsend.

And why should she credit anything Noah Hubbard said? He was a jealous, angry, hate-ridden man only too anxious to believe the worst of someone else, especially if he could gain by it.

But if Noah could be believed, the spy had been giving the regulators information on a steady basis. One of the men who'd come with Noah and Lucius could be the source but Delilah couldn't get away from feeling the spy lived at Maple Hill.

But who?

There was no way to tell. She would have to select one person to watch. If that person proved innocent, she would have to observe the movements of a second. But where should she start?

Why not with Priscilla? At least it might be interesting to discover where she had been going.

"Someone tipped off the government militia," Reuben told Delilah, rage burning in his eyes. "They knew where the regulators were going, the route they traveled,

283

when they were supposed to get there, and who was leading them. If I didn't know better, I'd swear it was one of our own men who did it."

"Did they try to close the court anyway?"

"They didn't get a chance. The minute they learned the militia had government warrants for the leaders' arrest, they scattered to their homes. But Governor Bowdoin wasn't satisfied with running us off this time. He sent more than a hundred and sixty horsemen to comb the countryside for Adam Wheeler, Henry Gale, and Job Shattuck. Shattuck went to a friend's house, but somebody tipped the cavalry off, and they found him. They had to cut the cartilage in his knee before they could take him. Now he's rotting in a jail in Boston."

"And the rest of them?"

"I don't know where they went." He turned on his sister. "I bet your Mr. Trent knew what was going to happen."

"Boston is halfway across the state. Nobody here has any idea what goes on there. Certainly not Nathan. He's too busy with his own concerns."

"So it's *Nathan* now?"

"We all call him Nathan when he's not around. That's beside the point."

"Maybe it is the point," Reuben insisted doggedly. "Maybe you're so concerned about Nathan you forgot about your own family."

"Damn you, Reuben," Delilah cursed, tears of pain glistening in her eyes. "I wouldn't be here if it weren't for you. Nor would I stay, not with Jane needing me. If you don't believe me, pay your confounded debt. I'll be glad to go home."

"I didn't mean that," Reuben said, the fight driven out of him by the unpalatable reminder that Delilah was working off an obligation he couldn't pay. "It's just my temper. And hate for Governor Bowdoin. They're not doing anything for Shattuck. If he doesn't die of gangrene, he'll be crippled for life."

"I'm sorry for Job Shattuck," Delilah said, "but I won't be held responsible for what happened to him. Nor will I let you hold Nathan responsible. His friends don't trust him any more than you do. In fact, they're certain someone at Maple Hill is spying for you. They accused me."

"But you haven't given us a single scrap of information."

"Nathan even told them he made sure I didn't have access to any details, but I doubt they believe him. In any event, they're making their plans somewhere else now."

"It's just as well. If they thought you were spying, no telling what they might do."

"They wouldn't do anything. Nathan wouldn't let them." Delilah didn't stop to think how that sounded until it was too late. Reuben frowned at her, suspicion in his eyes.

"Is that man making up to you?"

"I didn't say it right," Delilah said, trying to avoid answering the question. "Nathan is very protective of everyone at Maple Hill. Very lord of the manor. Maybe it's his English background."

But Reuben couldn't be sidetracked so easily. "I didn't ask you about what he learned in England. I want to know what he's doing right now."

"I guess you could say he's protecting me." Delilah said, then quickly added when Reuben started to swell with wrath, "His aunt is always trying to give me the worst jobs. If Nathan hadn't stopped her, I'd be doing the laundry and oiling the floors in addition to cleaning the grates and helping in the kitchen and the dining room."

"That's too much for forty shillings. I think I'll step inside and have a talk with Mr. Trent."

"I'm *not* doing those things because Nathan already

285

said it was too much. And he's just as protective of Mrs. Stebbens and Tommy."

If Reuben went up to see Nathan, there'd be a fight. Delilah knew her brother. And right then she knew if it came to a choice, she would protect Nathan before Reuben.

The realization shocked her profoundly. All her life she had been taught loyalty to her family before all else. She had always put them first. That was her reason for coming to Maple Hill. She had been taught to hold the needs of her community in next importance. Somewhere way down the list came duty to the government and respect for rich landlords.

Now, much to her shock, Nathan had leap-frogged all the way to the top of the list. For all she knew he had been firmly entrenched in first place for weeks now. In a way that thrilled her. Up until now, knowing Nathan loved her had been the most wonderful thing to happen to her. Now she had discovered that to be in love was even more wonderful. It was as though every weight had been removed from her soul. She still cared about the troubles of her people, but they no longer had the power to weigh her down with despair, to burden her with heartache. Love had given her a freedom such as she had never known.

She wanted to dance and sing with happiness.

But she didn't. It was going to be difficult enough to explain things to Reuben when she moved back home. Right now it would be impossible.

"Are you sure you're not covering for him?"

"You can go ask Mrs. Stebbens if you don't believe me, though I wish you wouldn't do it just now. She's trying a recipe I taught her for steak and kidney pie. I doubt she'll get it right if you take her mind off what she's doing."

"So he's got you cooking, too," Reuben said, firing up.

"No, he hasn't. Mrs. Stebbens sews better than I do,

286

and Nathan likes food cooked like it was in England, the way Granddad used to like it. I help her out and she does some of my sewing."

"So you're doing the sewing now, are you?"

Delilah had never realized how tiresome Reuben could be or how irritating his temper and his suspicions were.

"Serena gave me some material to make a dress. And if you say one word about my being too good to take handouts I'll brain you, Reuben Stowbridge." Her brother, intending to make just such a complaint, subsided at once. "Mrs. Stebbens offered to help cut it out," Delilah continued more calmly. "It only seemed fair to help out with the cooking, especially since I've been preparing some of those dishes for years."

"I still don't like it."

"Well, I'm satisfied, and I'm the one who has to work here, so we'll say no more. Tell Jane I'm well and looking forward to being home at Christmas. Tell her to save the cooking until last."

Delilah breathed a sigh of relief as she watched Reuben head back down the road. As much as she loved her brother, it was nearly impossible to keep him from flying into a rage over one thing or another. She had more sympathy for Jane than ever.

She sighed again, this time a little sadly. She hated lying to Reuben. She wasn't looking forward to going home for Christmas because it meant she wouldn't be with Nathan. Already she'd found herself looking for ways to remain at Maple Hill. But she knew Reuben. If he suspected the truth, he might never welcome her into his home again.

No, as much as she hated it, it would be best to go home, tell Reuben and Jane after Christmas, and give them a short time to get used to the idea before she and Nathan were married. Maybe the insurrection would be over by then. If so, it would make Reuben's acceptance of her marriage a lot easier.

287

But anger over Shattuck's ill treatment was liable to make things worse before they got better.

The news that Nathan had ridden out while she'd talked to Reuben irked Delilah. She was bursting to share the happiness of knowing she loved him. She wanted to tell him right now that she would marry him, and even though his absence thwarted her, she went about looking so much like the cat who swallowed the canary that Mrs. Stebbens taxed her more than once about keeping secrets.

"It's not a kind thing when a body is as curious as I am," Mrs. Stebbens protested. "And there's no use saying there's naught the matter with you. I can see it in the way you walk, like your feet don't hardly touch the ground."

"I really can't tell you."

"So I figured, but I'm so eaten up with curiosity I'm tempted to squeeze it out of you."

Lester refused to exhibit curiosity, but he managed to be present whenever Delilah and Mrs. Stebbens were together.

Tommy showed no interest in anything but his dinner and getting out of as many chores as possible. It had rained heavily all afternoon, and all outside work had come to a halt.

"I must have forgotten to tell you Nathan said he would be away until late tonight," Serena said when she and Priscilla sat down to dinner. She directed her words to Lester, but her eyes were on Delilah. "It's a shame Mrs. Stebbens went to the trouble of cooking this pie for him. Neither Priscilla nor I will touch it."

Delilah felt sorely tempted to dump it over Serena's head. The irksome woman knew Delilah had taught Mrs. Stebbens to make the dish, and she had *forgotten* Nathan's message for that very reason. But Delilah was so happy that not even Serena's barbs could destroy her mood. Nathan loved her, and she loved him. Nothing else mattered.

Nine o'clock found Delilah in her room, reading one of the books she'd borrowed from Nathan's library, waiting for him to come home. The rain had stopped hours earlier. The moon shone so brightly she could watch for him out her window.

Sometime after ten, she finished her book. Rather than go to sleep just yet, she decided to get another one. She didn't bother to take a candle. Enough light poured in the windows for her to find her way and the candle Nathan kept in the library would serve to look for her book.

But when Delilah reached the library, the mesmerizing view of garden and river caused her to forget about candle and book. The moonlight turned the river to liquid silver, and trees, bare of their leaves, cast crooked limbs against that silver backdrop, looking like cracks in a smooth surface. The scene was profoundly peaceful, and Delilah delighted in knowing that for the rest of her life she could enjoy this spectacular view at any time she wanted.

With a sigh, she turned back for the candle, but just then she heard a board in one of the stairs creak. Without stopping to think why she did it, Delilah crossed the room and crouched down behind the high-backed settle against the far wall.

Seconds later she heard the door handle turn ever so slowly. Then someone entered the library with whisperlike footsteps and closed the door. Whoever it was crossed the room, and Delilah heard a key turn in a lock.

Nathan's desk! It was the only thing in the room that was locked. Taking infinite care to avoid making even the slightest sound, Delilah leaned forward until she could see around the end of the settle. A woman's back was to Delilah, but it was easy to identify Priscilla Noyes.

What did she want from Nathan's desk? The light was barely strong enough for Delilah to see Priscilla take a paper from one of the small drawers, close the drawer, and lock the desk. She had known what she was looking for and where to find it. Delilah drew back in her hiding place before Priscilla could turn around, and Priscilla hurried away, closing the door behind her.

Delilah hurried over to it, turned the knob silently, and eased the door open. A light disappeared up the steps. Delilah breathed a sigh of relief. Priscilla was going back to bed. Whatever she had taken, she didn't mean to take it from the house.

Delilah lighted the candle, picked out a book, snuffed the candle, and left the library. She had barely placed her foot on the third step when she heard one of the bedroom doors on the second floor open. She dashed into the drawing room across the hall. Keeping the doors slightly ajar, Delilah watched until Priscilla came down the stairs. She wore a cloak and heavy shoes, the kind she'd wear if she planned to go out.

Priscilla was the spy!

She padded softly toward the back of the hall. Then Delilah heard the back door open and close. Book in hand, she scurried down the hall and through the pantry into the kitchen. She watched Priscilla round the corner of the house and head toward the river. Racing back down the hall, Delilah reached the library window in time to see Priscilla go down through the garden and take the path heading north along the river.

Once more Delilah hurried to the kitchen. She grabbed an old cloak Mrs. Stebbens kept hanging by the back door, then looked down at her slippers. They would soon be ruined by the cold, wet ground. Her gaze fell on a pair of boots Tommy had put by the back door in case of snow. She stuffed her feet into them before letting herself out the door and hurrying toward the garden.

Delilah pulled the cloak more tightly around her. Despite the rain, it was bitterly cold, and the temperature was dropping rapidly. The ground would freeze before morning. She hoped Priscilla wasn't going far. They both might catch pneumonia.

Delilah had to run to catch sight of Priscilla. The exertion sent blood hurtling through her veins, and in fifteen minutes Delilah didn't feel the cold so much.

Forty-five minutes later, Priscilla was still striding along. They had already passed several houses, their presence being heralded by barking dogs on two occasions. Delilah breathed a sigh of relief when Priscilla at last took an inland path, but she cursed her luck when she lost sight of her as the path twisted and climbed up from the river bottom through the trees. She would never have known where to look if she hadn't seen a light coming from a small cabin once she came to a clearing.

Being very careful not to make any noise, Delilah approached the cabin from one side and then crouched down until she was next to a window. Very slowly she stood up and looked just far enough around to be able to see inside. She was rewarded by seeing Priscilla and Hector Clayhart together. Priscilla handed him a piece of paper. It had to be the note she had taken from Nathan's desk.

It must be the list of insurgent leaders, but what good was that now? Everybody already knew the leaders. Still, there must be something important about it. Otherwise they wouldn't have gone to the trouble of stealing it and meeting at night.

Whatever it was, Delilah had to stop them.

She stepped out of the bracken and dead leaves under the window and went up on the porch. Priscilla and Hector were kissing passionately when she opened the

291

door. They leaped apart, shock and surprise on both their faces.

"Now I understand why you didn't want to marry Nathan," Delilah said.

"What are you doing here?" demanded Priscilla. "How did you find us?"

"I followed you. I was in the library when you stole that paper from Nathan's desk."

Hector looked down. The paper was in his hand. Instinctively he put it in his pocket.

"You couldn't have been. I saw no one."

"I was hiding behind the settle. Does Nathan know you have a key to his desk?"

"I didn't take anything important."

Delilah decided she had to appear to know more than she did if she was to force any information out of them. "You took the list of names Lucius Clarke gave Nathan. Why?"

Bull's-eye! Both Priscilla and Hector lost color.

"It's a letter I wrote to Ezra Buel long ago," Hector told her. "I asked Priscilla to get it back for me."

"Let me see it."

"It's private."

"I won't read it."

Hector made no move to remove the paper from his pocket.

"Why did you take the list?"

Neither of them answered.

"I know you want to use it to incriminate Nathan."

"No." Priscilla's protest lacked conviction.

"Give it to me, and I'll forget all about it."

"No." That was Hector.

"Either you give me the list, or I'll tell Nathan the minute I get back."

"You won't if you don't leave here."

"What do you propose to do? Keep me locked up here until you've ruined Nathan? Or something worse?"

"No," Priscilla said, fright causing her to lose any desire to remain silent. "Hector wouldn't hurt you. He only wanted to give the note to Shays so he'll—"

"Shut up!" Hector commanded.

Now Delilah understood. "You're the one who informed on Shattuck. You've been spying for both sides." A flash of scorn hot enough to scorch Hector's cheeks flashed from her eyes. "I could understand your helping either side as long as you believed in its goals, but to lie to both of them!"

"I didn't lie."

"You accepted their trust. It's the same thing." She seemed to have difficulty finding adequate words to describe her feelings of disgust. "If Reuben ever finds out what you've done, he'll shoot you. As for your friends . . . I imagine you'll end up wishing Reuben had gotten you first."

"Nobody will know anything about it because you won't leave here." Hector pounced on Delilah and dragged her to a low-backed chair and forced her to sit down. She didn't even try to escape. She just glared at him scornfully.

"Are you going to kill me?"

"Of course he isn't," Priscilla answered when Hector didn't reply immediately.

"I'll keep you here while I decide." He began to tie Delilah to the chair with a sheet pulled from the bed.

"You'd be better advised to let me go. Nathan will search the countryside inch by inch when he finds I'm missing."

"Why should he care about a serving wench?" Hector asked sarcastically.

"Because he's asked this *serving wench* to be his wife." Hector stared at Delilah in patent disbelief.

"Ask Priscilla if you don't believe me. He even kicked Serena out of the house because she was rude to me."

"He'd kill you himself if you hurt her," Priscilla said.

"Nathan Trent?" Hector laughed cynically. "He's too much of a dandified fop to box his own shadow."

"You're wrong," Priscilla said. "He may seem quiet, but he's a dangerous man."

"If Nathan doesn't get you, Reuben will," Delilah said, making no attempt to get away from Hector. "I don't imagine you think he's too foppish to fight you."

The look on Hector's face showed how much he feared Reuben.

"Of course if I can get that paper back in Nathan's desk before he finds it missing, nobody need ever know it was taken," Delilah said.

"Why would you want to protect us?" Priscilla asked.

"I don't. I'm interested only in protecting Nathan," Delilah explained. "If people think he has anything to do with spying, even if it's not true, they'll never accept him."

"But why should you care?"

"No woman wants her husband to be an object of suspicion and dislike."

"What will you do for us?" Hector asked.

"Isn't keeping Nathan and Reuben from killing you enough?" Delilah asked. Hector flushed.

"Hector didn't do this without a good reason," Priscilla said, equally willing to defend the man she loved. "He was only trying to get back some of what Noah and Lucius took from him."

"Why didn't you go to Nathan?" Delilah demanded. "Surely Nathan would help the man you mean to marry."

"How did you know?" Priscilla asked.

"No woman would do what you've done unless she loved a man very much," Delilah said in a softer tone.

"Her mother won't let her marry a pauper," Hector said, his broken pride manifest in his unsteady voice.

"Then don't ask her. Talk to Nathan, work something out, but let me return that note before it's too late."

"You won't tell anyone?" Priscilla asked.

"I'll never tell a soul unless it's to protect Nathan."

Priscilla looked undecided.

"Are you crazy?" Hector exclaimed. "We can't let her go."

"I thought this was a mistake from the beginning," Priscilla said. "I begged you to talk to Nathan, but no, you had a better way. What has it gained us? Not one damned thing. Delilah's right. If people find out what you've done, they'll kill you. Maybe not Reuben or Nathan, but somebody will."

"Maybe I should have talked to Nathan, but it's too late now. We can't let her go. Come on." He grabbed Priscilla's arm and pulled her toward the door.

"We can't leave her here. She'll freeze to death."

"She should have thought of that before she followed you," Hector said, pushing Priscilla out the door before him. He turned and faced Delilah. "Let Nathan comb the countryside. By the time he finds this place, you won't be able to tell him anything."

Delilah tried to pull her hands free, but she'd been so confident Hector and Priscilla would give her the note she hadn't noticed he had tied her so securely she couldn't move her arms or her feet. She looked around the cabin hoping to get an idea about how to free herself, but except for the bed, the cabin was bare.

She tried to stand up and pull her hands over the back of the chair, but Hector had tied them to one of the slats. She couldn't free her hands unless she could find a way to break the slat.

With a painstaking effort, Delilah jumped her chair in the direction of the doorway. If she could beat the slat against the door frame, maybe she could crack it. One attempt convinced Delilah she'd break her hands long before she broke the slat. Winded, she slumped in the chair while she considered her problem.

Clearly she could not untie the sheet. Therefore, she

295

had to attract someone's attention and keep herself warm while she waited for Nathan to rescue her. By hopping around the room, she was able to locate some matchsticks on a shelf. It was impossible to reach them with her hands, but she nudged them with her nose until several fell to the floor.

Before she could even think of the pain it would cause, Delilah turned her chair over.

The sheets bit into her wrists and ankles, but instead of thinking about the pain, Delilah twisted her chair around until the matches were within reach of her fingers. It wasn't difficult to pick them up, but she didn't know if she could strike one. A fire was already laid. If she lighted a matchstick, her next problem would be to ignite one of the slivers of lighting wood next to the fireplace and somehow insert it in the grate between the pieces of wood.

That was a lot of ifs, and everything depended on her being able to light a matchstick. Ignoring the pain in her wrists, Delilah maneuvered her chair toward the fireplace until she could reach one of the bricks. She would use its rough surface to light the matchstick.

The first one broke. So did the second, but she managed to light the third. However, once it was lighted, she was unable to pick up the piece of lighting wood. Just as she was about to drop the matchstick, let it burn out on the floor, and try again, she smelled burning cloth. Somehow her wrists were twisted about so the match flame reached the sheet. She couldn't see what part of the sheet was being burned, but if she could burn it through, maybe she could free herself.

She could only guess when the flame went out. She broke three more matchsticks before she lighted another. She could hear cloth tear when she pulled with her full strength, but it held. Delilah used up all her matchsticks before she was able to light another.

And still the sheet held.

296

She began the agonizing journey back to the shelf. From it, she dislodged two more matchsticks. This was her last chance.

She broke the first one. She broke the second as well. Her only choice now was to search around for one of the broken pieces and hope it was long enough to burn through the rest of the sheet. She had to roll the chair until it was practically on her hands before she could reach a broken matchstick. But was it enough to burn through the rest of the sheet?

Luck was with her. She was able to light it without breaking it again. Soon the gratifying smell of burning cotton assailed her nostrils. She held the matchstick in place until it scorched her fingers. Dropping the charred end, she said a short prayer and pulled with all her strength.

She was rewarded with a satisfying rip. Two more tugs and Delilah's hands were free of the chair slat. With great effort, she was able to raise her arms over the back of the chair. Tucking her body into a tight knot, Delilah passed her feet through her arms and brought them in front of her. In a matter of moments she had untied her ankles. She had just cut her wrists free with the knife she'd found on the shelf next to the matchsticks when Priscilla entered the cabin.

The two women stared at each other.

"So you got yourself free."

"Yes."

"What were you going to do?"

"Why did you come back?"

Priscilla hesitated then held out her hand. "To give you this." It was the note.

"Does Hector know?"

Priscilla shook her head. "He's sleeping. I made a copy. This is the original." The note had the additions and deletions in Nathan's hand. "You promise you won't say anything to anyone."

"Not unless I must to protect Nathan."

Priscilla handed the note to Delilah. "I'll give you the key when I get home."

"You're not coming?"

"I have to stay. If Hector knew I gave you the original, he'd follow you."

"He's not worthy of you," Delilah said.

"He's the only man I want."

Loving Nathan as she did, Delilah could understand. "Don't stay too long," she said, and left without a backward look.

It was past three o'clock when Delilah finally crawled between the sheets on her bed. She meant to stay awake until Priscilla returned, but she fell asleep less than an hour later.

Nathan wakened her with a kiss.

Delilah struggled to fight through the bonds of sleep, aware of the softness of lips upon her own, of feathering kisses across her eyelids, of the soft brush of his warm breath against her skin. Her arms encircled his neck, imprisoning him. He laughed softly.

"Open your eyes."

"I can't," she murmured sleepily.

"Don't you want to look at me when I talk to you?"

"I've memorized every part of your face." Something nagged at the back of her mind. Something she wanted to tell him.

Nathan sank down on the side of the bed. "Very well, lie there like a sleeping Venus. Just listen. I have to be away for most of the day, but I'll be back before nightfall. Will you be waiting when I return?"

That was what she wanted to tell him. "I'll always be here. I'll never go away."

"I hope you mean that," Nathan said, his kisses tender and sweet.

"I do." The mists of sleep began to close in on Delilah. "I have something else to tell you," she said, trying to free her brain of the fog which clouded it.

"You can tell me later."

"I must tell you now." But it was hard to wake up. Easier to sink back into oblivion.

"It'll keep until tonight. I've never seen you look so tired. I'll tell Mrs. Stebbens not to wake you."

"It's important," Delilah said, but she was already drifting away.

"Tell me tonight," Nathan said.

He kissed Delilah back to sleep.

Delilah came awake slowly. She lay in bed, eyes closed, and stretched luxuriously. Her legs ached as never before. What on earth could she have done to make her so stiff?

Then she remembered Priscilla and Hector and the note.

Her eyes flew open. The sun poured in her window. It must be close to noon. Delilah jumped out of bed and dressed at a record speed. She was driven by pangs of guilt at leaving Mrs. Stebbens and Lester to cook and serve breakfast alone. Then she remembered Nathan would be gone for the day, and she slowed down. Priscilla and Serena never came down to breakfast when Nathan was absent.

Still she had her work, she had to get the key to the desk from Priscilla so she could return the note, and she had to tell Nathan she loved him more than anything else in the world.

She pinned her cap to her hair, adjusted the neckline of her dress, and hurried downstairs to face Mrs. Stebbens's probing questions, Lester's inescapable scolding, and Tommy's complete indifference.

Chapter Twenty

Delilah was irritated. Even though Serena hadn't gotten up until noon, she had immediately sent her off on an errand. Though Delilah had been allowed to take the buggy, she still got behind in her work. Everything seemed to fall to her today. Worst of all, she couldn't find Priscilla. The young woman had disappeared; no one knew where she had gone. Desperate to return the paper before Nathan returned, Delilah ventured to speak to Serena.

"Priscilla's whereabouts are no concern of yours."

"There is something I must ask her."

"Tell me. I'm completely in her confidence."

"It's rather private."

"What can you possibly have to say of a private nature to my daughter?"

It required all of Delilah's ingenuity to get away without telling Nathan's aunt everything. Then, to completely ruin her day, Priscilla came in five minutes before dinner and rushed up to her room to change. Delilah probably wouldn't be able to return the paper until everyone had gone to bed. She hoped Nathan didn't look for it this evening.

The back door to the kitchen burst open, and Nathan strode in, mud-spattered from riding over countryside still soggy from yesterday's rain. Nonetheless, Delilah thought him the most beautiful sight she'd ever seen.

Oblivious of everyone else, he swept her into his arms and kissed her soundly.

She blushed furiously.

"I thought I'd better warn you to set a place for me," he said.

"Your place is already set," Delilah said as she tried unsuccessfully to wriggle out of his arms.

"What do you mean coming in the back door?" Mrs. Stebbens asked, scandalized. "If people get to hear of it, they'll think you're touched in the head."

"I wanted to kiss Delilah without having to explain to my aunt and cousin," Nathan said without the least show of embarrassment.

"In that case, it's all right," Mrs. Stebbens said. "Anybody who knows Mrs. Noyes can understand that."

Nathan took a more secure hold on Delilah. "What was it you wanted to tell me this morning?"

"Not now," she hissed.

"What did you say?" Nathan teased.

"I'll tell you later," she said, still in a whisper.

"I suppose it's the cold in my ears, but I can't understand you."

"There's nothing to understand," Delilah snapped, out of patience with his joking. "It's been so long I've forgotten. Besides, I'd never talk confidences here, not with three pairs of ears straining to hear every word I say."

"If this meat stays on the spit much longer, it's not going to be fit to eat," Mrs. Stebbens announced. "Lester's ready to ring the bell. You'd better hurry if you want to change your clothes."

Nathan didn't want to leave.

Mrs. Stebbens vacillated. "Of course I could hold off a spell if you wanted to have a quick chat."

"He may, but I don't," Delilah said. "He took the whole day to get home. He can wait another hour to hear what I have to say."

" 'Tis a cruel maid you be," said Mrs. Stebbens, grinning from ear to ear. "Take care he doesn't seek consolation elsewhere."

"If he gets discouraged that easily, he's welcome to look anywhere he pleases," Delilah snapped, becoming truly angry. Didn't anybody understand that she wanted to talk to Nathan alone, that this was not something she could joke about? She wrenched herself out of his arms.

"I've got work to do. And you have to get dressed."

Nathan looked a little surprised and hurt.

Mrs. Stebbens started to make a remark, but the expression on Delilah's face caused her to change her mind.

"You'd better hurry up and get dressed, Mr. Nathan. I think I smell the haddock. It's about done."

"In the library, after dinner?" Nathan asked.

Delilah looked a little less irate. "When I've finished helping Mrs. Stebbens clear away."

"Is it worth waiting that long?" Imps danced in his eyes again.

"Nathan Trent, if you can't wait a few minutes for something that'll affect the rest of your life, then you'd best not waste any more time."

Nathan studied her so closely Delilah couldn't prevent a telltale flush from flaming her cheeks.

"Change your clothes before I change my mind."

Nathan grabbed her and kissed her soundly again. "Will it mean I can do this every night?"

"Get out of here this minute, or I'll take a rolling pin to you," Delilah threatened, but she was smiling too broadly for her words to have any meaning, at least the one she'd intended.

"I've decided I'm not hungry."

"And I've changed my mind," Delilah exclaimed. "You'd exhaust the patience of a saint, and God knows I'm no saint."

"I'm a sinner, too. Can we sin together?"

Delilah took refuge in the larder and locked the door behind her.

"I think you'd better go," Mrs. Stebbens said, grinning more broadly than a proud mama. "You've flustered her so much she may leave Lester to do the serving alone."

"Wish me happy, Mrs. Stebbens. Wish me very happy."

"I do, sir. We all do. Now get along. Other people have to eat even if you've lost your appetite."

Mrs. Stebbens chuckled as Nathan left the kitchen. "You mark my words, there'll be wedding bells before the month's out."

"There'll be murder when Mrs. Noyes hears about it," Lester prophesied. "She ain't never going to let herself be displaced by no serving maid, not if she dies for it."

"She won't have any say. You knock on that door and tell Delilah it's all right to come out. Unless you've a hankering to serve the dinner by yourself."

"The old master must be turning in his grave to see what's going on in his house."

"He's turning all right," Mrs. Stebbens declared, emphatically, "but it's on the devil's roasting spit. If anybody ever went straight to hell, it was Ezra Buel."

The door opened and they both stared in shocked silence. Serena had entered the kitchen.

"Mr. Trent has returned home. Be so good as to set a place for him." She spoke with such condescension, such hauteur, Mrs. Stebbens was moved to respond.

"Mr. Nathan's already been to the kitchen with his orders. Dinner's to be put back ten minutes."

Serena cast Mrs. Stebbens a fulminating glance and stalked out.

"That's done it," Lester said. "You're in for it now."

"I'm not in for anything, and if that old crow doesn't know I'm more important to Mr. Nathan than she is, it's about time she did. And that ain't a spot on what Delilah is to him."

303

Delilah thought the meal would never come to an end. Serena seemed determined to postpone each course until every dish arrived at the table cold or overcooked. Priscilla, who hadn't bothered to pay attention to Nathan in weeks, acted as she had when Delilah had first come to Maple Hill. And Nathan kept making leading comments to Delilah, which caused her to blush, Priscilla to watch her covertly, and Serena to glare at her with lethal menace.

She nearly sighed with relief when she heard the furious pounding on the front door.

"Why would anyone come visiting during dinner?" Serena asked after Lester had been dispatched to discover the meaning of the disturbance.

"They probably heard about our superb cook," Nathan said, fully enjoying a beef brisket Delilah had worked two weeks to help Mrs. Stebbens learn to prepare to perfection. "I didn't find anyone in Boston who could cook English dishes as well as this. Where did Uncle Ezra ever find her?"

That question was destined to remain unanswered. Lucius Clarke, followed by Noah Hubbard, Tom Oliver, Asa Warner, Eli Beck, and a half-dozen others burst into the dining room despite Lester's efforts to convince them to wait in the drawing room.

"They've closed another court, and Shays has sent out another letter," Lucius announced without preamble. "Listen to this:

The seeds of war are now sown. I request you and every man to supply men and provision to relieve us with a reinforcement. We are determined to carry our point. Our cause is yours. Don't give yourselves a rest and let us die here, for we are all brethren.

304

"Does that sound like a man who wants peace or one who means to start a war?"

"I think we should go into the drawing room," Nathan said. It was impossible to continue their meal with so many men squeezed into the room.

"How can you care where you are?" Lucius demanded.

"Because I can't think in this crush," Nathan said. "If you wish my attention, you'll have to come to the drawing room. Delilah, bring some ale for our visitors."

"Behold!" Noah shouted as though he had just become aware of Delilah's presence. "There stands the spy."

Every head in the room turned to Delilah, the men's looks so angry, so dangerous, it was all she could do to stand her ground.

"Anyone charging a member of my household with treason had best have proof," Nathan said. The look Delilah knew so well affected even such an emotional person as Noah Hubbard.

"But our spy said so," Noah insisted.

Nathan ignored Noah. "Into the drawing room. Lester can bring the ale," he said to Delilah just before he left.

"I'll bring it. I've done nothing, and I'll not run away."

"I wonder what he means by 'our spy'?" Serena said to Priscilla. "I would give half of everything I own to prove that little slut a liar."

"I'm sure Delilah would never sell information to the regulators, but she was in the library last night."

"How do you know?"

"I heard her."

"Why didn't you tell me?"

"Nathan said she could use it any time she liked. I figured she went down to get a book."

Serena jumped to her feet and ran to the library as fast as her feet would carry her, too quickly to see the smile of malicious triumph on Priscilla's face.

305

"Now what about this letter of Shays?" Nathan asked as soon as the men reached the drawing room.

"It's not so much the letter," Lucius explained, "but the fact he named a committee of seventeen, mostly former officers in the Continental Army, to raise companies in the county of Hampshire. They're all to be under Shays's command."

"As long as the legislature does nothing about his petition, it was to be expected."

"But those seventeen are the very ones on the list I gave you."

"How can you know that?"

"Our spy told us," Noah chimed in. "He said Shays joked that Lucius Clarke had chosen his lieutenants for him. There's only one copy of that list, and I saw you lock it in your drawer. If Shays knows about it, he had to learn about it from someone in this house."

A coldness encircled Nathan's heart. He tried to keep his mind from thinking what it was impossible not to admit. He tried to tell himself there was an obvious explanation for all of this, one that had nothing to do with Delilah, but fear had taken hold in his heart and was rapidly putting down roots.

"Numerous people have seen that list," Nathan pointed out. "Names have been crossed out and added several times."

The doors opened, and Lester followed Delilah into the room with ale and mugs.

"Lucius Clarke thinks you took a list from my desk," Nathan said to Delilah as she set the tray of pewter mugs down on a gateleg table.

"I never took anything from your desk," Delilah said, looking at Nathan rather than Noah. "How could I, without a key?"

"It was a list of the insurgent leaders."

"I don't know the contents of any such list." And she didn't. She had refused to even look at the piece of pa-

306

per before she'd thrust it into the small drawer in the drum table next to her bed.

"It doesn't have to be Delilah," Nathan said.

"Who else could it be?" demanded Noah.

"It's possible your spy is either misinformed or lying," Nathan said. "If he's lying to Shays, he could be lying to you as well."

Lucius and Asa Warner couldn't ignore the logic of Nathan's argument, but Noah would have none of it. "I've known this man since he was born. He's as loyal as anybody in this room."

"Who is he?" Nathan asked.

"I won't tell, not even if Delilah and your man there were to leave. I don't trust you, and I don't care who knows it."

"What reason would I have to help Shays?"

"What reason do you have to keep visiting all those farmers? Most of them are insurgents."

"I've figured out how they can pay their debts and make a little money for me at the same time."

"I don't believe it," Noah said. "Ain't nobody paying debts."

"How?" Asa asked.

"By making use of what they can do," Nathan explained. "I suspect the source of Noah's distrust has to do with my taking over Gilbert Eells's credit and demanding payment in cash."

"You tried to ruin me," Noah cried.

"What did I do that you haven't done to dozens of others?"

"This isn't solving the question of who's spying on us," Lucius said.

"I don't think there is any question of spying, not if that list is all you've got," Nathan said. Noah tried to protest, but Nathan cut him off. "Everybody knows the rebel leaders by now. Lucius has accosted most of them in the street. Maybe that's what Shays meant."

Nathan's argument was too logical to ignore. Talk had been general between both sides for months.

"Besides, what would be the point of giving Shays a list of his own men?"

"He'll know who we suspect," Noah suggested.

"He knows that already," Asa insisted. "As Nathan said, they don't hesitate to show their faces. I say we forget about spies. The more important question is what are we going to do about Shays's call to arms."

"I say we ask the governor to raise the militia," someone said. "And they got to come from the eastern counties. Nobody's going to fire on relatives and friends. We've already seen that."

The discussion was joined. Nathan relaxed and turned to Delilah. He winked surreptitiously. She turned away to fill more mugs rather than let anyone see the answering smile she knew danced in her eyes. Her eyes gleamed with admiration for the way Nathan had handled Noah's accusation, and her heart swelled with pride.

It also beat so hard it seemed to throb in her throat. She had to find a way to return that paper tonight. She couldn't go through another evening of tension like this.

The drawing-room doors opened with such a resounding crash that the discussions, several of them quite heated, stopped in mid-sentence. Serena Noyes stood in the doorway, a look of triumph transforming her from a defeated middle-aged woman into a gloating witch. One hand held a piece of paper aloft. The other clasped a bent knife.

Delilah stood as though turned to stone. She knew what was written on that piece of paper. A glance at Nathan told her he did too.

"I hold the proof right in my hands that this Jezebel has betrayed those who clothed and housed her," Serena announced, her voice shaking with emotion.

Noah Hubbard snatched the note from Serena's hand.

"Where did you find this?" he demanded, when he had read it.

Serena pointed dramatically at Delilah. "In a drawer in the table next to her bed."

Nathan turned to Delilah, the shock of betrayal distorting the features she knew so well. She wanted to suspend time so she could explain, she wanted to remove that horrible expression from his face. But events rushed forward carrying her along.

"How do we know it's the right list?" Asa asked.

"All the names are on it," Serena said.

"But who wrote them? She might have been making a list of the names she heard us mention."

"Is that your hand?" Noah demanded of Nathan.

Nathan continued to stare in Delilah's direction. Yet she could tell his gaze wasn't focused on her; rather, he was looking at something only he could see.

"Is it your handwriting?" Noah asked again.

For a moment it seemed Nathan still hadn't heard Noah, but then he turned to look at the paper held up before him. He nodded his head.

"There!" Serena was triumphant.

"Did you give it to her?" Asa asked.

Nathan turned toward Delilah once more. For one horrible moment she thought he was going to lie to protect her.

"No one gave it to me," Delilah said, tearing her gaze away from Nathan's. "I found it."

"Where?"

"She got it from Nathan's desk," Serena cried. "I found this in her room, too." Serena held up a knife with a bent blade.

"What's that for?" Noah asked.

"Come, I'll show you."

Everyone poured out of the drawing room behind Serena. Delilah didn't know what would be found, but she knew it would be something to damn her even more

309

thoroughly, if that were possible. She looked at Nathan, but he wasn't looking at her now. He was staring at the people streaming out of the room in Serena's wake.

"Nathan, I didn't lie. I didn't take that list."

He couldn't speak. Couldn't move. He was in the grip of a rage at once more powerful and more all-consuming than the fury that had consumed him for months after Lady Sarah Mendlow's betrayal. Every piercing emotion, every stab of pain, every agonizing moment of that time years before swept over him, suffocating him like the incoming tide. It blocked his ability to think, destroyed his reason, and deadened him to anything but his own great suffering.

"Look at me," Delilah begged when he acted as though she hadn't spoken.

But the look Nathan turned in her direction made the next words die in her throat. She had never seen such a blaze of fury in anyone's eyes. It was as though he hated everyone in the world, as though he wanted to kill every person he could get his hands on, himself included.

Delilah didn't know what to do, what to say to reach him. The fire in his eyes told her she couldn't, to stay away. It warned her he was dangerously close to losing control.

Delilah had never been more terrified in her life, but when he turned from her to follow the others into the library, she ran after him. She wouldn't hang back like a coward.

The sight that met her eyes shocked her. Someone had used a knife to hack a way into Nathan's desk.

"Priscilla!" The word escaped involuntarily as she whipped around to seek out Serena's daughter. Priscilla stood just behind her mother, a dogged look of surprise on her face.

"Did you do this?" Noah demanded.

Nathan seemed to struggle a moment before he could drag his mind from its dark thoughts. "This is my

310

house," he said in a soft but dangerous voice. "No one interrogates my servants."

"I didn't do it," Delilah stated. The look in Nathan's eyes was tearing her apart.

"Did you take the list from my desk?"

Delilah wanted to keep her promise to Priscilla, but she was fighting for her happiness. Besides, Priscilla had already broken their agreement by ruining the desk and telling Serena about the note.

"No. I have never been in your desk."

"But Serena found it in your room," Noah burst out.

One look from Nathan quelled Noah.

"After all that talk of spies last night, I couldn't sleep," Delilah explained. "I came down to the library to get a book to read. I heard someone coming after me, and I hid behind the settle. It was Priscilla."

"Liar!" cried Serena.

"I never left my room," Priscilla said.

"She took a paper from an inner drawer. I followed her when she left the house. She took it to Hector Clayhart." Delilah had to raise her voice to be heard over gasps of surprise, murmurs of disbelief, and the shuffling movement of nervous people ill at ease. "Hector wanted something in your handwriting so Shays would trust him."

"Aha! We've got you there," Noah shouted with glee. "Hector is our spy, has been from the first. He's the one who told us the leak was coming from this house."

"Of course he did. Priscilla's taking him information. He's spying for both sides."

The clamor of astonishment and skepticism grew louder.

"How can you let that girl vilify your own flesh and blood?" Serena exclaimed.

"Why didn't you tell me?" Nathan asked.

He didn't believe her. He wouldn't let himself. Delilah could see it in his eyes, hear it in his voice, see it in the rigidity of his stance.

"I wanted to, but you left before I woke. Besides, I thought it would be better if I just put it back. As long as no one knew, no one would be hurt. It wasn't the information they wanted, just something in your handwriting."

"Why should Priscilla do a thing like that for Hector?"

"She's going to marry him," Delilah said.

"She is not!" Serena declared over the hiss of whispered exclamations. "You have my oath Priscilla hasn't set eyes on Hector Clayhart in two years. I won't allow my daughter to throw herself away on a penniless farmer."

"Hector's been making up to Miriam Dickinson," Tom Oliver said. "Her ma said he's been haunting her doorstep for a month."

"I'm not in love with Hector," Priscilla said, "and I didn't leave the house last night."

"She's lying," Delilah said as calmly as she could. "I followed her down the river path. She met Hector in one of his cabins."

"Nathan, are you going to stand here and let that *female* accuse your cousin of having midnight assignations?"

"But I saw them," Delilah insisted. "She was there."

"I never left my room," Priscilla repeated.

Delilah sensed that Nathan didn't believe her. Priscilla had trapped her so effectively her story sounded false.

That made Delilah so angry she started to shake. Though why she should waste her time getting furious over Priscilla's treachery when her whole life was disintegrating right in front of her she didn't know. Nothing Priscilla could do mattered when Nathan stared at her as if she were something to be trod underfoot.

How could he love her as much as he'd said he did and not believe her? She had always thought when you fell in love, you had complete, unquestioning faith. She

312

felt that way about him. Why couldn't he feel the same way about her?

His disbelief hurt more than she could ever have imagined. But with the pain came anger. She didn't deserve this. If she hadn't been trying to protect him, none of this would be happening. If he believed her, it still wouldn't be happening.

"How do you explain the desk?" Nathan asked. His eyes were cold, empty, the eyes of a stranger.

"Why ask me?" She couldn't keep the angry edge from her voice. "You don't believe anything I've said."

"There's too much evidence against you," Noah said.

"Why can't you trust me?" Delilah asked Nathan.

Trust her! God help him, he had trusted her. He had believed in her implicitly, had offered to give up everything he possessed for her. He had gambled everything on her love, her loyalty, her truthfulness. Once again he had been made to look a fool.

Nathan could almost hear Lady Sarah Mendlow laughing at him. He shook his head, but he kept seeing her, hearing her false accusations, feeling the bitterness of ostracism. Anger spurted in him like a hot geyser. He'd never trust a woman again.

Struggling to put aside his personal emotions, he strove to see Delilah's treachery in the same light as the others. His private anguish must remain buried forever in his heart.

"You once said you would choose Reuben over me," he said, addressing Delilah as soon as he had himself under control. "I didn't hold that against you, but this goes beyond repeating information you might overhear. You've lied, stolen, destroyed property, and tried to ruin the good names of others. I can't have anyone in my home who would do that."

His words stunned her. Somehow she had thought she would have a chance to talk with him alone, to convince him she was telling the truth. To have everything be-

313

tween them severed with such horrifying finality pierced her to the core.

"Nathan, please . . ."

But he didn't hear her; he didn't see her. The wall of anger rose between them until he stared straight through her as though she no longer existed.

"I will have Jacob Pobodie take you home first thing tomorrow morning. Be ready at daybreak. Until then, stay in your room."

"*Nathan* . . ."

The cry came from the depths of her soul, but Nathan hardened himself against it. He had thought nothing could be worse than the agony he suffered, but the look of pain and despair in Delilah's eyes before she turned and ran up the stairs was almost more than he could bear.

The worst irony of all was to be forced to play out this comedy of errors, this tragedy of spirit, before Serena and Noah Hubbard. All the people who disliked him, despised him for being British and owning more of their country than they did, could enjoy seeing him made the fool. He who was so shrewd, who thought he knew Americans better than the Americans themselves. Well, they had their laugh now.

Nathan schooled his features to a look of indifference. He hadn't been brought up in England for nothing. He hadn't suffered more grief than any of them without learning to show an impassive face to the world. He would play out this scene without letting them know he was dying inside if it cost him every ounce of will he had left.

"If you would care to continue your discussion, I suggest we return to the drawing room."

But the mood was broken. Even Noah Hubbard felt the need to be free of the oppressive atmosphere. A few stayed long enough to finish their ale, but Nathan ushered the last guest to the door only fifteen minutes after

Delilah had rushed from the library.

"Serena, I wish to speak to you in the drawing room. Alone," he added when Priscilla started to accompany her mother.

"I don't see why," Priscilla replied. She seemed prepared to argue.

"Don't try my temper any further tonight." Nathan bit each word off sharply. "I'll have something to say to you in the morning. Go to your room."

"I will not be ordered about," Priscilla answered sullenly.

"Go or be carried."

Priscilla took one look at the cold fury in Nathan's blue eyes and hurried up the staircase.

"Now," Nathan said to Serena as he closed the doors behind him, "I have just a few words to say. Listen well, because they are the last you will ever hear from me."

"What do you—"

Nathan ignored her interruption. "I told you once before I would not tolerate your meddling in my affairs. I also told you never to search another room in my house."

"I never entered your room."

Nathan did not respond to her statement. "On numerous occasions you have demonstrated your unwillingness, or inability, to abide by my wishes. And you have done everything in your power to discredit Delilah even though I ordered you to do otherwise."

"But she's a spy. A traitor."

"I don't care what she is!" Nathan exploded, his tight control unraveling like a frayed rope. "I love her. Can't you understand what that means? Or are you so twisted inside all you can do is sit in your room swilling brandy and thinking of ways to make other people's lives as miserable and hate-filled as your own?"

Nathan turned his back on Serena. Not to hide the tears which welled up in his eyes despite his efforts to

315

hold them back. He was afraid he couldn't look at his aunt without strangling her.

"I wanted to marry her. I've never wanted anything so much in my entire life. I would have sacrificed Maple Hill, the money, everything for her."

He whipped around to face Serena, a look of such ferocious rage on his face she shrank back in terror.

"But you ruined all that, you and your bitch of a daughter. Who cared about that list? Everybody knew what was in it. It wouldn't have made any difference if she had handed it to Shays herself."

Terror prevented Serena from uttering a sound.

"You couldn't rest until you destroyed her. But you also ruined yourself," Nathan said savagely. "Until the moment you die, I will never let you forget, not even for one moment, what you've done tonight."

His hands snaked out and grabbed Serena by the throat. She tried to scream, but his thumbs cut off the sound. "I ought to kill you, but I'm not going to. Instead I'm going to make you live in a kind of misery you've never imagined."

He released Serena, and she collapsed into a chair.

"You're going to live on a farm in Vermont. I'll give you just enough money to survive—if you work very hard."

"No, please. You can't—"

"There won't be anybody to help you except one old man. You are not to leave the farm or try to communicate with me in any manner. You will take nothing from this house but your clothing and the jewelry your husband gave you."

Serena sobbed uncontrollably.

"If you write me, if you try to see me, I will cut off your funds."

"Priscilla—"

"She will remain here until I decide what to do about her."

"But Delilah stole the list."

"I know!" Nathan cried, the anguish in his heart spilling out in those words. "But why did you have to tell me? Didn't you know I would have given you Maple Hill and everything in it if you had burned that piece of paper rather than bring it in here tonight?" He picked up a small drop-leaf table and threw it against the wall. Serena's scream was accompanied by the sound of splintering wood and breaking glass.

"But you had to expose her, you had to do your utmost to convince everyone she was a traitor. Well, what do you have, Aunt Serena, for all your scheming and conniving and changing orders behind my back? What do you have for all your hating and your lying and your cheating? You have exactly what I have. Nothing! Not a goddamned thing!"

Nathan cursed violently.

"Get out of my sight. If you don't, I may kill you yet."

Serena fled.

Nathan remained. For a long time he simply stared through the open doorway after his aunt. Finally, he closed the door, poured some ale into a mug, and took it over to the window. But he didn't drink.

So it had happened again. A different time, a different place, a different woman, but he had fallen victim just as easily as before. And just as publicly. He would once more be the butt of tavern jokes and polite tittle-tattle. Once a fool, always a fool.

Damn, damn, damn! Was there no woman who really was what she seemed? Were they all Delilah's? Would he ever learn to stop handing them the means to destroy him before they even asked?

He wasn't sure what hurt more, the loss of Delilah or the loss of an ideal. Maybe it was impossible to decide because this time the two were inseparable. The agony had been intense with Lady Sarah Mendlow because she

317

was his first love, and because the destruction of his trust had been intertwined with the destruction of his father's business. But after the hurt had gone away, he had realized he'd been in love with an image, an ideal which had very little to do with the woman herself. He would always despise Sarah for the motive behind and the manner of her rejection, but he knew the mistake of thinking her worthy of his love was his own.

But Delilah was different. He had started by being wary of her, wanting to stay as far away from her as possible. It was Delilah who had convinced him she was genuine. From her words, her deeds, the way other people reacted to her, he had come to believe he had found a woman who would always be honest with the man she loved even if it cost her dearly.

God knows he had given her plenty of opportunity to take advantage of him, and she had always refused. She had even sacrificed her reputation to save his. And no matter how badly Serena had treated her, she had shown compassion for that hate-filled woman. Her loyalty and love for her family had been unswerving. Fool that he'd been, he had believed she might someday come to feel the same way about him.

And all the while she'd been waiting for the chance to steal a list nobody cared about. All her smiles were lies. All her promises were lies. Everything he'd thought of her had been only a fabrication. It was all false, base, a portrayal to be cast aside as soon as her real object was achieved. Never mind that he had come to love this deceptive portrayal, that he had embraced it with little hesitation. It had nearly destroyed him and his hopes for building a new life in America.

Because nothing was as important as that little piece of paper.

Nobody would ever have paid any attention to the damned thing if it hadn't been for Noah Hubbard. When he'd waved that slip of paper about, his face wreathed in triumph, Nathan had felt an almost mad compulsion to strangle the man. Only the presence of the others had prevented him from beating Hubbard until he begged for mercy. But it wasn't just Noah. He hated them all, them and their greed and stupidity and their cowardly fear of a few farmers armed with little more than their own courage.

But hate requires continuous fuel for its fires, and as the night dragged by, Nathan exhausted his fodder. He was left with the skeleton of his hopes and the ashes of despair.

For hours he stood, a motionless figure, staring out into the black night. The ale turned warm and still he didn't move. First one candle guttered. Then another. He didn't stir. The last candle flickered and went out. Still he didn't move. When dawn came, Nathan remained standing before the window.

The first sounds of movement in the house caused him to tense, but when no one attempted to interrupt his solitude, the muscles in his shoulders relaxed. Then a buggy rounded the corner of the house, and he tensed all over again.

Delilah. She was going home.

Nathan watched her until the buggy disappeared into the woods. Then, with a vicious curse, he flung the still-full glass of ale through the window and rushed from the house out to the stables. Minutes later he was riding at a gallop in the direction of Hector Clayhart's farm.

Chapter Twenty-one

"He hasn't eaten enough to keep a bird alive, not since she left," Mrs. Stebbens said to Lester, "and Priscilla doesn't eat at all as far as I can tell. I don't know why I bother to cook."

"She avoids him," Lester said. "Ever since he sent her mamma away, Mrs. Noyes screaming like a madwoman, she's been scared to death of him."

"I can't say I blame her. The way he goes about looking like he'd like to cut your liver out is enough to give a body a nasty turn."

"I don't see you acting any different," Lester said. It rankled that Mrs. Stebbens should feel comfortable around a man he feared.

"It doesn't do to go about quaking in your boots," Mrs. Stebbens explained. "Encourages people to act like tyrants. You ought to know. That Mrs. Noyes was the worst I've seen."

"I wonder how the poor lady is doing." Lester had a soft spot for Serena. She had given him importance.

"She'll make out. So will her daughter. It's Mister Nathan I'm worried about."

"Him!" Lester exclaimed. "He's as strong as a bull and twice as mean."

"It's the strong ones that suffer the worst when things go to pieces," Mrs. Stebbens stated. "They're not used to it, you see. They don't know how to depend on anybody. Your Mrs. Noyes, now, she knows how to squeeze a body for every last drop. She even twisted that dried-up piece of rind Noah Hubbard around her finger."

"I wonder what he's going to do about Miss Priscilla."

"I don't know, but if I was her, I'd be looking about me for a husband."

Nathan pushed his account books away. It was ironic. If things continued on their present course, he would collect most of his debts in cash without having to confiscate any more property.

And all because of Delilah.

He couldn't even allow her name to enter his thoughts without feeling the pain which tortured him day in and day out. There was no place he could go in the house and not be reminded of her—the way she'd looked in that blue gown, the way she'd smiled at him when Serena wasn't looking, the way she'd blushed when he'd caught her looking at his body. His desk had been repaired, but he had only to look at the drawer that had been forced to hear her denial.

That denial hurt him the most. Why had she lied to him? He didn't care about the note. Neither did he care that she would steal to help Reuben. He had always been jealous of her loyalty to her brother, but now he realized her love for her family would always be a part of her.

That same fierce loyalty would have encompassed him if she had become his wife. But would she have married him?

She had wanted to tell him something that evening. From the way she'd gotten embarrassed and then angry when he'd teased her, from the way she'd kept looking at him all during dinner, he was certain she had decided to marry him. Why else would she have been so happy? And she had been happy, even though she had gotten angry with him in the kitchen.

But how could this have been true if she had had the note upstairs at that very minute? How could she possibly have expected to get away with it when evidence of forced entry to his desk was there for the first person who entered the library to see?

The only answer that made any sense was that she was innocent. Nathan longed to believe that, but he couldn't find any evidence to support it.

The morning after Delilah left, he had traveled the river road to Hector's place. The cabin was bare. If anyone had ever used it, every sign of occupancy had been removed. Only the vague smell of something burned hinted that a vagrant might have spent the night there. Someone had trampled the brush under the window, but the circle went around the house as if it had been made by someone looking for a way to break in.

If Delilah was telling the truth, someone had covered his tracks well.

Delilah had been gone from the house long enough for Priscilla to break open the desk, but that didn't make any sense unless Priscilla and Hector were selling information. But why would they? What reason could Hector and Priscilla have to turn against their own people?

Nathan had gone over the same ground at least once every day since Delilah had left, and he always came to the same conclusion. The Delilah he knew—the woman he loved, the enchantress he wanted to marry—would never lie to him. She would have told him she'd taken the information. She would have told him with pride, defying him to do anything about it.

But everything else pointed the other way. How could he believe her when no one else did, when his common sense told him she had to be guilty? And could he chance opening himself up to betrayal again?

Nathan shoved the account books into his desk and hurried out of the house. He couldn't keep these thoughts from driving him crazy unless he was in the saddle, visiting the people who worked for him, oversee-ing their work, trying to come up with new ways to make money. He had to be away from Maple Hill.

That was why he had decided to sell the place and move to Boston.

Delilah would never have thought she could be so miserable at home. She loved Reuben, liked Jane, and adored David and Daniel. She had been feeling guilty for months because Jane had had no one to help her with the heavy work around the farm, anxious to get back to a place where she belonged and was needed, so it was a cruel shock to find her place had been filled.

Reuben had gone off to look for Shays the minute Delilah had told him Hector was spying for both sides.

"I told Daniel he couldn't trust him," Reuben raged as he gathered up musket and powder horn and prepared to go out into the bitter cold. "I told Daniel, 'He's one of them for all he's nearly lost his farm. You can't trust nobody who's willing to sell out his own kind.' Daniel would have it he wasn't putting too much faith in any-thing Hector said, but others did."

"It's good to have you back," Jane said with less en-thusiasm than Delilah had expected. "To be sure I was glad to have Polly stay, but Mother will be wanting her to help with the holiday cooking."

And except for Reuben's insistence that he was going to serve Nathan a bad turn for sending Delilah away in disgrace, that had been it. She was home, things were back to normal, and there was no reason to remember she had ever been at Maple Hill.

But things weren't the same. In the four months she had been away, Jane had taken the management of the household into her hands. Delilah felt annoyed when she had to ask what to do next. She felt resentful because

Jane's sister had occupied her bed. Still, she understood, and she tried not to feel hurt.

But she did.

No one spoke about her time at Maple Hill. She knew it embarrassed Jane and Reuben, that they were grateful for her sacrifice but didn't want to be reminded of it. She understood and tried not to resent that.

But she did.

Maybe worst of all, at least in her own eyes, was the way she felt about her home. In the tiny cabin, with rough materials used for clothing and bedding, old and chipped plates, and rough-hewn furniture, its small space occupied by five people, she felt poor for the first time. She tried not to resent the knowledge that people like Lucy Porter, Noah Hubbard, and Tom Oliver had far more than she was ever going to have.

But she did.

"This has nothing to do with fitting into the family or feeling poor," she lectured herself aloud late one afternoon as she set out to do the evening milking. "It has to do with Nathan Trent and nothing more."

And of course, that was true.

She cried herself to sleep every night knowing she would never be his wife, that she would probably never see him again, that he would never know she loved him so deeply it was impossible for her to think of loving anyone else.

She wouldn't allow herself to dwell on that final, horrible evening when all her dreams had come hopelessly unraveled. Instead she remembered the many hours they had spent in the library, arguing over each family's skills and what Nathan should do to help them. She thought of his smile when he was happy, of the incredible strength of his embrace, of the warmth of his kisses, and of her wonderful feeling of contentment when they were together.

She worried about him. Was he getting enough sleep?

He tended to work too late and spend too much time in the saddle. And his eating habits were terrible. All that food and wine every evening. She had gotten him to moderate his habits a little, but she was certain he would go back to sitting down to supper well after dark, eating enough food for five people, and drinking enough brandy to send him to an early grave.

And she could see Priscilla encouraging him. If he died, Priscilla would have all the money Hector needed.

A shaft of fear pierced Delilah's thoughts and stayed her hands in the act of milking. The cow turned an inquiring gaze in her direction, but in a moment Delilah resumed her rhythmic squeezing and the cow went back to chewing her cud.

She knew Serena had been sent away. That was the talk of Springfield within an hour of the departure, but Delilah distrusted Priscilla more than her mother. Serena was supremely selfish, but she was predictable. Priscilla's duplicity had proved her ruthless, dangerous, and willing to stop at nothing to get what she wanted, at least when it concerned Hector. Nathan held notes on everything Hector possessed. Would Priscilla see Nathan's death as a way to give her lover back his holdings?

There's no need to worry my head about it. Even if I knew what Priscilla planned to do, nobody would believe me. They would set it down to spite because she exposed me.

Nathan wouldn't believe her either. She had embarrassed him in front of his family and his peers. Men hated that. And to his mind she had compounded the sin by lying, trying to implicate a member of his family, and destroying his property. He would never forgive her.

But Delilah's dreams continued to be haunted by a smile which made all the harsh realities of her life fade into insignificance, a pair of arms which offered all the comfort she wanted.

Sometimes she saw Jane watching her out of the corner of her eye. Delilah knew her brother's wife was aware of her unhappiness, that Jane was afraid somehow she and Reuben might have been the cause of it. And Jane was hurt because Delilah didn't share the problem with her.

But Delilah couldn't confess that she would do almost anything to be back at Maple Hill. She couldn't tell Jane her heart was heavy, tears suddenly filled her eyes, and she had dark circles under them because she longed to be near the man Reuben and Jane still thought of as the spawn of the devil. She couldn't say her love for this man left her no pride and little desire to live outside his arms.

Jane would swear she was mad.

Delilah could hardly listen to Shays's plans without screaming that she would tell Nathan if they so much as thought about turning their muskets against him. Though Nathan was more and more frequently mentioned with respect by the townspeople, and the insurgents often made him an exception in their universal condemnation of the merchant class, Delilah saw them all as Nathan's enemies, even the handful of merchants turning to Nathan as the only person who could help them avoid confrontation. She had to tell herself at least half a dozen times a day that it was pointless for her to want to run to Maple Hill and warn Nathan. He could take care of himself.

So she watched as Shays organized his army, and silently prayed Nathan would find some reason to go to Boston before the fighting started.

Nathan stared at the portrait, conscious of a growing sense of dissatisfaction with it. At first he couldn't understand why. This was his best work. Not even his portrait of Lady Sarah Mendlow compared with this one.

Then he knew what was wrong. He had painted an ideal, not a woman. In the same flash of understanding

326

he realized he had tried to do the same with Delilah. He had made such a point of her honesty, venerating her for being what other women in his life had failed to be, he had almost turned her into someone to be worshiped rather than loved.

He accepted human frailty in others, even himself, but when Delilah had fallen short of perfection, he had been too dazed, too embittered to try to separate the ideal from the woman. Nor had he seen the need to do so. He had turned his back on her.

But he wasn't in love with an ideal. He loved a real woman. Delilah.

No ideal could replace the genuine warmth of her smile, the determined jut of her chin, or the sinuous sway of her hips. Flawlessness could not counterbalance her energy, her concern, her joy in life. Nor could it replace the imperfections which had become so dear to him: her generous mouth, her stubbornness, her inability to see when she was being imposed upon.

Every trait that made her real, desirable, absolutely necessary to his existence could be considered a flaw. Yet he wouldn't change any one of them.

He looked at the portrait again and cursed himself for a fool. He covered it, intending to put it in the attic and forget it, but he knew he wouldn't. Flawed though it may be, it was all he had of Delilah. He couldn't give it up.

He looked at the presents piled around the room. He *had* bought the necklace of blue stones and the velvet, as well as a lot of things from as far afield as Hartford, Newport, and Providence. Now they sat in his room, a monument to much more than an empty holiday season.

Nathan struggled with himself. Even though his mind continued to tell him Delilah was guilty, his heart told him with increasing insistence that she was innocent, and he could prove it if he but figured out what had really happened. He had gone over everything said that

327

evening until he could recite the dialogue word by word. After finally admitting he couldn't sort truth from lies, he realized he either had to accept Delilah's statements or Priscilla's.

That made everything simple. He had never trusted Priscilla. He had only believed her because other things had pointed to Delilah's guilt. And because of Lady Sarah Mendlow. Once he'd accepted Delilah's version, a great weight lifted from his heart. He now had hope. He would get to the bottom of the incident and prove her innocence, but most important of all, he believed in her again.

Suddenly decisive, Nathan gathered up all the presents. He would take them to Delilah. That would give him a chance to see her, make certain she was all right.

Delilah saw him coming and felt a dizzying rush of joy. She had believed she would never see him again, yet here he was, looking just as she remembered. Before she knew it, she had flung away her basket of eggs and was running toward him. She didn't have time to think of anything except how much she wanted to feel his arms around her.

Nathan had spotted her even before she spotted him. He could hardly believe it when she immediately started running toward him. He whipped his horse into a gallop so as not to waste a single precious second.

They met at the corner of the house. Nathan held out his arms, and Delilah literally leaped into his embrace. She laughed and cried with happiness, her tears making their desperate, hungry kisses wet and salty. But Nathan didn't seem to notice. His hungry lips covered her mouth, and there was no gentleness in this reunion. Later, perhaps, but now their need was too urgent.

But not even the cloud of euphoria which surrounded

them could long withstand the sharp pricks of reality, so Nathan slowly allowed Delilah to slip through his arms. The moment her feet touched earth, common sense, like an evil talisman, returned with dreadful finality.

"I think I dropped my eggs," she said, looking for anything to say except the words in her heart.

"You have nothing in your hands," Nathan replied. His hands touched her face, caressed her skin, felt the wetness of her tears, absorbed the warmth of her flaming cheeks. Simply being with her brought life to the cold, barren plain of his soul.

"Jane will be angry."

"Maybe she won't notice."

"She notices everything." *But not the most obvious thing of all, that I would trade everything in the world to be back in this man's arms.*

"Are you getting along all right? Are you glad to be back home?"

Delilah's throat closed; she couldn't answer. How could she tell him she had never been more miserable in her life? How could she explain that he had changed her life forever? The things she did with her family, the house, her room — they used to give her pleasure and happiness, but no longer. Now everything reminded her of him. She feared he no longer loved her, that he would never love her again. In the end, she didn't give him any answer.

"How about you?"

"Mrs. Stebbens tries to spoil me. She's convinced I'd be happier if I ate more. You'd be appalled at the food she puts before me."

It was a small confidence to share, just one of the threads that bound their lives together.

"Her cooking's not quite what it used to be. I think she misses you in the kitchen."

Even if everything came out of the kitchen burned to a cinder, Nathan knew he couldn't miss Delilah more than he did already. He'd been so absorbed in saving his fortune he hadn't realized how much he had come to depend on her being in the house.

She was his ally, his secret companion, his advisor. She gave him encouragement when he was disheartened; she praised him when others looked at him with hard, calculating eyes. It was as essential to him to know she was in the house as it was to spend time in her company.

"Where are your brother and his family?"

"They've gone to visit Jane's parents. He wanted to take the presents early so we can spend all of Christmas Day together."

"They've left you to do all the work by yourself?"

He sounded so worried, so indignant on her behalf, she had to fight back the tears. Don't be a sentimental fool, she told herself angrily. A little bit of caring changes nothing.

But it did. This proved his feelings for her weren't dead, that no matter what he thought of her, some part of him still wanted to know she was being cared for. Just like a man, she thought, worrying about a little physical labor when it's the two feet of space between us that's breaking my heart.

"All the chores have been done, and Reuben will help with the feeding when he gets back. I was just collecting the eggs to have something to do. I don't know what Jane will say when she learns I broke them all."

"I'll buy you some more."

"No," she said quickly. "I can tell her I stumbled or was frightened by a snake."

He smiled for the first time, the same old smile that caused her to go weak in the knees and silly in the head.

"Have you ever stumbled, or been frightened by anything?"

She had to return his smile. "No, but I've been acting

330

so peculiar lately she'll believe anything."

Delilah hadn't meant to let that slip. Funny, she'd been trying so hard not to tell him she still loved him, still thought of him every minute of the day.

"I brought the rest of your clothing."

She had hoped he'd never know she'd left behind the dresses Priscilla had given her and the ones made from the material he had provided.

"I was checking to see if you'd left your trunk."

He hadn't been checking anything. He'd been going to her room every day, sometimes more than once, just to stand at the window, sit in her chair, or read some of the books she had brought up from the library. It made him feel closer to her when it was too painful to look at her portrait.

"I've brought some other things, too."

"I couldn't have left so much."

She had checked everything several times. What else had there been to do through the long hours of that dreadful night? Since it had been impossible for her to close her eyes, she had filled the long, cold hours by packing and sorting through her things, deciding what she would leave . . . remembering the times she had worn each gown, the look in his eyes when he had seen her, the sly comments he'd made when she had passed close enough for him to whisper, the swelling of his body in their more private moments.

"They're Christmas presents."

Delilah didn't know how much more she was going to be able to take. Why had he come here asking after her, worrying about her, bringing her gifts? Didn't he know everything was over? How could he throw her out of his house, look at her as if she were the lowest form of life, and then turn around and give her presents? Tears gathered at the backs of her eyes. If he kept on, she was going to cry right in front of him. She knew how much men hated crying, but it would be his own fault. He just didn't know when to stop.

Nathan took a small package from the buggy seat. He pried open her clenched fingers and unwrapped the paper. A stream of blue and silver flowed into her hand. Speechless, Delilah stood looking at a necklace of blue stones. It was the most beautiful thing she'd ever been given.

And the one thing she couldn't accept.

"I brought the velvet, too," Nathan continued, opening one package after another.

But she didn't see what was in the other packages. Her eyes never left the necklace in her hand. Inexpensive it might be, but it represented all they had shared that was priceless. She didn't think of the house and the clothing, the silver and china, the security she would enjoy as Nathan's wife. They would be nice, she would appreciate them; she'd been poor all her life. But she would happily go on being poor if she could just have the man she loved.

She thought of those damned tight breeches. Would she ever be able to picture Nathan without seeing his muscled thighs? She wondered if Jane felt that way about Reuben, and decided that she herself was probably a depraved woman who would be ostracized by society if they knew what went on in her mind.

Then she recalled Nathan's kisses, the strength of his arms, the wonderful comfort of being crushed in his embrace, his inflamed groin against her fluttering stomach, her aching breasts against his hot hands. She thought of the portrait hidden in his room. Somehow that was the greatest compliment of all.

Then the tears started to fall. Not a delicate, captivating tear dangling from a lash, not even a moist trail down soft cheeks. No, Delilah couldn't cry in a feminine, seductive manner. She was certain she looked as though someone had dashed a bucket of water in her face.

332

Then, wonder of wonders, Nathan enfolded her tightly in his arms, one hand pressing her head against his chest as he kissed her hair.

That made her cry all the harder, great gusty sobs which should have disgusted him. But he held her more closely, and before she knew it, her arms were wound around him.

"I can't take the necklace," she said between sobs. "I can't take any of these gifts."

"I want you to have them."

"Don't you understand that everything has changed?"

"I couldn't give them to anybody else."

She pulled away enough to be able to look up at him. "You're the one person in the world I can't take anything from."

"I don't understand."

"For one thing, Reuben would shoot you and Jane would never speak to me again. But that's not the real reason," she added when he would protest. "An unmarried woman should never accept gifts from an unmarried man. . . . That's not the real reason either, and you know it."

"You mean—"

"The situation has changed," she said, afraid if he spoke first he would further shake her resolve. "Had things continued . . . if we had . . . if you still wanted . . ." Words failed her.

"If we were going to be married, you could accept them as bridal gifts," he said for her.

Delilah nodded.

"Can't they just be gifts from a man who loves you?"

Delilah's gaze flew to his face. As incredible as the words seemed, confirmation was written in his eyes, in the tightening vise of his arms around her body.

"But how? Why?"

"Don't ask me that. Don't ask me anything. All I know is I love you more than ever. I've been nearly crazy since you left. I can't sleep I can't eat. I can't concentrate on my work. Someone will be talking to me, and I won't hear a word. Everything I see or do reminds me of you. At times I just stand around, trying to remember everything I can about you. I'm going mad."

Delilah had thought she was cried out, that she had no more tears in her body, but they began to flow afresh, even more copiously now. She didn't draw back when Nathan lifted her off her feet and kissed her with a harsh urgency that matched her own need of him. She didn't protest when his tongue forced her lips apart and plunged into her mouth, seeking her tongue, renewing its intimacy with frantic haste.

Even though she knew it was useless, that it would only make telling him to go that much more difficult, Delilah threw her arms around his neck and kissed him with equal intensity. She gave no thought to being observed, to Jane and Reuben coming back early, or to Shays or one of his men stopping by to see her brother and finding her locked in a passionate embrace with one of his enemies. She only cared that Nathan loved her, that he wanted her, and that she was in his arms.

For that moment Nathan was enough.

"I've thought about holding you in my arms so long it has become an obsession," he whispered.

"I've thought of you too," Delilah said, squirming in his embrace as his tongue tickled her ear. "Every night I tried to think of the things I needed to do for Christmas, but all I could think of was you."

"I remembered the way we used to share secret looks during dinner," Nathan said. He nuzzled her neck, making his words hard to understand. "That day down by the river, the night I waited for you in your room, the hours we spent together in the library. I remember most the way you looked that evening in the drawing room singing love songs. I always imagined you sang one to me."

"I did, when I was alone. I never realized until then how powerless words are to express our deepest feelings. I wanted to touch you, but I didn't dare."

"You can touch me now," he murmured as his lips trailed searing kisses across her bosom. She knew she should object—she would be ruined if anyone saw such an intimate display of feeling—but she didn't want to stop him. She felt his loins begin to swell, the pressure against her abdomen increasing, and a molten core of heat expanded and flowed through her. Her arms encircled his waist and drew him closer.

She would have to live without him for a lifetime. *Just a few minutes more.* Then Nathan's lips touched the tops of her breasts, and she knew her moment of decision was near. She had to stop him while she still could. His tongue snaked down below the edge of her gown, pushing down the linen lining until it reached the hard, aching, swollen nipple just waiting to be caressed.

Delilah gasped when he gently removed her breast from the confines of her gown and suckled it with his hungry mouth. Her body grew rigid with tension, alive with expectation, demanding in its hunger. The now familiar uneasiness came to her stomach; it spread through her body until every nerve stretched to the breaking point. She felt the warm moisture between her thighs grow hot, felt her hips loosen, her muscles quiver with eagerness.

She grasped Nathan's head to press him closer to her breast, hoping his nearness would relieve the growing ache inside her. His mouth loosely cupped her swollen nipple while his tongue's rough edge teased it. Then ignoring her nipple, his impudent tongue traced circles around its sensitive base before laying trails across the warm underside of her breast.

Desperate to relieve the delicious ache that tortured her, Delilah roughly guided Nathan's lips back to her

335

throbbing nipple. He eagerly took it in his mouth and sucked, hard.

Delilah gasped at the sweetness of this agony.

In that moment she wanted Nathan more than she wanted life. Every day, every hour, every second of the last four months had been leading up to this moment. Now that it was here, Delilah wondered that she had never seen its inevitability—and that she didn't want to escape it.

She offered no objection when, with a groan of throttled passion, Nathan swept her up in his arms and carried her into the house. She offered no protest when he laid her upon the bed and uncovered both her breasts to provide a feast for his hungry mouth and seeking hands. This was an affirmation of her love. Above all else she wanted him to have that.

Fulfilling a wish which had bedeviled her for months, Delilah placed her hands on Nathan's bottom and caressed the firm, muscled mounds of his buttocks, feeling muscles tense and quiver under her fingertips, his body move and shudder against her, her own body become more heated. Even as Nathan tortured her breasts, the center of her need changed.

A burning sensation centered itself in her loins. Dimly perceived at first, it continued to grow in intensity and breadth until the whole lower half of her body was on fire. She couldn't remain still. She wriggled and squirmed until she brought her aching flesh with its mounting need into contact with Nathan's body. There was no reluctance, no twinge of regret. Unconsciously her hips relaxed and her legs opened.

Nathan uttered an agonized groan when she pressed herself against his swollen groin, then peeled her dress and shift down to her waist. From there it was a simple matter to slip it from under her hips so Delilah lay naked before him.

It happened so quickly it took Delilah's breath away.

For a moment the cold air made her conscious of her nakedness, but soon the heat from deep within her core warmed her entire body until she felt she would burst into flame. She wanted Nathan. She had to have him. Her seeking hands found his groin.

With a strangled protest, Nathan snatched her hands away. "I can't control myself if you touch me," he muttered.

Delilah didn't understand, but as Nathan's hand slid along the line of her leg, over her thigh, and directly to the sensitive spot between her creamy white thighs, it ceased to matter. No hand had ever caressed her. She had never allowed anyone to explore her body, but she didn't draw back. This intimacy, this sharing of what had always been hers alone, was her gift to Nathan. She entreated him to possess her.

Her body tensed as Nathan's fingers skimmed over hypersensitive skin, igniting a trail of sparks, each lighting up a different nerve center until she squirmed beneath his touch.

But nothing compared to the shock of Nathan's fingers parting her flesh and driving deep inside her. Delilah's entire body rose off the bed. The feeling was indescribable. It was as though she had been invaded, plundered, and possessed by a force beyond her power to resist, yet at the same time finally liberated, taken outside of her corporeal self to a plane where she and Nathan could truly become one.

Fighting to retain some control over her limbs, Delilah unbuttoned Nathan's shirt and pulled it off his shoulders. She let her fingers play over his chest, across his back and his tight abdomen. But the feel of his body under her fingertips was almost blotted out by the blaze he had kindled deep within her. As his hand sank deeper inside her, her hands became more insistent in their searching. Again she found his groin, and again he groaned in pain as he pushed her hand away.

"Don't. You'll ruin everything," he said as he slipped out of his clothes. Nathan barely had his body under control. He trembled with the urgency of the need that filled his every living cell. He was trying to prolong each precious moment, but it took all his willpower to keep from falling upon her right then.

Before Delilah had time to see the beauty of his naked body, Nathan moved above her. His hand plunged inside her once more while his lips sought out and suckled her tender nipples.

She thought she would cry out in sweet agony. Then she felt something larger, softer, more insistent between her legs. The pressure increased and she instinctively opened wider to accept him. Slowly Nathan entered her, stretched her until she was certain she could never hold all of him. No matter how impressive he had been in his tight breeches, he seemed even more enormous inside her. Then, without warning, he drove deep into her until she sheathed all of him. The sharp, unexpected pain stunned Delilah, and she lay still, fearful of what would come next.

When he began to move inside her, slowly withdrawing and then, just as deliberately, sinking his full length into her, Delilah's fears receded before the sweet intoxication that gripped her. Her abdomen tensed, the muscles in her groin expanded and contracted with his movements. Nathan methodically stoked the fire he had built within her, careful to keep it growing, careful to keep her balanced on the edge of the abyss.

Until his lips found her swollen nipples once again. That was too much. Delilah could no longer control her body. Unable to further endure this slow buildup, to wait for the explosion she instinctively knew was coming, she wrapped her arms around his neck and kissed him with all the longing and fear and desperation and hunger that had haunted her from the moment she'd left Maple Hill. She wanted to get her fill, to absorb enough

338

of him to keep her from ever again feeling so desperately in need of him.

Nathan's lips covered Delilah's neck and shoulders with kisses. Even as he plunged deep into her, as the rhythm of his lovemaking increased to a headlong rush toward fulfillment, his lips worshiped her body. The feel of her soft skin under his fingertips, the taste of her sweet mouth, her feathery, warm breath on his cheek, the salt of her tears of happiness, the smell of her fresh clean skin mingled with the fine moisture of desire and combined to stir his passion as much as the wet, welcoming flesh he buried himself in.

Delilah's body responded, adjusting her rhythm to his, an ever-expanding wave of pleasure radiating from her belly, cutting her off from the trammels of her ordinary being and leaving her free to meld—heart, body, and soul—with Nathan. Delilah surrendered to this swell, this never-ending series of swells, which carried her along on its powerful crest. Higher and higher, deeper and deeper, until, utterly disembodied, she was completely free.

She felt Nathan react to her quickened tempo, her more aggressive response, with an increase in his rhythm. Absorbed by the sensations which rocketed through her limbs, Delilah surrendered and let herself be carried along by the quickening pulses.

Abruptly Nathan's body went rigid, his strokes became irregular, his harsh breath came in quick, uneven gasps. Instinctively Delilah's muscles clamped down on him, trying to absorb him deep within her. Then, from her core, she felt a wave of sweet agony grip her body, turning it inside out as waves of pleasure rolled over her, tossing her upon stormy swells until she felt she could stand no more. She held tight to Nathan as she drifted to the edge of consciousness.

He groaned aloud as the exquisite pleasure of repeated explosions racked him, giving his body, so long

339

denied, its natural release. Firmly in the coils of the most intense consummation in his life, Nathan was helpless until the spasms of pleasure had run their course.

Then, gradually, they both relaxed and lay still.

Chapter Twenty-two

Delilah and Nathan remained in each other's arms without speaking long after their breathing had returned to normal and their hearts had calmed in their breasts. To speak would have been to break the spell which, sheltering them in its care, allowed them this short, precious time together.

Time. She had so little time to tell him what this day meant to her, to explore the body which seemed to be the other half of her own. She had stolen surreptitious glances for months, but how little she actually knew of the body that had so recently worshiped her own.

Nathan was so unlike Reuben. The two men were equally tall, but Reuben was built for strength. Thick, powerful shoulders and legs gave him the look of a Goliath, while Nathan reminded her of a fine carriage horse. He was tall and strong of limb, but lean. His chest was broad and powerful, yet his waist was greyhound slim.

And he wasn't hairy like Reuben. As her hands traveled over Nathan's limbs, she was glad his skin wasn't marred by rough hair. Just a light sprinkling in the center of his chest and around his navel highlighted the wonderful smoothness of his flesh.

There was something powerfully exciting about exploring a man's body intimately. It was as though she had been allowed to pass through a barrier which kept out every other person in the whole world. She alone, no one but Delilah Stowbridge, would be allowed to run her hands over Nathan's torso, to gently massage the muscles in his shoulders until he moaned with contentment.

It was almost as though she owned him. No, that was wrong. He had made her a gift of himself. What an awesome demonstration of faith, the act of surrendering oneself to another. Odd, Delilah didn't think it so incredible that she should have done the same for Nathan. That seemed natural. But that he should have done it for her!

She could hardly believe it was happening.

Her hand slipped down Nathan's side, over his hip, and around his buttocks. She didn't know what it was about this part of his anatomy that aroused her so, but even now she could feel her nipples begin to harden. She brought her hand forward over his hip but Nathan intercepted it and guided it gently to the safer region of his stomach.

Delilah melted into his embrace. The feel of his warm skin against her sensitive nipples was almost as exciting as the feel of his lips and tongue had been a short while before. She pulled away just a little. She wasn't ready for another round of such passion as they'd experienced. She wanted to lie still and absorb as much of his nearness as possible. She would always welcome his love, but her soul received its richest nourishment from these moments of quiet.

She traced his jaw with the tip of her finger. His skin was so clear, so closely shaven; his chin was so strong. And his lips were soft, just moist enough for them to catch on her finger. That tickled his lips, and she smiled when he twisted away.

His hair fascinated her too. Every man she knew wore it long and gathered at the back with a ribbon. Nathan's thick, blondish-brown hair was cut so short it barely touched his collar. She combed it with her fingers. Next to her nearly raven tresses, his locks looked lighter than ever.

She took his face between her hands. Would she ever

tire of looking at him? Would this time together be enough to last her through all the empty years ahead? A tiny sob broke from her throat.

Nathan propped himself on an elbow. "What's wrong?"

She shook her head and nestled in the crook of his arm, trying to recapture the mood, but his words had broken the spell.

Delilah sat up and reached for her dress. "You have to go. Reuben and Jane will be home soon."

Nathan pulled her back down next to him. "Not yet."

He tossed her dress aside, but she picked it up again. The moment was irretrievable.

Nathan made no attempt to convince her to come back to bed. Maybe he could tell from the way she put on her clothes that she wouldn't change her mind. He began to dress as well.

"When can I come again?"

Delilah kept her back to him. "You can't," she said, softly. "We can never do this again."

"Then why did you—"

"I don't know." She turned to face him. "Yes, I do. I wanted something of you I could remember, something I didn't have to share with anyone else, something to remember when you're gone."

"Delilah—"

"Don't say anything, please," she begged, cutting him off again.

"I was just going to offer you a job," Nathan said.

"A job?" Delilah asked, taken completely by surprise.

"I need someone to supervise the flax spinning. I've got weavers now as well. Mrs. Wheaton doesn't like the responsibility."

Delilah almost jumped at the chance to have a legitimate reason to see Nathan. Not even Reuben could object to her going to Maple Hill if she had a job.

But she couldn't do it. And not because of Reuben or Jane. Because of herself. Being around Nathan regularly, knowing she could never be anything more than his lover, would tear her apart. Better to have nothing to remember than something she would someday come to regret. "I can't."

"Is it because of Reuben?"

"No. It's because of me. You don't understand, do you?"

He shook his head.

Why couldn't he see it? Didn't anybody in England ever fall truly in love? "I can't be around you and know we can never be more than lovers."

"I want to marry you."

"But you also think I betrayed you."

"Not anymore. I don't know what happened to me that night—sometimes I think I lost my mind—but I don't believe you betrayed me."

Delilah's elation was short-lived. She could see that, as much as he *wanted* to believe she was innocent, he would never be completely sure she was telling the truth until he could prove it to himself.

Still, she had hope now. Nathan loved her and wanted to believe her. That was more than she'd had when she'd gotten up this morning. It might be enough if she was smart enough to figure out how to make Hector or Priscilla admit what they had done. She didn't know whether she could do it, but she was going to try.

In the meantime, she couldn't keep seeing Nathan. She had no willpower where he was concerned. If she gave into him again, she wouldn't be able to refuse him after that. Then, if he didn't marry her, she would despise herself.

"When you've proved to your satisfaction what I said was true, offer me the job again."

"At least let me give you some money."

That made her angry.

"I don't need your money," she said scornfully. "I won't be kept by any man."

344

"I didn't mean it that way."

"Then what did you mean?"

Nathan gestured to the crude, bare cabin. "You must have very little. I could help. Mrs. Stebbens cooks more food than we can use, and there's much more in the storage rooms."

"Thanks for the offer, but now that Reuben's debt is paid, we have enough for our needs."

Not until Nathan's face registered hurt and bewilderment did Delilah realize how cold and hostile she'd sounded. But she couldn't have felt otherwise. To have Nathan treat her family like a charity case shocked and embarrassed her. It also infuriated her.

"I didn't mean to hurt your feelings. I just thought since I have so much—"

"And we have so little, you'd give us some of it," she finished for him. "Thank you, but Reuben and Jane would choke on anything from your hand."

She regretted her words the moment they were out of her mouth. The fact that they were true didn't make it any easier.

"You'd better go before I say anything else," she said, going to the door and holding it open for him. "Besides, if you stay much longer, someone is bound to come by."

"You won't let me see you again?"

"If you love me, you won't ask it of me."

He looked so hurt, so downcast, Delilah kept to her resolution only with difficulty. But as she watched him walk away, she wondered if she could stand not seeing him again. She had loved him for months, but the hour she'd spent in his arms had united them even more deeply than any promise made with words ever could. He had become as essential to her as her own body.

"Governor Bowdoin has ordered up forty-four hundred militia from the eastern counties," Lucius told Nathan.

345

"They have orders to start for Springfield on the seventeenth. Even in this bitter cold, they ought to be here in three days."

Nathan had to pull his mind away from thoughts of Delilah to answer Clarke. He had been back three times, but she had not seen him since that day before Christmas. Once Jane had told him she wasn't there. The other times he'd been told Delilah didn't want to see him. It had taken all of Nathan's control to keep him from forcing his way into the house.

"You're going to have to declare yourself," Lucius said.

"What do you mean?"

"Come up with some money to help pay the militia," Asa Warner explained. "The legislature isn't in session so the governor can't get any money. If the militia comes, we have to pay for it."

"It's already coming," Lucius said.

"And if I don't agree to pay anything?"

"You'll be marked down as supporting the regulators," Noah Hubbard said, malicious pleasure gleaming in his eyes.

A sudden inspiration made Nathan smile right back. "Put me down for the exact amount as Noah."

He almost laughed at the reaction. Lucius looked embarrassed, Noah turned red with rage, and Asa Warner tried to hide his amusement.

"How much do I owe, Lucius?"

"I haven't paid my full amount yet," Noah said before Lucius could answer. He directed a look of pure hatred at Nathan. "I'm short just now."

"I'm a little short myself," Nathan admitted. "I'll pay when Lucius shows me a receipt for your payment."

"The governor appointed Major General Benjamin Lincoln to command the militia," Lucius said before anyone could say anything else. "He commanded troops in the War of Independence. He's . . ."

But Nathan's thoughts were far from General Lincoln

and his qualifications to command the militia. He was thinking about how this would affect Delilah and her family. And how that would affect her relationship with him. No matter which way he looked at it, it could only make things worse.

It wouldn't matter that these were a lot of strangers from across the state. If Nathan supported them and they shot at Delilah's family, that would be the same as if he held a musket himself.

It wouldn't matter if he never paid a cent toward the cost of the militia. He would be held as accountable as any of the other River Gods. Nor would it matter that he had counseled caution from the first or that he'd gone out of his way to help dozens of his debtors. He would be as guilty as the rest.

He cursed.

Nathan turned over, slammed his fist into the pillow, and tried to get comfortable once again. He had been restless ever since Delilah left, but he was having more trouble sleeping tonight than usual. And the mice on the third floor were making it harder. He'd meant to remember to tell Lester to set some traps, but every time he'd thought of the floor above, his mind had focused on Delilah and the mice had gone completely out of his head.

The noise was much worse tonight. In fact, it sounded as though rats were up there. That was an unpleasant thought. A few field mice always found their way into a house during the winter. You got a cat or set traps. Either way they were no problem. But rats. That was something else again. He'd see about it tomorrow.

He turned over once more, but he was even less sleepy than before. Now the possibility of rats in the house was keeping him awake.

"Damnation," he said as he lunged out of bed. He might not be able to do anything about Delilah's absence, but he could do something about the rats.

Nathan pulled on a pair of stout boots, wrapped himself in a thick dressing gown, and lighted a candle with a hurricane globe. Search as he might, he could find nothing to use as a weapon. He then remembered the walking stick which had lain unused in the bottom of his trunk since he'd left London. It took only a minute to find it. Thus armed, he ascended to the upper story to do battle with any rodent so unwise as to expect to live out the winter on his bounty.

But as Nathan's gaze reached the level of the third floor, he froze on the stairs, one foot about to be set down on the next step. A light came from under the door of Delilah's room.

Nathan considered returning to his room for a pistol. Instead he blew out the candle, set it down on the step, and took a two-fisted grip on his walking stick. Being extremely careful not to make the slightest sound, he climbed the last eight stairs. He tiptoed across the landing to Delilah's door and listened intently, but the noise had stopped. Light still came from under the door, but there was complete silence in the room. With a quick, decisive movement, Nathan turned the knob and threw open the door.

Hector Clayhart sat up on Delilah's bed with a start.

He stared at Nathan with a half-expectant, half-surprised look. He wore a nightshirt. Obviously he'd intended to spend the night in Delilah's room.

"What the hell are you doing here?" Nathan demanded, entering the small chamber.

"H-how did you find me?" Hector asked.

Nathan's expression relaxed. "I thought I heard a rat. I was about to beat you to death with my cane."

Hector seemed to relax, too. "I had to find some place to stay. Ever since Delilah accused me of spying for both sides, nearly every man in Hampden County is out to kill me."

Nathan could understand why Hector wouldn't want to be caught hiding in another man's house—it made him look like a coward—but there was something about his expression Nathan couldn't decipher.

"How did you get in here?"

"It was easy. You're gone all the time, your cousin never leaves her room, and the servants stay in the back of the house. I can practically come and go as I please."

"What about food?"

"I can get what I want whenever I go out."

"I'll tell Lester to bring you something."

Nathan was certain Hector was about to refuse. Instead he said, "That'll be a lot easier than trying to get back to my place without being seen."

Nathan couldn't explain his suspicion that something was not right. Hector's explanation seemed so reasonable. Still, he couldn't get over the feeling that no matter how innocent Hector's being in his attic might be, he hadn't been told the entire truth.

Quite suddenly Nathan knew what had been wrong with Hector's expression when he'd burst into the room. Hector hadn't looked upset. He had looked surprised. But why surprised? Surely he hadn't been expecting somebody else? There wasn't anybody else.

Or was there? An explanation flashed into Nathan's head. It came with startling clarity.

"You expected Priscilla to open that door, not me. That's why one of our plates is sitting next to your bed. She brings you food after we've retired. You don't go out to get it. You don't leave this room at all."

"No! That's not true."

"You did spy for both sides, and Priscilla helped you."

"I didn't! I only pretended to."

"You had to have that note to prove your credibility with Shays. Had he started to doubt you?"

Nathan heard a near-silent footstep behind him. He didn't turn around.

"Why did you do it, Hector? Why did you turn against people who've been your friends all your life?" Nathan asked.

Hector glanced over Nathan's shoulder, and his attitude changed to spiteful anger. "Because Noah and Lucius drained me of every cent I had," he growled.

"Why not go after them?"

"How? You hold notes on every acre I own."

"Then you should have come to me. I'd have been happy to help you against Noah."

"I told you to go to him," Priscilla said from behind Nathan. Anger turned her voice from a breathless whisper to an ugly hiss. "Then you could have had your revenge and money too."

Nathan turned around and looked into the barrel of the musket in Priscilla's hands.

"What do you plan to do with that?"

"That depends on whether you plan to turn Hector in."

"And if I do?"

"I'll kill you."

"And if I don't?"

"I may kill you anyway. I don't trust you."

"Make sure that's the real reason. If you're hoping to inherit Maple Hill, you'll be disappointed."

"Who else would get it? You don't have any relatives except Mother and me."

"I made a will when I was in Boston. Delilah inherits my entire estate. If I die, you and your mother will be destitute."

Priscilla turned white.

"She gets nothing?" Hector asked, dazed.

"Even the clothes on her back would belong to Delilah," Nathan told him.

"If I don't shoot you?" Priscilla asked, recovering some presence of mind.

"I might decide to help you, for a consideration."

"Such as?"

"Hector has to let it be known he spied for both sides. I want Delilah's name cleared of all suspicion."

"No! You know what Lucius will do if he finds out."

Nathan looked from Priscilla to Hector, a question in his eyes.

"And if we agree?" Priscilla asked.

"I'll see you have enough money to make a start somewhere else."

"In a town. Hector doesn't want to farm."

The prospect of being able to get away from the farm he hated caused Hector's resistance to collapse. "I want the money in one lump sum."

"You'll get regular quarterly payments for three years only."

"I've got to have it all at once," Hector insisted.

"How will it be paid?" Priscilla asked.

"I'll set up arrangements through an agent in Boston."

"Who'll guarantee the money?" Hector demanded.

"I will," Nathan replied, disgust creeping into his voice. "You'll receive it as long as I have it to give."

"Where will we go?" Hector asked.

"I don't care."

"Ipswich," Priscilla said. "My father had family there."

"I want to go to Boston."

"Maybe we shall, once we've gotten established."

"My cousin and I have a few details to discuss," Nathan said, and before either of them could object, he ushered Priscilla into the hall and closed the door.

"You don't have to marry him," Nathan said, not mincing his words. "You deserve a better man."

"I've got the man I want."

"You've got a weak man who will always blame someone else for his failures."

"But I'll be there to see he doesn't fail."

"You want that?"

"Both my father and my uncle were strong men. My father beat my mother, and my uncle made her work like

351

a slave. I hated them both."

"Not all strong men are like that."

"Maybe, but I don't want to take a chance. Hector loves me. Now that I've been proved right about this, he won't question my decisions again."

"I'll have a lawyer draw up the papers. You will have no claim on me after the three years are up."

"What about Mother?"

For a moment, as he remembered Serena had been the cause of Delilah's disgrace, cold anger flared in Nathan's eyes, but it gradually died as he realized she was a tortured, miserably unhappy woman. She probably couldn't have acted any other way. As he contemplated the happiness he looked forward to with Delilah, he found it within himself to set aside his rancor.

"I can never allow her in my home again, but I'll make her an allowance sufficient to permit her to live anywhere she wants. Boston if she likes, but I think she ought to live with you. I don't think she's capable of living alone."

"You're generous."

"I would have done more if . . ." He let the sentence trail away.

" 'If' is a useless word," Priscilla snapped. "It holds out hopes which never come to pass and delivers only heartbreak. I want no ifs. You'll soon discover you and Delilah have more than your share."

Nathan knew the moment he rode up he should turn back. Reuben's two little boys squatted in front of the cabin, their gazes fixed on the closed door. He could hear the murmur of women's voices from inside. A loud moan broke through, and the soothing murmur rose to a higher level, then fell off only to rise again to another moan. Common sense told him to go away and come back after the crisis had passed, but he couldn't wait to tell Delilah that Hector's confession had cleared her name. He also had to tell her he wanted to marry her as soon as possible.

He remembered the bigger boy's name. "Daniel, is your aunt inside?"

Daniel nodded his head.

"Would you tell her to come out?"

Daniel shook his head.

"Would you tell her I want to see her?"

Daniel shook his head again.

Nathan muttered under his breath. "Will you take her a message if I give you a coin?"

Daniel thought a moment and then nodded.

"Tell her Mr. Trent wants to speak to her."

Daniel was gone so long Nathan began to wonder if the child intended to come back.

"She can't come out," Daniel said when he finally emerged from the cabin. "Go away."

"Tell her I'll wait. Go on, tell her," Nathan said when Daniel seemed reluctant to go inside again.

"Mama's not feeling good. She said go away."

"Tell her I'm not leaving until she comes out."

Daniel shook his head and sat down. Nathan's patience ran out. "Either you take her the message or I go inside." Given that kind of choice, Daniel got up and went back inside the house.

Delilah came out.

"I told you not to come back."

Nathan drew her away from the house, away from the two boys. "You didn't think I could stay away, did you? Not with you so close."

Guiding her around the corner of the house, Nathan took her into his arms, and kissed her with all the urgency of a man who's had to hold himself in check for weeks. Delilah tried to resist. When she found she couldn't, she gave in and kissed him back just as passionately.

"We shouldn't be doing this, not with Jane inside hav-

353

ing pains. I told you to stay away. It's no good."

"I want you to marry me, Delilah Stowbridge. I want you to go with me right now to post the banns."

"Nathan, you know we can't. You said yourself you could never trust me."

"I said a lot of things I didn't mean that night."

"But you know you'll always wonder."

"No, I won't. Hector has confessed to everything. Within a few days everyone in Springfield will know the truth about that note."

Delilah's heart leaped with joy. She had never realized how desperately she wanted to marry Nathan. Being constantly aware of the many barriers that separated them, she had held herself in check, never allowing her emotions full rein. But now everything seemed possible, and her heart soared with happiness

"But how? Why?"

"I'll tell you later. All you need to know is he and Priscilla left Springfield for good. Now can you think about us?"

Jane chose that moment to let out a long wail.

"I've got to go. I only came out because you threatened to come inside."

Nathan didn't know whether he wanted to strangle Jane or shake Delilah until she forgot she ever had a family. Didn't she care anything about her future, or would Reuben's family always have first claim on her?

"Don't you understand what I said? I want to marry you. I want you to be my wife, the mother of my children. I want you to leave here and come with me to Maple Hill."

"I can't leave Jane," Delilah said, apparently shocked that he would even suggest such a thing. "Jane is in her seventh month and having pains. And do you know why? General Lincoln is marching from Boston with an army and Shays has ordered the men to move out on the seventeenth."

"They won't be here for days."

"It's what will happen when they get here that frightens me. They wouldn't be coming unless they meant to fight."

"They wouldn't be coming at all if Shays hadn't written that last letter," Nathan said. "That convinced the governor he wanted war."

"But Shays doesn't want a fight."

"Then he shouldn't have given the order to march."

Delilah realized they were arguing about things neither of them could control. "This is pointless," she said.

"Then let's talk about something else."

"Nathan, I can't stand here gossiping while Jane's suffering."

"If you won't marry me, will you be my housekeeper?"

Delilah gaped at him. "Absolutely not. You know perfectly well I couldn't be in that house and stay away from you."

He grinned broadly. "That's what I was counting on."

"Be serious. I can't leave here no matter what. Jane could have her baby at any time. And it's too early."

Nathan's expression turned grave. Anger flared in his eyes. "Can't you see they're using you? Every time something happens, they turn to you. It doesn't matter whether or not they can handle it themselves, they expect you to do it for them. Worse than that, they expect you to agree with everything they do. If you don't, they make you feel guilty, make it a question of loyalty, of patriotism. Beware of people who call upon patriotism and God when their arguments can't win your support. They're depending on your better nature to get you to do what their project can't."

"All this may be true"—she looked at him, his honest face lined with worry, his mouth tight with anger, his eyes reflecting the pain of rejection—"it *is* true, but that doesn't change anything."

"I don't mean to ask you to choose between us, but isn't there somebody else who could stay with her?"

"It's not a matter of choosing," Delilah said. "I couldn't marry you with Reuben going to war at any minute. How could I face Jane if my husband's men killed her husband—my brother."

"They're not my men."

"I couldn't face myself if I left her and the boys. They took me in when Mother died. They never asked for anything or made me feel I was anything but a cherished member of their family. I would not leave her now if I loved you more than anything else on earth."

"Do you?"

"I thought I did. Do you remember the morning I overslept, the time you came to my room to tell me goodbye?"

Nathan nodded.

"I wanted to tell you right then, but by the time I was awake, you were gone. Then you came back just before dinner. You kept teasing me, trying to get me to tell you right then. I couldn't do that in front of Serena. It was too private. Then Lucius came and Serena found the note and you didn't believe me."

"I've already told you I was wrong. I knew the next day that you were innocent."

"But you didn't believe my story. You thought I made it up."

Nathan had no answer for that.

"You once said if I wanted to marry you, I had to be willing to choose you over everything else, even my family. Well, if you want to marry me, Nathan Trent, you're going to have to believe me before you believe anybody else."

A long, anguished moan from inside the house interrupted them. "I've got to go," Delilah said. "Jane needs me."

Nathan reached out and caught her by the arm. "I need you, too."

Delilah went into his embrace. Her arms encircled his

356

neck and she kissed him tenderly. "I know, but I have to go."

"You shouldn't be here," Nathan said. "If there is going to be fighting, you don't know where it will start. I want you to come to Maple Hill."

"I've already told you I can't leave Jane and the boys."

"They can come, too. And whoever is inside with her now. There's room for everybody."

Delilah hardly knew whether to kiss him for his kindness or hit him over the head for being so obtuse.

"You haven't been through a war, so you can't know what it does to people. It creates fear in everyone, it separates them from their neighbors, it forces them to hate their enemies even if they loved them the week before. Jane will never set foot on Maple Hill, if she dies from not doing it. Reuben would turn her out of the house if she did. They hate you, Nathan, you and all the others who've been squeezing them for years, the merchants who let them fight for the land and the rights they're now trying to take away. You don't seem to understand. If war comes, they'll shoot at you, and they'll shoot to kill."

"Doesn't anything I've done since I got here mean anything?"

"You've helped too few, and there are so many."

"So as long as I own Maple Hill, there's nothing I can do to change their minds about me?"

"There might be something, but I don't know what it is."

"So where does that leave us?"

"Where we were in the beginning. On opposite sides."

Nathan grabbed Delilah by the shoulders. He had to do something to make her see, to make her understand what she was saying.

"Reuben can come, too. He doesn't owe anyone any money. It's not his fight any longer."

Delilah took Nathan's face in her hands and kissed him gently. "I think it's wonderful you love me enough to lie

357

to yourself, but if you could hear what you're saying, you'd blush with shame. You don't believe a word of that. You're just saying anything you think might change my mind. But you know it isn't that simple. Reuben can't change any more than you can."

"Then leave them all if they won't come."

"Would you desert your family if they were in danger?"

Nathan shook his head.

"Well I can't desert mine."

"But they're wrong, Delilah. And their blindness is going to cost us our happiness."

"Would you desert your family just because they were mistaken?"

Nathan knew he hadn't deserted Priscilla or Serena even though he disliked both of them, but he was more interested in future happiness now than in naked truth. "This has nothing to do with what I might have done. This is now. The choice you make will determine both our futures."

"Don't make me choose, Nathan. I can't, not now. I love you. I'm sure I always will. If I don't marry you, I'll be miserably unhappy the rest of my life. If I desert Reuben and Jane right now, I'll despise myself until my dying day. I can live with unhappiness. I can't live with hating myself."

Nathan racked his brain for an argument which could change her mind, but just then Reuben and Captain Daniel Shays rode into the clearing. The major reason for her inability to marry him stood before him.

Chapter Twenty-three

Nathan hoped they would go into the house. He didn't want a confrontation, but the moment Reuben saw him, his face became twisted with fury and he came toward them at a run. Daniel Shays was right behind him.

"What are you doing here?" Reuben grabbed Nathan by the coat collar. "I ought to kill you for what you did to Delilah."

Nathan knocked Reuben's hands from his coat.

"I've told you a dozen times it was Lucius and Noah," Delilah said, trying to step between the two men. "Besides, he came to tell me Hector confessed."

Nathan moved Delilah to one side. "I also came to invite your family to stay at Maple Hill. If fighting breaks out, they may not be safe here."

"Why would you do a thing like that?" Reuben asked.

"Because I don't want to see Delilah hurt," Nathan said, deciding it was time to put his cards on the table. "Since she seems determined not to leave your wife's side while you're away, I decided the best thing to do was invite them all to stay at Maple Hill."

"Why are you so concerned about Delilah?" Reuben demanded. "She's done working for you."

"I love Delilah. I've asked her to marry me."

Delilah turned white, Captain Shays's jaw dropped, and Reuben exploded in fury.

With a bellow of rage, he threw himself at Nathan. Delilah cried out, expecting to see Nathan battered and broken under Reuben's furious rush, but she could hardly believe her eyes. The result was extraordinary. Reuben lay on the ground while Nathan remained on his feet, looking barely ruffled.

"Being English may be a curse in your eyes, but it has one advantage," he said, breathing a little more heavily than usual. "I was taught a very scientific method of wrestling and boxing. If you don't want more of the same, you'll curb your temper and listen to me."

"I'll listen to you when hell freezes over," Reuben said, charging to his feet. Delilah jumped between them, but Nathan quickly set her aside. Reuben came barreling in again. Nathan didn't escape unscathed this time, but the results were the same.

Undeterred, Reuben climbed to his feet, prepared to charge Nathan again.

"That's enough, Reuben," Jane said. Unnoticed, she had walked up behind them. "You've made your point, but so has he."

"I can't allow him to talk about my sister that way."

"His words can't hurt your sister, but his fists can hurt you."

Turning fiery red with chagrin, Reuben was about to rush in again when Delilah stepped in front of him.

"Don't you dare. I'm not a Lucy Porter to be fought over."

"You want people to know what he said about you?"

"He said he loved me, that he wanted to marry me. What's so wrong with that?" demanded Delilah.

"Him?"

"Surely you expect Englishmen to fall in love," she snapped. "They must. There're so many of them they have to keep sending the extras to Massachusetts."

"But he's—"

"You say one word about people owing him money and I'll scream. He only sold up Uriah Douglas because I told him to. Uriah is a lazy liar. Nathan would never

360

have gotten a cent of his money."

Reuben looked at his sister as if she were a stranger.

"He's got dozens of people working for him, and you know it, so let's have an end to this continual wrangling about debts. If you want to fight because of what people owe Noah Hubbard and his like, go ahead, but leave Nathan out of it."

"Delilah, what's come over you?"

"Sitting for hours over his books, trying to think of ways for people to pay what they owe. Going over figures to see if it was working."

"You helped him?"

"I accused him of wanting money no matter how he had to get it. He challenged me to help him. And you'll find people like Isaac Yates are glad I did."

"Aye, Isaac never misses a chance to sing your praises," Shays said.

"Then why don't you listen?" Nathan asked. "If Isaac and the others can work something out, maybe the rest of them can as well."

"Not every merchant is willing to give the farmers a chance," Shays said. "For most it's easier just to take what they have and sell it. It's those men we want to stop. We don't want a war. We just want to keep our homes."

"Then disband your army before General Lincoln gets here. Go to Boston, speak to the members of the General Court, explain what you need," Nathan advised.

"We're poor men, Mr. Trent. We can't afford the cost of travel or lodging for the time it takes to seek out so many."

"It only takes a few men. Surely you can raise the money among you."

"Mr. Trent, some men in Springfield haven't seen silver coin in two or three years. Will the Boston innkeepers accept a piglet or a goose in payment? Noah Hubbard won't."

"Then talk to the merchants. Bring force to bear on them if you must. Noah Hubbard will back down. The man is a coward."

"Maybe, but if we disarm one Noah Hubbard, a hundred more will appear in his place. You see, the Boston merchants are being driven to the edge of ruin by the London merchants. Since the war they've demanded coin for everything they ship to us."

"Not every merchant demands coin."

"Possibly not, but there aren't enough who don't to make a difference. Our people are desperate. To them this is the only way."

"You'll lose everything you've gained if you try to fight General Lincoln," Nathan warned. "Bowdoin has convinced the legislature you mean to overthrow the government. If you force them, they'll raise the full might of Massachusetts to crush you."

"We can't stop now," Reuben said. "They've finally started to pay us some attention."

"Delilah, can you make your brother see that kind of attention could get him and his friends killed?"

"The time for talking passed long ago," Shays said. "We held town meetings and country conventions. We sent petitions and emissaries. They've all been ignored."

"Then vote them out of office."

"We mean to, but if we don't get some relief now, many of us won't have anything left by the time elections come around."

Nathan gave up. "You won't come?" he said to Delilah.

"You know I can't."

"The offer to your family still stands."

"None of my kin will ever set foot on Maple Hill," Reuben stated.

"Even though you must be the most pigheaded, stubborn, blind, obstinate, obtuse, bigoted man of my acquaintance, I intend that one of your kin will be my wife," Nathan stated with savage energy. "And she surely *shall* set foot on Maple Hill."

Then before Reuben could recover from that verbal assault, Nathan pulled Delilah into his arms, gave her a swift but thorough kissing, and strode off toward his horse.

Reuben, recovered from his shock, started after him, but was stopped in his tracks by Delilah's words.

"You step one foot after him, Reuben Stowbridge, you so much as touch him, and I'll marry him this afternoon in the middle of Springfield Square."

Reuben spun about, unable to believe either the words or the voice could belong to his sister.

"You must have a fever to talk like that," he said, unable to account for it any other way.

"Why should I be the one who has a fever? I'm not going about putting muskets into the hands of every idiot in the countryside. I'm not going from town to town scaring honest citizens half out of their wits and getting the governor so mad he's raised an army to send after us. I don't attack everybody who's English when my own grandfather was London born, I'm not getting ready to leave a wife due to deliver and so worried she's having early pains.

"No, Reuben, I'm just a woman who has to stay behind and work the farm and feed the children and fight off any soldiers who might want to help themselves to your produce—or your women. I'm just one of the females who will be left to grieve when a husband or son or brother doesn't come home and she's left to struggle on alone.

"I must be a dumb woman, too, because I can't have any thoughts of my own. I can't have any opinion on the war. I can't even be expected to understand what I'm told. I certainly can't be allowed to question anything you decide to do—I can't even make up my mind when I'm in love. Surely even anyone as stupid as a woman would know she couldn't possibly be in love with an Englishman, particularly a rich Englishman."

The enormity of the unfairness of her situation almost caused Delilah to break down, but she fought back the tears.

"Well, I do love an Englishman. I love him more than anything else in the world. I think I always will. He wants me to marry him. He's willing to take my family in even though they make no effort to disguise their hatred for him, though they attack him at every opportunity. He wants to love me, to take care of me, to protect me from harm, want, hurt—to make me happy. He *wants* to do all this for me, Reuben. Not for anybody else. Just for me. And do you know what I told him?"

No one dared make a sound.

"I told him I couldn't marry him. I told him there are too many things between us for us to ever be happy. I sent him away. And do you know what's keeping us apart? You, Reuben. Your hate and your friends' hate and our neighbors' hate and Shays's hate. Everybody's hate. And Jane and the boys, your love, my love, your loyalty—all good things, all wonderful things, but all turned to evil because they're tinged with hate."

"Delilah, you can't—"

"So when you describe your heroic battles, the way you showed the government what it meant to have Reuben Stowbridge mad at them, you remember who stayed home and you remember what it cost me. Because I'll never forget, Reuben. And I'll never forgive you for it."

Delilah burst into tears and ran into the house.

Jane rolled from side to side, moaning, clutching her stomach.

"All she wants is Reuben," said Polly. "If he doesn't come, I'm afraid she's going to lose the baby."

"You can't lose a baby just from worry."

364

"You wouldn't think so, not a healthy woman like Jane, but there was many who did during the war. Peggy Wilkins for one and Betty Stout for another. Of course Betty didn't take to the bed until after she heard her Will was dead, but she was feeling poorly before that."

They were all worried. General Shepard had fired on the regulators when they'd tried to capture the Springfield arsenal. Only four men had died, but their deaths brought home the stark realities of war, all too recent in their memories.

"I don't know where Reuben is."

"Mama said they fled north to Pelham."

"How does she know?"

"Some men have already deserted. Ran away as soon as Shepard fired that cannon. Others quit after a day or two of walking in the snow. There's a steady stream of people coming in each day ready to swear loyalty to the government just so they won't have to freeze and go hungry."

"You can bet Reuben won't be one of them. If we want him, one of us is going to have to go after him." Delilah didn't know whether to be proud or angry.

"If you're thinking about going to fetch him, you'd better do it soon. I hear they're heading north again, maybe as far as Athol."

"That's twice as far as Pelham. Next thing you know they'll be in Vermont."

"They'd go all the way to Canada to escape Lincoln."

But Delilah wasn't thinking about evading General Lincoln. She was thinking about Reuben and how much better it would be for both him and Jane if he came home. They had lost, their ragtag army scattered across the countryside, helplessly fleeing before the armed might of the Massachusetts militia. General Lincoln had offered amnesty to everyone who laid down his musket and sword. She might not be able to convince Reuben to swear loyalty to the government, but if he did lay down his weapons, maybe they wouldn't care.

"I'm going after Reuben first thing in the morning," Delilah announced. "I'll bring him home if I have to tie him to a saddle."

"How are you going to get to him?" Polly demanded. "We don't have a horse, and it's too cold and dangerous for you to go on foot. Besides, it would take you so long to walk to Pelham the army is bound to have moved on."

But Nathan had horses, more than he needed. Delilah knew he would let her have one. She just didn't know if she could talk him into letting her go after Reuben alone. Well, she'd have to try, or take the horse without asking. Either way, she had to find Reuben.

"Don't tell Jane where I've gone."

"What should I say? You know she'll ask for you. She always does after five minutes of being with me."

Delilah couldn't help but smile. Jane and Polly loved each other, but each had a sister's impatience with the other. Especially since Polly thought all of Jane's troubles were in her head.

"Where're you intending to get that horse?"

"Never mind."

"You're going to Maple Hill, aren't you?"

"Where else could I get a horse?"

"Tom Oliver would give you one straight out."

"I'd walk before I'd take anything from Tom Oliver," Delilah snapped. "Lucius Clarke, too. You may not like Nathan, but he's always treated me honorably."

"I don't dislike him. I think you ought to marry him. You'd be a great fool to let a man like that get away."

Realizing the doubtful wisdom of saying anything to a chatterbox like Polly, Delilah restrained her impulse to confide in a sympathetic ear. "You make sure Jane doesn't know what I've done. She's got enough to do, worrying over that baby."

During the long walk to Maple Hill, Delilah racked her brain for a way to convince Nathan to let her have a horse. Knowing how he felt about her safety and about the foolishness of the armed rebellion, she wouldn't put it past him to refuse her the horse and to order her to return home. It would probably be easier just to take one.

Nevertheless, she could hardly wait to see him. Ever since that morning they'd spent together, he had hardly left her thoughts. There were times—the nights were the hardest—when she desperately wanted to forget her resolution and throw herself into his arms. Every time she relived each glorious moment of that morning, her body writhed on the bed, racked by a yearning only Nathan could satisfy. When she remembered his kisses, his touch, his filling her body, she had to hold on to the side of the bed to keep from dashing out of the cabin in the middle of the night.

She was still trying to get her mind off Nathan and onto the horse when she entered the Maple Hill kitchen through the back door.

"It's about time you got back with that wood," Mrs. Stebbens said without turning around. "I've told you a dozen times if I've told you once, it's got to be cut thin so I can control the heat."

"I didn't bring any wood, but I'll get some if you want."

"Miss Delilah!" Mrs. Stebbens exclaimed whirling about so fast she lost her balance and had to steady herself against the table.

"When did I get to be *Miss Delilah.*"

"Ever since the master said you'd be coming back as his wife."

"He said that?"

"At least a dozen times a day. Whatever are you doing here? Mr. Trent is away for the day."

Delilah's disappointment over Nathan's not being home was much greater than her relief that he wouldn't immediately refuse her the horse and send her home.

"My sister-in-law's not well. I have to go after my brother, and I need to borrow a horse."

367

"I don't know when he's coming back."

Lester entered the kitchen in time to hear the last remark. He looked straight at Delilah but didn't acknowledge her presence. "A cook's got no business knowing the master's doings."

"If he expects to get any dinner, it'd better be my business," Mrs. Stebbens announced.

Delilah could tell, even though Lester pretended he still controlled the household, Mrs. Stebbens's mastery was at last complete.

"You get your long face out of here or you'll be going to bed with an empty stomach. That man's worse than a dose of castor oil," Mrs. Stebbens said, making sure Lester heard her last words before he closed the door behind him.

Mrs. Stebbens chattered on while making preparations for dinner. Delilah listened, but her mind was on Nathan. Where had he gone? Was his business going well? Was he lonely living in this big house by himself? Were people nicer to him? Did Mrs. Stebbens still cook his favorite dishes? Did Hepsa mend his shirts?

She was still thinking of him when she slipped under the covers in her old room. It hadn't taken her very long to realize coming back to Maple Hill made her feel she was coming home. Now she understood the uncomfortable feeling she'd had since going back to live with Reuben and Jane. It wasn't their fault; it was hers. She had become a visitor there. Here, she felt at home.

She wanted to be at Maple Hill. She would never really feel at home anywhere else. Somehow she must find a way to take her place beside Nathan.

Nathan hadn't returned home by morning, so Delilah took one of the horses. She felt a little uncomfortable about not asking, but on the whole she was relieved. Whatever terrible things Nathan might say upon her return, she would already have brought Reuben home.

She took the river road. The day was bitterly cold, the winter clouds were low and dark, and the countryside lay under deep snow crusted hard enough to support a small man. Fortunately for Delilah, the feet of the many men and horses traveling north had beaten the snow down and cleared the drifts. Progress was slow and miserably uncomfortable, but it was steady.

A light rain started an hour later. Her thick cloak with its great hood kept her dry, but the damp cold soon chilled her to the bone. It was nearly mid-morning by the time she reached South Hadley. She stopped at a tavern for information, to get warm, and to rest her horse.

The rain turned to sleet.

"Best go on back home," the tavern keeper advised her. "We're in for a good storm. Probably five or six inches of snow before it's done."

But Delilah couldn't go back—she had to find Reuben—and she couldn't stay at the tavern because she had no money. She had no choice but to get back on the road.

Conditions worsened rapidly, and a light snow was falling when she rode into Hadley. But she found out the troops were still at Pelham, only ten miles away. She had to keep going. She couldn't stop now.

It wasn't hard to find Reuben once she reached Pelham. Everyone knew Shays's huge, fiery-tempered second in command. She was told he'd be at the tavern with all the other officers.

"You must be daft to think I would leave now!" Reuben exclaimed when Delilah told him why she had come. "Lincoln is following us. If there's a fight, Shays will need every man he has."

"Your wife needs the *only* man she has," Delilah shot back, her patience completely exhausted by Reuben's blind attachment to the regulators' cause. "What's more important than being at her side when she has your baby?"

"She's not going to have the baby now. She's not due for another month."

"She's having pains."

"Jane always has *pains* when she doesn't want me to do something. She had them with Daniel when I wanted to go join the fighting in Virginia. She had them twice with David, when I wanted to go to the convention in Worcester and again in Pittsfield."

"You don't think she's in any danger?"

"Jane's healthy as a horse. She'll have that kid on the morning it's due and be up and about before nightfall. She did with the other two."

Delilah didn't know whether to be madder at Reuben or Jane. There was clearly no point in saying anything else to her brother. Just now the battle was the most important thing in the world to him. Delilah decided only a man could hold such an opinion. The birth of a child had to be the most important occasion in any woman's life.

But if Jane had caused her to make this long ride just to try to get Reuben to come home where he would be safer, then Delilah would have a few pithy comments for her sister-in-law when she returned. It was one thing for Jane to attempt to play tricks on her husband. It was quite another for her to rope Delilah in on it. And Delilah meant to tell her so.

"I'd better see about finding you a place to stay."

"I'm going back," Delilah said. "If I leave now, I can be home before dark."

"You won't get to Hadley on foot."

"I have a horse, one of Nathan's if you must know," Delilah said defiantly when her brother looked at her accusingly. "You surely didn't expect me to travel by foot in this weather."

"I didn't expect you'd be traveling at all. Now give over and wait here while I talk to Shays."

"I'm leaving now."

"I say you're not."

"Let's get something straight, Reuben Stowbridge. You forfeited all right to censor my conduct when you left us to go off on this mad gamble. If you think I'm capable of taking care of your farm, your children, and your wife, then I'm also capable of deciding whether or not I'll return to Springfield today."

"It's crazy. Look at the weather."

"I made it here. I'll make it back."

But thirty minutes out of Pelham Delilah wasn't so sure. The snow had become heavy, the wind suddenly picked up, and the temperature seemed to be dropping. She pulled the cloak more tightly around her and lowered her head to keep the snow out of her eyes. She didn't need to watch the road. The horse would do it for her.

She passed through Amherst and Hadley without stopping, but she paused in South Hadley long enough to warm her frozen fingers. The tavern keeper urged her to stay inside, but he wasn't nearly so anxious for her company when he learned she had no money.

The storm turned into a blizzard an hour out of South Hadley and Delilah began to wonder if she would ever reach home. Her entire body felt frozen stiff. She kept her head bowed to keep the snow out of her face even though she could no longer feel the sharp needlelike flakes when they hit her cheeks. She couldn't move her fingers either. Snow began to collect in the hollow formed by her body as she hunched over the saddle.

She thought to pull off the road and ask for shelter at one of the houses along the way, but the snow had obliterated all landmarks. She couldn't discern any roads, not even the one that led to Hector's cabin.

After a time Delilah started to feel drowsy. She was relieved to find she didn't feel so cold anymore, but she didn't want to doze off. If she did, she might fall out of the saddle. Her body was so stiff from riding all day she doubted she'd be able to mount again. The snow was coming down so heavily, the sky was so dark, she couldn't even see the river, though it was sometimes less than ten feet away. She fought the drowsiness that continued to creep over her. But she couldn't help it, she was just too sleepy to stay awake.

Her horse jerked up its head. She sensed an increase in its energy, a quickening of its stride. She tried to understand what was happening, but she was so sleepy she couldn't think.

"Delilah!" It was a cry out of the darkness, and in the next instant Nathan was at her side. "My God, you're frozen stiff."

"Nathan." That was what she tried to say, but the faint sound that left her lips was ripped away by the driving wind. Delilah felt herself lifted out of the saddle and placed before Nathan on his mount. He opened his cloak and wrapped it around her, holding her against him and the life-giving warmth of his body.

Then, driving his heels into the sides of his mount, he rode for Maple Hill as though her life depended on it.

Nathan burst into the kitchen in the midst of dinner.

"Merciful God! She's not dead, is she?" Mrs. Stebbens cried when she saw who it was Nathan held in his arms.

"No, and she won't be if I have anything to say about it. Tommy, I want a blazing fire in my bedroom in less than five minutes. Lester, bring some brandy and all the extra quilts we have in the house. Mrs. Stebbens, bring every hot water bottle you can find, filled, as soon as you can get water hot."

"He's wasting his time," Lester said after Nathan had gone from the kitchen. "I've seen people freeze to death before. She has death written all over her face."

"There'll be death written over every part of your body if you don't get that brandy upstairs quick," Mrs. Stebbens said, interrupting her preparations long enough to make Lester understand the true state of affairs at Maple Hill. " 'Cause if Mr. Trent don't cut your gizzard out, I will."

Tommy had a fire blazing in the hearth and Nathan had Delilah buried under quilts by the time Mrs. Stebbens brought up the first of the hot water bottles. He sat by the bed, spooning straight brandy down her throat as fast as she could swallow it.

"I'll bring up more bottles directly," Mrs. Stebbens said as she studied Delilah closely. "She doesn't look good. Too pale and listless."

"I tried to make her walk, but she's too weak."

"She doesn't need walking. She needs to be warm. The heat's all drained out of her."

"I told Tommy to lay in enough wood to keep the fire blazing all night. I've got ten quilts on her now. I can't see how any more could help."

"Whatever you do, she's got to be as warm as you can keep her."

"I'm giving her all the brandy she can swallow."

"That ought to help."

But Mrs. Stebbens didn't seem so sanguine when she came up again with fresh hot water bottles.

"I don't like the looks of her. She ought to have come around a bit by now, have some color. She's pale as skimmed milk."

Nathan picked up Delilah and all the bedclothes and put her on the floor as close to the fire as he dared. She'd hardly swallowed any brandy the last two times he'd tried to give her some. He was frightened.

"You've got to do something else or she's not going to make it," Mrs. Stebbens said when she came up again. "I don't like the sound of her breathing."

"What can I do?"

"She needs body heat, somebody to lie down on each side of her and keep her warm. Pity she isn't at home."

"Keep bringing up hot water bottles every thirty minutes," Nathan said. "If you get too tired, wake Lester and

373

tell him I said he's to take over."

"I'm not going to bed, sir. Not while Miss Delilah's still got a chance."

The minute the door closed behind Mrs. Stebbens, Nathan began stripping off his clothes. Then he crawled between the sheets next to Delilah. Even with the hot water bottles and the overpowering heat from the blazing fire, Delilah's body felt like ice. He opened her gown and pressed as much of his body against hers as possible.

That's how Mrs. Stebbens found them when she came in half an hour later. Nathan had been afraid she would shriek in shocked surprise, but she took it all in stride.

"She's not looking any better, but at least she's not any worse."

"Put the bottles against her back and make up the fire before you go," Nathan asked. He was so hot rivulets of perspiration ran down his forehead.

The long night hours brought no comfort to Nathan. If he had been worried that lying next to Delilah might ignite passions he couldn't control, he was mistaken. He was too afraid her slow breathing might stop altogether to think of anything but her next breath, the warmth of her body, whether she moved even the slightest bit.

Odd how simple your wants become when they are reduced to the most elemental level. He had wanted money, security, friends, success, recognition, any number of things over his lifetime. Now he would have traded all of them just to have Delilah wake up.

He couldn't think of a future without her. If she didn't marry him . . . There was no completion of that thought. Just a void. He hadn't realized until now that everything he had done in the last two months had been prefaced by or predicated on the assumption she would become his wife. He had come to believe that was the only way things could end.

But now he knew there was another way. He knew the fragile woman in his arms was not immortal, not invulnerable to the vicissitudes which affected everyone else. He hadn't given much thought to the consequences Reuben's death might have on his family. But now he understood what hurt that could cause, and he swore he would do everything in his power to see that no harm came to Delilah's brother.

It struck him as ironic that Delilah could be so cold and he could be so warm. This seemed a reflection of their lives. Always on opposite sides, always pulling in different directions, always looking at the same thing with different eyes. He wondered if it would be different after they were married. One thing was certain. He'd see to it she didn't go out in any more blizzards. If he ever found out who had let her place herself at the mercy of yesterday's storm, he'd choke the life out of him.

Mrs. Stebbens returned several times before she saw a change in Delilah.

"She's got some color, Mr. Trent." She felt Delilah's forehead. "And she doesn't feel so clammy cold."

"I noticed the change just after you left last time," Nathan said, so exhausted from worry and heat he could hardly keep awake. "I thought one time she even moved a little, but I guess I was mistaken."

"You stay right where you are. Go to sleep. You look like you need the rest. I'll look after the both of you."

"But you've been up all night, too."

"No matter. I can go to sleep when she gets better. You've got to be awake then, so you'd better sleep now." She winked and grinned. "And don't you worry none about Lester or Tommy popping their heads inside to see how she's doing. I told them I thought she was sickening from the influenza. I said you might send the first one you saw out for a doctor."

"Nobody could survive in this blizzard." It was still snowing as fiercely as it had been when Nathan found Delilah.

"They know that."

Nathan laughed. "Thank you."

"No need to thank me. You're doing exactly what the doctor would have ordered had he been here. I can't help it if their minds are too small to understand."

Nathan didn't know whether Mrs. Stebbens's mind was any larger than Lester's or Tommy's, but it was certainly of a more romantic bent. She was seeing a wedding in the future. And Nathan was going to do everything he could to make sure she wasn't disappointed.

Delilah fought to open her eyes, but she felt so tired she gave up. She couldn't move. Her whole body seemed weighted down. She tried to think, to remember what had happened, where she was; but she kept wandering in and out of consciousness. She finally gave up. She was warm and comfortable. That was enough.

Delilah felt something rough against her cheek. She moved and it hurt. She tried to move away, but she couldn't. Why? What was hurting her cheek? With a great effort, she overcame her lassitude and opened her eyes.

She recognized Nathan's room. She had only been in it a few times, but she knew it as well as she knew her own. And she was lying, wrapped in what must be a dozen blankets, before a blazing fire. It was Nathan's unshaven face that had scratched her cheek, the weight of his body that kept her from moving.

My God! They were both naked! They lay in the middle of the floor like man and wife. Delilah couldn't immediately recall how she'd come to be there, but she was certain she wouldn't have forgotten her own wedding.

When the door opened and Mrs. Stebbens entered, Delilah flushed crimson from head to toe.

"Praise be!" Mrs. Stebbens cried. She was so overcome

she had to sit down on a chair to wipe the tears from her eyes. "There was a time I thought you'd never blush again in this world."

"How did I get here?" Delilah asked. She was mortified to be caught like this by anybody, even kindly Mrs. Stebbens who didn't seem to find anything unusual about it, but there was no use being modest now. She had to know the truth.

"Mr. Trent found you on the river road well-nigh frozen solid. We wrapped you in quilts, put you next to the fire, and poured brandy down you, but nothing worked until Mr. Trent lay down beside you. It would have been more proper with another female, but I didn't figure he would do you any harm, not with you cold as a mackerel and me popping in with hot water bottles every half an hour."

"Not to mention the fact I have an aversion to taking advantage of women when they're lying at death's door," Nathan muttered, still half-asleep. "I know you'll say it's just the English coming out in me, but I can't help it. We're funny that way."

Delilah blushed furiously all over again.

"I've got to get up. I can't stay here," she protested.

A wicked, teasing light came into Nathan's eyes. "Do you want to go first, or shall I?"

"Seeing as you're both mother-naked, I can't see that it makes any difference," Mrs. Stebbens remarked.

"Since you're the invalid," Nathan said to Delilah, "I shall rise first."

Both women reacted to his throwing off a layer of quilts with shocked protests.

"Does this mean you want to get dressed while I watch?" Nathan teased.

"No, it doesn't," Delilah assured him.

"You're a wicked man," Mrs. Stebbens said with a chuckle.

"It means you have to cover your eyes while I get up,"

Delilah explained. "Once Mrs. Stebbens has helped me dress, she will leave, I'll cover my eyes, and you can get dressed."

"How do I know you won't peep?"

"As if I would," Delilah replied hotly.

"I was warned about American women. I was told they could be shockingly familiar."

"It would be hard for any woman to be shockingly familiar around you," Delilah stated. "By the time you were done with *your* familiarizing, there'd be nothing left to shock."

"Give over you two. You're not getting dressed, Miss Delilah. You're getting in that bed and you're staying there until I say you can get up. You came as close to dying as a mortal can and still be in this world. Mr. Trent will turn his eyes away while I help you into the bed."

"Am I not to have even a tiny peep?"

"Not a one," Mrs. Stebbens told him, punctuating her comment with an indulgent chuckle.

"After sleeping on the floor and giving generously of my heat, I think myself sorely used."

"If you want to really be sorely used, you just peep," Delilah threatened.

It took just a moment for Mrs. Stebbens to help Delilah into a thick, flannel gown and get her into the bed. She immediately pulled all but one of the quilts off Nathan and spread them over Delilah.

"Now that I'm of no further use, you don't care if I freeze to death," Nathan said.

"You're more like to suffer a heat stroke," said Mrs. Stebbens, fanning herself. "I don't know how you stood it all night."

"Neither do I," Delilah said, no trace of amusement or mock seriousness in her voice. "I owe you my life."

"If you keep me lying on the floor, you'll have my life in exchange." It was easier to joke than to yield to the emotion which threatened to overwhelm him. Relief and happiness that Delilah was well made it difficult for him to speak.

"I'm going," Mrs. Stebbens said. "Don't be long in dressing."

"How will I be sure she won't look?"

"Because she's a decent woman," Mrs. Stebbens declared. "And decent women don't have any interest in men's bodies. Make sure you keep your eyes closed good and tight, Miss Delilah. I wouldn't put it past that man to do something disgraceful just to shock you."

Chapter Twenty-four

Delilah was deliriously happy. For two days Nathan had barely left her side. Though he had temporarily moved into the room he had used before his uncle's death, he treated his own room as though it were still his. He came in and out at any hour upon the flimsiest excuse. If Mrs. Stebbens thought Delilah might like a thick soup, nothing would do but for Nathan to inquire personally. He checked the fire every few minutes to make sure it never fell below a roaring blaze. If Delilah wanted to take a nap, he had to tuck her in. If she wanted to sit in the drawing room, he would wrap her in twice as many quilts as she needed and carry her downstairs so she wouldn't tire herself.

"I never thought I could be cossetted too much," Delilah told Mrs. Stebbens after Nathan had spent ten minutes deciding the room was too large to heat properly and that a screen he remembered seeing in the attic would help protect her from drafts. "After being the one expected to do the cossetting, I find it surprisingly uncomfortable. And I thought I would like it so much."

"Fair unsettles you, doesn't it? Don't worry. It won't last. He'll come to himself soon enough."

But he didn't. The weather made going out impossible, so nothing prevented Nathan from giving Delilah his full attention. She finally decided if she didn't soon find something for him to do, he would set her recovery back a week.

"I've been meaning to ask you something, but I don't know if I should," Delilah said.

"You know you can ask me anything."

"It's about that painting of me, the one in the other room. I found it when I was putting away your things."

To her surprise Nathan wasn't angry at all. Rather, he looked like he'd been caught in a guilty secret.

"Why didn't you tell me you could paint?"

"I suppose it's something I wanted to forget."

"Why? I can't wait for you to finish it."

"I doubt I'll touch it again."

His tone of voice upset her. It wasn't angry or petulant. It was final, as if after a long struggle Nathan had finally put something behind him.

"I don't understand."

Nathan pulled his chair up to the bed. He took her hand and squeezed it tight.

"I guess it's about time I told you a little about myself."

From the expression on his face, Delilah decided he wasn't going to enjoy making these revelations.

"My father decided if his sister could marry the son of an earl, his son could marry the daughter of one. When he found I could paint, he decided I should become a portrait painter. Gainsborough and Reynolds were making huge amounts of money just then. More important, they had entree into almost any house in London.

"He sent me to an expensive school and hired the best art teachers he could afford. By the time I was twenty-two, I was being asked to paint portraits for people who couldn't afford Gainsborough or Reynolds. Mother decided I was to marry one of the Earl of Glencoe's daughters. Fool that I was, I didn't see anything wrong with the prospect. I even obligingly fell in love with her."

"Who was she?"

"Lady Sarah Mendlow. She was the fourth daughter and even more beautiful than you. She was willing to marry me as long as I was rich. Unfortunately, my father chose that time to lose his business and with it the only reason

Sarah had for marrying anyone like me. I would have understood if she had simply broken off our engagement. I was never so deeply in love I didn't realize she wouldn't have married me without the money. But she felt shamed, and she determined to ruin me. She chose a time when the house was full of guests to accuse me of attempting to force myself upon her. She even ripped her gown to make it appear I had tried to take her against her will."

Delilah didn't need Nathan to tell her the humiliation he must have endured. His face went blank, like a mask, all lines of expression smoothed away, and his voice was even, low pitched, dead, as if he were telling a story that bored him slightly. His eyes, focused on something she couldn't see, were empty.

He was like a living shell.

"The earl, shouting that he would ruin me, had me thrown out of the house. By the next day all my commissions had been withdrawn. There wasn't a footman in town who would allow me to leave my card. It was as if I had never existed."

Nathan was silent for a few minutes.

"I went to work for my father, as I should have in the beginning. I may be a good painter, but I'm a good businessman, too. Unfortunately, we discovered this too late. We were at war with the colonies then, and other merchants refused to give them credit. My father thought the colonies would lose and all accounts would be collected by the British army. He gave credit to everyone who wanted it. By the time he realized his mistake, it was too late. I held things together for a time, but in the end we lost everything. Even though I begged him not to, my father wrote his noble brother-in-law, but the earl refused to answer his letters. He even put an announcement in the *Times* saying he would not be responsible for my father's debts. My parents died of shame and poverty."

"So that's why you hate Americans so much."

"I used to think it was their canceled debts that ruined my father, but I realize now he ruined himself. He was too

382

concerned with pushing me into the upper class to pay proper attention to his affairs. And he made a bad business decision because he wanted to make a lot of money fast."

"And your painting?"

"I only began the portrait when I thought I would never have you."

"I think you ought to finish it. Not just because of me. You ought to be very proud you can create something as beautiful as that."

"Do you really like it?"

"Very much."

"I'll think about it. In the meantime, it's time for your nap. You'll never become strong again without your rest."

"But I'm always sleeping. Can't I stay up a little longer?"

"Not today. If you continue to do so well, Mrs. Stebbens says you can start getting up for a few hours tomorrow."

"Mrs. Stebbens has nothing to do with it. It's you, and don't think I don't know it."

Nathan grinned, not at all abashed at being found out. "We worked it out together."

"Bosh," Delilah said, but she took her nap.

Jane came over in an ox cart.

"I want to see my sister-in-law," she announced to Mrs. Stebbens. "I know she's here."

"Sit yourself down," Mrs. Stebbens said. "You don't look like you ought to be out and about."

"I've got to see Delilah."

"You might as well take a seat. Nobody's going to see Miss Delilah without Mr. Nathan says so."

"She's my sister-in-law," Jane began.

"Then you ought to keep her at home instead of letting her go about in blizzards. Sit down. I ain't going to hurt you."

Jane sat.

"Now you enjoy a nice cup of coffee while I go find Mr.

Nathan. It's a nasty cold day out, it surely is."

Nathan entered the kitchen in less than a minute. Mrs. Stebbens discreetly remained in the butler's pantry.

"I'm Jane Stowbridge, and I've come to take Delilah home," Jane announced the minute Nathan stepped through the door.

Nathan didn't bother to fence. "How did you know Delilah was here? I've strictly forbidden anyone to breathe a word."

"I guessed. I got a message from Reuben, saying he was all right and not to worry but that I was to keep Delilah from going after him again. I knew then she'd left Pelham. This was the only place between our farm and Pelham she could be."

"As long as she was alive and able to get here."

"Nothing's happened to Delilah, has it?"

"Yes, something did. She nearly died."

Jane went dead white. "And now?"

"She still has to spend most of the day in bed, but she's recovering. I don't think she'll have any permanent damage, but I'm worried about her lungs. She has a persistent cough."

"I'll see she gets the best possible care once I get her home."

"You may see her, on conditions, but she's not going anywhere until I'm satisfied she's fully recovered."

Jane's expression hardly changed, but her indignation was easy to see. "May I remind you she's my family, Mr. Trent. Not yours."

Nathan's eyes grew hard. "Pity you didn't remember that before you let her go off to Pelham."

"I was ill. I didn't know."

"It was your business to know."

No one, most especially a stranger, had ever taken Jane to task for anything. She could only stare at Nathan in surprise.

"I'm taking care of her now. As soon as she's strong enough, we're going to be married."

Jane's body stiffened, and her eyes grew cold and hard. "I wasn't aware she had accepted an offer from you."

"It seems to me, ma'am, that all you are aware of is your husband and your hatred of anybody he hates."

"I won't sit here and be talked to like this."

"You will if you want to see Delilah. I won't have you upsetting her by making her feel it's her duty to be home, waiting on you hand and foot. You're going to tell her she should stay right where she is until she's completely well. You're going to tell her you can do without her for a while longer. And you aren't going to tell her anything about Reuben that will upset her."

"And if I don't agree?"

"You're welcome to some more coffee before you leave."

Jane studied Nathan carefully, but she couldn't see much of the man Delilah had described. He looked just as cold and implacable as Ezra Buel ever did. It was easy to believe they were kin.

Jane made up her mind. "I dislike you, and I don't trust you, but I'll do as you wish because I believe you have Delilah's best interest at heart. And because I believe you will do what you can to insure her reputation is unharmed."

"Delilah has done nothing to be ashamed of."

"After being here alone with you for a week, I doubt the rest of the world would agree."

"The rest of the world can go to hell, which is where I'll send anyone who tries to hurt Delilah."

"I'm her sister-in-law. I love her."

"Prove it by trying to think of her first instead of Reuben or yourself."

Nathan didn't think much of Jane, but he had to give her credit. She'd taken his accusations without flinching. The woman had plenty of courage. Why hadn't she used it instead of bleeding Delilah dry?

"Jane," Delilah cried happily when Nathan ushered her sister-in-law into the room. "You shouldn't have come to see me. What about your condition?"

Jane was shocked to see Delilah looking so pale and weak.

"I'm fine. I came in the cart. How are you feeling?"

"Much better. If Nathan's not after me to rest or eat some soup, Mrs. Stebbens is up here making sure I don't get out of bed for as much as a glass of water. I'll be thoroughly spoiled by the time I'm better. I won't be fit for work. How is Reuben?" Her face tightened with worry.

"He's fine. I don't know where he is just now, but I've heard no reports of fighting."

Delilah relaxed. "Maybe there won't be any more. Now tell me about the boys. Daniel was trying so hard to act like a little man."

Nathan left the two women to catch up on family news, but he made a note of the time. Jane would get twenty minutes and not a second more, even if she did have to travel nearly an hour each way.

Still, he would have to make some pretense of feeling more charitably toward Jane. Delilah loved her family, and if he didn't want to give her pain, he must do his best to get along with them. But the Stowbridges would have to do some of the giving. And they weren't going to keep plaguing her the rest of her life. If he had to, he'd take Delilah someplace where she'd never see them again.

"She seems weak still, but she's in good spirits," Jane said when she met Nathan in the downstairs hall.

"She nearly died. She's lucky to be alive."

"I appreciate the care you've given her."

"Damnation," Nathan cursed. "I didn't do it for your appreciation or out of Christian charity or any other laudable reason. I did it because I love her. Why is it so hard for you and your husband to believe that?"

Jane's expression didn't change. "At least you've made her stay in bed. It's more than I could have done."

Nathan's attitude softened a little. "It's easier here. At home she would want to help. Here she knows we won't let her lift so much as a spoon."

"Can I see her again?"

"Come anytime. I'll send the buggy for you. I only ask that you do not tire or upset her."

"It may seem hard for you to believe, Mr. Trent, but we love her, too. We just see her differently. I'm used to her being a tower of strength. You see her as someone fragile to be protected. I suppose both of us might be right."

"It doesn't look the way I remembered it," Delilah said. Nathan had brought his easel into the bedroom so he could put the finishing touches on her portrait.

"What's wrong?"

"Nothing. I can't put my finger on it, but it's different somehow."

Nathan thought it wiser not to tell Delilah he had re-done the painting as a portrait of the woman who had nearly died in his arms. Someday, if she asked, if she guessed . . . he knew he would tell her regardless, but not today.

"Where will you hang it when it's finished?"

"In the drawing room if you think it's good enough. In the attic if it's not."

"I wouldn't let you hide it in the attic."

Nathan stepped back, decided the last stroke had achieved what he wanted and dropped the brush into a jar of cleaner. "I'd burn it if I thought you didn't like it."

"I'd keep it even if I hated it. I never thought anybody would paint a picture of me. That only happens to truly important people."

"And women whose future husbands happen to be portrait painters."

"Are you really going to be my husband?" she asked. "I know we've talked about it, but . . ."

"I keep asking, and you keep refusing—you're a very stubborn woman—so I decided to keep you here until you agree to my outrageous demands."

"Do you mean I'm well enough to go home?"

"You are home."

"You know what I mean."

"You're well enough for just about anything except going back to Jane and the boys."

"You're not just saying that to keep me here?"

"Would it?"

"No, not if they needed me. But if you wanted me to stay . . ."

Nathan was at Delilah's side instantly. "I've never wanted anything more. I would marry you tomorrow if I could."

"We can't," Delilah said with a happy laugh. "We have to post the banns first."

"I know."

"I can't stay here after that."

"Are you still worried about what people will say?"

"Not really. I could have had you take me home that next morning, or have asked Jane to stay with me, if I'd been concerned about wagging tongues. I didn't suggest it because I knew Jane would probably stay, and I so desperately wanted you all to myself, even if it was to be for just a little while."

Nathan's happiness disappeared.

"Just a little while? You're not thinking of going away again, are you?"

"I have to go, but I'm coming back this time."

"You won't let anybody stand in your way?"

"That's what I wanted to tell you that night. I knew then I loved you more than anyone else in the world. I couldn't explain that to Jane, though she feels the same about Reuben."

"I know. She doesn't see how you can love me."

"I'm afraid she'll always feel that way. Reuben, too."

"If you can accept Serena and Priscilla, I can accept Reuben and Jane." Nathan sat next to her on the bed, put his arms around her, and drew her close. "We have strange families, the two of us."

Delilah put her arms around him. "I don't want to think of our families or the war or anything—except us."

Nathan feathered a kiss on her cheek.

"And you can stop treating me as if I'm made of porcelain. I may have gotten a little too cold, but I'm plenty warm now."

Nathan didn't need a second invitation. They fell back on the bed, wrapped in each other's arms. "I was afraid you might not be strong enough."

"I know. I decided if I didn't say something, you might never touch me again."

Nathan kissed the delicate shell of her ear. "You like my touch?"

"Very much," Delilah said, turning her head to make it easier for him to continue his attentions. "I've been thinking about it for days."

"And I've been thinking about touching you ever since I saw you," Nathan admitted. His tongue played along the edge of Delilah's ear sending shivers of delight all through her body. Her stomach knotted and then shot tendrils of delicious tension into every muscle. Now Nathan was blowing gently on the wisps of hair behind her ear and along the side of her neck. More shivers, more tendrils of tension, until she squirmed away from him. But the harder she tried to twist away, the more Nathan tormented her until she captured his teasing lips in a hungry kiss.

"You know that drives me crazy," she said in a breathless whisper.

"Not half as crazy as being next to you for months and not being able to touch you," Nathan replied, once more snuggling in the crook of her neck.

"You did touch me."

"If I had touched you the way I wanted to, we would have created a scandal that would have been heard from here to Boston."

"Oh," Delilah replied. She turned to face Nathan and blocked his path to her tortured ear.

But Nathan did not give up so easily. He kissed the tip of her nose and then gently kissed her closed eyes. His tongue bathed her eyelids in soothing warmth. His fingertips traced the line of her cheekbone; his lips followed with a trail of kisses. Delilah tried to recapture his mouth, but Nathan seemed famished for the taste of her body. His tongue traced arabesques down one shoulder, then made a gentle arc back until it arrived at the mound of her breasts.

"It's only fair for what you did to me with those tight breeches," Delilah managed to say. "I couldn't take my eyes off you."

Nathan lifted a breast from her bodice and gently kissed its burning surface. "That's how I felt about your blue dress."

Delilah's body tensed, her breasts hardening as Nathan slipped her gown over her shoulders and down to her waist. Then he lay very still, his lips exploring the side of her neck, his warm breath teasing the tiny hairs at her nape, his fingertips doing a slow ballet across her breasts.

"Those breeches caused me to have such shocking feelings I was afraid I was a wanton at heart. Nobody ever told me I was supposed to feel that way."

"Like this?" Nathan asked as he alternately cupped her breasts and feathered his fingertip around each hard, puckered nipple. With a groan, she pulled his head down to her breast, somehow relieved when his lips tugged at the painfully sensitive nipple until she moaned with pleasure. She ran her fingers deep into his thick hair and pressed his head against her body. A gentle nip of Nathan's teeth caused her to utter a tiny scream of delight.

"I've always wanted to undress you," Delilah confessed as she pulled at his shirt, eager to feel the warmth of his skin beneath her hands. Her entire body was ablaze, yet she wanted to touch even more of him. "Does that shock you?"

"I've spent hours every day practically sitting on my hands so I wouldn't undress you," Nathan replied.

Delilah felt abandoned when Nathan deserted her breasts to slip her gown under her hips and drop it to the floor. But as the tension in her body spiraled down like a leaf in the wind, his lips and tongue traced a curving trail across her ribs and down her abdomen. Then, as she was once more swept up in the vortex of desire, he advanced to her very threshold. As his lips traced another path toward her still throbbing breasts, she felt his hands part her creamy white thighs and uncover the nub of her very existence.

Delilah forgot everything else.

Ever so gently he stroked her with his fingertip. Delilah moaned and moved against his hand, fire shooting through her like bolts of lightning. Nothing had ever so overpowered her, held her helpless in its toils. She could feel the waves of sensual delight increase in force and frequency as they washed over her.

Nathan's lips found her breast once more and new currents of aching pleasure racked her. Delilah moaned and arched against him, but the waves of pleasure from this gentle sucking were nothing compared to the sweet agony he had caused between her thighs.

She tried to rip the clothes from his body, but he wouldn't be deterred. She tried to roll away from him, but he held her prisoner. He was going to torture her until she died of pleasure.

"Please don't wait," she begged, as she pulled his head away from her breasts. "I can't stand it much longer."

But Nathan's hand never left her. By the time he had removed the rest of his clothing, Delilah had crested a series of waves to achieve a shattering climax. As her exhausted body slumped to the bed, she thought nothing could be any more devastating than this.

But the moment Nathan eased himself into her moist heat, she was in the toils of a physical desire for him that was so strong, so overpowering, that even though seconds before she had felt exhausted, burned out, she now felt starved for the only force on earth which could reach the kernel of need buried at the center of her.

Nathan. Only Nathan.

Delilah arched upward at the same time she took his firm buttocks in her grasp and forced him deep inside her. The urgency had left her when Nathan had withdrawn his hand, but as he started to move within her, hot waves of need returned, stronger than before.

It was impossible to remember that only a few days before she had been too weak to get out of bed. It didn't matter that her body was drenched in sweat from a shattering climax only moments ago. She felt she was about to explode with energy, and still more was building inside her. She wanted to cling to Nathan until she absorbed him, wanted him to wrap her in his embrace until she became part of him. Her whole body seemed to be expanding, absorbing, encompassing, filling the space around her until the universe was part of her being.

She forgot yesterday, forgot five minutes before; she was aware only of each instant, time having been brought into incredibly sharp focus, momentary slivers of it having been stretched into slow motion by the forces which had rendered her utterly powerless, which even now were depriving her of conscious thought.

She was only vaguely aware of Nathan's increasingly rapid breathing as she slipped into complete fulfillment.

Polly burst into the library unannounced. "Reuben's in jail. He's been sentenced to hang."

Delilah gasped in horror. "When did it happen?"

"In Sheffield," Polly said. "We heard about it only this morning when they brought him to Springfield."

"I'll be ready to go in half an hour. How did you come?"

"I walked."

"Can I borrow the buggy?" Delilah asked, turning to Nathan. "Jacob can drive us."

"I'll drive you myself," Nathan said, but his hand restrained Delilah when she would have left the room.

"I understood that all the insurgents had been pardoned," Nathan said to Polly.

"You knew he was captured?" Delilah asked.

"No, only that some insurgents had been. I was told they would be pardoned if they swore loyalty to the government."

"Most of them were pardoned, but they said they're going to hang six as an example."

"Nathan, can you . . . ?"

"I already have, but apparently I wasn't persuasive enough."

That look was on his face again. Delilah didn't know who had inspired it, but she hoped it was Noah Hubbard or Lucius Clarke. She was certain they had tried to insure that Reuben would be the example. From Nathan's anger, he was sure of it too.

"If they mean to hang him now, they mean to do it despite anything I can say."

"But you'll talk with them again? Plead with them if you must?"

"I'll do what I can."

"I've got to go. Jane must be frantic."

Nathan's grip tightened. "Would you leave us alone?" he said to Polly. "Mrs. Stebbens would be happy to bring you some refreshments in the sitting room."

Both women looked at him without understanding, but Polly shrank from the fierce look in Nathan's eyes.

"I don't know where it is."

"The last door on the left," Nathan told her.

"Nathan, what did you mean by that?"

"Sit down. I want to talk to you a minute."

"I don't have time. Jane will be in a state—"

"Ever since I've known you, Jane has been in a state or Reuben's been in a temper or they've both fallen down and bruised their shins. And you always run to them. Do you think that once, just this once, you could think of someone else?"

"You?"

"I was thinking of yourself, but I'd love it to be me."

"But this is different. They really need me."

"It's always *different*. Every time they *really* need you. But that didn't stop Jane from letting you go off after Reuben, and it didn't stop him from letting you head off in a storm."

393

"But he couldn't stop me."

"I'd have stopped you. I'd have tied you to a bed, a chair, anything before I'd have let you nearly kill yourself."

Delilah sat down. "Was I really that sick?"

"For twelve hours I thought you were going to die. I never prayed so hard in my life."

"You prayed for me?"

"Why should that be difficult to believe?"

"Nobody ever prayed for me before."

"If it makes you feel any better, I've prayed for you since, prayed you'd have better sense than to do something like that again. What were you doing out? You've lived here all your life. You know you can die in a storm like that."

Delilah realized Nathan had never asked her why she'd been out in the storm. "I went to find Reuben. Jane grew so upset over the battle in Springfield she began having pains again."

"That's twice I can remember, but she's been fine every time she's come here. Can she have pains anytime she wants?"

Delilah dropped her eyes. "That's what Reuben said."

"Yet she let you go all that distance?"

"Jane didn't know where Reuben was, and nobody knew the weather was going to turn so bad."

"Reuben must have."

"He tried to get me to stay, but I wouldn't."

"For your family you'll practically kill yourself, but for me you can't even—"

"Don't say it."

"Can't you see they're still using you?"

"Don't say that, either. Reuben's in jail, sentenced to hang, and Jane's expecting a baby. What do you want me to do? Tell them I'm having too much fun, that I'll come later?"

"No. I always knew you would go. I only hoped I would be able to make you understand what they're doing.

They'll always need you. They will always have some reason why you can't come back."

"I'll come back. But now I have to be with Jane. You once said if I loved you I would have to choose you over my family. And I have. But I can't choose you all the time. Someday it'll be our children, maybe even our grandchildren. Today it's Jane."

There was nothing more to say. All he could do was watch her go and hope she would come back.

Chapter Twenty-five

"The General Court made the decision to pardon all but six of the leaders," Nathan told Delilah and Jane. "They can't hang Shays and Day because they fled the state, so they chose six men from across Massachusetts."

"Isn't there anything else you can do? Someone you can talk to?"

"I've seen everyone with any power to affect the decision. If Reuben would write a letter of apology and send it to the Governor's Council, they might decide to grant him clemency."

"Reuben would never do anything like that," Delilah declared. "He'd hang first."

"He will not," Jane stated. She had been nursing her infant daughter, but she handed the little girl to Polly, buttoned up her dress, and came over to Delilah and Nathan. "Tell me what the letter should say. I'll write it down. Reuben will copy it over and sign it."

"But it goes against everything he's ever stood for," Delilah protested.

"Getting himself hanged goes against everything I stand for," Jane stated flatly. "He'll sign it if I have to club him over the head."

Delilah never knew how Jane did it, but Reuben did write to the Governor's Council:

Feeling the deepest sorrow and remorse and in full knowledge of the evils of my conduct, I now admit

396

great shame and guilt. I was never an officer in the regulators, but having a good horse and a foolish fondness to be thought active and alert I was persuaded to take an old cutlass and ride at the head of a column during the attack on the Springfield arsenal. I had left home unarmed and was guilty merely one of uttering foolish and wicked expressions for which I am deeply ashamed. My part in the engagement at Sheffield was strictly defensive, being merely of a party that was out foraging for provisions when we were ambushed. I humbly ask the mercy and pardon of the most gracious and loving, fatherly Governor and Council.

Delilah offered to carry the missive to Boston, but Jane wouldn't hear of it. "It'll be more effective if it's delivered by his wife, especially if she's also suckling a babe."

When Nathan heard Jane intended to travel to Boston alone, he insisted upon driving her himself. He invited Polly to help with the baby. Delilah would stay home with the boys.

Delilah endured several days of miserable suspense. People came by to express sympathy, but they also came out of curiosity. She tried to shield Daniel and David, but the lads knew. They had known almost from the first. Neither boy said anything until one evening when Jane and Nathan had been gone four days.

"Donny Hubbard says they'll hang Papa," Daniel said. "He says it won't make any difference what Papa does now. He says they got to hang somebody, and it's going to be Papa."

Just like Noah Hubbard to poison his child's mind with hate, Delilah thought.

"Your father wrote a very nice letter," Delilah said. "I'm sure the men in Boston will give it special attention, particularly with your mama taking it personally."

"Donny says Nathan's going won't do any good either. He says people don't like him."

"Who's Nathan?" David asked.

"He's the man who's driving your mama and Aunt Polly to Boston."

"Donny says—"

"I don't want to hear any more *Donny says*," Delilah snapped. "He's only repeating what his father says, and Noah Hubbard is a miserly, mean-spirited, hateful man. I'm sorry I didn't scratch his eyes out when he accused me of spying on Nathan."

"What happened?" David asked.

"Nathan threatened to beat him senseless."

"I like Nathan," David said.

"I do too," Delilah answered, tears in her eyes.

"Will he threaten to beat the men in Boston senseless?"

"He will if they keep on wanting to hang your father."

"Then I like Nathan, too," Daniel said. He thought a minute. "I think I'll beat up Donny Hubbard. If he says anything else about Papa," he added when Delilah looked at him askance.

"Let's hope your mama brings us good news. Then no one will have to beat up anybody."

From the look of dejection on Jane's face, Delilah could tell before they reached the house they had failed.

"They wouldn't even see me," Jane told Delilah.

"They said they had already considered the issue as much as they were going to," Nathan explained. "I think that was primarily the governor's doing. He's furious about the rebellion and is determined to punish somebody."

"Isn't there something you can do?" Delilah asked Nathan when they were outside.

"I'm going to get some more people to write letters, particularly people like Noah Hubbard and Lucius Clarke."

"How can you do that? Noah's been telling everybody they'll hang Reuben no matter what you do."

"If I make Noah pay me what he owes me in coin, it will ruin him. He'll write that letter, but I don't know if it will have any effect. Bowdoin is determined to have somebody's blood. I don't know how I can stop him."

Delilah had managed to keep up her courage until now, but in the face of Nathan's statement, she burst into tears.

Nathan couldn't think of a thing to say that would do any good. This wasn't a time when words could help much, only love would. His love would help her survive the waiting and the healing.

So he held her close as she cried, told her how much he loved her, and let his own strength support her now that her own had given out.

But he hated this feeling of helplessness. It weighed on him worse than when his father had lost the business. He had done everything he could to help him. He'd worked until he was so tired he could hardly think, he'd talked to everyone he'd ever known who could possibly help; but it had been to no avail.

Now it looked as though his efforts were for naught once again. Oddly enough he wasn't thinking about money this time. He would probably come out of this far better off than Uncle Ezra would have been, but that wouldn't count for much if Delilah lost her brother. He had always been jealous of the loyalty and love she gave Reuben. More than once he had wished Reuben would disappear and never be heard from again. He privately considered the man a hotheaded fool. But no matter what else Reuben might be, he was the only family Delilah had. That was something no amount of money could replace.

Nathan vowed that somehow he'd see Reuben didn't hang.

"Nathan's going to get Colonel Clarke and some of the other River Gods to write letters," Delilah told Jane later. She had dried her tears and washed her face after Nathan had left. He might not mind seeing her crying, but it wouldn't do Jane any good.

"They won't do it. I know they won't."

"Nathan said they would, so they will."

"You think a lot of him, don't you?"

"I love him."

"I wasn't talking about that. You think he can do anything he sets his mind to. If he says it'll be done, as far as you're concerned, it will be."

"I never thought about it like that, but I suppose I do. Nathan is a very determined man."

"I know," Jane said, remembering her encounters with him during Delilah's illness. "Do you think he'll be able to save Reuben?"

"I don't know," Delilah admitted. "Nathan might be able to bend everyone in Springfield to his will, but he doesn't have any influence in Boston. You found that out for yourself."

"Then we have to help Reuben break out of jail."

"How?" Delilah didn't hesitate. She didn't stop to think that it was illegal, that they might get caught and all end up in jail. She only asked how.

"I don't know, but we've tried everything else. We've got to think of something."

"Who's the guard?" Delilah asked after the two had sat for several minutes in silence.

"There're several."

"Name them."

"Let's see, there's Rufus Silliman, Ephraim Trumbull, and Caleb Parsons."

"When does Caleb come on duty?"

"He's been coming on at night, sometime after supper."

"Then that's when we'll do it," Delilah declared, buoyant with excitement.

"Do what?"

"Break him out of jail."

"How?"

"Caleb's fond of rum. We're both going to visit Reuben. We need to pick a night when there's no moon and it's as cold as can be. You go inside, and I'll see Caleb drinks so much he passes out. He used to do it nearly every time he came to my uncle's tavern."

"What's Reuben to do?" Jane asked.

"Run as soon as I call out."

"But suppose somebody recognizes him?"

"Think of some way to disguise him. Maybe he could wear one of your dresses."

"He can't wear anything of mine."

"Then make a dress for him," Delilah said, exasperated by her sister-in-law's lack of imagination.

"He'll never pass for a female, not as tall as he is."

"Maybe not, but by the time they figure out who he is, he'll be gone."

They had to work out a few more details, but that was the plan they settled on.

"Are you going to tell Nathan?" Jane asked.

"No."

"Why?"

"I don't want him involved in this."

"You think he'd help us?"

"Maybe, if he had to, but he disapproves of breaking the law. He'd be bound to do what he could to stop us."

So for the next three nights Delilah and Jane visited Reuben together. Caleb remembered Delilah from the tavern and was perfectly content to sit talking with her while Jane visited inside.

The fourth night turned bitterly cold. Caleb didn't question Jane when she came bundled in a lot of clothes.

"I brought something to keep you warm," Delilah whispered after she and Caleb settled themselves on the rough bench in front of the jail.

"Why are you whispering?"

"I don't want Jane to hear," Delilah said. "I remembered how fond you were of rum. I brought you some."

"I can't drink on duty."

"Nobody will see you," she whispered encouragingly. "Besides, they wouldn't care if they did. It's bitter cold."

"I can't."

"Suit yourself," Delilah said, "but I wouldn't have brought the stuff if I hadn't thought you'd want it." She pouted. "I had a terrible time sneaking it past Jane. She doesn't like spirits. She gives Reuben the devil every time he has a drop."

"Sure keeps a man warm though," Caleb said, looking longingly at the bottle.

"I'd better see how Jane's doing. She might not want to stay so long tonight. It's terribly cold."

"Why aren't you wearing that dress?" Delilah demanded when she saw Reuben still in his own clothes.

"He won't put it on," Jane told her.

"I can't be seen wearing a dress," Reuben protested. "I'd be a laughingstock. I'd never be able to hold my head up again."

Delilah itched to slap Reuben hard enough to knock some sense into his head. "You won't have to hold it up at all if they hang you," she told him, furious. "The rope will keep it plenty high."

"You don't understand—" Reuben began.

Delilah thought of all she had done because of Reuben, the months of hard work at Maple Hill, that terrible trip to Pelham, the weeks of worry, the times she had turned Nathan away because of him, and she got so mad she wanted to hit him. How could anyone be so foolish at a time like this? Didn't he know what they had gone through?

She realized for the very first time that Reuben had no real understanding of anyone except himself. He wasn't deliberately heedless of others. He simply couldn't see beyond his own point of view. He would never understand the consequences of what he had done, how much he had caused her to suffer. He simply wouldn't see it. Delilah glared at her brother as no woman had since he'd been a little boy.

"I understand, Reuben Stowbridge. I've been your sister for nineteen years, but for the first time I understand you perfectly. It's all right for you to start wars, shoot people, spend weeks tramping through blizzards, and get yourself sentenced to be hanged. It's okay for Jane to travel all the way to Boston to try to see the governor, for Nathan to make everyone he knows write letters for you, for me to get Caleb Parsons drunk on duty; but your stupid pride is more important than your life and your family's future." She ground her teeth in frustration. "I can't help being born your sister, but it's a shame Jane had to marry such a fool."

"Delilah!" Jane exclaimed, shocked at her sister-in-law's conduct.

Quite suddenly Delilah knew she had had enough. "Get him in that dress if you have to knock him out," she said as she turned to leave. "Caleb passes out quickly and recovers even more quickly."

"But suppose he won't do it?" Jane asked.

Delilah glared at Reuben. "Then I'll shoot him in the leg. Maybe we can drag him out." She spun on her heel, leaving her brother and sister-in-law too astonished to speak.

Delilah was relieved to see the level of liquid in the bottle had dropped while she was inside. She sat down next to Caleb, thankful he had drunk too much to notice she was still in a temper. He offered the half-empty bottle to her.

"Keep it. If Jane finds me with it, she'll skin me alive."

Caleb took a swallow while Delilah talked about things he didn't remember or care to be reminded of. He took another, then another, and finally a long drink. Moments later he staggered to his feet.

"I feel sick," he announced, and wandered off behind the jail.

Delilah ran inside. Reuben was in the dress. "He's gone. Quick."

But just as they stepped outside the jail, Delilah heard a groan behind her and turned to find Caleb staring at them.

"Oh my God," he moaned again, holding his head. "Help!" he cried. "Help! Jail break."

Delilah tried to distract him, but Caleb was only conscious of the horrifying fact that the prisoner was about to escape because he had gotten drunk.

"Help!" he cried again.

Townspeople began to arrive as Reuben and Jane vanished into the dark.

"Where did he go?" someone asked, and immediately ran off in the direction in which Caleb pointed.

Delilah was taken by the arm and pulled away from the light. "Was this your doing?"

It was Nathan.

"Yes." He walked her, as rapidly as possible, away from the hubbub.

"Was that Jane or Polly?"

"Jane."

"He'll be caught, you realize. And you'll both be brought before the sheriff."

"We had to try something," Delilah hissed. "I couldn't just let him hang."

"I told you I was working on some letters."

"You also told me Governor Bowdoin was determined to hang him. I didn't figure a few letters were going to change his mind."

"They've postponed the execution."

"That only means we'll have to wait longer for the same results."

They did catch Reuben. The dress proved to be a virtual beacon in the night. Everybody noticed him. The sheriff returned him to his cell and chained him to the wall. Caleb, also in jail for his part in the jailbreak, loudly placed the blame for the whole incident on Delilah. Only Nathan's interference kept her from being arrested.

The sheriff looked upon her crime as so severe he took her and Jane before the Court of Common Pleas and General Session. With Jane conspicuously nursing her baby during the proceedings, the judge probably wouldn't have done any more than warn them, but after Nathan's impassioned defense, he actually praised them for their ingenuity and their courage. He did, however, caution them to find a better way to exercise it.

Even though Delilah and Jane were given a reprieve, Nathan found himself just as thoroughly out in the cold as ever. Clearly, as long as Delilah's family continued to be in crisis, they would first call on her. She would probably slight her own children for them.

Nathan decided he couldn't accept that. If they were ever to have a normal life, Reuben would have to be safe. Forever. He didn't know how he was going to accomplish that, but he got an idea of where to start when he heard the election results.

"Governor Bowdoin and two thirds of the legislature have lost their seats," he told Delilah. "It may take a little while, but I'm sure you'll see some changes in the laws."

"But that won't help Reuben."

"I'm still doing everything I can to free him."

"I know, and I don't mean to sound ungrateful, but I can't be cheerful or thankful when Reuben is about to die. I'm tempted to find Noah Hubbard and Lucius Clarke and shoot them both."

"You sound like Reuben."

"I *feel* like Reuben." She looked furious enough to commit murder. Then, in an abrupt change, she threw herself into Nathan's arms. "What am I going to do?" she sobbed. "Jane will never survive if Reuben dies. She won't be able to run the farm and take care of the children."

Nathan could see Delilah's family standing between them for the rest of their lives. In one last desperate attempt to salvage his future, he said, "I don't know what I'm going to do, but Reuben will not die. I'll have to be away for a few days."

Delilah grasped his coat as if she would never let go. "Where are you going?"

"To Boston."

"You can't leave now. They're going to hang Reuben in six days," she said, incredulous.

"I'll be back, I promise. You stay with Jane and keep

your courage up. It's not over yet. We have a new governor. There's a chance he will see Reuben's case differently."

But he left so quickly, visibly anxious to get away, his thoughts obviously on something more than his leave-taking. Delilah felt stunned. It had never occurred to her he would leave in this, the greatest hour of her need, but neither had she thought his goodbye would make her feel as if he were already gone.

As the days rolled by and she heard nothing from him, she began to wonder if his love for her had diminished. He'd been in love with her for months. He'd asked her to marry him several times, but even though she had finally agreed, she'd never allowed him to post the banns. She had put him in second place every time there'd been a crisis. She had always come back, but she'd never stayed.

Jane was too preoccupied with Reuben to notice whether Nathan was present or absent, but Delilah could tell from Polly's looks she thought he had gone away.

"A woman won't give up," Polly said one afternoon when her question about Nathan's whereabouts caused Delilah to break into tears. "She'll keep on waiting and hoping. But a man's different. His pride can't stand being put off so many times."

Had she turned her back on him too many times? Had she finally damaged his pride? By the morning of Reuben's hanging she thought so.

Jane refused to stay at home. Everyone tried to talk her into changing her mind, but she was adamant.

"If Reuben has the courage to fight and die for a cause," she told her father when he threatened to lock her in the house, "then I have the courage to be there to support him. How would you feel, Papa, if you were about to die and none of your family was with you?"

"We'll all be there, hon."

"You're not his family. The children and I are, and we'll be there to watch him die."

It looked like all of Springfield and half of Hampden County were there.

"It's ghoulish," Polly said to Delilah, whispering so Jane and the boys couldn't hear. "They've come to watch Reuben like he's some freak at the county fair."

Delilah muttered some response, but she was searching the crowd for a glimpse of Nathan. Common sense told her he wouldn't be there, but she couldn't give up hope, not until she had seen every face.

By the time they reached their position next to the scaffold, Delilah knew Nathan was not present. She felt certain he wasn't going to be.

He was gone.

He had left her, and she had nobody to blame but herself. He had told her months ago she would have to learn to put him first. She had told him she would, that she had, but that wasn't true. And, unable to believe she would change, he had finally gotten tired of waiting.

Why couldn't she have seen it? Everyone had told her what to do, but she never took advice. She even had Priscilla's example, but she had continued to believe Nathan would always be there when she wanted him. It wasn't the war or their differences or Reuben's family that kept them apart. It was her own inability to see what was important, to make up her mind as to what she wanted.

Now she didn't have to decide. Nathan had done it for her.

Exactly at noon, a drum roll captured Delilah's attention, and cold terror ran down her spine. They opened the prison door and brought Reuben out. The crowd was so dense by now she couldn't see him. People behind her craned their heads in an attempt to get a glimpse. In a moment Delilah could spy a double line of marching militiamen, drummers in front, coming toward her. Her heart pounded painfully in her chest as the procession came closer. She saw Reuben, head held high, hands behind his back, walking between the rows of militia.

Involuntarily she looked at Jane, but her sister-in-law

had eyes for no one but her husband. The boys gripped their mother's skirts. Today, at least, none of them needed to hold on to Delilah. They stood alone, as a family.

They didn't let Reuben stop and hug Jane and the boys. They didn't even let him speak. They pushed him toward the platform.

But even as they forced him to mount the steps, a bayonet in his back, Delilah heard the galloping of a horse. *Someone afraid he is going to miss the spectacle.* But the sound didn't go away. As the ministers spoke to Reuben and then addressed the crowd, the thundering hooves grew louder. They came on and on, the hoofbeats audible over the sound of the drummers' dreary, thumping rolls.

Soon the horseman would be in the middle of the street filled with people. The crowd began to crane its necks to see what madman would gallop into the center of town. Even the sheriff looked toward the approaching horseman rather than the man he was about to hang. Then the crowd parted with screams and shrieks, and Delilah's heart stopped beating as the horseman galloped to the very foot of the scaffold.

It was Nathan.

He vaulted from the saddle, bounded up the steps, and thrust a rolled-up piece of paper into the sheriff's hands. The crowd held its breath as the sheriff started to read:

"By the order of the Governor and the Council of the Commonwealth of Massachusetts, in their infinite mercy, the man Reuben Stowbridge is granted a reprieve. . . ."

Epilogue

Delilah snuggled contentedly in her husband's arms.

The sounds of early summer filled the warm air of the garden: the swish of the river eddying around the roots of trees growing along its banks; the rustle of the afternoon breeze through the fresh green leaves of elms, maples, and oaks; the chirping of two robins as they built their nest; the loud chatter of two squirrels as they argued over ownership of a particularly fine beech tree.

Some late tulips still dipped and swayed in the wind, but the spring garden had given over to the heavy scent of lilac, apple blossom, and flowering poplars. Already the hum of bees heralded the butterflies, hummingbirds, and dragonflies of summer.

"Do you think they'll be happy in New York?" Delilah asked Nathan. She didn't seem particularly concerned about his answer. She rested in the circle of his arms, her head against his shoulder, her eyes closed. She was utterly at peace.

"Why shouldn't they? He's got a hundred acres of bottom land, another three hundred for grazing, and that much again in virgin timber."

"You didn't have to be so generous. I didn't think Reuben was going to be able to speak for weeks after you told him."

"I thought they would be happier away from Springfield. It'll be easier to forget."

Delilah could still feel the sadness of her family's departure. They had stayed until after the wedding. After Nathan's gift of land, it would have been unthinkable for them not to remain, but it had been a difficult time. Reuben would never like Nathan. Delilah wasn't sure why, but she knew it was so. And she realized that Nathan didn't think much of Reuben. They were too different. They saw the world in different ways, but her great love for both men would never change that.

Jane had changed, though. From the moment Nathan had put that pardon in the sheriff's hands, he'd become a deity in her eyes. She allowed no one, not even Reuben, to say anything against him. And when he'd given them the farm . . . well, there didn't seem to be any words good enough to describe Nathan Trent. It was already understood that the Stowbridges' next boy would be named Nathaniel. Delilah guessed the one after that would be called Trent.

"I know why you gave them that farm," Delilah said. "You don't have to get upset," she added when she felt her husband tense. "You sent them away so they couldn't turn to me when things go wrong."

"They can visit as often as they like," Nathan said.

"Visits are different. Confess now. Am I right?"

"Do I have to admit all my sins?"

"Yes. I've been confessing for months. It's your turn now."

"Very well," Nathan turned so he could look into her eyes. "I confess I want you all to myself. I don't want to share you with a brother, a sister-in-law, or nephews and nieces. I want every moment of your time, every bit of your attention, and every scrap of your love. There, I've said it and I'm glad."

Delilah laughed.

"You sure you can't stand to share me at all?"

"Not one minute."

She snuggled even closer. "You'll be tired of me by fall. You won't mind so much then."

"I'll never tire of you, not this fall, not any fall."

410

She rested against him, her face averted, her smile blissful.

"Suppose you had to? Suppose you had no choice?"

"Dammit, Delilah, I didn't consign Reuben's family to the end of the earth for you to dredge up somebody else to mother. It had better not be Priscilla. I'd make her a widow before the week was out."

"It's not Priscilla. In fact, it's no one you know."

"Then don't let them come." Nathan paused. "You know, you're not making any sense." He put a hand under Delilah's chin, raising her head. "You're playing games with me, woman. Just what are you talking about?"

"A visitor."

"I won't have any visitors."

"A tiny permanent resident."

"Delilah . . . Delilah?"

His wife gurgled with happiness.

"I think it'll be just in time for Christmas."

"Do you mean . . . ?"

"Yes, you silly man. I'm going to have our baby."

Nathan jumped to his feet. "Are you sure?"

"Positive."

He picked Delilah up and whirled her around. She laughed with happiness.

"You keep that up, and the child's going to come out with addled wits," Lester said, as he approached them along the garden path. He handed Delilah a shawl. "Mrs. Stebbens says you got to put this around your shoulders. Otherwise you'll get a chill and that baby will have the sniffles for the rest of its born days."

Mrs. Stebbens had been promoted to housekeeper, with a cook, two maids, and a washwoman under her. She still tyrannized Lester and Tommy.

"Am I the only one in the house who didn't know you were going to have a baby?" Nathan demanded.

"I just told Mrs. Stebbens this morning. I guess she can't keep a secret."

"A strainer can hold water better'n that woman can keep

411

secrets," Lester said.

"She can't wait to have a baby she can spoil," Delilah told Nathan. "She's already making plans on how to rearrange the household schedule so she can be his nurse."

Nathan directed a piercing look at his wife. "Do I detect the approach of someone who will oust me from first place in your heart?"

"There's nothing more important to a woman than a baby," Lester volunteered. "To hear my mama talk, you'd think she was put on this earth to love nothing else."

Nathan looked thoughtful. "I wonder how soon they accept children at boarding school," he mused.

"Nathan!"

"They'll be sent to England, of course."

"Nathan Trent!"

"Until then they'll need a full nursery, including a wet nurse. Hector's old place ought to be just perfect."

"You will not install my baby in some nursery miles away," Delilah said. "And especially not with a wet nurse."

"Then you'd better make the nursery big enough for two cribs."

"Why? I'm not having twins."

"The second one's for me."

Delilah stifled a gurgle of laughter.

"See, I have no pride, and it's all your fault. I'll do anything, even to sleeping in the baby's room, to keep you from forgetting me."

Hugging Nathan more tightly to her, Delilah looked into her husband's eyes. "This is your baby as much as mine. It will bring us closer together. It won't separate us. I want you in the nursery. I want you to hold our baby, to see our child learn to turn over or crawl or laugh aloud. But just as important, I want you to be with me. I can't live without you."

"Always?"

"Always."

Author's Note

In the years immediately following the American Revolution, economic collapse threatened many of the new states, but nowhere were economic conditions worse than in Massachusetts, where an alarming uprising known as Shays's Rebellion flared up in the western counties in 1786. Impoverished backcountry farmers, many of them Revolutionary War veterans, were losing their farms through mortgage foreclosures and tax delinquencies. In August at a Hampshire County convention of some fifty towns, the delegates condemned the Massachusetts Senate, lawyers, the high costs of justice, and the tax system. Led by Captain Daniel Shays, a veteran of the American Revolution, these desperate debtors demanded cheap paper money, lighter taxes, and suspension of mortgage foreclosures. Hundreds of angry agitators attempted to enforce their demands by closing the courts. Insurrection in eastern Massachusetts collapsed with the capture of Job Shattuck on November 30, but the insurrection in the western counties continued to gain momentum.

When Shays and his followers attempted to capture the federal arsenal at Springfield, state authorities raised a small army under General Lincoln. Supported partly by contributions from wealthy citizens, forty-four hundred men enlisted for one month to march on Springfield in January, 1787. Several skirmishes occurred—at Springfield three Shaysites were killed and one was wounded—and the movement collapsed. Daniel Shays and several other leaders were condemned to death, but were later pardoned.

The uprising had the effect of inducing the state legislature not to impose a direct tax in 1787 and to enact laws lowering court fees and exempting clothing, household goods, and the tools of one's trade from the debt process.

While the condemned rebels of Massachusetts awaited what the General Court called "condign punishment," delegates from every state except Rhode Island met in Philadelphia "in order to form a more perfect union, establish justice, and insure domestic tranquillity." More than any other single factor, the lack of justice and of domestic tranquillity, as evidenced by Shays's Rebellion, caused the Continental Congress to call that convention.

The miraculous result of the delegates' months of labor was the Constitution of the United States. John Quincy Adams would say that it had been "extorted from the grinding necessity of a reluctant nation," and that "Shays's Rebellion was the extorting agency." Historian Charles Francis Adams would write that Shays's Rebellion was "one of the chief impelling and contributory causes to the framing and adoption of the Constitution."

The people of Massachusetts, farmers and merchants alike, could see the republican form of government the Constitution guaranteed to every state promised protection for all classes. In spite of some querulous opposition from the diehard westerners, they were among the first to ratify the document and to swear to abide by its provisions.

I have tried to remain faithful to the historical sequence of events and to the roles played by specific leaders. For the sake of clarity, I have exaggerated the role of Daniel Shays in the early days of the uprising. The text from Shays's letters, the letter Reuben wrote to the senate begging forgiveness, and Reuben's pardon are taken from the actual documents.

Other than the rebellion's leaders and a few other persons, such as Governor Bowdoin and General Lincoln, all the characters in this book are products of my imagination. Any likeness to an actual person is purely coincidental.